"THE PAIN IS GONE. COME WITH ME. DREAM."

The sharp edge cut through the skin, deep and deeper, until the jugular vein opened wide and hot blood gushed. She dropped the blade and bent to press her forehead to his.

The dreams were fleeting, but time slowed in this place. Her hand in his, she brought him to the Ral world, then even further into realms of beauty and color that she had no idea existed in her mind.

"The game's about to start," she whispered.

Other Avon Books by
L. Dean James

SUMMERLAND

MOJAVE WELLS

L. DEAN JAMES

AVON BOOKS • NEW YORK

MOJAVE WELLS is an original publication of Avon Books. This work has never before appeared in book form. This work is a novel. Any similarity to actual persons or events is purely coincidental.

AVON BOOKS
A division of
The Hearst Corporation
1350 Avenue of the Americas
New York, New York 10019

Copyright © 1994 by L. Dean James
Cover art by Dorian Vallejo
Published by arrangement with the author
Library of Congress Catalog Card Number: 93-90957
ISBN: 0-380-77324-4

First AvoNova Printing: June 1994

AVONOVA TRADEMARK REG. U.S. PAT. OFF. AND IN OTHER COUNTRIES, MARCA REGISTRADA, HECHO EN U.S.A.

Printed in the U.S.A.

RA 10 9 8 7 6 5 4 3 2 1

For my little brother,
Rick

Thank You

Behind every writer is a bunch of good people willing to help with research, ideas, and far-out theories. Thanks so much to Bill Parnell and Homicide Detective Jim Conley of the Anaheim Police Department. Thanks also to Shirley Meibos and Gloria Hale for their invaluable support, and to Dr. Kathy Henkins, without whom this book and several others would never have seen print.

Chapter One

HANOVER SAID EVERYTHING would be all right. Hanover said there was absolutely no danger. Now Hanover was dead, and John Caldwell was scared out of his mind. He left the house quickly, closing the door on the empty silence within, but his internal shuddering refused to stop.

Overhead, a fat autumn sun westered, still full of fire and heat—another hot Southern California November, another hot dry Thanksgiving. John's car was parked in the drive behind the professor's aging Ford station wagon. He climbed behind the wheel of the Jeep and backed it into the street. Brittle leaves scattered and crunched under the mud treads. At the house directly across the way, holiday visitors had arrived. Children piled out of a small blue sedan and raced up the walk to the open arms of an elderly couple.

Run, John, run—anywhere, only go! He gunned the engine, aware of the neighbors' curious eyes on him, and sent the Jeep speeding through the quiet tract. Thirty-year-old stucco houses with neat green yards flashed by. His fingertips were still numb, as well as the skin on his face. God! The terror grabbed him again, and heart pounding, he fled.

II

Sergeant Nate Curtis, fifty-two, tall, and heavyset, hadn't recovered from Turkey Day yet. His wife Janice's giblet stuffing was caught somewhere between the pumpkin pie and the cranberry sauce, and none of it had found its way out of his stomach. He popped another couple of

1

Rolaids as he turned down Vista Road in search of 1483 East. Easy enough to find. There were three dark blue county M.E. wagons parked in front, two black-and-whites across the road, and a hell of a crowd of onlookers gathered on the walk to either side of the house, just outside the yellow tape barriers.

There were also parked in the drive of the two-car garage a red Toyota Camry and an ancient green Ford station wagon behind a new white Probe. Nate glanced around. Nice neighborhood, older, wealthier. Professor Hanover was some sort of bigwig at University of Orange. *Was* being the key word here. A young uniformed officer—Jason Kelly, Nate remembered—came down the walk to greet him. Under short-cropped blond hair, the kid's long narrow face was white, and the sergeant's already unhappy stomach did a queasy roll.

"What have we got?" he asked brusquely.

"Four children, eight adults."

"Jesus H. Christ," Nate muttered, though he'd already heard some of it through the dispatcher. "Cause?" He really didn't want to hear the bloody details.

Kelly shook his head. "Can't tell. Looks like they all sat down to dinner. And just died." He held up a couple of small paper filter masks. "Forensics says we should wear these."

Grunting, Nate fitted the elastic string around his head while Kelly opened the front door to let the sergeant through. The kid continued to talk. "The folks across the street said there weren't any lights on in the house last night, which got them to wondering. So this morning, Dorset—he's the neighbor—came over and knocked on the door. When he got no answer, he looked in through the dining room window. And saw this. . . ."

The carpet underfoot was worn but clean, the house full of bric-a-brac and nice furniture, which Nate observed only peripherally. Most of the family still sat at the table, slumped over their plates. The children—a toddler in a high chair and three preteens at a folding card table—had been placed near the kitchen door. An elderly graying man, possibly the professor, lay just inside the room, a large turkey on the floor beside him.

The sight of the golden-roasted, and now shriveled, poultry carcass made Nate dig in his pocket for the Rolaids. Several men in plastic surgeon's gloves and paper booties moved about the area. Nate glanced at the windows, then stepped toward them. A team member dusted white fingerprint powder gently over one pane, avoiding the small, vaguely round hole in the center of the glass. When Nate reached a finger out, the man said, "Careful, sir. Sharp."

It was indeed sharp. Around the hole, the glass was razor thin, but rippled outward, growing thick and distorted by the time it reached the wooden frame. The pane in the other window was the same, a slight breeze whistling into the room through the opening.

"What the hell did this?" the sergeant asked.

"No idea, sir. Never seen anything like it before. No broken glass outside or in, and no other windows affected, just these in the dining room." The fellow glanced over his shoulder. "The drinking glasses on the table are extremely thin on the one side away from the windows and thick on the other. Like they melted somehow."

"Is that possible?"

"As far as I know, it can only be done with superhigh temperatures. That would've burned everything around them, though. Unless of course, it was done somewhere else and the glass brought here, but there's not much sense in that."

"No," Nate muttered, and returned to the table and the bodies seated around it.

Kelly glanced at the sergeant. "You know what I think . . . I think it was food poisoning."

"Yeah?" Nate was already processing the information his eyes gave him. "Doesn't look like there's any food on the plates to me. Doesn't look like they had a chance to take a bite."

"Hors d'oeuvres," Kelly stated. "Hors d'oeuvres could do it."

"You got any idea how long it takes for food poisoning

to come on? These people were dropped in their tracks by something." Assuming the professor had the chair at the head of the table, Nate nodded to a second empty chair with a plate before it. "Who do you suppose was sitting there?"

"Dorset says there was a young guy here yesterday. One of the prof's grad students. He didn't know his name, but this student's been here a lot the last few days. Drives a dark green hardtop Jeep, and he left in one big hurry around 3:00 P.M. Think he could have killed them?"

Nate ran fingers through his thinning gray-brown hair, thinking out loud. "So he's invited to Thanksgiving dinner—the professor's gofer. He sits down to eat, and wham! the whole bunch keels over." The sergeant walked carefully around the table. "But not him. No, he's still alive. But does he call 911? Does he try to help? No . . . he walks out that door, gets in his car, and drives away." Nate tapped one of the forensic team members on the shoulder. The man was leaning over the body of a plump, pretty woman in her fifties. "Who're you?"

"Garrett, sir."

"You're new, right?"

"We met on the Swenson homicide, Sergeant. Last year."

"Shit, yeah. Whatcha got here?"

"Cause of death?"

"That'd be nice."

Garrett shook his head. "No wounds that I can find. No obvious cause. The lividity's much heavier than usual, lot more blood pooling in the lower parts of the bodies. This is pure speculation, mind you, but it coulda been poison. Some sort of anticoagulant. Gas maybe, or something that's absorbed through the skin, though there's usually some external bleeding with those. From the nose or mouth. Best not to touch anything with your bare hands."

Nate had already taken an involuntary step back from the table. "So who's heading toxicology since Weldon retired?"

"Takamura. Can we bag these bodies now?"

"Okay by me." Nate deserted the dining room with its

dozen bodies and odd windows and headed into the gracious, spotless living room. "Kelly!"

The young man trotted after him. "Do you think the grad student killed them?"

"Hell if I know. But I want him. I want him bad. He's the only one can maybe tell us what happened. You check the rest of the house?"

"It's empty."

"So where'd the prof work? He's got an office here somewhere. All these fancy educated professor people do."

"There's a study," Kelly offered. "Full of all kinds of crap."

The sergeant followed the young officer down a long narrow hall. Three bedrooms, two baths, all designer decorated by the late Mrs. Hanover most likely. A fourth bedroom, the last one on the right, was the study. Large area, impossibly cluttered, and completely out of sync with the rest of the house. Light poured in through a wide north-facing double window with white filmy curtains. Once white, Nate amended; they were now slightly yellowed. The prof had been a pipe smoker, and the room was permeated with a sweet tobacco scent. Two aquariums, sporting large iridescent fish, bubbled cheerfully. Then there were the terrariums, a half dozen on crowded tables.

Nate peered with distaste into one with a very large, very hairy spider. And very alive. Whatever or whoever had killed the family hadn't disturbed the creatures in this part of the house.

"Tarantula," Kelly said. "They're supposed to make real nice pets."

The young officer was serious. Nate rolled his eyes and checked out another tank that appeared empty at first. A closer look revealed two dark eyes in a triangular head buried in the sandy bottom. Rattlesnake. Nate shuddered.

"So?" he asked casually. He'd arrived at the desk finally. "What was it the prof taught at the college?"

"He was head of the anthro-archeology department."

"Into old bones, huh?"

Kelly smiled. "That and other things. The neighbor,

Dorset, thinks the professor was a few bricks short of a full load. He says Hanover was also into old UFOs."

"What?"

"There's these aerial photos. See here on the bulletin board." Kelly tapped a finger on some eight-by-ten black and white glossies fastened to the board with colored stick pins. "Huge fancy designs made on the ground thousands of years ago. Some people figure they were like landing signals, or directions for someone to see from way overhead. Like in space. . . . Like in UFOs. . . ."

"Bullshit!" Nate snorted. He leaned closer, squinting. The pictures were grainy; small dark arrows, circles and lines in an unknown lighter background. No way of judging size. "You read up on this stuff?"

Kelly looked uncomfortable. "Saw it in a Time-Life book on unexplained phenomena." Now he looked guilty. "And I sorta looked at the papers on the desk. I was careful, though, not to mess things up."

"Good, 'cause I want forensics to go over this room, too." Nate stared at the desktop, then gently shifted things aside to look at a thick red folder. *Creation Myths of the Serrano Indians.* By J. R. Caldwell. Who in hell were the Serrano Indians? The desk calendar beside the folder was well used. Under yesterday's date was the notation, John for Thanksgiving. Touching only the edges, the sergeant turned the calendar pages back. Under Sunday, November 19, he found J. Caldwell, Devil's Playground, 5 A.M.

"You ever heard of this Devil's Playground?" Nate asked.

Kelly gave him a blank look and shook his head. "There's a faculty picture here on the wall."

Nate scooted around a table with terrariums and checked the photo. A dozen scholarly types, young and old. The dead man from the dining room stood in the background, tall, stately, a younger, shorter man beside him. Nate checked the list of names underneath. Sure enough, it was Doctor Arnold Hanover with John Caldwell, T.A. T.A.? Teaching assistant? Maybe.

He lifted the framed picture off the nail. "Take this

across to the neighbor, what's-his-face, and get an ID. Make it quick."

"Sure, Sarge." Kelly received the photo and left Nate alone in the study.

"Well, well," Nate muttered, eyeing the address book beside the calendar. With a stubby pencil from his breast pocket, he located the C's. John Caldwell, 356 W. Francis, Brea. Nate pulled a Kleenex from the box on the desk and wrapped the handpiece on the phone. The pencil was used to punch in the number.

On the fourth ring, someone picked up the line. "Hello?" The male voice sounded hoarse, sleepy.

"John?"

"Yes?"

Nate smiled. "John Smith?" Hell, not very original.

"No. . . ." The voice hesitated. "You—"

"Must have the wrong number. Sorry." The sergeant hung up, then took a peek out the window. Kelly was coming back across the street. Good. Impatient, Nate waited. "Well?" he demanded as the young officer arrived.

"It's him, all right. John Caldwell was here yesterday."

Nate scribbled the address onto the pad from his pocket. "Call Brea and ask 'em to get a squad out there immediately to pick this guy up. The little SOB's at home. Hustle it! Oh, and Kelly . . ." the sergeant called after the young man. "Tell 'em to approach with caution. Just in case."

"Got it," Kelly said.

"Well, well," Nate muttered again, eyes on the faculty picture. Whether he was a killer or not, and whether he wanted to or not, John Caldwell was going to help Nate figure out just what the hell had happened here during that fatal Thanksgiving dinner. Absently, he pulled his paper mask down and popped another Rolaid in his mouth.

III

Deputy Mike Nichols woke in an excellent mood. Outside the windows of his round-shouldered Airstream trailer, morning light gave a soft golden glow to the desert sand rolling into the distance. The Shadow Mountains were low, dark mounds to the northwest—the very first thing he saw when he opened his eyes.

He climbed out of bed, unmindful of the chill, and padded to the tiny bathroom, where he showered and shaved meticulously, an unusual procedure for his day off. But today was special. Today Mike was taking the Dodge to Sid's for a tune-up.

Happy, he dressed in his good slacks and a good shirt, then stopped. Stupid to go to the garage in his best clothes. He changed into worn jeans and a faded red flannel shirt, pulled on his Wolverine cowboy boots with their scuffed heels and toes. His dark hair, still damp, was carefully brushed. Maybe should have gotten a haircut yesterday, but too late to worry about it now.

Only eight-thirty. Time enough for a bowl of cereal and a cup of instant coffee. He set a pan of bottled water on to heat before getting out the cornflakes and a bowl, then sniffed the milk carton from the fridge before pouring the contents over the cereal. Only he wasn't hungry. Too damn nervous. Crazy, a thirty-one-year-old law officer with butterflies in his stomach. The flakes went soggy and were dumped into the plastic-lined garbage pail under the little sink. That had killed twenty minutes.

Mike donned his jacket and took the coffee with him to the door, smiling in anticipation. This time he'd find something witty to say, not just sit like a lump. This time, he'd have the courage to ask. The three narrow metal steps had a little ice on them still, and both the blue and white Jeep Cherokee and red Power Wagon parked in front sparkled with melting frost. The starter on the Dodge ground slowly until the engine finally caught, backfiring several times. No doubt about it—time for a tune-up.

His only neighbor—Doc Charlie in his big new RV—wasn't stirring yet. The Mojave Wells Trailer Park boasted all of two occupants, while the whole town of Mojave Wells had a population of forty-six. More than half of the community was age sixty-five and over. Mike backed the pickup around. A gust of cold desert wind swirled up a dust devil of dead leaves from the Chinese mulberry in front of his trailer. In summer the tree provided much-needed shade; now it was pretty much nude, letting the late fall sunlight through.

Mojave Wells lay a little more than a mile north from the isolated trailer park. Sid's shop was at the far end of town, closest to where the 137 ran into Highway 15. Mike drove by the liquor/grocery store, the tiny post office, and the one-room school building. There were several cars and big rigs parked in front of Hannah's Cafe, and just past it, he pulled into the Bowers' Garage with its three ancient gas pumps and corrugated tin building with two small work bays. The big front door was up, an older sedan on the lift. He could hear Sid clanging around behind the vehicle.

"Hello!" Mike called.

The clanging ceased, and Sid Bowers wandered into view, dressed in greasy coveralls, a giant screwdriver in one greasy hand. A strand of dark blond forelock had escaped the red bandanna tied around her head, and she brushed it out of deep blue eyes. Even covered in grime, Mike thought she had to be just about the finest looking woman he'd ever seen.

"I haven't finished this brake job—" she began.

"That's okay."

"So pull it in and leave it. I'll call you when it's done." Sid turned and disappeared behind the sedan again.

Mike slipped in an oil puddle when he followed her, and she eyed him with displeasure.

"My insurance doesn't handle customers in the work area."

Deputy Nichols felt his face heat. "That's okay. I got medical coverage through the county." Stupid! Clumsy!

"You know, Nichols, it'd be a helluva lot cheaper if you did the tune-up yourself." Sid was adjusting the right rear brake shoes, screwdriver inserted into the little hole in the drum to turn the star wheel on the cylinder.

"I don't like getting greasy," Mike blurted into the silence. More stupidity. Shit!

But Sid only smiled grimly. "Neither do I."

"Want some coffee?" the young officer asked, hoping to divert the conversation in a direction he could handle.

"You buying?"

"Well, sure . . ."

"Cream, no sugar." She continued to work.

Dismissed, Mike headed across the empty lot to Hannah's, replaying the conversation, his frustration level rising. How on earth was he ever going to get through to this woman? Everyone in town knew Sidney Bowers was having a rough go of it. In the year since Dale's death, she'd managed to keep the garage alive. Barely. No one had expected her to stay, let alone take over the business, and Mike was only one of the many gentlemen callers in the past months. Sid treated them all with equal, though gentle, contempt. She and her husband, Dale, hadn't been just lovers, but partners and friends—closer than Mike had ever seen a couple.

Depressed, he pushed in through the glass door to the cafe. Klutzy, inept Mike Nichols didn't stand a chance against the memory of Dale Bowers. Hannah peeked out through the kitchen slot, plump face ruddy with the heat from the stoves.

"Howdy, Deputy Mike!"

"Hi, Hannah."

The woman popped through the door, swathed in a great filthy apron, her short dark hair plastered by sweat to her skull. A plate of eggs and toast was clutched in her thick fingers. "Ah, honey! You're lookin' about heartbroke. You been chasing after Sid again, ain't ya?" She dropped the eggs in front of Abner Skoats at the counter.

Mike felt another rush of heat in his cheeks. The half dozen customers, all neighbors and friends, were offering quiet sympathy from their stools.

"Where's Joel?" the deputy asked, just to change the subject.

"Hell if I know," Hannah groused. "Didn't come in this morning. You ever get tired of being a cop, hon, I'll hire you on the spot."

"As a cook? You'd be sorry."

"Honey, I'm sure you're good at other things." She flashed him a wicked grin.

That brought laughter, and Mike's face turned a brighter red. Joel was Hannah's husband as well as her cook, and she was always offering his job to eligible men.

Eyes twinkling, the woman caught Mike's gaze. "Breakfast, hon?"

"Coffee. Two, please. To go."

"Can you ride, Mike?" Hannah filled a couple of ceramic mugs with steaming black liquid.

"What?"

"Can you ride a horse?"

"Sure."

"Just a thought, honey. But she's got those two damn horses over there behind the shop. She and Dale used to ride all the time. Why not ask her to take you out in the desert sometime? Worth a try."

Mike poured cream in one cup, sugar in the other. "Okay. Thanks, Hannah."

"Thanks, nothing. That'll be a buck-forty-two for coffee and advice. Remember to bring the mugs back or I'll charge a deposit next time."

More laughter. Mike paid and hurried off, the coffee slopping over the rims. Sid would never go for it, not riding. No one could ever take Dale's place, or ride his horse or drive his stock car, which was parked in back like the animals. The Dale Bowers Memorial Shrine. Give it up, Nichols, he told himself. But he couldn't.

IV

John had put himself to sleep finally with a pint of tequila. The phone woke him at nine-thirty, a wrong number. But it jolted him awake, allowing all the horror to flood back into his consciousness. At least there'd been no bizarre, otherworldly dreams this time. He lay back on the bed a moment longer, head swimming from the aftermath of the alcohol, his bladder making dire threats. The studio apartment, cluttered with research material, seemed to close in on him.

Run, John, run! Anxiety and panic mixed equally with the horror to goad him, now. He got up and staggered into the bathroom to relieve himself, then back to the combination living room–bedroom–kitchen. At the dresser, he began tossing underwear and shirts into a small plastic suitcase. Toothbrush, razor, deodorant, a mindless assortment of necessaries. His hands shook and his mouth tasted dry and foul. Hanover, you bastard! Was there gas in the Jeep? Not nearly enough to take him beyond the limits of nightmare. He rubbed fingertips together, staring at the soft pink scholar's hands. There was feeling in them, at least.

Run, John, run! He fled the apartment. The keys were still in the ignition, the Jeep parked half out in the street just as he'd left it yesterday. Yes, the tank was almost full. He vaguely remembered filling it before heading to Hanover's for dinner. Swift Friday traffic greeted him at the boulevard. He needed to find the freeway, but his mind refused to make the most rudimentary of connections. Turn right, he decided. Yes. A green sign overhead directed him into the left lane to pick up the Orange Freeway north. He'd driven this way a thousand times, but everything seemed frighteningly different—frighteningly strange. Take the 57 north to the 60 east. Somewhere out there would be the 15, climbing over the Cajon Pass to the Mojave Desert.

They'd gone to the Devil's Playground that day, and Hanover had made a deal with the devil, all right. Only he'd traded John's soul, the bastard! A week ago—less than a week really—John had picked Hanover up before dawn. The old man was excited, yet subdued. John had seen the pictures, the aerial photos of that stretch of desert called the Devil's Playground, and they didn't look all that promising. Hanover was convinced otherwise. The faint broken ridges in the sand were too straight, he'd said, the curves too concentric to be natural. A man-made landing marker for the chariots of the gods, for galactic visitors, and constructed thousands of years ago.

Hanover was crazy, no two ways about it, but he was John's dissertation adviser and, despite himself, John

Caldwell, confirmed cynic and perennial student, found himself almost hoping the professor was right. The universe seemed an awfully lonely place if humans were the only ones in it.

The sun had cleared the horizon last Sunday just as they'd gone over the top of the Cajon Pass with John's elderly Jeep straining on the last leg of this last grade. The Mojave spread out just below them, purple and hazy in the distance. It was a series of great desolate valleys cut off eons ago from the Pacific Ocean's life-giving moisture by the Sierra Madres. To add even more insult, nearly half of the desert had been allocated to the military to bomb and strafe and march over in perpetuity.

In the early morning light, John had watched a small squadron of jets speed in tight formation just above the desert floor, made soundless and toy-sized by the miles. Hanover didn't notice. He had a photo turned to the light, and muttered under his breath while they cruised past Victorville. John continued to drive while loaded buses heading toward Las Vegas zoomed around him. The highway ran boringly smooth and the Jeep hit top speed—sixty. The rattle and rumble of the vehicle precluded conversation. John phased out, his eyes wide open, his mind sound asleep.

"The Mojave Wells turnoff, Caldwell!"

John jumped a foot off the seat. "What?"

"We turn off at Mojave Wells!"

"Right, right. I got it." He swung over, turning southeast on 137, a narrow two-lane with chuckholed pavement. Mojave Wells was only one short step away from ghost town status. The buildings were sun-bleached and tacky, each with a huge evaporative swamp cooler on top or hanging in a window. They passed a garage, a cafe, and a store, and the town ended abruptly. A little farther down the road and under an optimistically large sign that read, Mojave Wells Trailer Park, sat a trailer and a fancy RV. A blue and white county sheriff's Jeep was parked next to the weathered Airstream. Jeep Cherokee, John noted with a touch of envy.

Hanover pored over his aerial photos and his topo

maps, looking up to stare out into the desert to the west. The Devil's Playground. Lost in thought, the professor chewed at his graying mustache.

"We need to drive out into it, Caldwell," he said finally. "Too far to hike."

Resigned and just a little uneasy, John pulled off the pavement and climbed out to lock the hubs in four-wheel drive. Windy. Cold. The sun was only now getting some strength. He slipped back in behind the wheel and put the Jeep in gear, found the faintest of car tracks to follow out into the sand. The tires spun and caught. Greasewood and mesquite dominated the sparse flora with occasional yucca and Joshua to stand above them.

"Bear right," Hanover ordered.

The track bore left. Hell. The steering was sloppy—too much play in the wheel—and the Jeep fought him for control. John forced it down into a small gully and up the other side. Hanover, face pressed to the side window, continued to stare at the landscape. Caldwell stepped on the brake pedal.

"No, no. Don't stop here. Keep going."

"Can't, Professor. If we go any farther, we won't make it back out." Maybe the Jeep could do it, but John wasn't a particularly good driver, or aggressive. Anything more than a thirty-degree slope had him convinced that the vehicle would roll over, four-wheel drive or no.

Grumbling, the professor climbed out with his haversack and small canteen. John shut the engine down, then joined the older man.

"The area looks all wrong for this," Caldwell said, remembering other impromptu digs the old man had dragged him on.

Hanover gave him the imperious glare he was famous for. "Is that a professional opinion, you little pea-brained twit?" He checked his watch, and stalked away westward over a low rise.

John swallowed his anger, then started after the professor, fighting the terrain. On the slopes, his feet sank and sand leaked into the tops of his Wellingtons. The bitter wind cut through his thin jacket, and produced a deep chill. If this was the Devil's Playground, then it was indeed a cold day in hell. Caldwell found himself struggling to keep up. The old man's legs were longer than his, and as much as John hated to admit it, at more than twice his age, Hanover was in far better physical shape.

In the bottom of a shallow debris-cluttered gully, the professor checked his wristwatch once more, and halted to inspect the ground. Crouching, he swept sand away with his hands until a narrow line of dark porous rock appeared.

"This is it," Hanover stated. For some reason there was none of the usual excitement in his tone that such a discovery should cause.

John opened and closed his mouth, afraid of the man's acid scorn. It was only igneous stone, a natural formation, nothing more. Hanover moved away, and began the same process a short distance west, his salt-and-pepper head bowed. Again, a narrow line of lava was exposed to the sunlight. John squatted by the first discovery, sweeping more sand away. Those might be chisel marks on either side of the rock. In fact they had to be. Certainly, the wind and sand would not have worn the formation in so precise a manner. He glanced around him.

The debris scattered in the gray sand was white—not sticks as he'd first thought, but tiny bleached bones, even whole skeletal remains. Rodents, John decided. But why so many? He followed the professor westward in a straight line and passed the still form of a rattlesnake. The curious row of curved lines on the ground beside it were the peculiar marks of the sidewinder. It had not been dead long enough for the wind to erase the tracks. An odd dread filled John.

"W—What are all these bones doing here?" he asked, unable to hide his unease.

Hanover's nostrils flared in obvious disgust. "Simple explanation. We're near a coyote den." He pulled the collapsible shovel from his pack and unfolded the blade, locking the telescoping handle in place. "Here, dig!"

The shovel was pushed into John's hands, and as always, he obeyed. The sand seemed to dribble into the little crater as fast as he emptied it. Impatient, Hanover hovered over him. The blade finally struck something solid a short way down the ridge of black lava. With careful fingers, John cleared the sand away from a small rectangular box. He looked up into Hanover's face. Now, the man's dark eyes glittered with some intense emotion.

"What is this?" John asked.

"All the proof we'll ever need, Caldwell." The professor peered at his watch again. "Wait here. I've left my notebook in the car."

"I'll come with you."

"No! Stay here. It'll be all right, I promise you. You're in absolutely no danger. But don't leave this spot. We might not find it again so easily."

Absolutely no danger. What the hell did he mean by that? John watched him trudge up the slope and disappear behind the lip of the gully. Damn. He gazed at the box, as black as the lava it was anchored against, and found the courage to touch it with his fingers. Cool. Not metal or stone. Perhaps a high impact plastic, then. Solid, no seams, and somehow fused to the rock. Unwillingly, his eyes tracked to a miniature skull only inches away in the sand. Except for the size and overlong incisors, it might be human. A tiny perfect backbone with attached rib cage lay near it.

John stared. A coyote would eat such small prey whole. A coyote . . . Thunder rolled over the desert suddenly with a jet close behind the sound. It slammed by overhead, so low, he could feel the wind of its passing, see the rockets fixed under the wings. Shit!

Realization struck him hard, and he looked down into the hole. This box was no evidence of UFOs, but some experimental weapon the military had set out long ago, then likely lost in the bureaucratic shuffle. Had to be. The thing had lain here all this time pouring out enough lethal radiation to kill the small wildlife that wandered into range, and now it was killing John Caldwell.

He scrambled toward the slope on hands and feet, desperate, but halfway there the world imploded. He felt himself snatched back, sucked into a vacuum and spewed out, scattered in a wave of particles. Then the process reversed itself again. Dimly, he thought there should be pain, but there was nothing—only a state of nonexistence. Death.

Water splashed into his face, into his mouth. Hanover leaned over him, the canteen in his hands and faded blue sky behind his head.

"Four hours, twenty-three minutes and eighteen seconds," the professor said, voice trembling. "What did you experience?"

John's fingertips were numb, his toes and the skin of his face without feeling. Four hours . . . Somehow he managed to snag his hands in the old man's jacket.

"You bastard . . . You knew. . . ."

"It's alien, Caldwell. I thought it might be a signal device at first, but it somehow breaks down and re-forms living cells. For all we know, it could be a spontaneous transporter. You have to understand the magnitude of this find."

"So I'm the guinea pig." John let his hands fall limply to the sand. "You killed me."

"By all rights, you should already be dead." There was no remorse in Hanover's voice.

"Radiation . . ."

"No. I've had bones from the area tested. There's no radiation, but whatever the physical forces, they seem to have a disruptive effect on the internal organs. Now tell me, what was it like? I saw you dissolve and resolve twice. What did you feel? Is there pain?"

John kept silent. A heavy hatred filled him slowly.

"Caldwell, don't be selfish. You've got to tell me before . . . while you're still able."

"Fuck you," John snarled, and struggled to his feet. The lower limbs still worked well enough to carry him up the slope.

"Wait!" Hanover shouted.

He was busy filling in the hole, covering his alien artifact with sand. Hiding it. John hadn't waited. And he hadn't died. That seemed to disappoint Hanover at first. They had returned to Brea with the professor driving for fear his student might decide to keel over at the wheel. And the resentment and hatred John had felt gradually dissipated. Simply by staying alive, he'd become the most important thing in Dr. Arnold Hanover's life—proof that human beings just might be able to put to use what he'd discovered in the Mojave.

John was no longer the used and abused teaching assistant then, but a valued ally, a colleague, spending much of those last few days at the professor's house. Under close observation, no doubt. There'd been periodic bouts of dizziness and numbness, usually coinciding with Hanover's four-hour timetable. John hadn't minded until he'd sat down with Hanover's family for Thanksgiving dinner . . . Then, even from so great a distance, that alien force had unraveled his being again and killed everyone around him.

The Jeep wandered into oncoming traffic, and the blare of horns shocked John Caldwell back to the here and now. He was already in Barstow with no memory of the drive. Hands tight on the steering wheel, he continued east on Highway 15.

Chapter Two

SID BOWERS SNUGGED the last spark plug down. *Tight, but not too tight,* she imagined Dale's whisper in her ear. Leaning over the right front fender, Mike Nichols watched her every move with intense gray eyes. God, she hated that. It felt like everything she did was under close scrutiny, like he was just waiting for her to foul up. At least the deputy wasn't one of those bozos who snatched the tools out of her hands, saying in a grand and masculine voice, "Here, little lady, let me do that for you." Sid pulled another spark plug from its cardboard and cellophane package.

Mike was different in a lot of ways from the guys who showed up at the shop, most of them looking for something more than a mechanic. Sid even liked him—the way you liked an overgrown puppy—but she would never let on. No sense in encouraging him. The last plug was tightened.

"Bring me that box on the workbench," she ordered, and dutifully, the deputy turned to fetch it. Ignition wires. The big Dodge pickup was in pretty good shape considering its age, but the spark plug wires and fan belts were disintegrating. Sid took the box from Mike, then began systematically replacing the worn wires.

It was cold. The wind found its way unhindered into the garage, and even though Sid had two layers of clothes on under the coveralls, the chill got to her. Her hands were the worst, stiff and numb, but the space heater cost too much to run. She looked at the grime under her nails, the gouges in her knuckles that never seemed to heal, and wondered briefly why any man would find her attractive.

19

Mike Nichols had placed his elbows on the fender once more, peering intently at those same greasy hands while they worked. Hell. He was a strange one—not a tough guy like a lot of the law officers she'd known, and when he wore his uniform, the holstered gun looked almost out of place. But then Mike spent most of his time rescuing stranded motorists out on the 15. And most of those broken-down cars ended up here in the shop, thanks to the deputy—which was likely against regulations, but she appreciated the work.

Occasionally Mike worked with the Highway Patrol on wrecks, so he did see his share of blood and destruction and vehicular violence. Now, he shifted his weight from one foot to the other, and bowed his head.

"It's been backfiring," he muttered as if embarrassed to tell her.

"I'll check the timing in a bit." Sid used a long pipe cheater bar to break the nut loose on the fan pulley, and even so she had to struggle with it. Mike never moved or offered to help, which irritated and pleased her at the same time. Dale had been the same way, letting her figure out on her own what she was capable of. Dale had . . .

When they'd first married, Sid had realized that if she wanted to be with Dale Bowers, it would probably mean spending a lot of time under the hood of a car. But she had always been curious about how things worked—why they worked.

At first, Dale had just answered her questions, explaining the combustion engine in great fascinating detail, then one day, he started putting tools in her hands. Tools, he'd said, were the one thing that made us truly different from animals, and to be a good mechanic, you had to know your tools, what they were for and how to use them. From then on she began her hands-on training. She was given carburetors to rebuild and engines to tear down, and her fine logical mind served her well.

They'd had such dreams together, she and Dale. Just another few months and the car would have been ready. He was going to race the Trans Am on the stock car circuit, and Sid was to be in the pit crew. But all it had taken was one drunk driver to end those dreams—one drunken Air Force officer on a lonely stretch of desert highway.

She cut that line of thinking abruptly, but her eyes had already blurred. Sid turned and rubbed the moisture away with a fairly clean wrist.

"Got something in your eye?" Mike asked from behind her.

"Yeah," she grunted and stared at the big three-quarter-inch ratchet in her hand. In this shop was Dale's legacy, well over a hundred thousand dollars worth of tools and diagnostic equipment. If Sid sold the shop and the Trans Am out back, her daily fight for simple existence would be over. But how could she? Dale was here in every tool she touched, in every direction she looked. Cold comfort, but comfort nonetheless.

"Got another customer, I think," Mike said.

Sid looked out past the lot to the road beyond. A battered dark green Jeep, steam billowing from under the hood, rolled off the street and up to her little row of round-shouldered pumps.

"Wait here," she ordered. "I'll be right back." The deputy followed on her heels anyway as she crossed the cracked, gray pavement.

The driver pushed the door open and climbed out, a young man of average height and build with longish wavy brown hair. Sid halted, a sweet pain twisting in her gut. Then she noticed the guy's shirttail was hanging halfway out and his face was deathly pale. He kept rubbing his thumbs over his fingertips.

"Trouble?" she asked, forcing herself not to stare at the high cheekbones and wide-set dark brown eyes.

The fellow only looked bewildered. "Yes . . . maybe you could . . ." He glanced at the deputy hopefully.

Mike shook his head with a wry twist of his lips. "She's the mechanic."

"I don't have a lot of money on me." Now the man looked morose. There was an edgy nervousness about him that bothered Sid. She popped the hood loose, and a great cloud of steam boiled out.

It took only moments to find the problem. "Broken radiator hose. You got fifteen bucks?"

The guy nodded.

"All right," Sid muttered. "I can get to it in about forty minutes."

"Do it now," Mike said. "Mine can wait."

"Is there a bathroom?" the new customer asked, face even paler.

"'Round back." Sid pointed her chin, and returned to the shop with the deputy again close behind—as if he were on a damn leash. Irritating as hell. She dug through the shelves in the tiny storeroom for a piece of one inch woven water hose, aware of Mike standing beside her.

"Looks a lot like Dale, doesn't he?" the deputy observed gently.

Perceptive son of a bitch. "Not really," she lied and kept herself busy. Her memories were both crystal clear and hazy. Nowadays, she saw Dale in the checkout line at grocery stores, in cars passing on the street, but the driver of the Jeep resembled him closely enough to bring chills. Mike reached out suddenly to put a hand on her arm.

"Sid . . . I was thinking . . . maybe . . ."

"Don't," she snarled, knocking his hand away. She grabbed up a length of hose and fled the storeroom.

II

The Jeep overheating was bad enough, but when John pulled into the garage at Mojave Wells, his fingertips had already begun a warning tingle. With forced calm, he'd managed to carry on a fairly coherent conversation before taking himself as quickly as possible behind the building and away from the lady mechanic and her friend. The numbness spread much faster than the last time. In panic, he glanced around. How far must he go before they were safe—the lady mechanic and her friend?

There was a small house behind the garage, set some hundred feet back. Its dry desert yard held nothing but tumbleweeds, and the arid open landscape beyond swept away into the distance—into the Devil's Playground. A shrouded vehicle and a faded red Toyota pickup were parked beside the weathered white clapboard house. Three nearby pipe corrals had occupants, two horses, and a little donkey that had the pen closest to the garage. Beyond them, to the right of the shop, were a dozen wrecked cars behind a chain link fence. The cafe hemmed him in on the left. Whichever direction he went, death and destruction might follow in his wake.

Desperation goaded him. Run, John, run! But there would be no escape—it was already too late. A sudden vibration rippled through him. He glanced down and saw his hands dissolve, then the world itself dissolved around him, the sensationless void swallowing him whole. The maelstrom whirled him once more into nothingness. Again, there was no pain, only a dim molecular awareness, a nanosecond of nonexistence before he was rejected.

Sick with disorientation, he opened his eyes on reality. A sharp rock dug into his cheek and cold sand had molded itself to his body. Through the pipes of the corral, he focused on the still form of the donkey. It had collapsed to the ground, its neck outstretched, its legs folded under it. The horses were crowded back against the far rails, their bodies tense with alarm. John Caldwell dragged himself upright, wondering vaguely just what they had witnessed.

He staggered into the tiny cubicle that passed for a bathroom. The sink was black with grime, the floor covered with grit. With shaky hands, he splashed icy water onto his numb face. Rejected. That had come as a certainty, an understanding from something outside himself. Why?

He leaned forward on the filthy porcelain and stared into the mirror, then touched his cheek. The nerve endings were still dead. His right eyelid ticked, and he focused there. In the dim light from the door, the pupil appeared dilated, but even so, he could see an odd discoloration in the iris. Yellow streaked the deep brown now, and the white around it looked jaundiced. Not in the left eye, though. That one was normal.

Oh, God, what was happening to him? The panic

churned in his stomach again, and John pushed himself away from the mirror, then forced his legs to function as near normal as possible, to carry him back to the Jeep. Eyes averted, he passed by the poor little donkey lying dead in the dirt.

The lady mechanic was hanging over the front of the Jeep where it was still parked by the pumps. The cowboy—the tall lanky man in boots—passed her a screwdriver, then looked up. Something in the guy's cool light-colored eyes made John straighten. Suspicion, doubt. Got to keep it together, Caldwell. He tucked his shirt in, ran a hand through his hair as he approached.

"Kinda tired," John mumbled and watched the woman start his motor. "Drove all night."

The cowboy leaned a hand on the fender. "Better take a nap somewhere, then. I get real tired of scraping people up off the highway."

The woman straightened. "Lay off the customers, Deputy Nichols. You're not on duty." She dragged a hose over and began to fill the radiator.

John managed a weak smile. So that was professional suspicion and doubt in the guy's face. He was a cop. Brakes wheezing, a sixteen-wheeler with a black and chrome tractor slowed out on the road and pulled in across the cafe's lot.

"Lucas is back," the lady mechanic said. Her eyes followed the truck, then turned on John. "All finished. Need a receipt?"

"Uh, no." John pulled his wallet out and dug through the few bills, found a ten and a five. He held them out to her. "Thanks."

Somehow, he got into the Jeep, got it started, and headed down the road toward the Devil's Playground. The man called Nichols watched him until the vehicle finally drew out of sight beyond the cafe.

John drove carefully through town. The shabby buildings of Mojave Wells disappeared behind him, and now the bleak countryside seemed to spread unendingly in all directions. He found at last the faint trail leading south off the road, then took the Jeep deep into the desert over terrain that once would have scared the hell out of him. But he couldn't have walked it, not in his present condition.

Tires churning the loose sand, he forced the vehicle at an angle up the side of one more steep gully, and finally tipped it over. The seat belts were long missing. John clung stubbornly to the steering wheel, felt his head thump into the roof as the Jeep did a lazy roll. It righted itself and went over again. His head hit the ceiling once more, and the car came to rest upside down in the bottom of the gully. The engine sputtered and died. Carefully, Caldwell untangled his legs from under the dash, then used his feet to kick the passenger side door open as far as it would go. His nose was bleeding profusely and movement brought pain from a number of body parts.

"Shit!" He lay back on the roof that was now a floor and let the blood trickle into his throat. Just rest a moment, he told himself, until the bleeding stops. Rest. Slowly his eyes closed.

III

It was still Friday, near midnight, and Nate Curtis's stomach was still in revolt. He moved down the long dim hallway to the isolation postmortem room of the morgue at the Orange County Sheriff's Station. This was, what? the third roll of Rolaids. At this rate, he'd have to buy them in those damn big bottles.

Dr. Edward Fry, swathed in green surgical scrubs and mask, looked up when Nate entered the observation room. There were four carts with shrouded forms on them around the pathologist. A fifth sat empty, the occupant presently on Ed's stainless steel table. It was Professor Hanover himself. Safe behind his glass window, Nate nodded a greeting.

"Save some of those Tums for me," the pathologist said, his voice slightly distorted through the microphone. He wiped his brow with the back of a gloved wrist.

"They're Rolaids," Nate answered loudly, trying to keep his eyes from the blood-smeared gloves and the gaping cavity in the pale corpse's torso. A squeamish homicide cop. Hell. "What killed them?"

"Take a look." Ed indicated the abdomen.

"Wouldn't know what I was looking at."

The pathologist scooped something out of a hanging scale that resembled the ones you weighed produce in at the market. "Red Jell-O instead of a liver. The kidneys are goo. We got complete disruption of the internal organs in every victim." He held his prize close to the glass for better viewing, and Nate tried hard not to cringe.

"Can a poison do that?"

"Don't know how. Happened all at once." Ed slung the Jell-O back into the scale. "I'd say these folks were microwaved to death, but nothing's cooked, it's just shook to pieces. Disrupted. Was Hanover somehow connected with the military? I mean, there's no way of knowing what those idiots at the Pentagon will come up with next, but if it kills quiet and quick—well, that's just up their alley."

Nate shook his grizzled graying head. "He was an archaeology professor and a mean son of a bitch according to everyone, but no military ties. Not that we can find."

"An answer with a qualifier. I'd dig deeper, if I were you. *Something* killed twelve people damn quick. Have you asked the military?"

"Problem with asking them is they'll start asking back. I don't want those bastards in my face. I'd just as soon keep a lid on this whole mess for a while."

"What are you gonna tell the press?"

"Already told 'em," Nate grunted. "Told 'em we suspect food poisoning. Botulism from home-canned green beans, but that you're still checking into it. The toxicology tests alone will give us six weeks grace. So that's the official bullshit story—at least until I can get my hands on the Caldwell boy." His stomach twinged, and he popped more Rolaids. It occurred to him then that maybe he had an ulcer. But no, Janice's stuffing did this to him every year.

Ed eyed him curiously. "I'm going to do one of the children next. Want to watch?"

"God, no!"

That violent a reaction made the pathologist chuckle. "Well, get the hell out of here so I can get back to work."

"How come you're all alone in there?"

More chuckling. "Had Nelson and Web helping me, but they both got sick and went home—too much Thanksgiving dinner. You're not the only one with a weak stomach. Hey, leave the rest of those Tums, please."

"Rolaids," Nate said and tossed them on the little white table as he left.

IV

In the upended Jeep, John Caldwell was lost in exhausted sleep. Unconscious and unknowing, the numbness had taken him again, unraveled his being, then collected the molecules and re-formed him. Even that failed to disturb him. Night had fallen and still he slept, lost in a terrifying dream. He drifted in visions, trapped without a frame of reference in an alien reality. Pale humanoid creatures with huge almond-shaped black eyes moved through these visions—tall, slender people dressed in dark armor. They had lipless slits for mouths and fluted nostrils that opened and closed as they spoke.

He stood with a small group now in a sealed chamber barren of doors or windows or furnishings. Over and over, they tried to communicate their desires to him, but John had no understanding of the words or the gestures that accompanied them. One creature, taller than the rest, moved toward him at last. In each of its two hands, it carried a black box similar to the one Professor Hanover had found in the desert. These were placed on the floor at John's feet. The creature squatted beside them, and with long, double-jointed fingers, opened one. Within were threads of colored light woven like wires, but intangible.

Words and gestures followed, and still John watched, uncomprehending. Patient, the creature pointed a narrow hooked fingernail at this purple light and that green one. These movements were repeated carefully many times. "On, on," his tutor said. The others in the chamber echoed the word, chanting. John stared, frustrated and fearful. He shook his head violently, and his nose began to bleed again, a thin stream of red that splashed onto the seamless white floor. Silence fell, and the small group backed away from him, fading through the walls. He was left alone with the two boxes.

Light flared in the opened case, and once again John was soundlessly torn apart. This time resolution brought pain, acute. In the side of his left hand came searing agony, and he screamed. And woke up. Pale blue moonlight glistened on the sand beyond the open Jeep door. A gust of wind drove grit against the metal behind his head. Warm blood flowed over his lip and down his chin, and his hand still ached dully.

He dragged himself on his elbows out of the vehicle, squeezing past the half-open door and into the light. The left hand, held out to the moon, looked somehow deformed. Closer scrutiny showed the little finger to be slightly longer and jointed in four places instead of three. A narrow claw topped it. No ... Afraid and angry, John bit into the strange yellowish flesh and felt pain. Not a dream, then. He buried his face in his arms and gave way to tears.

V

Nate started home from the hospital, then changed his mind. He turned the little Datsun sedan around and went back to Vista Road. The tract homes along the narrow street were mostly dark. There were few street lamps, and in the headlights the shrubs threw vague shadows on stucco walls. Sergeant Curtis parked two doors down from the professor's, then pulled on his rumpled gray suit coat and walked the short distance to the house. The November night had gone chilly.

He pulled the official yellow tape loose from the door, ignoring the "Crime Scene—Keep Out" sign and a health department notice. The key Officer Kelly had given him turned the dead bolt easily. Nate flipped the living room lights on as he passed through to the hall. He didn't have a mask, but instinct told him it wasn't necessary. In the shadowed living room, the windows were invisible. The drinking glasses on the table were still exactly as found. What melted glass and killed people from the inside at the same time? Nothing; they couldn't be related. But they were by God, they were. Somehow.

Nate turned and headed down the hall past empty, silent bedrooms. Hanover's office was much as they'd left it, except that faint white powder had been dusted on the phone and file cabinets, the tables and chairs.

It was to the cabinets that the sergeant went first, not entirely sure of what to look for. The files under A were too academic to arouse interest, the Bs were positively boring, but the Cs offered up a thick folder marked Chariots. This was pulled and set carefully on the big desk while he rifled through the rest, drawer after drawer. Nothing more caught his attention. On the slender table under the bulletin board, Nate eyed the prof's computer setup. The logo at the bottom of the monitor screen didn't strike any chords. The keyboard mocked him. Somewhere in the contraption was probably all the information he needed, but the sergeant didn't know diddly about computers, despite the fact that most of the officers on the force couldn't do a damn thing without them anymore.

He dug through the little floppy disk file box and found two worth taking. One was marked Chariots, the other said simply, Devil. Janice was the family computer whiz. If she couldn't open them up, then someone at the station could—probably Kelly. Nate checked his watch. Nearly 2:00 A.M. Hell. The floppies were pocketed carefully inside the coat. You didn't bend the things, that much he knew. He reached for the light switch, then paused, gazing at the terrariums.

There was a sister of Hanover's back east—Rhode Island—but she couldn't come out to L.A. for another few days. Long time to go hungry. Hell. There was a round container of tropical fish food near the aquariums. Nate dumped a little in each tank. Nowhere could he find a bag of Purina Tarantula Chow though. Or Rattler Chow. A quick search re-

vealed a small tin filled with something foul-smelling and
sporting a multitude of insect legs and papery wings.

The spider didn't seem particularly thrilled when he
shook some into its glass-walled cage. The snakes, Nate
gave up on completely. Even if there'd been a few handy
mice around, he wouldn't have had the heart to serve them
up as dinner.

"Sorry fellas, you lose." He made a mental note to have
Kelly—if he hadn't already done so—find someone to
take care of the prof's critters, then took the folder and
floppies back out to the Datsun. The drive down Harbor
was fairly quick. Even at this late hour, there was plenty
of Friday night traffic. Disneyland had shut down over an
hour ago, and there were still cars trickling out of the gates
as he passed by.

The Anaheim police station was fondly called Disneyland North and often referred to as a real Mickey Mouse
operation, no offense taken. All around the Happiest King-
dom On Earth were city streets with their fair share of
crime, no more, no less, and the Anaheim police handled
it all with professional efficiency. But twelve unmarked
bodies in one upper–middle-class dwelling sure made a
man wonder.

He pulled the Datsun into the garage next to Janice's
new silver Oldsmobile Cutlass. It tickled him to think of
tiny Janice in the great big Olds, and him squeezed into
the 210, his head pressed into the roof. She'd been trying
to talk him into a new car, too, but the Datsun was as
comfortable as an old shoe and ran like a top. When they
were first married thirty years ago, his wife had worried
that her money would bother him—the fact that she had
plenty and he'd never had any. They'd had their hard
times emotionally, but it had never been over money. Nate
liked money, appreciated and respected it, but it had never
held any real power over him.

Despite the fact of Janice's wealth, they lived moder-
ately. Neither of them had much use for "things." They
had no children, and somehow that hadn't bothered them
either. There'd been plenty of nieces and nephews to spoil
and send home—the best of both worlds. No, money had

never bothered Nate, but it might have made him too self-reliant, maybe a little lazy even. He was too easily content, happy to stay a homicide sergeant for over a decade instead of working his way up through the ranks. One of his partners was captain now, but responsibility kept you tied down. Nate preferred to be responsible for his own actions, not the actions of others.

The garage door closed slowly behind him, and he put his own key in his own lock. The house smelled good, of spices and Janice's favorite perfume, Hawaiian White Ginger. The lady loved Hawaii, her one true vice, and every year they spent his vacation there, exploring the islands by plane, by boat, even on horseback—just another pair of happy *hoales*.

Nate passed out of the kitchen and into the dining room, which was also Janice's home office. The floppies were laid carefully on the computer desk, but the folder was carried with him down the hall to their bedroom. Janice slept deeply, tousled blond head buried in a down pillow. Sometimes he felt guilty, as if his life had been too good, and he didn't deserve it or this good-natured, pretty, middle-aged woman.

Best to climb into bed with her, snuggle up, but he loved a mystery almost as much as he loved her. Twelve dead bodies was too enticing a puzzle. And the melted glass. He took himself instead into the living room and pulled his bifocals from his breast pocket, then began to read the first typewritten page of Professor Hanover's theories on the Chariots of the Gods.

VI

The wind grew stronger sometime in the night. It rocked the Airstream hard enough to eventually wake Mike Nichols. He listened to it moaning around the glass louvres of the windows. An old friend, this wind. As a kid, he'd climbed high in the branches of the old black locust in his grandmother's yard right here in Mojave Wells—so the dry desert wind could rock him. Eyes closed, he drifted on the gentle motion of the trailer, but sleep would not return.

Cactus was dead. Sid had discovered the little burro in its corral behind the shop just after she'd finished the tune-up on Mike's rig. It had shaken the young woman, shaken her hard, though she'd tried to hide the fact. They'd raised the orphaned animal, she and Dale, not long before his death. But it went that way with horses and donkeys sometimes—a twisted gut, colic. Mike had tried to convince Sid that she wasn't to blame. His sympathy and kindness had only made her angry.

Remembering only served to make him miserable. He turned restlessly on the hard, narrow bed. Set his sights too high, this time, but wasn't that always the way with him? Maybe if you always pursued the unattainable, you didn't really have to worry about attaining it. That made a convoluted kind of sense. Only he was tired of being alone, and Sid needed someone in her life besides a ghost. Not because she was a woman or a widow, but because they'd be good for one another. Gut instinct told him that, not ego.

And poor little Cactus was dead. Finally Mike drifted into sleep, but the last conscious memory was of the burro, its legs folded back under it, its neck stretched out, blind eyes focused on infinity. Death had somehow caught the little animal unaware—sudden, complete, unalterable. Sad.

VII

Blood and mucous drizzling from his nose, John finally gave up on the tears. He'd come here to relocate Hanover's cursed black box, to try and undo the damage it had caused. Deep inside, he sensed that it was already too late, but to give up now was impossible. He crawled back into the Jeep, and mostly by feel, found the two-foot crowbar and the professor's collapsible shovel in the jumble of his belongings.

With thin blue moonlight to guide him, John climbed out of the gully and headed west. There were landmarks he remembered—a huge old Joshua tree and a jumble of sandstone boulders. Things looked different by night, but this was the way. He discovered finally the tiny Valley of Death with its litter of white bones and the narrow ridge of igneous stone exposed here and there through the sand.

At first, he dug with only the right hand, but that was awkward. The left, with its ugly little finger, functioned perfectly, and the pain had gone. Might as well use it. The hole grew deeper, and almost, John thought he'd guessed wrong, until the shovel blade glanced off of something smooth, hard. Trembling, he uncovered the box, then remembered the dream, the vision. There had been two boxes in it. Why two?

The strip of chiseled lava ran east–west. Close on the south was a low rise, to the north the floor of the gully spread and beyond that, another rise. John used the shovel to probe the sand across the gully bottom and struck more stone, some ten feet from the first igneous ridge. This too had been shaped by hands, human or otherwise. Panting with effort, he dug at the spot most parallel to the first box.

The second one lay two feet below the surface, on the same level as the other. It was also anchored to the side of the black stone in some unknown fashion, but John had the crowbar. It turned out to be not so easy a task. He tried every angle that gave him purchase, anything to use as a levering point. Nothing worked. Finally, in frustration, he beat on the second box with the crowbar. The black material seemed even more impervious than the stone.

Cold night wind absorbed the sweat on his face and tugged at his hair. Once more near tears, he collapsed in the sand. If the boxes could not be freed, then they must be destroyed. But how? On his stomach now, he reached into the excavation and ran fingertips along the slick dark surface. No seams, no latches, but there was a row of tiny holes on the underside. The claw on the left hand snagged in one—not by accident. A small burst of understanding filled him. He slid his hand to the farthest mark in the row and pushed the nail into it firmly. The box dropped free of the rock.

John pulled it out of the hole with difficulty. At no more than six inches on a side, the thing weighed at least forty pounds, more like fifty. He found the holes by touch again, eight of them, equidistant from either side. Again, he somehow knew what next to do. The claw tip was slipped into the second hole, then the seventh. The smooth black top slid soundlessly aside. No treasure here. The box was empty. Dead. Broken. This one was set aside.

He removed the first box, now, in the same manner as the other. The effort to drag it from its sandy bed left him panting. The lid slipped back easily, revealing a miraculous swirl of bright color and light, star threads woven in complex beauty, complex purpose. "Purple and green," John muttered to himself, staring into the box with awe. "Purple and green."

Somehow these wires of light were bent into patterns, into the circuits of this alien device. But dream memory would not serve him here. There were slender fins protruding a short way from the inside walls. The myriad colors were repeated over and over, but a single purple and a single green thread were twisted through the rest. He dug through his pockets and found a battered business card, which he tore in half. The colors faded when one piece was wedged between the fins over the spot where the purple light was emitted. The threads of light winked out altogether when he covered the source of the green light. Now the box was as lifeless as the second one. But not broken. No.

Relief washed through him, however unreasonable. He'd bought a little time, no more. Hanover had been right; these black boxes were of the utmost importance. With them, mankind might gain the stars . . . or bring itself complete destruction. John only wanted his life back. He removed his jacket despite the cold and placed both boxes on it, then, dragging them behind him, headed north toward Mojave Wells.

VIII

"Janice . . ."

Even in the dead of night, she woke with a smile for him, expression curious, not angry. "Hmmm?"

"Think you could help me with something?"

Tired blue eyes blinked up at him. "What's the problem?"

"I got these computer disks. I think they might help me with the Hanover case."

Janice swung her small shapely legs off the bed and reached for the light robe on a nearby chair. "It is a homicide, then." A statement, not a question.

"Still not sure." Nate handed her the disks.

She peered at them in their little white sleeves. "At least they're high density. Do you know the program? IBM maybe?"

"All I remember is the little TV's called a Vendex." At her blank look, he growled, "Janice, you know I don't know jack about computers."

"You're going to have to learn someday, my dear." She was smiling again.

Nate only grunted and followed her down the hall to the dining room, watched her turn everything on and push the first disk, the one marked Devil, into the larger of her computer's two slots. Hanover had stuff to back up every one of his crazy theories. His papers were thorough, and by the time Nate had finished reading them, he was half-convinced planet Earth had been visited through the ages by galactic visitors.

The odd thing was, Nate could better believe the prof's theories because the man had never actually seen a UFO himself, only what he believed was evidence of them. Evidence was Nate's stock-in-trade. Of course, evidence could be falsified. Still . . .

"We're in luck," Janice said, her eyes on the monitor screen. "I've got a DOS file list here on the Devil diskette. What do you want to see?"

"All of it."

Now his pretty wife positively beamed. "Come here. You're going to have to print them out, but I'll show you how to call the files up and start the printer, then I'm going back to bed."

Chapter Three

JUST BEFORE LIGHT, Sidney Bowers woke for another of her nightly trips to the toilet. Outside the little bathroom window, the chill night was quiet, but beyond the pipe corrals, a thin strip of light shone around the back door to the garage. She blinked and stared into the dark, still half-asleep. All the shop lights were doused at the end of the day to keep the electricity bill down. She'd never forgotten to turn them off, not once.

The alternative answer frightened her, then made her angry. She felt her way down the short hall and into the murky living room. Dale had always kept a loaded .44 in the bottom drawer of the desk. It was still there, untouched in well over a year. Sid, in flannel gown, slippers, and robe, carried the pistol with her out the door. The chill wind immediately cut through the thin clothing.

She should call Mike—he could be here in five minutes or less. But first Sid wanted to make absolutely sure she wasn't going to embarrass herself. No need of a flashlight with the moon so bright, not quite so full as last night, but setting later. The horses stirred as she moved by them, and the Overo pinto, Candy, nickered in hopes of an early breakfast. A motionless dark mound lay in the last corral—Cactus under a canvas shroud. She would bury him as soon as she could borrow Abner's little tractor with the backhoe. Sadness tugged at her momentarily, then the lights in the shop drew her on.

No movement, no sounds behind the corrugated metal walls. Maybe she *had* left the lights on. There was always a first time. Only the hasp was broken from the doorframe, and the padlock hung at an angle, still hooked to the latch.

The heavy pistol dragging at her wrist, Sid pulled the door open just a crack. The blue-white glow of the fluorescent lights over the workbench showed her little, except a couple of odd black boxes on the stand. Not hers, no. The tools and equipment looked undisturbed.

She took a step inside, the door hinges creaking, the .44 held out before her, elbow tucked against her side to steady the weapon. Something lay in the shadow of the bench—a body. Caution made her approach very careful. Still no movement. Slowly, she squatted beside the inert form of a man, then caught a shoulder in a firm left-handed grip and pulled him over partway, the gun ready.

It was the guy with the old green Jeep. Blood and sand encrusted his nostrils and the nose was flattened across the bridge, swollen, bruised. Dried blood streaked his chin. An accident? A fight? Sidney considered the matter a long moment, then put a finger to his neck and found a strong pulse. Next she checked the knuckles of his right hand. No bruises. His injuries weren't likely to be from a brawl, then. She noted the sturdy nails, clean, slightly long, but well kept. Soft uncallused palm. Not a laborer, this one.

Not that it was any of her business. The wall phone was four steps away, behind her cluttered desk. Time to call Mike, then call an ambulance. Instead, she felt for the unconscious man's back pocket and tugged his wallet free. The driver's license named him John Caldwell, born in 1968—a few years younger than Dale, younger than Sidney. The awkward smiling face in the photo hardly resembled Caldwell now, but it did strongly resemble Dale.

There were also a couple of credit cards, a student ID for University of Orange, library cards, four one-dollar bills, a five, and a twenty. None of it explained what he was doing here.

"Caldwell," she said sharply. "Wake up!"

No response. At the filthy sink against the back wall, she filled an equally filthy coffee cup with water and carried it back to the bench with her. The contents were dribbled into Caldwell's face. He stirred finally and moaned, then woke with a start, eyes wide.

"Why did you break into my garage?" Sidney demanded, clutching the gun tightly against her thigh.

Caldwell focused on her with some difficulty, and muttered, "Please, I—I can't hurt you. Don't be afraid."

"What makes you think I'm afraid?" Sid brought the pistol into view, not exactly pointed at him, but not exactly not. "Now tell me real quick what you're doing here."

"It's broken," the young man answered willingly enough. "I thought maybe with the right tools I could fix it—"

"What's broken?"

His gaze shifted away. "I'm not exactly sure. . . ."

"I'm going to call the cops."

"No!"

Caldwell's left hand wrapped around the wrist with the .44, and she nearly pulled the trigger out of reflex. His fingers were strong, tight, and the two struggled briefly, until Sidney saw the pinky finger, its yellow skin stretched taut over four broad flat knuckles that curled around her wrist. The nail was more claw than anything else, digging into her flesh.

"Dear God!" Sid wrenched free and scuttled back, truly shaken now.

"Please," Caldwell begged. "No cops!"

There were tears rolling down the man's cheeks, and Sidney felt a sudden ache in her chest. Dale had never cried. Never. But this wasn't Dale, no matter what her eyes told her or what her heart wanted to see.

"Jesus," she whispered. "What happened to you?"

Caldwell hid the hand behind the other, ragged sobs caught in his throat. "It changed me."

"What did?"

"The black box . . ."

Sidney glanced at the bench with a sudden rush of alarm. "You brought them here?"

"One's broken, the other I turned off. They can't hurt you. *I* can't hurt you, now."

This was crazy, beyond belief. She tried to remember earlier in the day when he'd paid for the work on his car. The vision came bright and clear. He'd held the wallet in his left hand, and there'd been nothing wrong with the fingers. No. A finger like that could not have been missed.

Caldwell's eyes closed, but the sobs still shook him. Sid glanced at the phone, struggling with indecision.

"Please," she heard him say again and found his gaze on her once more. "I'll leave. I'll go away and I won't come back. I promise. Only please don't call the police."

"But where will you go?"

Silence for an answer, and those deep brown eyes, full of despair.

"Maybe a doctor . . ." she muttered.

He shook his head.

"Is your Jeep here?"

Again a shake of the head. "I rolled it . . . out in the desert."

Sid laid the pistol aside on the cement floor, wondering at her own actions even as she did them.

"There's an extra bedroom in the house out back. I want you to clean up, then rest. Later you can tell me exactly what you think is happening. There's a retired doctor who lives in the trailer park. He's a little eccentric, but a decent guy. Maybe he can help you."

John Caldwell broke down again, tears streaking the blood and sand even more. "Thank you," he sobbed.

"Don't thank me yet," Sidney advised.

II

An early morning call from Avery Sands brought Brigadier General Alden S. McKinley into his Pentagon office around 4:00 A.M. There was minimum staff on duty, and he paced the corridors alone, thoughtful, and just a little curious.

There was a folder already on his wide empty desk. McKinley took the upholstered executive chair and considered the "TOP SECRET/EYES ONLY" stamp on the front. The door swung open silently, and the general looked up.

"Mornin', Avery," he grunted at the slender, medium

height man standing on the threshold. "What brings you to this neck of the woods?"

A rhetorical question. Avery Sands probably spent as much time in Washington as the general. He was one of many civilian advisers to the Pentagon, but he was also a presidential adviser and had the presidential ear. In his mid-thirties, his hair was blond and straight and baby-fine, which made him appear all the younger.

He just happened to be a consulting NASA scientist, too. But most important, McKinley liked and trusted Avery, something that couldn't be said for most of the people he worked with. The scientist had a brilliant, aggressive mind, yet somehow managed to hang on to the little things—like loyalty, ethics, and a sense of humor.

Sands had a familiar quirky little smile on his lips, now. "Looks like Project Majestic may get reinstated."

The general took a deep breath and let it out noisily. "I thought we were through with that crap. All the research, all those billions spent on radio telescope setups, and nothing to show for it."

"It's a big galaxy. . . ."

"And don't give me that needle-in-a-haystack bullshit. This needle Earth's been stabbing at every part of space for fifty years. If there was someone out there, they would've sat on the sharp end by now." McKinley glared at the "EYES ONLY" folder before him. "What makes all you scientists think we'd have a friendly long-distance phone call anyway? We can't get along among ourselves, how're we gonna get along with nonhumans? If there *is* anyone out there, I'll bet they're keeping their mouths shut. In which case, they're a hell of a lot smarter than us."

Avery, who'd heard this speech many times before, watched him in silence, then, "Feel better now, Boss?"

"No," the general growled. "So what's happening?"

"Remember a university prof from California named Arnold Hanover?"

McKinley scratched at his thick white hair. "We've got him on file, don't we? He's published on UFOs."

"Right," Avery nodded. "He's dead. His whole family's

dead, and it could be connected to something he found in the Mojave Desert a couple of weeks back."

"Something military?" The armed forces shared the Mojave Desert, and accidents involving civilians weren't unheard of.

"Maybe . . . But not our military. Not any on Earth."

"Jesus H., Avery. This has happened before. Every time some nervous Nellie thinks he sees an XT in the bushes, we start getting top secret headaches around here."

"Read the report," his friend advised.

The general sighed heavily, then broke the seal on the folder with a blunt thumbnail. There wasn't much inside, but what there was started a sharp, bright pain behind his eyes.

"We're going to have to move fast," he said finally.

"That's what I figured."

"I want those bodies collected, and anything Hanover had on this find of his. What about the student . . . Caldwell?"

"Local police have no leads so far."

"Well, hell."

"We have another problem. . . ."

"What now?"

"Robert Candliss has the jump on us."

"Candliss . . ." McKinley repeated. "That's that Air Force bastard I kicked off the UFO Work Team." The general grew thoughtful. "The guy's ambitious as hell, a real hotheaded pain in the ass, but maybe we'll let him run with the ball a while. Let him pull things together for us. If it's a false alarm, he can take the heat for blowing federal funds. If it's not, we'll just step in and take over when it suits us. What do you think?"

Avery Sands looked doubtful. "I think we should get rid of him. He's too damn heavy-handed, Boss."

"What about SETI?" the general demanded, ignoring Avery's advice already. "Do they know?"

"There's nothing happening at the Mojave facility, but Candliss has been in contact with Fenwick."

Great. McKinley groaned. Twenty years of staring at computer screens and listening to the stars had turned

SETI scientist Quinten Fenwick into a complete space cowboy. Neither he nor Candliss had much of a grip on reality, and together, they could sure wreak havoc.

"Hell, this is all a wild-goose chase anyway." The general closed the file. "I'm giving it to you, Avery. You're in charge. I want constant briefings on the situation. Let's see what Candliss and Fenwick come up with before we start stepping on toes, but clean up after them. And clean up good. I don't want a word of this to get to the media. Understand?"

"You got it, Boss."

"So go."

Avery paused with his hand on the doorknob. "Alden . . . Why did you take over the UFO Work Team? It's obvious you don't believe in any of it."

"Because, my friend," McKinley said, "someone's gotta keep you dreamers' feet on the ground."

III

Nate pulled into the station parking lot around 9:30 A.M. Janice had let him sleep in. She'd called Rick Laughlin and asked him to take the morning meeting for Nate. Grateful for the extra couple of hours sleep, but still more than a little tired, the sergeant unfolded himself from the Datsun, then pulled Professor Hanover's file from between the seats. This case had all the earmarks of a real whodunit, promising to be the most mind-boggling puzzle of Nate's law enforcement career. The more he'd read through Hanover's papers last night—the more information he gathered—the more complicated things grew.

Of course, the easy explanation laid all the responsibility on John Caldwell—the frustrated and angry T.A. who takes revenge on a slave-driving, foul-tempered professor and his family, using some obscure poison that causes a cellular breakdown of the internal organs. The next explanation was a paranoid's dream—Hanover, dabbling in something he shouldn't, is eliminated by . . . what? Extraterrestrial agents? Government agents?

Smiling at such wild conjecture, Nate strode through

the crowded lot, through the civilian and police vehicles. It was a fine fall morning, the sky clear and blue. Later it would be hot, but now the air was perfect and smog-free. He pulled his badge case from an inside coat pocket and opened it, letting the little red security eye beside the station's rear entrance scan his magnetic key card. The door unlatched with an audible click and let him through.

There were nods and hellos from the busy folk passing in the halls. Nate headed straight for Homicide. The pathologist's preliminary findings should already be on Nate's desk. He found the wide outer room with its desks and file cabinets nearly empty, a redheaded man lounging alone in a chair. Detective Rick Laughlin was a bright young officer in his late twenties. At the moment, he drank coffee from a Styrofoam cup.

"You really should bring a mug from home," Nate said from the doorway. "Polystyrene won't break down for a thousand years."

"Yeah?" Rick said, as if he hadn't heard the same line a hundred times before from at least a half dozen officers.

"So what's happening? Did I miss anything important?" Nate passed him on the way to the sergeant's office, a little cubby with a desk and a small glass window that looked out on the other room. "Has anyone gotten a line on the Caldwell kid, yet?"

Rick didn't answer, but he followed Nate into his office. "Captain wants to see you."

Somebody had rearranged the desktop, and not very well. The sergeant laid the file down and looked up, perplexed and annoyed.

"What does he want to see me for?"

Detective Laughlin hesitated, obviously uncomfortable.

"Where's the lieutenant?"

"With the captain . . ."

Uh-oh. Nate did a quick backtrack of the last few days' events. This could only mean that somehow, someway, he'd fouled up and was about to be called on the carpet. Damn. He stared at the desktop.

"Who the hell's been at my papers? Where're the

Hanover reports? Kelly should've had them on the desk early."

"Captain Wallace has 'em. You're supposed to take anything else you've got on the case with you."

Nate tugged at his lower lip. This was going to be far worse than being chewed out—they were taking the case from him. But why? Rick had wisely retreated out of the office. Irritated, the sergeant gathered up Hanover's Chariots file and walked back into the hall. Bren Cassidy hooted at him through the open door of the Burglary Division, which was ten times larger than Homicide and ten times busier. Nate managed a smile that faded the moment he was beyond Bren's view.

The Captain of Crimes Persons was James T. Wallace. He'd been Jimmy twenty years back when he had worked with Nate. Times had changed, and power tended to make assholes of some men. But then maybe that was a requirement; maybe it took an asshole to keep a whole lot of people in line. Nate had never cared to find out. Despite the distance of years and politics, he still liked Wallace. *Captain* Wallace.

The captain's door was closed. Nate paused before it, then knocked—loudly, but not too loudly. Lieutenant Ford answered the knock with a grave expression on his pleasant, thin face. Nate kept his own expression neutral. They knew that he knew what was coming.

"Lieutenant. Captain." He nodded at them both, then gave Wallace a direct look. "You wanted to see me, sir?"

"Have a seat, Sergeant, please."

Ford had returned to his own seat. Nate took the hard wooden chair directly in front of the massive oak desk. Wallace, a year or so older than Nate and with only a ruff of gray hair left, shuffled the papers on his desk. Nate waited.

"The Hanover case has been taken out of our hands," the captain said a long moment later. "We're to give up everything."

"To who?" Nate asked carefully.

"It's really none of our business."

"But why? Hanover was a local professor. We've got

twelve deaths in our own backyard. If that isn't our business, I don't know what is."

"Nate." The lieutenant leaned toward him. "There's nothing we can do about it. For us, the case is closed."

"We don't know that they're homicides, anyway," Wallace added.

"And we don't know that they're not. The tests will—"

Ford shook his head. "That's all gone, too. Taken this morning."

"Have you brought everything else you have pertaining to the Hanover investigation?" The captain put his elbows on the desk, and Nate set the Chariots file in front of him. Wallace looked up. "That's all of it?"

"Yes." Over the years Nate had learned to read people pretty well. All kinds of little things could give a man away. He'd also learned to use that knowledge to his advantage. With just the right touch of regret, he said, "That's all of it."

Captain Wallace looked satisfied, but Ford sent Nate a quick sharp glance.

The captain gathered the folder to him, smiling. "Good. Excellent." The smile widened. "Lieutenant Ford says you've got two weeks coming. I think you should take them now. I'll see that the scheduling is arranged. Hawaii, isn't it? Every year, you and the wife?"

Nate smiled back, but he thought dolefully, I am a creature of habit. Aloud, he said, "Is there anything else I can do for you, sir?"

Wallace's smile was painted on. "Just enjoy yourself in Hawaii, and forget about Hanover."

"Yes, sir."

The sergeant stood up, and Ford got hastily to his feet as well. Nate beat him out the door without being too obvious.

"Nate!" The lieutenant caught up with him as he turned a corner in the corridor. "Hold on."

"Bullshit!" Nate growled, voice low, still in motion. "Who the hell called this play? Do you even know?"

"It was the World Health Organization."

"A disease, then. Some bug got loose in a government

lab somewhere and just happened to end up on the professor's Thanksgiving table. Now they come to clean up, but we should forget it."

"Nate . . ." Allen Ford was a regular cop who just happened to also be a lieutenant. Nate could be honest with him, vent his frustration, and Allen would always listen. "Nate, I don't think it was a bug."

The sergeant halted. "Why?"

"Ed Fry says there was no big fuss when they took the bodies. They were careful, but not that careful."

"Yeah? The W.H.O.?"

"That's what they said, but that's not who they were. We're talking dark suits and very short hair."

"Spooks?" Nate's eyes widened a touch.

"Of some sort." Allen caught his gaze. "You gave the captain everything?"

"Everything, dammit."

"Then let go of it. Take your vacation. Take Janice to Hawaii." The lieutenant glanced at his wristwatch. "Look . . . uh, I've really got to run. I'll set up the scheduling and get Captain Wallace to approve it. See me before the shift's over." Allen Ford turned back, headed in the opposite direction.

Nate returned alone to Homicide. Laughlin was there, and Conner and Hansen. They kept themselves busy at their desks. Good. He was in no mood for conversation. The sergeant closed the door to his office—something rarely done—and seated himself behind his own desk. There were two other new homicide investigations, both with suspects arrested. Both would be slam dunks by the look of them. The Anaheim Homicide Division wouldn't suffer too much if Nate went to Hawaii a week or so early.

He pulled the phone closer and dialed home and got the answering machine. Hell. Janice wouldn't appreciate a change of plans. She, too, was a creature of habit and looked forward to Christmas in Hawaii. He stared at the phone for a long while, then grabbed up the handpiece and punched in the number for the Orange County Sheriff's Station.

IV

John slept with his face turned to the wall, the blankets pulled over one shoulder. Sidney stood a moment in the bedroom doorway, watching, then took a hesitant step toward the bed. To see that familiar dark hair against the flowered pillowcase disturbed her, but not nearly so much as the hand that clutched the blankets. She moved around the bed and leaned closer.

In an age with special effects and fancy molded plastics, John Caldwell's one odd finger might be a clever fake. To the touch, though, it had been icy cold, rough skinned, and those four broad knuckles had flexed—she'd seen them do it, felt their grip. This couldn't be, and yet it was.

Caldwell stirred, but didn't wake. His eyes shifted under the lids, and his face contorted. Whatever the dreams, they did not make him happy.

"What have I done?" Sid whispered. "What can I do?" Open the shop, get to work, let the poor man sleep. There'd be time later to see if any sense could be made of all this. Maybe he'd be gone when she came back to the house for lunch. She almost hoped he would as she left the bedroom, headed for the front of the house.

Tired already from rising so early, Sid gathered the keys off the kitchen table and took herself outside, forgoing breakfast. Cold wind, same as yesterday and last night, same bright ineffectual sun. The phone in the shop was ringing, but she stopped to throw hay into the horses' mangers and check the level in their fifty-five-gallon water containers. A thin layer of ice floated in the drums.

It was easy enough to get in the shop with the hasp on the door broken, but the phone had already quit ringing by the time she was inside. Pushing up the one huge front door took a little extra effort. She paused with the sweet, dry wind gusting into the garage.

There was a gunmetal gray four-door sedan at the pumps. An E car, government issue. She'd seen enough of them as a child to know. The driver side door opened immediately, and a slender man in a neat dark suit and tie stepped out. A sheet of paper fluttered in his grip.

"Sidney Jane Bowers?" he said as he approached. His fair hair was cropped so short that pink scalp showed through, and there was an extremely serious expression on his youngish face.

A real tight ass, Sidney decided, just like her father had been. "Yes?"

"Henry Teal, D.O.D. May I ask you a few questions?"

"Depends. What's the D.O.D. stand for?" She already knew.

"Department of Defense, ma'am," Henry Teal said, playing along. No doubt the man knew everything about her, knew that her father had been in the CIA, had died in an unknown Central American country on an unspecified mission. "This won't take long." Teal flashed an official gold and silver badge and an ID card in a leather wallet, then held out a black-and-white fax photo to her. "Have you seen this man?" The wind tried to snatch the picture, but Teal caught the edges with both hands and straightened it.

This man was John Caldwell. Sid's empty stomach did a quick flip-flop. Too long a pause, though, might make Teal wary. So tell the truth, Sidney, but not all of it. She fixed her attention on the photo and nodded.

"He was here yesterday just before noon. I replaced a radiator hose for him and he left." She looked into the agent's face and saw only a schooled dispassion with just a touch of superiority, but his eyes were on her as well, and she returned her attention to the picture.

"Could you describe the vehicle, his clothing?"

"Older Jeep hardtop, dark green. White shirt, tan pants, I think. Don't you need to write this down?"

"Was he carrying anything? Did you see anything in the vehicle?"

"No . . . usual junk in the car, but I couldn't say what. Maybe if you tell me what you're looking for . . ."

Teal ignored the question. "Time you last saw him, please. And the direction he drove away in."

"I don't know the exact time. He was here maybe fifteen minutes, and he headed south. Just why would the Defense Department be looking for him? Is he . . . a spy or something?"

"I really can't say, ma'am. Thank you for your cooperation." Agent Teal turned abruptly and headed back to his car.

"You're welcome," Sid called after him. "Need any gas?"

But the E car started up and made a tight U-turn, heading back toward Highway 15. Sid finally allowed herself a shiver, then looked back into the shop. The boxes were still on the bench. They had to be what Teal was looking for. She could have told him about them—should have told him—but her distrust and hatred of the whole covert bureaucratic system was still strong. Damn! John Caldwell was in deep shit with the government, and now, so was Sid.

V

Mike Nichols was cruising west on the highway when his cellular phone began to beep. It was a new toy, an unwilling donation to the San Bernardino Sheriff's Department by a Barstow drug dealer. By right of confiscation, law enforcement agencies could now utilize the high-tech toys and money taken in drug busts. That meant the bad guys were supporting the good guys and helping them catch more bad guys—an irony Mike thoroughly enjoyed. The phone beeped again, and he picked it up.

"Deputy Nichols."

"Nichols, this is Sergeant Curtis, Homicide Division, Anaheim Police." The call faded in and out as the Cherokee rolled past a power station near the town of Baker. "Your people say you cover some territory called the Devil's Playground up near Mojave Wells. That right?"

"Yeah. Why?"

"There's a case I'm working on locally that may be tied in to that area of the desert."

That sounded curious. "Yeah? How so?"

"Look. Has anything out of the ordinary happened up there in the last few days?"

"In the Playground? Haven't heard of anything. It's not a real popular tourist spot, especially this late in the year."

"Anything . . ."

The voice faded completely for several seconds. Mike waited for the static to dissipate. "Come again?"

"I said, anything unusual anywhere around there? Mysterious deaths maybe?"

A homicide, Mike would definitely remember. The sergeant had to think he was dealing with a real country hick. "This is a quiet area. Nothing much happens besides auto accidents. We haven't even had any highway fatalities in over a month. And the last homicide was over ten years ago."

"Wait a minute," Curtis snapped. "I'm not necessarily talking about murder. Just a death with strange circumstances. Do you understand what I'm saying?"

"No," Mike said flatly, then paused. "Well . . ." This would sound particularly stupid and hicklike. "A burro died." That was a little out of the ordinary, but not much.

The silence that followed made the deputy think the line had gone dead. Then, "Tell me how it died."

"Don't know for certain. It just keeled over. I figure it was probably just a twisted gut."

Another long silence. "Maybe a very twisted gut. You wouldn't have seen a young guy 'bout five-foot-ten with brown hair and brown eyes around the time that burro died?"

Now it was Mike's turn to hesitate. "There was a guy like that . . . driving a dark green Jeep."

"Son of a bitch! That's the one! When did you see him? Is he still in the area?"

"Wait a minute. Are you saying he had something to do with the burro's death?"

"Look, is he still in the area?" This was said slowly and carefully, and Mike was insulted.

"The guy was in Mojave Wells yesterday late morning, then he left, headed south on Highway 137. That's the last

I saw of him. Is there a warrant out? You want him picked up if he shows again?"

"Deputy Nichols, you'd best stay clear of him for now. I'll be in touch."

"Hey, come on ... I want to know what this is all about."

But the line had gone dead. Cursing, Mike slowed the Jeep, and waited for traffic to clear, then swung the vehicle around and sent it back toward the Mojave Wells turn-off.

VI

The damn black boxes were in the way, but it took a long time before Sid found the courage to move them. John Caldwell said they couldn't hurt her, but then he wasn't in very good shape physically or mentally as far as she could tell. She nudged one of the boxes with a pair of channel locks first, then reached out a tentative finger. Odd smooth surface, sleek, cool, and hard, yet somehow resilient. Like nothing she'd ever felt before. And heavy. Solid lead wouldn't be so heavy.

With shop rags wrapped around them, Sid lugged the things to the back of the garage and set them on the wooden boards on the concrete floor with the batteries. Finally she donned her coveralls and pulled Laura Kelsey's VW Bug inside, then started on the front wheel bearings. Traffic rumbled lightly out on the 15, an occasional jet thundered by in the distance, but these were ordinary, everyday sounds, almost subliminal. Sidney kept her mind on the work, refusing to think about the man asleep in her house. Laura, a retired schoolteacher who lived in town, would need the car by this afternoon for her weekly trip to see her sister in Barstow.

Sid hooked the small wheel-puller's claws over the outside bearing and began to cinch the puller down against the end of the axle. Outside, a car drew up close to the wide door. The driver killed the engine, and she could hear the monotone voice of a female dispatcher. Mike Nichols was here or one of the CHP. The thought of either made her nervous.

A car door slammed. "Sidney!"

Shit. "I'm really busy, Mike."

"Did you bury Cactus yet?" the deputy demanded, squatting beside her. He was in uniform, long-sleeved tan shirt, green Levi's, the holstered pistol hooked to his utility belt. A padded nylon khaki green jacket was tucked over his arm.

"I have to borrow Abner's tractor first."

Mike stood abruptly, pulled on the jacket, and headed around the outside of the building. In alarm, Sid abandoned the car to chase after him.

"What the hell are you doing?"

Deputy Nichols had climbed through the pipes into the end corral and torn the tarp back from Cactus's sad little body.

"Mike . . ."

He hunkered down and felt through the shaggy winter coat, along the bloated stomach, along the neck, then caught a hoof, and, with considerable effort, tugged the carcass over. Sid watched, confused and appalled, as he checked the animal carefully on the other side, also.

"What are you looking for?" she asked finally when he stood back, his lips pursed.

"A wound."

"Why?"

"Got a really weird call from a cop in Orange County. He asked if we'd had anything unusual happen up here, like a death maybe. When I told him about Cactus, he asked if some brown-haired guy was around when it happened."

Sid felt a little stab of fear in her gut. "You think he killed Cactus? But why?"

"Some people don't need reasons, just opportunities. The guy was back here alone. But I can't find any stab wounds, any blood. No marks of any kind." Mike slapped a hand in frustration against the upper rail of the corral. "I don't really know what the hell to look for. Never had any training in crime scene investigation, just how not to mess things up for the experts." He looked straight at Sidney, gray eyes suddenly intense. "Did he come back?"

She swallowed. "Who?"

"For Christ's sake, Sidney. Who do you think?"

"The guy with the Jeep . . ." Sid took a deep breath. "No."

"If he does come around, stay away from him. Call me immediately. This guy could be dangerous."

"I can take care of myself, Mike." Guilt and self-doubt made her hostile.

Deputy Nichols flipped the canvas back over the burro. "Everyone knows how damn well you can take care of yourself, Sid, so just get off your high horse. I've told you how it's gonna go. If you see the man with the Jeep, you'll steer clear and call me."

This was not the Mike Nichols she was used to pushing around—pushing away. Sid looked down on Cactus, then gazed at the little white clapboard house. Was he asleep? Was he gone? Or watching? All hell would break loose if John Caldwell walked out the front door at this moment.

"Sid, dammit!"

"All right. Fine. If he comes around, I'll hide out and call you."

"Thank you." Mike slipped through the bars. "I'm going to run south a ways, see if I can spot the Jeep. He may be long gone by now, but the sergeant mentioned the Devil's Playground."

He was talking to himself as he moved back toward the front of the shop. Sid followed slowly, her mind on other things besides wheel bearings.

VII

Nate made several more calls—one to his brother-in-law in Santa Ana to arrange borrowing a camper and pickup, then another call to Janice's younger sister in San Pedro. Donna was surprised to hear from him, even more surprised by his request, but willing. She and Janice had always been close.

Next, he tried home again, and Janice answered.

"Hi, hon. Look, my vacation's been moved up to this coming Monday."

"What? Why?"

"Something's happened here at work. I'm not going to be able to go with you to Hawaii, but Donna says she'd love to see the big island—"

"Now, hold on, Nate Curtis. What in the hell is going on? You've been looking forward to this as much as I have."

"It's the Hanover case, darling. It's getting more and more complicated by the minute, and I need to spend all my free time working on it." That brought a long silence.

"Are you in trouble?"

The lady was sharp, always had been. Nate grinned at the wall. "Not yet."

"Is it dangerous?"

"No."

"I spent enough years worrying when you worked the streets. Don't you dare get careless, Nate Curtis."

"Not me. Look, could you call the airline and change the flight? I'm kinda busy."

Janice sounded doubtful now. "I don't need to go to Hawaii. I'd really rather not. We'll go next year."

"Hey, Donna's really excited about the idea. You two will have a great time. . . ."

"Where are you going to be?"

"Following some leads. Don't worry."

"You and your mysteries. Just don't go for any rides in UFOs."

"How—?"

"I've had a look at those floppies you brought home. The professor was a crackpot, but he still makes too much sense." Janice paused. "I have to get back to work on the tax quarterly. We'll talk when you get home tonight."

After he hung up, Nate stared at the phone for a while. Janice would demand to know all of it, and Nate better have his story good and straight by this evening.

VIII

Nightmare grew distant, and reality shifted. No more running, no more fear. John dreamed. They were with him again, three tall, slender creatures, beautiful, peaceful. Their dark armor was made of the same smooth black material that encased the boxes, though it yielded with every graceful movement. They wore weapons. Beauty in war, peace in death.

John looked down at his hands, and they were golden with claw-tipped, many-jointed fingers. For some reason this didn't frighten him. He reached up carefully and explored the angles of his noseless face. His sharp tongue probed the bony ridges of his gums. So much more utilitarian without teeth to rot and wear away.

His companions watched his actions, huge dark eyes filled with expression—curiosity, approval. He showed them his hands, and they nodded, a slow tilting of the head from side to side. Their joy flooded through him.

"I'm not human anymore." The words were distorted by so strange a tongue, but clearly English.

" 'On, 'On," the others chanted, and he realized it was his name, just as distorted.

There were so many more things that he understood now. The tall one approached with the boxes again. She—the female leader of this warrior group—placed them once more at John's feet. He watched intently as she opened one, exposing its colored lights, then placed a nail tip to a point on one rectangular finned wall. John squatted, long knees in black armor tucked under his chin. The light was blue, the beam twisting, convoluted, through the others, but it was to the tiny lens that emitted the light that she pointed. With a gentle hook of her nail, she pulled the lens' free and held it out to him, a near-invisible speck. The lights had died. The miniscule lens was replaced, slowly, then everything repeated.

He watched her movements over and over, confused, until at last she took his hand and pulled him close, pressing her forehead to his. White light exploded behind his eyes and sent a jolt of terror through him. But fear must never be acknowledged. He jerked free of her grip.

" 'On."

"No!"

"Caldwell . . . ?"

"No!"

But that last voice was different. He forced himself to wake, to open his eyes. The lady mechanic stood at the foot of the bed, dressed in coveralls, a bandanna over her hair. The expression on her face was cold. John pushed his left hand into the folds of the quilt.

"Did you kill my burro?" she asked quietly.

His head ached dully, and he was too tired to lie. "Yes . . ."

"Why?"

"The box . . ."

"That seems like an excuse for just about everything with you." When he bowed his head, she stepped closer. "There was somebody here looking for you, this morning. A man in a suit with a shiny badge. From the Defense Department. Who the hell did you steal those boxes from?"

John's fear doubled at the thought of the government being involved. "Didn't steal them," he managed, his heart pounding erratically. "They're very old. The professor found them. You didn't . . . tell about . . . ?"

"Your damn boxes are fine. Professor who?"

"Doesn't matter now. He's dead, too." Caldwell pushed the blankets back and tried to sit up.

"What are you doing?"

"Leaving."

"No, you're not. I told you I'd help, and I will."

From somewhere, John dredged up anger. "You can't help. No one can help." He tried to stand, but his knees gave way and left him curled up on the floor between the wall and the bed. His left hand flexed on its own, and he used the right to trap the wrist. Something was happening—his body seemed to refuse even reflexive control, and his heartbeat was all wrong. Oh, God. He'd shut the one box down, but the changes were still happening.

The lady mechanic slipped her hands under his armpits and tugged him back onto the bed. She was strong, yet gentle.

"I'm gonna drive over to the doc's," the woman said, and pulled the blankets around John's shoulders. "It'll take maybe ten minutes. You stay put. Let the phone ring, don't answer the door. Maybe we can't help, but at least let us try."

"Why?" Caldwell asked. "Why should you?" But she was already gone.

Chapter Four

CHARLES T. DOWNING, M.D., took a great deal of pleasure in his simple lifestyle. He'd given up a third wife and a thriving medical practice in Century City over a year ago and fled to the hostile environs of the Mojave Desert without a single regret. This day, as every day, was spent watching sports on his big screen stereo television set. The black futuristic box took up almost the entire front area of his thirty-foot Winnebago.

Outside on the sandy trailer park grounds, the very latest, technologically advanced, satellite dish pointed its sensitive nose at the Toshiba Comm Sat, which lay in a geosynchronous orbit just above the eastern horizon. There were three such satellites available to Dr. Downing at the touch of a button, and he could watch sporting events from all over the world at any time. This, plus a well-spent six hundred dollars for a microchip that automatically unscrambled all the pay movie channels, brought unceasing joy to Charles's idle existence—this and a fridge well stocked with beer.

No matter that it brought his ex-wives close to homicidal rage. They were all lovely, conniving, greedy women who could sink their hooks into some other poor professional slob. Charles Downing had decided on relative poverty rather than supporting their high fashion lives. Nope. There were absolutely no regrets with this career move.

On the screen before him, mud-soaked men collided at the center of a distant field. Australian football was an all-out bloody exhibition in hostility and thoroughly absorbing. His beer can empty, Charles crushed it and dumped the aluminum into his recycling trash bag, then dug another can from the refrigerator, faded blue eyes still on the

TV. His world was observed almost entirely through a warm alcoholic glow nowadays, and that bothered him just a little—as did the growing beer belly on his otherwise slender middle-aged frame.

The sound of tires crunching on the gritty soil made the doctor glance out the little window in the door. Sid Bowers's ancient red Toyota pickup pulled up beside Charles's dusty Mercedes convertible. Well, well. A rare visit from the young woman was always delightful. He pushed the door outward as she climbed out of the cab.

"I was just about to fix a late lunch, my dear," Charles called. "Won't you join me?"

Sid shook her head, her short blond hair still wrapped in a greasy red bandanna. At least she'd removed the coveralls. Charles appreciated her approach, small round breasts bobbing behind the flannel shirt exposed under the open jacket. Her Levi's were just tight enough to accentuate her well-shaped posterior, and this Charles appreciated also. She climbed the steps and entered. He made certain to block the entrance just enough to force her to brush against him. After three disastrous marriages, Charles still loved women dearly.

"Well, then, to what do I owe this visit?"

"I need a doctor," Sid said without preamble.

"Are you ill? Have you injured yourself? I've told you, Sidney, that a mechanic's work is far too strenuous a profession for a—"

"It's not for me," the young woman snapped.

Charles sat heavily in his armchair. "I don't practice medicine anymore, Sid," he reminded her.

"But you could."

"But I don't. Would you like a beer?"

"Charlie, this is an emergency. This guy's got no place to turn."

"I'd advise you send him to Barstow, then."

"Can't. Looks like the government's after him."

Interest pricked, Charles leaned toward her. "Military? Is he AWOL? Sidney, best to stay out of it."

"No, I'm fairly sure this isn't a military matter—

nothing so ordinary." The woman's face was contorted with doubt. "You'll have to see it to believe it."

"How mysterious, my dear. What are we talking about?"

"Charlie, I don't know. Yesterday, this young guy drove into the garage with a busted radiator hose. I fixed it and he left. . . ." Sid paused, uncertain. "Then last night, late, I found he'd come back and broken into the shop. He was lying there on the floor, all beat-up–looking. And his left hand . . ." The doubt grew stronger. "Something's happened to the little finger on his left hand. It was normal when I first saw him, but now it's got more knuckles than it should and a claw instead of a nail."

Disturbed, Charles frowned. "Could that be why the government wants him? Is he maybe involved in some kind of secret experiment?"

"I don't know. He brought these two black boxes, small, but real heavy. Heavier than lead. Maybe they belong to the government, and he stole them. He denies it though, and he says the boxes changed him, that they're responsible for Cactus dying, too."

"Shame about the burro." Charles glanced out the window toward the deputy's small silver Airstream. The Power Wagon was parked in front, but the Jeep was gone.

"Will you at least come look?" Sid demanded. "If I've imagined all this, you can find me a nice padded cell somewhere."

"I certainly can't resist so bizarre a story. Let me just grab a jacket."

II

Quinten Fenwick fretted alone in his trailer at the Avawatz Mountain geological test site, which lay on the edge of the Fort Irwin Military Reserve some twenty dirt road miles north of Mojave Wells. He'd sat at the cluttered computer desk all day, studying the contents of Hanover's folders and diskettes by the light of a single gooseneck lamp, his thoughts in turmoil, his head aching.

Outside, an autumn wind gusted through the tiny high-fenced enclosure, whistling through the razor wire that topped the chain link. Inside lay a deep gloom, the air even colder than the desert beyond the heavily shaded windows. The gentle scrabbling in the corners came from sensitive Richter needles, not mice, and everywhere small amber and green lights glowed. Periodically, a series of high beeps sounded—the converse of machines.

The double-wide trailer held millions of dollars worth of equipment, including highly specialized electronics, number crunchers, small compact supercomputers capable of millions of calculations per second. With these and the help of a nearby eighty-five-foot radio telescope, Quinten listened to the black void beyond Earth's skies in hopes of a long-awaited message from other intelligent life-forms that might share our universe.

Hope and despair were common emotions to a SETI scientist. The Search for Extraterrestrial Intelligence had so far been a long and fruitless one. Until now. Quinten tried to control the wild excitement that still threatened to overpower him. Expectations too often brought shattering disappointments, and Arnold Hanover's discovery was almost too good to be true. If a message had finally arrived, it had not come across time and space. Chances were it had been here all along—not twenty-five miles from Quinten's lonely test site. The irony of that shook him.

This morning, Colonel Robert Candliss of the Air Force Intelligence Service had brought Quinten all the hard evidence of Professor Hanover's find in the Devil's Playground. Somewhere within these notes must be a clue to help unravel so tantalizing a mystery, but so far they had only raised more questions.

Quinten had known Professor Hanover for nearly a decade, had even called him a friend. They'd met at a SETI conference in New Mexico during the summer of 1982, and having similar missions in life, had exchanged information off and on over the years. This most recent discovery had been kept a delicious secret, though. Arnold Hanover had made the discovery of the century—of the millennium even—and most certainly had died because of it. How? Why? An accident? Or did mankind face some terrifying new force from beyond the stars?

Quinten refused to accept that last thought. Finally there might be solid proof that, in ages past, the earth had been visited by aliens, but not by the invading forces of Orson Welles's infamous 1938 radio show, "War of the Worlds." Hanover had simply stumbled upon a technology so far beyond man's present abilities that it had killed him. His own ignorance had caused his death. And somewhere out there was young John Caldwell, in possession of that same technology—possibly a danger to himself and to everyone around him.

The phone rang, a harsh buzz in the quiet, and Quinten jumped, spilling cold coffee and a sheaf of papers to the floor. Cursing bitterly, he snatched up the handpiece.

"Fenwick here."

"Teal just reported in." Quinten recognized Colonel Candliss's gravelly voice. "There's no sign of Caldwell, but we've verified his visit to Mojave Wells, yesterday around eleven hundred hours. It's time to send in the troops."

Quinten clutched the phone tighter. "No! Hold off on that, damn it. Let me check the area first."

"Too dangerous," Candliss snarled back. "Think of it, Quint. If there was one artifact, there may be others."

"That's precisely why we can't have a herd of unqualified military personnel trampling all over that part of the desert. There's no telling what kind of damage they'll cause."

"My men know exactly what to do—"

"Candliss, Dr. Renning gave me full authority. This is my decision."

"No, son, it's mine. I clued your boss in this morning, and he agrees. Besides, it's too late. My people're already on site."

"Jesus! You can't do this!"

"Calm down, Quint. Put your nose back into the professor's files and do what you do best. Leave the heavy work to me. I'll let you know what we find."

The line went dead, and Quinten resisted the urge to

throw the phone across the room—barely. Fucking Candliss with his military mentality. There were no fewer than twenty secret and supersecret government groups tangled in the UFO and alien intelligence search, and every one of them was determined to beat the others to the punch. The wonder of such a discovery was completely lost on them. Supersecret and superparanoid, they saw only threats and opportunities.

SETI, under the auspices of NASA, had been forced to accept the support and interference of these groups all along. Unfortunately that's the way the whole convoluted game was played. How else would one find the funding for million-dollar computers? Quinten sank back into his desk chair and forced his tired eyes to focus on the monitor. At the moment, there was nothing else he could do.

III

Mike set the Cherokee in four-wheel drive and sent it west off the road and into the desert. Someone had been out this way recently—someone in something far bigger and heavier than an old green Jeep, and it looked like more than one vehicle. The wind hadn't had time to erase the huge deep tread marks in the sandy soil. For lack of a better plan, the deputy followed them over the rugged terrain, past gnarled Joshua and spiky yucca.

The thump of helicopter blades came to him first, not far from the county road, then the machine swept overhead from behind the Cherokee, a U.S. Air Force gunship with rocket tubes on the sled rails. It swung to face him, weapons threatening, and slowing, Mike stared into the cockpit, into the emotionless faces of the helmeted pilots. The hair rose at the back of his neck. No matter that he was a civilian policeman with every right and good reason to be here on public lands—he could feel the cold animosity, the sense of total destruction hovering as close as the chopper.

But the fear passed, replaced by a surge of anger, and Mike pressed the gas pedal. The vehicle rolled forward into the downwash of the helicopter's blades. A little game of chicken, the deputy thought with grim amusement, and watched the chopper skate suddenly aside, then zoom upward and away to the west. Ha!

A mile farther into the desert, he found a deep gully that held an upended and familiar dark green Jeep. Abandoned. Mike halted beside it, and made a quick search of the interior. A fair amount of blood had dried on the worn upholstery. Again, someone had been here before him. Numerous boot tracks circled the wreck and the tread of huge truck tires led southwest out of the depression. Again, he followed.

Up another final rise and beyond a jumble of sandstone boulders the land opened up into a vast moonscape—the Devil's Playground, with its shifting sands and frozen lava flows. Mike slowed the Cherokee once more, eyes on the canvas-covered transport trucks parked in the distance. A small army of beige-garbed men swarmed over the area, shovels in hand.

The wisest thing would be to turn around and drive away. By sheer force of numbers, the military usually got its imperious way whether right or wrong, and this was obviously a military operation. Self-destructively, though, Mike headed right into the thick of it. Two air police with their white armbands and helmets met him on foot, blocking his path at the same time. One came around to the driver's window, and the deputy noticed the tall man wore a side arm. They both wore side arms.

"Sir. Please turn your vehicle around and return to the county road."

"Not a chance, fella." Mike smiled at him. "I'm on official business, and you boys seem to've wandered a ways from your base. Fort Irwin, right?"

"Sir," the man repeated, face neutral. "This is a matter of national defense. Civilians have no authority here. Would you like an escort?"

The deputy swallowed his irritation. "I'd like to see the officer in charge."

"Colonel Candliss is unavailable. We're acting on his orders. Sir."

"And I'm acting on the San Bernardino County Sheriff's," Mike bluffed. "Now move aside or hear about it from him."

The second man, off to the Jeep's right, had spent his time on a walkie-talkie. Now, he came to mutter in his comrade's ear.

"This way, sir," the taller man said finally.

They walked ahead toward the three trucks, and Mike let the Cherokee idle along after them. A lanky man with scalped gray hair and silver eagles on his shoulders met them. He motioned to Mike to step out of the car.

"Colonel Bob Candliss, Air Force Intelligence Service." He reached out a big square hand. "And you must be Resident Deputy Sheriff Mike Nichols. Out of Mojave Wells, right?"

"Yes, sir," Mike answered, taking the proffered hand.

Candliss turned and moved away, expecting the deputy to follow. "Look, son, it's not our policy to interfere in local law enforcement, but we've got a situation here that's a wee bit touchy, and I've got to ask for your full cooperation."

The two APs flanked the deputy as they strolled in among the trucks. The tires were nearly as tall as Mike.

"What kind of situation?" he asked ingenuously.

The colonel laughed. "You don't honestly expect me to answer that. . . ."

"Yes, I honestly do. This is public land, and you've got no jurisdiction."

"This is the US of A, deputy," Candliss's friendly tone hardened, "and I have every jurisdiction. We've lost a highly classified item here in the Devil's Playground. Once it's recovered, we'll be gone."

Boxed in by vehicles, Mike could see only a little of the action beyond them, men with shovels digging deep into the sand, their motions hurried but careful. The helicopter returned, only now there were two of them, flying a tight pattern over the desert in search of something above ground.

"You're looking for John Caldwell," Mike said with a sudden flash of insight, and regretted it immediately.

"You, young man," Candliss growled, jaw tightening,

"are just the type of stupid civilian that makes our jobs near impossible. I'm ordering you to get your fanny out of here and quick. You want to run crying to your sheriff about it, fine. . . ." The colonel pointed an accusing finger. "He knows better than to run afoul of the federal government. But if you show your nose around here again, Nichols, I'll put you in a deep, dark hole for the duration."

"Is that a threat?" Mike demanded, taking a step toward the officer. Something hard pressed into his ribs through the padded jacket, and he looked down at a shiny revolver in one of the AP's hands, its safety off, the hammer cocked. Jesus.

The colonel's smile returned, a bit strained. "I'm gonna have these fine boys show you back to the road, deputy. You're gonna keep out of our way and out of our business, or there'll be a knock on your trailer door late in the night. I do have that kind of power, I promise you."

Mike was too angry to respond. The other AP had relieved him of his own pistol. Candliss reached out and clapped the deputy on the shoulder, almost companionably.

"Just take it easy, son. Give us a few days, and we'll return your precious jurisdiction to you, none the worse for wear."

Dismissal. The colonel strode abruptly away, other, more important, things on his mind. Helpless, Mike let the APs herd him back to his blue and white Jeep. Both of them climbed into the vehicle with him, one behind the wheel, the other in the backseat. Their weapons had been holstered once more. Another military Jeep trailed them to the county road.

There, his handgun was returned, but not before the brass cartridges had been emptied onto the floorboards.

"Sorry, sir," the taller AP said politely.

The cold wind caught the dust plume from their retreating Jeep and tore it quickly apart.

"Shit," Mike grunted in disgust.

IV

Sid made sure Charlie brought his dust-coated medical bag. He grumbled about house calls, but she could tell he was thrilled at the prospect of adventure. Televisions and satellites could offer only so much diversion. Bundled against the cold, Doc crawled in beside her on the Toyota's bench seat. The heater had broken ages ago, but with the windows up, the autumn sun felt good.

"How come mechanics' cars never get repaired?" Charlie demanded, voicing the one true axiom of the profession.

"Probably for the same reason doctors don't operate on themselves."

"Hardly the same thing, my dear." The doc twiddled the dial on the radio and found that broken, as well. "You will, of course, show proper appreciation for my effort. Dinner at my place? Say Tuesday?"

"I'll think about it," Sid replied, knowing full well that other things besides dinner were on Charlie's mind.

The drive into town took only minutes, and she put the little pickup down the dirt driveway beside the closed shop. Charlie would know how to deal with this. Charlie, supremely calm and logical, could talk John Caldwell into seeking help. A tumbleweed bounced by, snagged momentarily by the corner of the clapboard house, then pushed on toward the cafe parking lot.

"I hope you've got a beer," the doc muttered as he opened the car door. The wind slammed it shut again. "Damn!"

"Need some help?"

"No. Let's just get this over with so I can go back to my nice warm Winnebago."

Sid led him onto the narrow porch and into the house. "He's in the bedroom. Here."

Only he wasn't. The bed was empty. The young woman stood frozen in the doorway. Blankets and top sheet were trailed across the bare wooden floor.

"Looks like there was a struggle maybe." Charlie scratched a silver brow. "They got him, Sid. Just be glad you weren't here or they might've gotten you, too."

"Who?" Sidney demanded.

"Them. The government, the military . . . whoever makes extra knuckles on a man's little finger and causes burros to die. Whoever owns those black boxes."

"The boxes!"

Charlie forgotten, Sid raced back out of the house and across the sterile yard, past the horses. Candy laid her ears back and galloped all of two steps in her tiny corral while Dale's bay gelding, Gomer, watched with little interest. The windowless shop was dark inside, its wide front door locked tight. Sidney felt for the light switch and flipped it on.

Charlie arrived panting as the fluorescent tubes flickered and caught.

"I put them here," she told him, "with the batteries."

The boxes, of course, were missing from the greasy acid-stained boards on the concrete, and Sidney felt an odd relief mixed with sorrow. Whatever had happened, it was no longer Sid Bowers's problem.

"Maybe I am crazy," she murmured.

"Or just forgot to make the bed. I suppose this means dinner is off."

"Shut up, Charlie."

Unoffended, Doc laid a gentle hand on her shoulder. "Sidney, my dear sweet thing, in the year that I've known you, you've never once led me to doubt your sanity. If I didn't believe what you told me at the trailer, I'd never have left my Aussie football game."

"Thanks, Doc . . . you're a good man," Sid said dryly and shrugged his hand away. "But I've never been real sure about *your* sanity." She glanced out the doorway into the fading late afternoon light. "I should just take you home, Charlie."

"Good. I have some single malt scotch. You look like you could use a stiff drink."

"No. I've still got a couple of jobs to finish." Laura

Kelsey hadn't been able to visit her sister after all, and Sid felt some guilt there.

Beside her, Charlie frowned. "Look, after what you've told me, I don't think it's so safe here. Cactus is dead, a strange man broke into the shop, and now he's been spirited away. You should spend the night at the trailer park." At her grimace, he hurried on. "If not at my place, then maybe at Mike's. I know our stalwart deputy would love a chance to defend you."

"Christ, that's all I need." And the last thing she wanted. "Got your bag? Let's go."

On the way back through the yard, Sid went slowly, studying the dry, wind-scoured ground. Tiny dust devils spun debris along the aisle beside the corrals. What tracks John Caldwell might have made were likely long gone. The broad windows of Hannah's Cafe faced out toward the street and unless one of the few customers had made a run to the outside bathroom door, it was doubtful anyone had seen what had transpired at the garage.

If anyone had taken Caldwell away by force, as Charlie proposed, they'd done so very neatly. Perhaps he was dead. No. The strewn blankets meant nothing, and it served no purpose to imagine government conspiracies around every corner. The man had simply retrieved his boxes and gone away into the desert somewhere.

"Wait!" Charlie said suddenly and halted. Head cocked, he listened, eyes widening.

Sidney heard it then, a spiraling muffled wail that came and went with the capricious wind.

"Tell me that's a dog," Charles Downing pleaded.

"It's not," Sid answered as the cry faded to silence. "And it came from the shop."

Already in motion, she rushed back to the door with its broken lock and flung it wide. Empty stillness met her. The lights, left on, flickered and buzzed over the workbench.

"John?" the woman called softly. "John Caldwell?"

No answer came. The shop was not particularly cluttered. Sid liked to keep the floor as clear as possible. Two big drums, one of kerosene, one of solvent, sat against the right wall. Other than these, the only thing large enough to hide a man was Laura Kelsey's VW Bug, its left front wheel still on the cement.

"Where is he?" Charlie murmured from behind her, and Sid jumped a foot.

"This way," she said and stepped around the little car.

Caldwell lay curled behind it, the black boxes near his head. The doc grabbed her arm, and she jerked loose to crouch beside the still form. He'd stuffed a filthy shop rag in his own mouth to stifle the cries. Sid slipped an arm under his neck and drew him half into her lap, gently pulling the red cloth free. Under the spill of dark brown forelock, the man's face looked different, something in the cheekbones, the chin.

John stirred and took a sharp breath of air, then his eyes opened. Now it was Charlie's turn to gasp. The whites of John's eyes had completely disappeared. Iris and pupil had flowed into one another, black and glistening in the reflected glow of the fluorescent lights.

"I'm still changing," John Caldwell said in a strangled voice. "The pain . . ." He held up the left hand. Both little finger and thumb had the extra joint, the waxy yellow skin.

"Shush," Sidney whispered and clutched him tightly. "Charlie's a doctor. He'll help you."

"No . . ."

In her arms, Caldwell suddenly convulsed. Lips drawn back from clenched teeth, he squalled, and the squall became an inhuman shriek. Sid clamped the rag back over his mouth and held on, afraid that he'd be heard all the way to the cafe.

"Help him!" she begged Charlie. "For God's sake. We can't let him suffer like this."

The doc had already dropped to his knees, and fingers shaking, tore things from his bag. "What?" he cried in panic. "How? I'm a plastic surgeon, not a goddamn exobiologist. Anything I do might kill him. Look! At his hand!"

It was the right hand this time, held clawlike away from the man's body. Sid watched the air around the index finger ripple as if from great heat. Flesh and bone distorted, rearranging itself, almost too quickly to follow. In moments the transformation was over, and taut yellow skin covered another grotesque many-knuckled appendage. Through the ordeal John lay rigid, his agonized wails muffled by the shop rag. Then the stiffened muscles relaxed, and his head lolled back.

"Jesus Christ," Charlie groaned.

"I told you," Sid accused. "I told you what was happening to him. You said you believed."

"And I thought I did. I just didn't have a wild enough imagination to prepare myself for this." The contents of his medical bag lay scattered around him, and he plucked nervously at the stethoscope in his hands. "Well, damn it, open his shirt." When Sid unbuttoned the bloodstained material, he laid the mike tentatively against John's chest, afraid to touch him. The instrument was moved several times before Charlie finally looked up, perplexed. "There's something happening inside, too. The heart seems strong, but the cardiac sounds are all wrong. There may be extra valves or chambers. Shit! I just don't know."

"There's got to be a way to help him."

Charlie shook his head. "Hannah says you and Dale were always bringing home some sorry critter or another, but this poor guy has to be the sorriest. And there's not a damn thing I can do, Sid. He needs the attention of whoever did this to him."

"He said the boxes did it to him."

"Then let's call in the Department of Defense. Give them the boxes and John Caldwell."

She'd been thinking nearly the same thing all along, but now that seemed the very worst solution. "No, we can't."

"Sid, what if he's dying? The government's his best bet for survival. They've got research going in exobiology . . . right now. It's supposed to be all speculation, but the scientists dream up alien worlds, then conjecture what kind of plant and animal life might evolve on them." Charlie's gaze came to rest on John. "Only maybe it isn't just speculation."

"No," Sidney said again and gestured at Caldwell's hand. "This wasn't cooked up in a lab."

The doc glanced down at the greasy floor under his knees. "I don't suppose it was. Then he brightened. "We'll go to SETI . . ."

"Who?"

SETI—the Search for Extraterrestrial Intelligence. They've got a place here on the Mojave, and this has got to be right up their alley." When Sid's jaw tightened, he rushed on. "They're good people, some of the best minds in the country, and most important, they believe. They've been hoping and planning for alien contact for decades."

"And they aren't government?"

Charlie winced. "Well, actually, I think SETI's pretty much government funded."

"Then think of something else, Doc."

"How the hell did I get elected to this post? You want my advice, but you don't want to follow it. This whole business scares the shit out of me. What if it's catching? What if we're already infected?"

"The boxes—"

"The damn boxes could be carrying some sort of virus. That's what viruses do, you know. They enter a cell and replicate themselves in it, destroying the cell in the process." The doc began to gather his things with slow deliberate movements, setting each item carefully in the bag. "You're a compassionate person, Sidney, despite that hard cold exterior. I always suspected as much. But your kindness is going to cost. We're in it deep, now. Even if this isn't catching, you and I will end up in quarantine for the rest of our lives."

"It isn't a virus," another voice muttered, and Sidney looked down into John Caldwell's strange, black eyes. "I'm being . . . translated."

'The patient is awake," Charlie said, a bitter edge to his words. "Translated? What the hell does that mean?"

"You aren't infected. There's a built-in safety device . . . in the boxes . . . so no bio life-forms can pass through in either direction. Nothing living can pass through, except the Ral."

The doctor opened his mouth, and Sid cut him off. "Pass through what? What are you talking about?"

"*They* told me. . . . The dream images of the Ral," Caldwell said dully. "They aren't real, though. The box made them in order to communicate its needs."

"*Its* need? The Ral?" Charlie snapped. "Are you talking honest-to-god aliens?"

John closed his eyes. "A people, a warrior race that found a way to explore the galaxies. Each world taken is a stepping-stone to the next. And on each new world that their ships find, they set up a portable gateway—these boxes—until the materials for a permanent one can be taken through. Only one of the boxes malfunctioned, and the Ral never came back."

"Yeah? So?" the doctor demanded in the long silence that followed.

"The undamaged box," John Caldwell continued softly, "waited until it finally found a way to perform its task. . . . I'm being translated physically from human to Ral so I can repair the gateway and pass through."

Charlie had settled more comfortably on the cold floor, and now he caught Sid's eye. "This gets worse and worse. And I'll bet it isn't in humanity's best interests to open that gateway for the Ral. What have you gotten us into, Bowers?"

"We'll destroy the boxes," Sid said, angry.

Caldwell gasped, his face contorted once more with pain. "No . . . you can't." He snatched the shop rag from her fingers and bit down on it, then every muscle in his body hardened.

Sidney, torn by helpless rage, hung on tight.

"I've heard enough, and I've seen enough," Charlie snarled. He climbed to his feet and backed toward the open door. "I'm going to get help."

"Doc! No!"

Chapter Five

THE MOJAVE WELLS Trailer Park, when first seen in the fading dusk, looked uninviting and lonely. There were two small floodlights at the bottom of the sign that stood beside the road, but one bulb had burned out. Only the faded red letters of the Wells and Park were visible. Nate wondered briefly just what the hell he was doing here, then sent his brother-in-law's elderly pickup down the rutted sandy road. The top-heavy camper swayed side to side.

Janice had chosen to be more amused than worried over this little adventure of her husband's and had sent him off late this afternoon with a kiss and a smile. But Nate was bothered some by his own behavior. Always the pragmatic law officer, this time he'd rushed headlong after . . . what? He'd convinced himself it was the extraordinary circumstances surrounding this case that kept him doggedly hanging on, but it might just be the sting of covert government interference. It hardly mattered which; Nate was here.

Of the park's two occupants clustered around one of the few trees, only the Airstream had lights on inside. It also had the official blue and white Jeep parked in front. Perfect. Nate pulled his pickup onto the neighboring concrete slab and shut the motor down. It took only a moment before the trailer door thumped open. The kid wore a cowboy hat, for shit sake, and high heel boots, all seen in the spill of light from the doorway.

Nate leaned out his window. "Howdy." Spreading it a bit thick, but what the hell.

"Hello," Deputy Nichols said, expression professionally serious. He was still in uniform. "I don't want to seem unfriendly, mister, but we got a whole huge trailer park here, and I've gotten kind of partial to the view."

Nate glanced back over the hood of the truck. Nichols's view consisted of a whole lot of desert and some low shadowy mounds against a darkening sky that might have been mountains once—a billion or so years ago.

"Want me to move?"

"Appreciate it . . ."

"Sure." Nate gave the kid an ingratiating grin and stuck an arm out for a handshake.

Nichols hesitated just an instant, then grasped the hand. Nate had read the faxed personnel report on the deputy, and the young man's grip only confirmed it—Mike Nichols was conscientious, but none too sure of himself. This was likely the best place for him, out in the middle of nowhere, where he couldn't get into too much trouble. Only Nate was probably about to change all that.

"Glad to meet you, Deputy Nichols."

The young man was surprised into a faint self-conscious smile.

Nate went on. "I spoke with you this afternoon . . . on the phone. Nate Curtis, Homicide Division, Anaheim PD?"

"Oh." The smile faded.

Nate didn't let that faze him. He pushed the car door open, and climbed out.

"This is going to take a while. Got any coffee?"

Mike Nichols watched in stunned silence as Nate took the three steps to the Airstream's threshold. The place was dinky inside, and the sergeant had to keep his head tilted under the low ceiling, but the sink wasn't full of dirty dishes and the table had only some paperwork laid out. Definitely conscientious. Approving, Nate settled on a thinly cushioned dinette bench.

The deputy had followed quickly enough. "Hey, do you mind—?"

"Coffee. Got any?"

"Just instant," Mike answered, his anger barely in check.

"Have to do, then." With his long legs out in the aisle,

Nate shifted his torso into as comfortable a position as he could. "Nice place. Kinda tight, though."

The deputy said nothing, only filled a small pan from a plastic water bottle and lit the stove. Cups were set out, while Nate talked.

"I didn't tell you much over the phone, but I'm about to remedy that. There's something very strange going on, and I'm gonna need your help to figure it all out." Mike Nichols maintained a polite silence while Nate considered his next words carefully. "Three days ago in Anaheim, twelve members of Professor Arnold Hanover's family died as they sat down to their Thanksgiving dinner. Eight adults, including the prof, and four kids. One was a baby."

Mike looked up from his jar of Folgers, eyes widening slightly. "Jesus."

"Exactly. They had one guest over, a young college student named John Caldwell. Lucky thirteen. Caldwell's the only one who survived. And I'd like to know why."

"I guess so." The deputy put his spoon down, interested. "You think John Caldwell murdered them?"

Nate drew a heavy breath. "I'm beginning to believe he killed them . . . but not on purpose."

"Hell of an accident."

Now that Mike began to warm to the subject, the sullen, put-upon attitude vanished. Smiling, Nate accepted his cup of hot coffee.

"Got any milk? So I was called in to investigate a possible multiple homicide. Only the next morning, the bodies, the evidence . . . everything was spirited away by the government, under the pretext of a possible epidemic of unknown origin."

Mike grunted, "Bet that pissed you off." He took the seat opposite.

"Sure did . . . in light of some files I came across in the professor's office. This is where you come in. Since I've been officially told to drop the Hanover case, you're going to help me get to the bottom of it all."

"Why me?"

"You've got a badge, and this is your territory. According to Hanover, there's something out there on the Devil's Playground, and I mean to find it. And John Caldwell."

Mike was shaking his head on which the cowboy hat was still perched. "Count me out. . . . I already had my hands slapped, but good."

"By who?"

"The Air Force. As far as I know, they're still systemically digging up the Playground. Colonel Candliss promised to lose me in a deep dark hole if I didn't stay clear."

"Shit . . ."

"So what killed the Hanovers?"

"We know why they died, but not how. Something turned their insides to jelly. All the internal organs were ruptured. And the glass in the dining room windows where they were found had holes in it, as if the glass had melted away. The drinking glasses on the table were affected, too. Weirdest thing I ever saw." Nate looked at his cooling coffee. "It's all tied to John Caldwell, though, and something Hanover found in the desert. Something that just may have come from . . . extraterrestrials."

Mike choked suddenly on a mouthful of coffee, and it took the sergeant a couple of seconds to realize the younger man was laughing.

"You always wear that damn cowboy hat in the trailer?" Nate snarled in irritation.

"Only when I'm feeling short," the deputy managed, forcing a straight face. "Candliss made me feel real short today, and you didn't help much. Only now I'm feeling better." He tossed the hat onto the kitchen counter, revealing dark wavy hair, a bit on the long side. "So tell me more about the spacemen."

"Since you want to play the skeptic, I'll do better than that. I'll let you read the printouts of the professor's computer files. He found a small black box made of an unknown material buried in the sand, a little over two weeks ago. According to him, every few hours this box would give off a pulse of some sort, which tended to kill anything close by in the desert—snakes and rats and stuff.

"The good prof, like a proper mad scientist, took his assistant, Caldwell, out to the Devil's Playground and subjected *him* to the pulse. Hanover says John Caldwell vanished and reappeared twice. Only the kid didn't die. *But* he continued to have side effects, tingling and numbness, disorientation, each time the box fired. This happened even in Anaheim, some hundred miles away. And I'm willing to bet, that's somehow connected to the deaths." Nate glared at the obviously amused deputy. "You got a better explanation, then let me hear it."

Mike shrugged. "Simple. Military. That's why they're tearing up the Devil's Playground. Candliss told me they lost a highly classified item out there."

"Classified, my ass. Hanover said we don't have anything close to the technology involved, but the military sure would like to."

Mike sat up, brows furrowed, but not from anything Nate had said, and then the sergeant heard it, too—a car bumping over the park road.

"That's Sid's truck," the deputy said by way of explanation. "Got a hole in the muffler." He stood and went to the door to call, "Hello! What's up?"

After a momentary silence, a man's voice answered, "Hi, Mike. . . . Nothing's up. Just had to borrow the Toyota to . . . haul some stuff."

"Come here. I want you to meet someone."

A car door slammed, and there were footsteps on the stair. Nate watched a smaller well-dressed fellow with iron gray hair enter, and rose to shake the newcomer's hand.

"This is Detective Sergeant Nate Curtis . . . from Anaheim," the deputy said. "Nate, this is my neighbor, Doc Charlie Downing."

"Charles," the neighbor was quick to amend. "God, you're a tall one. Ever play football?"

Nate chuckled. "In high school, but I wrecked a knee."

"Wide receiver, right?"

"Good guess."

"What's Sid up to?" Mike demanded.

Charles Downing paled somewhat, but the deputy didn't seem to notice. "She's . . . at the shop."

"Working late?"

"Yeah."

Mike turned to the sergeant. "Sidney's our resident me-chanic, and a darn good one." There was a proprietary pride in his voice.

The doc began to fidget. "Look, I just came home to find some papers and make a call or two, then I gotta get the truck back."

"Thought you had to haul some stuff," Nate said, just to see the man's reaction.

"That's right . . . and haul some stuff. It was real nice meeting you." Charlie squeezed past the deputy and rattled down the steps.

"Was he acting a little strange?" Mike asked, and Nate smiled.

"I could use some more coffee while we work out a few details."

The deputy looked slightly pained. "I'll fix you more coffee, but don't expect much else. I'm not a hotshot hom-icide sergeant, so I'll be the first casualty in any war of wills you plan on starting with the government."

"Son, you've got nothing to worry about. I know ex-actly how to deal with the bureaucracy. I just need some-one with some local authority to front for me. We'll make a great team."

What a load of horseshit that was, but Nate intended to keep piling it on until he got what he wanted.

II

Charles was shaking by the time he got his door un-locked. The TV was still on, but the Aussie game had ended long ago. Boxers, almost life-sized, dodged and danced across the screen. In a cabinet beside his favorite chair, he dug out a stack of magazines and began a hasty search.

His first thought as he'd left the shop was to find Dep-uty Mike, then call the paramedics out of Barstow, but during the drive, he couldn't lose the vision of Sidney's distress or John Caldwell's pain. There was an article in a recent *Omni* magazine about Dr. Quinten Fenwick and the SETI Foundation. Fenwick was stationed somewhere nearby on the Fort Irwin Military Reserve. If Charles could get through to the man . . .

Some outside advice was desperately needed. At last he found the article and a foundation number, but no one answered the phone. Fort Irwin answered on the first ring, and then left him on hold until the line disconnected. Angry, Charles tried again—three more times—until at last a tired voice answered.

"Fenwick here."

"Dr. Fenwick, my name is Charles Downing. I live in Mojave Wells, and I've got a big problem that you might be able to help me with. . . ."

"I'm sorry, Mr. Downing—"

"It's *Doctor* Downing, and this concerns SETI," Charles rushed on. "I've got a young man who is . . ." No, that might make the guy hang up on just another kook. "Look, we've got these two small black boxes found out on the desert that might be . . . extraterrestrial in origin. I think you should see them."

The silence seemed interminable, then Fenwick cleared his throat. "Two boxes . . . You said a young man. Is it John Caldwell?"

Oh, sweet Jesus. "Yes . . . Yes! He's in bad shape. Something's happened to him—caused by the boxes, he says—and it's nothing that I'm capable of dealing with."

"Bring him here—to me—as fast as possible."

"He needs medical attention—"

"He'll get it, just as soon as you arrive. Have you told anyone else about this?"

"Who would believe it?"

"Quite right. Dr. Downing, avoid coming through Fort Irwin. There's a road just east of you on Highway 15 that leads north out of Baker. Follow it to a dirt road exactly 10.6 miles from the town and turn west. You'll find my station another eight miles out. Hurry."

The feeling of relief lasted only moments after Charles hung up.

III

Despair and pain were all John knew. He could find no relief in sleep, though the dream images still haunted his mind. The Gatekeeper, with its near-sentient artificial intelligence, had set the pattern of change at a molecular level, and the program ran unhindered in Caldwell's body. The more cells translated, the faster the changes. Someone cradled his head, and he remembered vaguely where he was. Now he fought for coherency.

"Do you have your gun?" he whispered to the woman, the words mangled by strange thin lips and vocal cords meant to produce other sounds. The light hurt his eyes.

"What?" She leaned her head closer to his.

"Your gun . . . bring it to me. Please."

"No," the woman said firmly. "We'll find a way to help."

John curled long jointed fingers around her right wrist. "That's the only help I need. I'm dying anyway. . . . Who I am will be completely gone soon. What I become . . ."

How to explain the unexplainable? He released her arm and reached up, placing a hand on either side of her face. The woman flinched.

"Trust," John murmured, and she allowed him to pull her head close to his until their foreheads touched.

He closed his eyes and let the images form, vivid and clear. They stood in that same empty cubicle without windows or doors. This was the Pyn'ar, the dreaming room, in which all lives were equal—where only your visions had power. John felt an elation. He'd created this himself, without the help of the Gatekeeper. His control grew stronger, and that fleeting thought brought a stab of fear.

The woman—Sidney—stood beside him, frozen, uncertain.

"Here," John told her, "is a place of the mind." His words sounded hollow. "The greatest dreamers rule the People. More decisions are made here than in waking, because in dreams there can be no deception for the Ral."

She didn't understand, and he knew no other way to make it clearer.

"I'll call the ones from my memories. They're all I have. My visions are young, a child's yet. Don't be afraid. They can't harm you."

The female leader came first through the bare wall, tall and slender, encased in smooth chitinous armor. John had her smile, a twist of the lipless mouth that was truly frightening in human terms.

"'On,'" the female intoned.

Sidney backed away. "Caldwell! Stop it! Let me go!"

The terror in her voice caused a strange calm rage in him, an automatic response.

"Be still," he snarled, then managed a gentler tone. "Fear and weakness are intolerable. We . . . They've evolved from unbelievable savagery and kill without thought. Yet, the Ral have gained an inner peace that mankind will probably never know."

There was so much more he wanted to relate, but the vision melted, colors swirling into a red haze of agony. Bone and muscle twisted, and the pain dragged him down into dark night once more. Awareness returned slowly, then the stench of grease and oil filled his nostrils, gagging him. He lay alone, facedown, on cold cement.

"Sidney?" With effort, John Caldwell dragged his legs under him and tried to sit. Panic threatened. Her strong grip had become his anchor.

"Here . . ."

The young woman moved into view, close but out of reach. Her face had gone deadly white.

"I'm sorry," John said. Gravity tugged at him, weighed his limbs so they quivered and shook.

"Don't be," she answered, tone gruff. "This wasn't your choice. Or mine. And if I think too hard about it, I'll go crazy for sure."

"I want the gun."

"No. I don't know what Charlie's up to, but I trust him."

"You still don't understand. . . . They're warrior-hunters

with weapons beyond anything we've got. They'll come through if I open the gate."

"You won't."

He mustered some exhausted anger. "You don't know that. *I* don't know that."

"It was beautiful," Sidney said, abruptly changing the subject.

"What?"

"*It* . . . It scared me, but even then I saw the beauty. So tall and graceful . . . and fierce."

"She . . . I showed you a female. They're taller, and far more fierce than the males." John forced a smile. "But you don't want to be on the bad side of either. God! I'm so weak."

"Hold on. Just a little longer."

How could he explain the centuries that passed each time the changes came? "How do I look?" he asked instead.

Sidney's expression faltered. "Pretty awful."

John said nothing, only hid his face in alien hands.

IV

Mike listened to Detective Curtis, his interest fading. The big man was a lowlander, used to running things, and Mike didn't care much for his story or his pushy manners. And just what the hell was Charlie doing in his RV by the light of the television? For the hundredth time, the deputy glanced out the tiny window with its abbreviated view of the Winnebago.

"So the kid hasn't showed?"

Mike nodded distractedly, then focused on his visitor. "At least he hadn't at three this afternoon. They still had the choppers up, searching the Playground."

"I'd like to take a run out there . . . right now. Is the area visible from the road?"

"If they've got lights up, it will be."

"All right." Nate Curtis scratched the bristles on his chin. "A little look-see. We'll take your vehicle. If they've cleared out, they may've already found our boy. Which leaves me to spend my vacation in sunny Mojave Wells, hoping for crumbs of information handed out by the military. What a bunch of tight asses."

Outside the trailer, Sid's little pickup rumbled to life, exhaust chuffing through the hole in the muffler. Mike felt a sudden strong apprehension, and, snatching the cowboy hat from the counter, headed for the door. The sergeant followed on his heels.

"Got a feeling, huh?" Nate said, and slammed the passenger side door on the Jeep. He settled back. "You may be a better cop than we both think."

His words were heard, but failed to register. The pickup's cherry taillights bobbed in the dark toward the road, then disappeared. Mike gunned the engine.

"Not too fast," Nate Curtis cautioned. "You'll spook him. There's no traffic to hide in."

The deputy pulled out onto the pavement and turned toward town. Up ahead. Charlie's headlights swept across a broad curve.

"Use your running lights. You've got plenty of moon." Irritated, Mike obeyed.

"So where's he headed? Do you know?"

"Back to the shop, I imagine."

"But something's up. What set you off? Come on, kid, put it together."

"Hell, I don't know," Mike snapped. "Charlie's acting weird. Sid's all alone there. And Caldwell stopped at the shop yesterday. It's probably nothing."

Nate Curtis's teeth flashed white in the dimness. "But you don't think so. Instincts make all the difference in the world, deputy. I'm a firm believer in them."

"Well, I've never had much use for them, myself."

"Around here, I don't doubt it."

By the time they reached town, Charlie had disappeared. Mike pulled into the cafe lot. Hannah's was dark and deserted. The sergeant put a cautioning hand out.

"Don't go in just yet. Shut the vehicle down and wait."

"Come on, Curtis. These are my friends, not desperate criminals."

"You better hope so. You remembered your hat, but you left your utility belt back at the trailer."

"Shit! Why didn't you say something?"

"I feel safer with the only firearm. Now shut the damn vehicle down before you draw attention."

Son of a bitch. Mike put the Jeep into the moon shadows of the cafe and killed the engine. Resentment overpowered the embarrassment of leaving his weapon behind. This must be Police Science 101—big city cop come to instruct the small-town hick deputy. Hell.

Beyond the parking lot, Sid's house was dark and the shop closed up. The little pickup had disappeared altogether. Mike's uneasiness returned, stronger than before.

V

Charles parked alongside the shop as close to the back door as possible, then scrambled out of the cab and hurried inside.

"Sid! Is the house locked? We need blankets. Can he walk, do you think?"

John Caldwell turned fathomless black eyes on him from his seat on the concrete, arms hugging knees for support. In the half hour since Charles had left, the young man's features had made impossible changes. His clothes hung on him now, though the sleeves of his shirt and the legs of his pants were far too short. The doctor shifted his gaze aside, appalled and frightened.

"Where's Sidney?" he demanded to hide his reaction.

"At the house . . . to call you." The words did not come easily.

"The pickup's just outside. Can you get in the back by yourself?"

"No."

"All right. We'll manage somehow. Wait . . ." Gladly, Charles turned and ran for the house, careful in the darkness.

Sidney was already on the porch. "What took so long?"

"I had to make some calls. Come on. We need blankets

for the bed of the truck. We're taking him to Dr. Fenwick at Fort Irwin."

"No," the young woman said angrily. "Not the military!"

"He's a SETI man, and wants us to come in the back way so we can avoid the military." Charles pushed past her into the unlit house. "He said to hurry, and by the looks of Caldwell, I think we better. The blankets dammit! Let's go!"

Thin blue moonlight beamed in through the gauzy curtains over the bedroom windows. They stripped the beds quickly and hustled back to the shop, then together got John Caldwell on his feet and started toward the door. Charles's skin crawled to be in such close proximity, to touch that cold tight flesh. Jesus! How could a happily retired plastic surgeon end up in so bizarre a situation? Guilt nudged him. His plight was nothing compared to Caldwell's.

With the tailgate lowered, he and Sid dragged the young man into the pile of blankets and wrapped him up, then went back to lug the boxes out.

"I'll ride with John," Sidney announced and crawled to sit against the cab, with Caldwell's head in her lap once more.

"Hang on," Charles advised her. "This is going to be a bumpy ride."

John convulsed suddenly, caught again in the grip of his personal hell, but silent this time. Unable to do anything else, Charles Downing climbed behind the steering wheel and sent the Toyota in reverse past the shop and onto the road.

Chapter Six

CHARLIE DROVE LIKE a madman, and Sidney could do nothing but hang on to John and the side of the pickup. The black boxes, laid next to the tailgate, were kept from sliding into them by the blankets. A partial moon drifted high above, its glow still strong enough to banish all but the brightest stars. Sid watched the heavens and wondered from which direction in the sky *they* had come. Twenty-four hours ago, she would never have considered such a question.

But something had changed when Caldwell touched his forehead to hers earlier. The entire situation still terrified her, yet the weight of his alien head in her lap brought a strange comfort. The need to protect and defend him seemed almost overpowering.

Doc slowed for a sharp left turn, and the going grew much worse when the truck left the pavement. Between the jolts of potholes and an icy backdraft that deeply chilled her, Sidney endured as best she could. John, huddled in the blankets, was only a dark shape. Now the dirt road climbed steadily, though not steeply, and they followed its winding course until at last there was light; enough to turn this portion of the mountain from night to day.

Sid craned her neck to see. Someone had leveled a small flat and enclosed it in a high chain link fence—small, yet large enough to hold a new white double-wide mobile home. Two huge semitractors with long box trailers, also white, were lined up against the fence to either side. Charlie halted before a gate on which was hung a large sign that read, Avawatz Geological Test Site.

"Hey!" the doc shouted and hit the Toyota's feeble horn.

The gate rolled slowly aside. Sid cocked her head, listening to the almost subliminal background rumble of a generator, a big one. Charlie put the pickup through the opening, drove up to the edge of the central concrete slab, and cut the engine. The gate rolled back into place behind them and, uneasy, Sidney eyed the big loops of razor wire that ran the perimeter.

"John," she said gently and shook his shoulder. "John, we're here."

"You Fenwick?" the doc called, and Sid watched the grotesque shape of a man in what looked to be a white spacesuit crossing from the mobile home. They sure had a thing for white around here.

"I'm Quinten Fenwick." The man's voice quavered slightly through his helmet.

"You planning a trip to the moon?" Charlie demanded.

"It's an environment suit. Just a precaution, in case of . . . contamination."

The doc grinned. "Suit yourself, but I don't think it's necessary. Come on." He climbed out of the cab and led the scientist to the truck bed where Caldwell lay. "This is going to put you in the history books, Dr. Fenwick."

Almost reluctantly Sid peeled the blankets back just enough to give Fenwick a view. Under the bright floodlights, John Caldwell's misshapen face was all too visible, bizarre even, with his eyes closed. Fenwick, his own face contorted with fear or shock, turned to Charlie.

"Dear God, what's happened to him? You told me he was ill."

Charlie shook his head. "I said he was in bad shape."

"And what of the boxes?"

"They're right here."

Those simple words seemed to cue the next sequence of events. First came the almost explosive sound of heavy double doors slamming open, then on either side of them, a swarm of men in the same luminous white suits dropped to the ground from the backs of the long truck trailers and surged toward the Toyota.

"No!" Sidney cried when gloved hands reached for her.

She struck a curved plastic visor with the heel of one boot and sent the man reeling back into the others.

Fenwick, his voice cracking, began to shout, "It's all right! They won't hurt you. It's all right!"

"Bastard!" Charlie snarled at him, caught already in strong grips.

"There was nothing I could do—they were monitoring my calls. They only want to put you in quarantine. It's for your own good."

Sidney had taken to high ground—the top of the pickup's cab—but hands snagged her ankles and dragged her into the waiting arms of a half dozen men. Behind the clear masks were impassive faces, showing neither anger nor regret. Their silence was the most frightening thing of all. Caught tight, she and Charlie were forced toward the big tractor-trailer on the left.

The tailgate on the Toyota dropped open with a tinny bang, and Sid fought to turn enough for a look back. Another group pulled John Caldwell carefully from the blankets.

"Leave him alone!" she screamed, outrage and panic pumping adrenaline through her system. "John!"

He stirred sluggishly, confused by the bright lights and the strange surroundings, then shook off the hand that held his right arm. Sidney shouted his name again, and his head came up, black eyes narrowed in the glare. The suited men around him were divided now, some fearful, others determined to hold on.

One by one, Caldwell knocked them away and finally straightened, bare feet planted firmly on the rocky soil, his long slender height rising well above those who crowded around him. The weakness had passed, and so it seemed, had the gentle, frightened young graduate student. What remained resembled nothing these men had ever seen.

John pushed his way against a flood of shouts and white suits toward Sidney and the doc. Someone struck him from behind, and he turned so swiftly that the man had no chance to dodge aside. With a sweep of one clawed hand, Caldwell opened his attacker's environment suit from crotch to throat, and bright red blood spilled through the slashes. The man doubled over, howling, and John Caldwell was given a sudden wide berth by the rest.

"Stand away!" a voice boomed, and Sid looked up. Another man stood on the Toyota's tailgate, a pistol in his gloved hand. She opened her mouth to shout a warning just as the handgun fired. The sound was small, almost like a popgun, but the results were immediate. Caldwell hesitated, managed one last step in Sidney's direction, then collapsed. White suits swarmed in to block her view.

It didn't matter. She'd had enough. The lack of food and sleep had taken their toll, but worse, her reality had been turned completely inside out. Sidney Bowers finally snapped. The world came crystal clear around her, and rage heightened all her senses. With everyone's attention focused on the screaming injured man, it was too easy to break free.

In a matter of moments, she had torn the cloth and plastic helmets from the two closest men and bloodied one's nose. And then, even as they bore her to the ground, Sid managed to tear the sleeve of another with her teeth.

II

At the first glow of artificial light ahead, they found a small brush-filled gully along the road and stashed the Jeep. Not an ideal place, since morning light would still make it visible on the mountainside, but Nate hoped to be out of there before dawn. He'd been pissing Mike Nichols off, right and left, all night. Mike was a hardheaded kid and not much suited to intrigue. Then again, the sergeant wasn't much suited to it either, especially not in overweight middle age.

That damned cold wind continued to gust, and Nate's jacket did little to stop it. He'd never thought about a desert being cold, hadn't thought much about the desert, period, being more inclined toward tropical climes. The hike up the road had him panting almost immediately, but his long legs helped him keep up with the deputy's hurried pace.

The light formed a bright corona along the edge of the last bend. Sticking to the road was risky, and any moment a vehicle might come careening around a curve. Groaning inwardly, Nate grabbed Mike's shoulder, and, pointing to the steep side of the mountain, jabbed a thump toward the sky.

The deputy scrambled and tripped his way up through the shadows with youthful energy. Give him another twenty years, Nate thought glumly, and he won't be so spry. Rock and shale made footing chancy, but Mike forced the pace. When they'd just about gained the altitude necessary to take them above floodlight range, a shout rang against the mountainside.

"John!"

Beside him, the deputy froze for an instant. "That's Sid. . . ."

The shout came again, desperate, followed by a man's muffled screams of pain, and then the low pop of a weapon discharging. Mike threw himself forward, blundering over the last little rise. Nate managed somehow to snag him around the neck just as the young officer started down into the lights.

"Damn you!" he snarled in Mike's ear, dragging him back.

The choke hold worked. Half-strangled, the deputy was forced to relax, and Nate, cold but sweating, settled them both in the dirt behind a bit of thorny desert brush. Now they could look down into a small, fenced and crowded compound. Beneath them in the bright lights, the little red pickup was parked a short distance from the mobile home near the center. An army of white-suited men swarmed over the grounds between two long tractor-trailers lined up against the fence.

"Sid," Mike muttered and clenched his fists, watching the action below.

The young woman, visible against the sea of white, created her own brand of havoc, but to no real effect. In the end, she and Charlie were hauled into the back of the farthest truck. On the other side of the compound, two others, one in a bloodied white suit, were lifted bodily into the rear of the nearest semi. One, seen only briefly, appeared dead. The doors closed. Those left outside—nearly two dozen white suits—began to police the area. Some made sweeps with what might have been metal detectors, others seemed to be gathering debris. Two men collected a pair of small black boxes from the bed of the Toyota and carted them, with difficulty, into the mobile home.

Mike, still rubbing his throat, turned on the sergeant. "We've got to do something."

"Shut up." Nate put a hand up, listening to the grind of heavy gears in the distance, slowly drawing near.

The incoming vehicle arrived on the far side of the compound at another gate, and within the small enclosure, the men finished their tasks, then dogtrotted out through that gate to climb into the back of the olive drab transport—all but one, who climbed into the red pickup. Laboriously, the transport driver maneuvered the truck around, then sent it into the night, the Toyota following in caravan.

"That betters the odds," Mike muttered, "but not by much. So what's the deal?"

"What do you mean?"

"You're the self-appointed brains of this outfit. How do we break Sid and the doc out of there?"

"We don't."

"The hell you say. . . ."

"This is a government operation, deputy, and we've got no business even *thinking* of interfering." Nate shifted uncomfortably and felt the prick of stickers through his slacks. He considered the facts for a long moment. "They've got John Caldwell and the black box—*boxes*—now, apparently thanks to your friends. Which means I'm S.O.L. Case closed."

Mike hissed in outrage. "I'm not deserting Sid and Charlie."

"They're better off if you do," Nate said, his voice held low, his eyes on the enclosure beneath them, quiet and still. "The way you operate, kid, I wouldn't go to a picnic with you. You don't have the sense God gave a turnip.

You're just plain stupid—trying to run right into the middle of that mess."

Tired and cold and irritable, he was being unnecessarily cruel—something he would never do normally, but there was this strong desire to hop into his brother-in-law's old pickup and drive back to his smoggy, crowded, and ultimately less complicated city. He could still catch a flight to Maui and surprise Janice. After all, these weren't his friends or his problems.

"Look," he said finally, "they may keep them for interrogation, then turn them loose. Charging in after them will only make things worse. This is the federal government you're talking about—very touchy, very powerful people. Even if you could break your friends out, you'd be facing a long prison sentence or be on the run for the rest of your life. It isn't worth it."

Mike turned his head toward the sergeant, eyes glittering in the reflected floodlights, but he said nothing. God, how on earth had Nate managed to hook up with such a half-assed young law officer? The kid couldn't even remember his handgun when things got a little dicey, and he thought he could fight the U.S. Air Force.

"Come on," Nate growled. "Take me back to the trailer park, and I'll get out of your way. Doesn't matter what I say, you're gonna do what you want to. Never know, you might get lucky. I've heard God takes care of children and fools." He stood up wearily. "But I bet He's got His hands full with you."

III

The isolation room was dinky—the rear section of the trailer walled off from the rest by a thick sheet of Plexiglas. The brightly lit area within sported one molded plastic bench and a chemical toilet—a cheap camper john. At the moment, quarantine was a crowded affair. Sidney and Charlie had the bench, and squatting on the floor across from them were the three young men who had run afoul of Sid.

She eyed one of them thoughtfully. "How's the nose?"

"Fine, ma'am." He looked very much like the other two, except for the swollen purpling lump in the middle of his face.

They were regular army types, fresh-scrubbed all-American boys with ruddy cheeks and close-shorn hair. Probably embarrassed, too. They'd ended up in their government issue skivvies. Sid smiled at the air.

"John Caldwell was human, you know. Just last night. The changes'll start pretty soon, I guess. Of course, Charlie and I'll be the first ones to go. Horrible thing to watch." She held a hand up, fingers clawed, trembling.

"Don't be mean, Sid," Charlie grunted.

"I wanna be mean," she snapped. "I wanna break a couple more noses."

The soldiers said nothing, only stared at their knees, and Sid glared into the dimness beyond the clear wall. Figures moved around out there, and men sat at computers, their faces underlit with the green glow of electronics. A helpless fury burned in her, just below the surface.

"Are they cutting him up?" she demanded of the other captives. "Are they putting his insides into little jars of formaldehyde?"

Again Charlie answered. "He isn't dead. . . ."

"The bastards shot him."

"A tranquilizer dart. They're shortsighted assholes, but they'd want him alive."

Sid stood suddenly and slammed a fist against the Plexiglas. "Hey! Somebody! I gotta take a leak, but I won't do it in front of these military monkeys. Get 'em out of here! Get 'em out of here quick, or so help me, there's going to be blood all over the place, and it won't all be mine!" She swung around, and the closest soldier jumped up and tripped over his comrades to get away.

Someone knocked on the wall, and Sidney turned back. It was Fenwick. She recognized his weasel face and scraggly graying beard. Now he wore a lab coat and a very worried look.

"Mrs. Bowers, please . . ."

"Get them out of here."

"How? It's your fault they're in quarantine. Where would I put them?"

"That's your problem." But a thought occurred. "Put them back in your fancy environment suits. That should keep them until you can think of something better."

"Please, sir," said one of the young soldiers, with a hint of desperation in his voice.

"All right," Fenwick replied. "I'll see what I can do. . . ."

He headed away, until Sid shouted, "Fenwick, wait!" When the scientist returned hesitantly, she caught his eye. "Where is he? What have you done to him?"

"Mrs. Bowers, you must understand. I meant him no harm. We all have only his best interests in mind."

"Sure you do." The young woman sagged against the thick plastic shield. Alone, she might have given in to tears, but not here, not in front of an audience.

A short time later, three spacesuits were piled on the floor of the tiny air lock. The soldiers struggled into them and one by one, stood under the ultraviolet lamp and disinfectant mist.

"See you boys on the dissection table," Sidney called.

Behind her, Charlie chuckled morosely.

IV

Fenwick really had very little to say about what happened from here on out. The Foundation needed to be told, but the phone lines were under armed guard. Candliss had commandeered the test site and everything in it. He'd brought in his own surgeons, his own lab assistants and equipment. By the looks of the trailer interiors, Project Black Box had been put together hastily, but thoroughly. The unmarked semi rigs could pull out at any time and move to a new location.

Truth be told, Quinten was more than a little afraid of Candliss, and he felt certain that the colonel ran the operation without the complete knowledge of his own superiors. The man was a cold, ambitious bastard. The prize was his, and he intended to keep it for as long as possible.

Nervous, Fenwick followed Candliss's quick, sure stride across the enclosure to the second trailer. At least, the scientist had so far been allowed to tag along, if not participate.

Quinten stuck close when a back door opened just wide enough to admit the colonel. They climbed the stepladder and entered the chilly interior. Here, there were even more supercomputers than at Fenwick's. Printers chattered somewhere, and people moved purposefully through the crowded quarters.

"How's Corporal Metzger?" Candliss demanded of a medical aide who carried a stainless steel tray filled with instruments.

The young man glanced down. "Dead, sir. The slashes weren't deep, none of the internal organs had been pierced, and we got the bleeding stopped right away ... but we ... just couldn't seem to hold on to him. Captain Winslow says it was a histamine reaction, possibly to a foreign organism."

"Foreign," the colonel snarled. "That's putting it mildly. Poor kid. I want the body in the freezer, stat. We'll deal with that later when there's time."

"Yes, sir. It's already been done, sir."

"Good."

Candliss pushed past him roughly, headed toward the back of the trailer, and Fenwick hustled after, tripping over thick cables laid along the floor. Heavy-duty, clear plastic sheets had been draped and sealed around John Caldwell, forming a portable tentlike affair. He lay, eyes closed, on a long table, strapped across forehead, chest, and waist, as well as arms, wrists, thighs, and ankles. Nothing left to chance. The doctors worked with isolation gloves built into the plastic, poking and prodding the naked body with its waxy jaundiced skin. Quinten recognized only one of the three surgeons in attendance—Major Will Perkins, the largest, blackest man with the gentlest hands that Fenwick had ever known. They'd been friends for a lot of years.

"It's still unconscious," Candliss observed in irritation.

"No, Colonel." One medic pushed a stopper into a vial filled with a dark purple fluid, and Fenwick averted his eyes, somehow sickened. "He's just tuned us out. The tranquilizer wore off right away, and he's actually been quite talkative. Hard to understand some of it, because the tongue's formed differently, and he's got no teeth."

"You keep calling it he."

"Because that's what he is, General," Perkins said, his attention still on his work. His big hands, buried to the shoulder in gloves, drew another vial of alien blood. "We've got a fairly typical bipedal male, here—mammalian, I believe. The anatomy isn't that off, except the genitals are retracted into the body." The doctor glanced up, smiling wryly. "There's been more than once when I wished mine did. We've already had a quick look under the electron microscope. Ponnamperuma was right, our boy's got DNA—but far more complex than human."

"More advanced?"

"Far more evolved, and yet beautifully simplified. But just look at him. We can surmise a lot just by the physical appearance. The shape of the jaw and gums indicate that they're probably herbivores, but for some reason, they're built streamlined like predators. The musculoskeletal structure suggests our boy evolved in heavier gravity, and the eyes were developed for lower light levels. Not exactly nocturnal—more likely an elderly fading sun or one much farther from their world than ours is.

"We're setting up for a CAT scan next. We've already used the fluoroscope, if you want a look at the internal organs. The lungs are incredible. I suspect they were designed to utilize even heavy atmospheres—methane or chlorine maybe. Whatever, they're not *just* oxygen breathers. I'll need a lung section, though, to even begin to pin any of this down. As soon as we can handle it, I want bone marrow and spinal fluid, too. We're already running every other blood and tissue test we can."

Quinten listened to Major Perkins calmly relate all this and heard the barely contained excitement underneath. The man had been one of the first to dabble in the field of exobiology over twenty years ago. Still, his attitude bothered the SETI scientist.

"Will!" Fenwick said sharply, which got him unpleasant attention from Candliss.

Mystified, Will Perkins looked up. "What?"

"Less than two days ago, John Caldwell was human. . . ."

"I know, Quinten. This species doesn't adapt just through evolution, it's capable of a genetic manipulation that we haven't even considered. The possible applications are fantastic—"

"Damn it, you're missing the point." Despite the colonel's obvious anger, Fenwick rushed on. "As a medical doctor, how can you justify your treatment of this living, sentient creature, human or otherwise? We've been hoping for half a century for a message from neighbors in the galaxy, but this is *not* the welcome we had planned."

Perkins frowned. "Quinten, if I've been hasty, it's—"

"No!" The colonel ground his teeth. "This . . . *thing* killed one of my men."

"He defended himself!" Fenwick argued. "And for that you've given him undue suffering and pain."

An odd fluting whistle silenced them all. Within the plastic shroud, Caldwell had opened his eyes, and Quinten felt the weight of that dark alien gaze. The whistle came again from the fluttering of nostrils, an intaken breath.

"The pain means nothing," the creature said, words articulated carefully. "But to be restrained is unbearable."

Fenwick turned to Will. "He might submit to your tests, if you only ask. Set him loose, give him that choice."

"By God," Candliss snarled, "you'll do no such thing. Murphy! Fowler! I want this man out of here. Now!"

Two lab techs caught Quinten's arms and began to pull him away toward the doors.

"Will!" he cried over his shoulder. "Look at his face! You've seen it before!"

They dumped him unceremoniously onto the cold ground, and one had the nerve to smile and say, "Go play with your telescope, Dr. Fenwick," then the door was pulled tight and locked from the inside.

"Shit!" Quinten hissed.

Would Perkins understand? They'd both seen that face

over and over, these past years—in drawings from every part of the country, all slightly different, all essentially the same. These were the sketches made by people who believed they'd been kidnapped by aliens. It was all so incredible. The ripple of events spread swiftly outward, widening, carrying them into even more mind-boggling possibilities.

High above him, the stars already faded with dawn, but daylight wouldn't bring an end to this mad dream. They had chanced upon dangerous knowledge, and Quinten Fenwick felt a chill from more than the wind.

V

Johncaldwell was not a warrior's name, but then he was not a warrior—not without *mirik,* not without the dream mates. There had been a beginning, but they had taken her from him. Eyes closed, he listened to their voices, and ignored the discomfort. They had stabbed the thick skin on the underside of his wrist many times until a vein had been tapped.

They had probed every body cavity, and he, on his hard bed, was rolled to the equipment too bulky to bring to him. Because anger served no purpose, he chose to view the situation with grim humor. The Ral had treated humankind, in its dim animal past, in much the same manner.

"Caldwell . . . John Caldwell . . ."

He ignored the voice—Colonel Candliss—for as long as possible. His acute aural sense let him single out conversations all through the crowded trailer. It was a vicarious freedom of sorts, letting the mind wander where the body could not.

"Dammit, Will. Snap him out of it."

"Snap him out of what? He doesn't feel like chatting."

"Christ, but you're an uppity nigger surgeon."

Will Perkins gave him a nasty laugh for answer.

"What is it you wish of me, Bob?" Johncaldwell opened his eyes.

Using the shortened familiar form of the man's name would be the most demeaning. Candliss held his authority precious, and now, hovering over the plastic tent, his nostrils flared.

"What I wish from you," he growled, "is some information."

"Then ask."

"The black boxes . . . how dangerous are they?"

"Very."

"Are they responsible for the Hanover deaths?"

"Yes and no."

"Elaborate."

"No."

The colonel's jaw tightened. "We've had them in a lead-lined area with lab mice for over six hours and nothing's happened. Why?"

"Only be glad, Bob." Weary, Johncaldwell closed his eyes once more.

"I'm not through with you, Caldwell."

Throughout the subsequent demands and verbal abuse, he remained silent until Candliss marched angrily away. Only Will Perkins stayed, betrayed by a nervous habit, a thumbnail scratched rhythmically at the tip of his stubbled chin.

"This sterile field isn't really necessary, is it?"

Since it was a question already answered, Johncaldwell didn't respond.

"The molecular changes aren't catching," Perkins went on. "It isn't a disease. Is there any part of you that's still human?"

"My memories," he answered slowly.

"If I freed you, what would you do?"

Johncaldwell considered that with great care. "I would bring disaster and death on you all."

Chapter Seven

SILENT, MIKE DROVE his Jeep toward town and tried to let go of the anger. Up there on the mountain, Nate Curtis had only been painfully honest, and what he'd said certainly wasn't news to the deputy. Mike had always doubted his abilities as a law enforcement officer. Oh, he'd made it through training all right, and even garnered top honors on the written exams. Weapons practice hadn't been a problem either—every cardboard criminal that popped up on the shooting range, he'd drilled neatly in the heart or between the eyes.

A gun in the hand had a curious effect on most men—and women. It gave them a feeling of power, of strength. Not Mike. Weapons frightened him, but mostly, he found it was a fear of himself. Deep inside him lay a small darkness, cold and brutal. It caused him sometimes to act without thinking, which in turn caused him to think too much at all the wrong times.

On city streets, he would never have made it, but to give up his hard-earned place in the sheriff's department had proved impossible. So he'd requested the resident deputy post in Mojave Wells, and it had been granted. And why not? No one else wanted the job, while Mike Nichols had been raised on the high desert and had known the people in the area all his life—the perfect situation. There was never any real trouble here. Some car wrecks, nothing more. Until now.

Gray dawn light had crept over the barren countryside. For a long moment, he watched the trucks rumbling past on the interstate, then crossed to the 137. Mojave Wells had an almost eerie, ghostly appearance. The sergeant had

102

said nothing the whole way, and Mike thought he might be sleeping. Didn't matter. In sudden frustration, Nichols swerved onto the battered asphalt in front of Sid's garage.

"What the hell you doing?" Nate grumbled.

Mike only stomped on the brake pedal, and the Cherokee skidded down the drive, halting at the back of the shop. The sergeant watched him slam the driver's side door and disappear inside the corrugated metal building. Sid had left the fluorescents on. By their light, he found the three-foot-long bolt cutters and a pry bar the same length, then paused. What else? Think, dammit! There was a fence to cut through, and ... OK, sheet metal shears, gloves, rope, duct tape. God, this was hopeless. *He* was hopeless.

Now Nate watched him toss his motley collection over the back of the seat.

"Got everything?" the sergeant asked. "Cause I'd like that ride back to the trailer park."

"Sorry, this is the end of the line. You'll have to walk."

"Bullshit. It's a good mile."

"Mile and three-tenths," the deputy agreed. "I'm in a hurry."

"Aren't you forgetting something?"

"Probably. Come on, get out."

"Just run me back to the park. You don't want to forget your handgun this time."

Mike shook his head. "If I have a gun, I might have to shoot someone."

"Ah," said Nate Curtis with a knowing smile.

"Get the fuck out of my Jeep. Go back to Anaheim and investigate your nice safe little homicides."

"Why, when I can stay right here and watch a nice safe suicide?" The sergeant leaned toward him. "Hell, kid. You're going to have to wait until dark, anyway, so get in and close the door."

Mike obeyed and hated himself for it. Beyond Sid's front yard, the neon sign over Hannah's Cafe flickered pink and yellow in the growing daylight, and there were already a half dozen sixteen-wheelers pulled up in the parking lot. After gusting for over a week straight, the wind had died. The high desert air was still and bitter cold and tainted with diesel exhaust. Sergeant Curtis tried to straighten his long legs under the dash.

"How's the food at the cafe?" he asked, his eyes on Hannah's as well.

"Tolerable."

"And the coffee?"

"Better than mine," the deputy said sullenly.

"Good. Let's stop in for breakfast."

"How can you even think about food . . .?"

"What I'm thinking about is how we're going to manage tonight if we don't eat or rest."

Mike gazed at the man until the words sank in. We. He'd said we. Eat and rest . . . The deputy's nerves still thrummed, and his belly felt tied up in knots. "Christ, I don't think I can face a plate of Hannah's eggs."

"Then have pancakes," Curtis said cheerfully.

Mike started the car. Food would be bad enough, but facing Hannah and her good-natured nosiness would be far worse.

II

When the mice showed no adverse effects after seven hours exposure, Sergeant Rusty Dodd and Airman David Jessup donned lead aprons and attacked the problem firsthand. They'd been allocated a small work area in a corner of Dr. Fenwick's already overcrowded facility, and the young Air Force men knew well enough what danger they were in—they'd already suffered Quinten Fenwick's wrath over the shifting of some very delicate electronic equipment.

To be honest, the main room was a wreck. They'd hauled in the oxyacetylene tanks and the antiquated portable X-ray machine, which still had to be hung on a wall, and that had meant tearing the paneling out. Oblivious to the activity outside the mobile home, Rusty and Dave played with their little black boxes, both fascinated and afraid. Colonel Candliss stepped in alone about noon for a report. Dodd met him at the door and saluted.

"What have we got, Sergeant?"

"Sir, this material is invulnerable to any heat we can come up with—blowtorch and arc welder. We've used acid. We've used diamond carbide drill bits and saws and haven't even scratched the damn things."

"Could they be solid?" Candliss demanded.

"There's no way of knowing, sir. The X rays can't penetrate them. They're already denser than gold or lead, which doesn't make a whole lot of sense. And get this. One weighs in at twenty-nine kilos, 8.2062 grams. The other weighs exactly half a gram more."

"I need these things cracked, Sergeant, one way or another. What about the row of holes? They must have a purpose. . . ."

"No help there, sir. Not so far. I've poked everything but my dick into them."

Candliss managed a tired chuckle. "Well, hell, son. Don't stop there. If it'll fit, you have my permission to try."

"Yes, sir," Sergeant Dodd said, his mind already on a new tack.

The moment the colonel was outside, Dodd returned to the cluttered table they were using. "Jessup, bring me the tool case."

III

Sid was driving Charles up the wall. While once he might have taken pleasure in watching her lovely athletic body make nervous turns over the tiny bit of floor, the frenetic energy she threw off made his stomach churn. Or maybe that was the egg salad on stale white bread and lime Jell-O they'd been served for breakfast.

"Sidney, for Christ's sake, sit down. You're making me dizzy."

She ignored him as usual, studying the brackets that held the Plexiglas in place. That would do her no good— the brackets were on the outside of their cage. Next she checked the little air lock for the thousandth time. This was a bit more complicated, the outer and inner doors were solid aluminum, sealed by heavy rubber gaskets and opened automatically when cued by someone beyond the quarantine room. The rest of the walls and ceiling were zinc lined. Cool air sighed gently through a small vent above the inner door.

Charles ground the heels of his hands into tired, gritty eyes. An old man needed his sleep. Needed his beer and a good football game beamed from another hemisphere. This kind of reality just didn't appeal. And who would feed his cat? Except he dimly remembered Mocha, the feisty Siamese, disappearing not long after he'd moved into the trailer park. Deputy Mike said a coyote had probably eaten her. Poor thing. God, his mind wouldn't stop wandering.

Someone dressed in air force blue with shiny buttons and shiny silver birds on his lapels moved in close to the clear wall. A head honcho, and Charles was grateful for the distraction.

"Ms. Bowers . . ."

Contrary, Sidney strolled the six feet to the back of the room and found the toilet of extreme interest.

"Ms. Bowers . . ." This was said loudly.

"What can we do for you, General?" Charles asked from his seat.

The man ignored him. "Ms. Bowers, you were in contact with Caldwell the longest. I would like to ask you some questions."

"How bad do you want the answers?" Sid demanded, turning finally to face him.

"I can't let you out, if that's what you mean. There's still danger of contamination—"

"Bullshit. This is all bullshit. You're holding us illegally, and you're going to be one sorry son of a bitch, I promise you."

"Don't piss him off, Sid," Charles pleaded in a stage whisper.

"Who the hell are you, anyway?" the woman snapped at the visitor.

"The boxes. Did you touch the boxes? Did Caldwell tell you anything about them?"

"I touched them. And yes, he spoke of them." Sidney smiled into the long silence that followed.

Even in the dim light, the general looked irritated. "What do you want . . . within reason?"

"Some beer for Charlie."

"Oh, God bless you, child, Charles thought.

"All right."

"And I want to know what you've done with John."

The officer shook his head. "I'm afraid that's classified."

"Fine." Sid headed back to inspect the latrine.

"I could lie to you, if you like."

"And I could lie to you. Where's Fenwick? He'll tell me what I want to know."

"Out of the question," the man beyond the Plexiglas said, voice thick with anger.

Sidney only smiled again. "Give your questions to Dr. Fenwick and maybe I'll answer them."

Their visitor turned abruptly and strode away into the shadowy murk. All hope of beer vanished with him. After a moment, Sid Bowers settled on the bench beside her cellmate, thigh pressed against his, and Charles took warmth and comfort from her nearness, if nothing else.

IV

Quinten drank coffee in his kitchen—just about the only part of the mobile home still his. Past the windows, he could see the mess truck and the short line of men waiting for their noon meal, though it was closer to two o'clock. Project Black Box ran with typical military efficiency; the high-tech end managed well enough, while the tiny details tended to get lost in the bureaucratic shuffle. Fenwick wished the colonel nothing but sorrow of the whole deal.

With the wind no longer blowing, the day had actually gotten quite warm. The poor GIs, dressed in winter woolens, were sweating out there in the sun. Quinten observed them, vision hazed by lack of sleep. There seemed to be enough adrenaline in his system still to last him a lifetime.

And the bastards had thoroughly trashed his radio telescope system. Another debt for Candliss to pay, somehow, someday.

In the main room of the mobile home—some thirty feet from where Fenwick sat—a pair of soldiers worked diligently on the black box puzzle. The thought brought a thrill of fear. According to Hanover's journal, he'd left his original find buried in the sand, where it had pulsed every four hours and twenty-three minutes, destroying small wildlife within a ten-foot radius.

Yet for some insane reason, knowing full well the dangers, Arnold Hanover must have taken the box home. The Anaheim police report had noted the radius of affected area at the professor's house as twenty feet, double its earlier range of destruction. What might it do now? Quinten himself could be in grave danger, but he had absolutely nowhere else to be. He was a virtual prisoner in his own compound.

Candliss knew his time was limited, that soon someone higher up in the chain of command would discover Project Black Box and come to take over. Only by securing as much information as quickly as possible could he hope to hang on to some part of the project. So the colonel pressured his people into taking incredible risks. But by God, they would floor the world when news of this finally leaked out.

Someone rapped softly on the kitchen door, and Fenwick forced himself upright to gaze out the small, square window. Will Perkins stood on the wooden steps, still in surgical scrubs.

"Taking a break?" Quentin asked as he unlocked and opened the door. "How's your patient?"

"In better shape than I am," the black man grunted. "I need a cup of real coffee. You see what they've got over by the mess wagon? It's a twenty-gallon pot with a dirty dishrag full of coffee grounds floating in it." He slumped into a chair beside the Formica table. "You'd think an air force that can train astronauts, could train a goddamn cook."

Fenwick poured him some coffee only slightly better than the Air Force's and set the cup before him.

Perkins, shoulders hunched, stared at his hands. "What's happening to us, Quinten? I can't make sense of any of this. Caldwell's everything I've ever hoped for, but the more I learn of him, the more frightened I get. He radiates a kind of deep internal peace, and yet there's this sense of contained power about him.

"His brain size is nearly double ours, and there's no way of knowing what's really going on in that alien mind. I put it to him . . . asked him what he'd do if I freed him. . . . He said he'd bring death and destruction to all of us—just as calm and pleasant as you please, like some kind of sociopath. I don't think it was an idle threat."

"He isn't human now," Fenwick told the surgeon, returning to his own seat. "So you can't judge him against human behavior. But wanting to bring death and destruction to an enemy seems a perfectly logical concept for any sentient being. And we've gone out of our way to prove that's exactly what we are—his enemy."

"Quinten . . ." Will muttered, "you're not making me feel any better." He looked up from his untasted coffee. "I *have* seen his face before. The drawings . . ."

Quinten's hand tightened on his mug. "We've had visitors all along. All this time with never a shred of physical proof."

"Until now."

"Maybe. What we actually have are two black boxes of unknown origin, and something that was once human— none of which can be directly connected with any UFO sightings."

"Hell." Will grinned suddenly. "Who cares? We're still going to set the planet on its ear. Got anything to eat around here?"

Fenwick smiled back. "I've got microwave pizzas and assorted cheap frozen dinners."

"Anything's better than egg salad sandwiches and glow-in-the-dark Jell-O."

"What about Caldwell? Has he been fed?"

"Tell me what he eats and I'll send out. At the moment, he's tolerating a glucose drip."

"You should offer him an egg salad sandwich."

"I could never be so cruel." The surgeon pointed at the refrigerator. "So break out the chow."

Quinten pulled a couple of cardboard pizzas from the freezer. "Just how the hell did you end up on Candliss's team, anyway?" he asked casually.

"How the hell is right," Perkins grunted. "I was home in Washington, D.C., minding my own business. Colonel Whitebread pulled me out of bed Saturday morning about 3:00 A.M.. Poor Lorraine thought it was the Ku Klux Klan. I didn't even get to kiss my kids good-bye."

"Getting a little old for that, aren't they?" Fenwick remembered the two boys and one girl as tykes, but that was many years back.

"Fourteen ain't too old for this daddy to kiss." Will's grin returned. "Come to think of it, though, they're getting harder and harder to catch. Hey, put those damn pizzas in the oven."

Quinten never had the chance. Foolishly, he'd forgotten to relock the back door, and now it banged open. Bob Candliss leaned in.

"You have better things to do, Major," he growled at Perkins. "Out."

Perkins rocked forward, using the edge of the table to get himself up. "See ya around, Dr. Fenwick. Thanks for the coffee."

The colonel stepped away to let him pass, then climbed the stairs and entered the kitchen. Uneasy, Quinten Fenwick watched him close and lock the door.

"Have a seat, Doctor." Candliss sounded almost affable. "There's some coffee left, if you'd like some. . . ."

"I'll pass. Go on, sit down."

Quinten took a seat, though the colonel remained standing. After a long sleepless night, his appearance was still impeccable. Fenwick noted an expensive gold pen in a breast pocket of his uniform coat and tucked in beside it there was a fancy pocket calculator with what looked like the flat tip of a telescoping antenna at one corner. The scientist glanced up and found Candliss regarding him with bright lucid eyes. Well into his fifties, the colonel had always presented an ageless strength that intimidated even his superiors. Now, he rapped a fingertip on the Formica.

"Dr. Fenwick, I'm having some trouble communicating with the Bowers woman. So you're going to do it for me."

"Wait a minute . . ."

Candliss ignored him, pulling a folded paper from the same breast pocket. "These are the questions I want answered. Do your best, Doctor, or I may have to extract the information by other . . . less friendly . . . means. Do you understand?"

Quinten nodded, unable to trust his voice.

"Ms. Bowers will be expecting information from you in return. The answers you may give are also on the page. But should you forget yourself, be warned. You're dealing with classified intelligence, and the conversation will be videotaped."

"Go to hell," Quinten snarled, finding the courage from somewhere.

The colonel only straightened, smiling. "Spare me, Fenwick." He unlocked the door. "At eighteen hundred hours, a chopper will arrive with Brigadier General Alden McKinley—"

"Of the Joint Chiefs of Staff?" Quinten's eyes widened. "They know? You've told them . . . ?"

"Listen carefully. I don't want our visitor bothered with a lot of civilian whining and complaints. You're to stay clear of the whole business. Be a good boy, Dr. Fenwick, and we may put everything back together when we leave. Otherwise, your million-dollar MSA could have an unfortunate accident."

Shit. So he intended to use the Multichannel Spectrum Analyzer as a scientific hostage. Fenwick considered that and felt only satisfaction. Let Candliss play his little power games. Once the world knew for certain someone was out there among the stars, the search for extraterrestrial radio transmissions would be of more interest than ever. Funding for new equipment would be no problem.

"Are we agreed?" The colonel seemed annoyed by Quinten's silence.

The scientist nodded, eyes downcast, properly subordinate. "Yes, sir."

"Good! See the Bowers woman immediately." Candliss pushed the door open and stepped out to where his two aides waited, apparently with urgent messages. One handed him a cellular phone, and they moved off toward Truck One.

Fenwick sat a moment longer, staring across the threshold into the afternoon light. The mess wagon had disappeared, and activity within the compound had picked up again. Enlisted men hurried across the grounds, their arms loaded, while others filled heavy crates with equipment. A forklift bumped past. Project Black Box was obviously folding its tents. Quinten couldn't quite decide if that was good or bad.

A faint *clink-clink,* as much felt as heard, caught his attention. He looked down at the thin flooring beneath his feet. The sound came again, rhythmic and familiar. What? Quinten gathered the colonel's paper from the table and descended the stairs, closing the door behind him. Someone dogtrotted past, headed in the direction of the generator, then for a brief moment, Quinten was alone.

He squatted there beside the steps and took a quick look beneath the mobile home. In the shadows of that narrow space, light flickered off the chrome finish of a wrench in the hand of a man intent upon his work. Fenwick opened his mouth to demand what was going on, then saw the small package being strapped to the floor joist. Realization jolted through him. Dear God! The paper crumpled in his hand, Quinten backed hurriedly but quietly away, until he came up against the white side of Truck One.

Another pair of airmen bustled past. One raised a brow at the scientist, but kept on. Fenwick dared a look under the semi's trailer, then leaned deeper into the shadows and found it—another perfect little package, wired and set, with a tiny green light that glowed steadily in the dimness. It all made a dreadful sense. Candliss dealt with dangerous unknowns here. If things should get out of hand, he'd want a way to destroy that danger. And any evidence of his own mistakes.

The desert sun, angling in from the southwest, made Quinten's face prickle with sweat, but sick fear brought a chill. It had occurred to him that the colonel might well burn his bridges, no matter what. Accidents happened, and historically, the military offered an endless supply of scapegoats. Mind numb with the possibilities, Fenwick headed for Truck Two and his meeting with the Bowers woman.

V

Sid knew she'd won—at least one small victory—when the beer arrived. An ice-cold six-pack of Miller cycled through the air lock, and Charlie collected it almost reverently.

"Want one?" he asked.

"No, Charlie. They're all yours."

The man settled once more on the bench, and she heard the snap of a pull tab and then his sigh. They'd both managed to sleep a little in the last hour, Charlie on the bench, Sid tucked into a corner on the floor where she still sat. But soon, Dr. Fenwick would appear to ask his questions. Sidney Bowers waited and watched the darkness beyond her cell.

Three cans of beer later, the scientist finally appeared.

"It's fucking Fenwick," Charlie commented. The alcohol had taken the edge off of him. "Look, Sid. Shall we invite him in?"

Quinten Fenwick motioned to Sidney, and she stood slowly, then approached the Plexiglas. His thin face was the same ashen color as his hair now, and his eyes had dulled.

"Are you all right?" he asked.

"I'm fine, but you don't look so hot, Fenwick. Could it be your conscience is bothering you?"

"Everything, at the moment, is bothering me." The scientist held up a piece of wrinkled paper. "I have to ask some questions."

"So do I. Answer for answer, or no deal."

"Agreed. May I go first?"

Sid shrugged. "Sure."

"Have you seen John Caldwell use the black boxes?"

"No. He said one was broken and that he turned the other off so that it couldn't hurt anyone." The young woman pressed her hands to the plastic. "Now you tell me, and tell me the truth. Is John Caldwell still alive?"

Fenwick nodded his head once, almost surreptitiously, but said, "I'm not permitted to answer that question. Ask another."

"Bastard! Then tell me when the hell we can get out of here."

"Quarantine time has been set at a minimum of seventy-two hours, after which you will be debriefed. I'm truly sorry, Mrs. Bowers. Would you please describe the physical changes that you witnessed in John Caldwell?"

Sid closed her eyes, weary, and dredged up those unhappy memories, keeping her distance from the confusion and pain. Almost dully, she asked her next question.

"What will they do with him?"

"I'm not permitted to—"

"Damn it, Fenwick!"

"I don't know." The scientist glanced behind him. "I'm certain they're packing up to move him. Soon."

"Where to?"

"My best guess is Colorado—Cheyenne Mountain—to their underground facilities. But it could be anywhere." He smiled dryly. "Colonel Candliss is having this videotaped, you realize? And I can kiss my MSA good-bye. To the tune of 1.6 million—"

Sid cut in. "What are they doing with the black boxes?"

"Right now, they're trying to open them."

"Oh, Sweet Jesus . . ."

"If they do, you can kiss your ass good-bye," Charles Downing said with wry amusement and opened another beer.

VI

Airman Jessup hummed tunelessly while he worked at the grinder wheel. Bright sparks from the slender steel rod showered into his face, deflected by the safety glasses. Sergeant Dodd had decided they would fashion themselves a claw as similar to one of the XT's as could be managed. The Polaroid photos of the creature's hand lay on the workbench, but Jessup kept his mind on his job. The pictures had convinced him that he had no desire to see what the rest of their alien looked like.

Besides, *alien* was a forbidden word around here. Nobody knew nothing nohow—as usual.

"Jessup!"

The airman pulled back from the wheel, and slipped his earphones off. "Yeah, Sarge?"

"The colonel's getting antsy. We're gonna have to pack it in pretty soon."

"We're going with them, right?"

Dodd shook his head. "Not this time, kid. The general's calling in his experts."

"Expert whats? Shit. I know we can take these babies apart, if they'll give us some time."

"Time is what we ain't got." Sergeant Dodd eyed the curved steel in the airman's hand. "The point looks good, but the claw's going to have to be flattened more on the side."

Dutifully, Jessup caught up the mallet and laid the rod tip on the vise. It took three hard but careful raps to thin the metal claw.

"Shall we give it a try?" Dodd asked.

"Sure. But it won't work."

"Have a little faith."

The sergeant thumped the lighter weight box onto its side. After an initial leeriness, they'd gotten pretty careless in their treatment of the boxes. The more frustration they suffered, the more knocks and bangs were dealt out. Jessup gave this one a good crack with the hammer.

"For luck," he said and grinned.

Dodd wiped imaginary dirt from the end of his claw and inserted it into the first hole. As usual, nothing happened.

"Nice fit, though. Snug."

The next hole brought such an immediate response—a sharp hissing noise—that both men leaped back in unison.

"Whoa, darlin'!" the sergeant grunted, waving his steel rod. "Come on, baby. Be nice."

Arm extended, hand a bit shaky, he slipped the clawtip into the second hole again. Again, the box hissed, but this time the heavy black material at one corner turned liquid and flowed outward through the air toward the bench vise. It found the painted metal surface, attached itself with a gentle suctioning sound, and solidified. Dodd and Jessup gazed at each other, eyes huge, then whooped and began to pound each other on the shoulders.

"Wait, wait, wait!" the sergeant cried. "The damn thing's still closed tight. We ain't beat it yet."

To detach the box, they had only to insert the claw in the same hole. After that, nothing came easily. None of the other holes seemed to do a damn thing. Their first elation faded quickly. Dodd, jaw tight, flung the claw down after a time. Jessup scooped it up and started again, working a pattern of sorts; the first hole combined with the second, then the third and so forth. On the next run-through, using the third slot as the pattern base, he hit the jackpot, almost without realizing it.

"Jessup! Don't move!"

The young airman froze, the claw poised over the eighth hole, while Dodd turned the box upright carefully. The lid had opened soundlessly.

"Do you remember what you did?" the sergeant asked.

"I think so." Jessup pulled a gooseneck lamp closer. "It's empty. I can't fucking believe this."

The black interior seemed to suck away the light. There were tiny fins of all sizes and lengths protruding along the inside walls, but nothing else.

"This is some kind of extraterrestrial joke," the airman

growled. "Any moment now a little clawed hand is going to reach out, hit the switch, and close the damn lid."

"Try the other one," the sergeant ordered. "It's heavier."

"By five-tenths of a gram." Jessup ran his pattern on the second box and watched the top slide free. "Empty. No, wait."

They almost bumped heads trying to get a good look at the two pieces of white card stock wedged between the fins. There were words printed on the surface.

"It's a goddamn business card," Dodd growled. "Probably for the UFO Pick-A-Part junkyard. And these are used flying saucer batteries. Pull it out of there."

Chapter Eight

THE AIRSTREAM, ITS polished aluminum shell tarnished by age, had absorbed the sun's heat, and Mike Nichols woke in the late afternoon with sweat-soaked bed sheets tangled around his legs. Still drunk with exhaustion, he swayed there on the edge of the mattress, head in hands, and tried to pull his thoughts together. No easy task.

His little bedroom window offered up a view of Curtis's camper instead of the Shadow Mountains, but that brought more relief than irritation. The pessimistic side of Mike had expected the man to be long gone. Groaning, the deputy, dressed only in boxer shorts, got to his feet and staggered into the tiny bathroom. The trailer began to rock under him, and he braced himself between the close walls. Earthquake? No, just two hundred and fifty pounds of Anaheim detective.

"You got a couple of calls over the radio," Nate Curtis said from the narrow hallway, neck bent to keep his head from bumping into the ceiling. "Nothing serious, but San Bernardino's probably wondering just where the hell you are. And the phone's been ringing. We'll have to come up with some excuse for them." Mike only stared at him, stupefied. "Looks like you better drink this first."

A mug of strong coffee was handed in through the doorway, lukewarm and tainted with milk. Mike fixed his gaze on the cup.

"Best go in uniform tonight," Nate continued. "With your utility belt. If we get busted, we'll flash our badges, and they'll be a bit more careful how they handle us. Damn it, Nichols, drink the coffee and snap out

118

of it. We got some things to discuss before the sun goes down."

The old resentment welling, Mike did as he was told.

II

Jessup used long-handled tweezers to dislodge the first half of the business card. As it came loose, a faint sparkle of color materialized in the center of the box. Beside him, Dodd inhaled noisily. A tiny swirling cloud of light formed, misty, indistinct. They watched closely, but nothing more happened.

"The other one," Sergeant Dodd ordered. "Take the other piece out."

The young airman hesitated, uncertain of what would happen if he inserted the tweezers through that ghostly nebula. Curiosity outweighed reluctance though. With one quick motion, Jessup plucked the second half of the card free. The colors flared and brightened, then separated into strands no thicker than hairs that wove and twined and spread. The dance of lights mesmerized them momentarily, then the sergeant came to his senses.

"Jumping Jesus," Dodd croaked. "I think you better get the colonel. . . ."

Reluctant, David Jessup headed for the door.

III

Johncaldwell felt the Gatekeeper stir, and he welcomed it. The agony of translation had passed, but the energy still flowed between them. Already a tingling spread through his body, a gentle vibration. He felt the black man's gloved fingers adjust the long intravenous needle in his forearm. Despite everything, Major Perkins had not been completely unkind.

"Will," Johncaldwell said, frustrated by the less than perfect *wa* sound his mouth made. "You must leave."

The plastic-warped image of the major frowned down on him. "What?"

"Leave *il'ral*. . . . Your death is not required."

Another slighter form came to stand behind the surgeon. "What'd he say?" Colonel Candliss demanded.

"I'm not sure, sir."

"Caldwell, damn you. Don't shut down on me again."

Johncaldwell had already closed his eyes. Somewhere beyond the trailer walls, the Gatekeeper cycled, and he drew the power to him, let the weight of stars roll through and over him. A single box couldn't create the mass needed to distort space and open the gateway, but it did provide Johncaldwell with a terrible weapon.

The pulse lasted less than an instant . . . long enough. In its wake, computer monitors imploded, followed by the hiss and crackle of electrical fires. Other than that, silence reigned in the once noisy crowded room. But the straps that bound him were still tight. Resigned, Johncaldwell clamped his nostrils closed against the stench of burning plastic.

IV

"I'm sorry, sir, but you'll have to leave. Now."

The young AP was polite, but firm, and Fenwick dragged his gaze from Sidney Bowers's bloodless face. The videotape of this interview would damn Dr. Quinten Fenwick forever. Perhaps that's what Candliss had counted on—either a way to blackmail the scientist to gain his cooperation or discredit him completely.

"Fenwick!"

At Sidney's call, he looked back.

"Thanks," she said, but her eyes were filled with sorrow and pain. Downing remained hunched over his beer.

The hand on Fenwick's arm tightened. At least this time, he wasn't being manhandled, not in front of civilian witnesses. Dusk thickened into night outside the trailer, held at bay by the floodlights. Quinten took the flimsy stepladder to the ground. The AP didn't accompany him, only closed the heavy door with a thud. There was nothing left to do but return to his kitchen and await the colonel's pleasure.

Still no wind. Even so, the air temperature had dropped

sharply. Quinten hardly felt it. The generator rumbled quietly in the background and nothing stirred within the little compound. That seemed odd after so much activity earlier. His wristwatch read 5:15. The Air Force chopper carrying General McKinley should arrive at 6:00. Was Candliss in Truck One, readying the star exhibit in his galactic freak show?

Crates were stacked at the end of the aisle between the trailer and Fenwick's mobile home, ready for transport into Fort Irwin. He paused by his own back stairs, disturbed and angry. What madness to sit at the table with a cup of coffee and a load of plastic explosives under his very feet. He hadn't mentioned that to Mrs. Bowers. No reason to alarm her further, and Quinten hadn't checked their trailer. Colonel Candliss might have left that one truck unwired. No . . . not a chance. The man was nothing if not thorough. But soon enough, Project Black Box would be gone from here, and Quinten's secluded search of the stars could recommence. He'd pretend none of this had ever happened. He'd forget John Caldwell, the boxes, Sidney Bowers, and Charles Downing. Somehow.

The lights glared off the surrounding walls, bright enough to make Fenwick's eyes ache, and the shadows beneath the semitrailer across from him seemed absolute. Quinten almost reached for the kitchen doorknob, then paused, unsure of exactly what he had seen. Something glittering in the sand, and wary, the scientist stepped toward it.

A large star sapphire ring lay at the very edge of the light, but it was still on a pinky finger. Against his will, he leaned closer. Two airmen had collapsed in an untidy heap just under the high trailer floor. They'd been smoking. One cigarette still burned on the ground nearby, its cherry coal glowing in the dark. Fenwick reached out a shaky hand and touched a bare throat. The flesh felt hot against his cold fingers, but there was no pulse. Dead, both of them, though he couldn't see why. He bolted into the open area beyond as if something evil lurked in the aisle.

At the rear of Truck One, a door had been left ajar, and Quinten clambered up the stepladder. No one answered his knock, and the first niggling doubt became outright fear. That didn't stop him from opening the door a crack. Close, smothering darkness filled the trailer. The cold air held a bitter taste of burned wires and something far worse. Unable to stop himself, Fenwick pushed both doors wide to let in as much light as possible. Thin white smoke drifted out.

An AP lay slumped against the right interior wall, a carbine across his lap. Blood flowed sluggishly from nose and mouth, but Quinten could only stare at the bloody tears leaking from the corners of his open eyes. The veins in the whites had hemorrhaged. Panic gibbered in the scientist's mind. Run. Run! Instead, he gingerly unsnapped the AP's holster flap and pulled the revolver free. As if a bullet could stop this horror.

Fenwick picked his way through the destruction, blind to the dead bodies scattered around him, across desks, along the floor, male and female. By the time he reached the rear of the trailer, the stench of blood and fecal matter grew too heavy to ignore. The plastic shroud that tented John Caldwell had gone opaque. Candliss and Will Perkins lay on the floor, recognizable only by their uniforms. The force that had killed them all had been strongest here. Some enormous internal pressure had caused flesh and bone to explode outward.

Their bodies appeared to have been turned inside out, the buttons and seams of their clothing burst open to release the gore. Quinten, a hand clamped over nose and mouth, used the pistol barrel to break the now brittle plastic tent. Still strapped to the table, Caldwell opened his luminous black eyes.

"Did you do this?" Fenwick demanded, fear making his voice crack. "Did you kill them?"

"Yes."

But he'd known that already. Caldwell had simply destroyed his enemies. And Quinten was an enemy, too. He backed a step, and put a shoe into Will Perkins's ruptured intestines, then vomited until his stomach muscles knotted, helpless to move.

"Release me, Dr. Fenwick." It was an order, not a plea.

"N . . . no."

"I won't harm you if you do exactly as I say."

Numb, Quinten looked down on Candliss's corpse. The man's hand, fingerbones thrust through the flesh, seemed to be reaching for a blood-soaked breast pocket in his jacket. Oh, God. The scientist, stomach threatening another revolt, reached into the pocket and pulled the small hard plastic case free. It wasn't a pocket calculator, oh, no. He checked the single slide switch on the side, the little telescoping antenna, and the small red button on the front. The plastic had smeared, flowed like liquid, then solidified in a slightly distorted shape.

The moment he pushed the switch up, though, an almost inaudible electronic hum began. This had survived the devastation, even if Candliss hadn't. Fenwick's finger hovered over the live detonator button.

"Quinten? What are you doing?"

Where once Caldwell had seemed a helpless, even kindly, creature to be pitied, now Fenwick saw a monster, cold and calculating.

"You killed Will, you bastard," he said with quavering courage. "I won't turn you loose. I'll scatter you, me, and your goddamn black boxes all over the mountainside first. See this?" The radio detonator was brandished. "The colonel wired explosives under these trailers, and this is all I need to set them off."

That same odd whistling sounded as Caldwell inhaled. "I can't explain the forces contained within the two poles of the gate, Dr. Fenwick—within the boxes. I'm not even certain you have the capability to destroy them. But if you do . . . you'll crack this world in half."

Quinten clenched his teeth. "Then maybe I'll only kill you." He raised the pistol, pointed at Caldwell. "You *can* be killed?"

"Yes, but you'll have to hold the weapon steadier, I think." The creature watched him, unblinking. "A shot to the head is best. Aim for an eye . . . I told Will Perkins to leave. By the time he understood, it was too late."

"Why? Why did you do this to him?" Quinten broke

down, sobbing, cheeks already wet with tears. "He had a wife, children. He was a good man."

"Understand, doctor. The deaths of *il'ral* mean nothing. I do what I must. And whether I die or not, the Gatekeeper will continue to cycle, and your kind won't be able to resist such a puzzle. Another will be chosen to open the gate as I was. And another. Set me free, and go away, Quinten. Go as far away as you can."

Fenwick turned and ran, dodging the blood and death, breath held against the foul stink until he'd found cold and dry night air beyond the trailer. Caldwell's all-too-sane voice echoed in his head. None of it made sense. He'd referred to the boxes as a gate and a Gatekeeper. What did *il'ral* mean? The stepladder shuddered under his weight, and once on the ground, Quinten tried to scrub the gore from the soles of his shoes and the tears from his face.

The helicopter would be here in little more than twenty minutes, and a course of action must be decided on. Caldwell was right in one thing—the boxes would be too tempting. Was he right in another? Would an attempt to destroy them bring destruction to the world, too? Quinten shut the detonator off and pocketed it, then climbed the steps to Truck Two and rapped loudly on the door.

The same young AP who had thrown him out answered it. "I'm sorry, Dr. Fenwick. You no longer have clearance."

"Does this give me clearance?" Quinten said irritably and pushed the handgun into the man's face. "Don't!" he warned when the AP reached for his own pistol. "I want the Bowers woman and Dr. Downing released."

"You know we can't do that . . ."

Quinten thumbed the revolver's hammer back. "Order them released now, or so help me, I'll shoot you."

"Have you gone crazy, sir?"

"Yes," the scientist answered with all sincerity. "Do it!"

The man glanced over his shoulder. "I don't have that authority, sir."

"You do now. No, don't move. Just call Airman Willis. I warn you though . . . cross me, and you won't be the only one to die." Quinten grinned under the brilliant floodlights. "Remember what they say about shooting fish in a barrel. I can't miss in this crowded trailer."

V

Shouting started at the rear of the trailer, and Sid peered out through Plexiglas. There seemed to be some confusion, personnel milled about in the dimness, then both doors of the air lock hissed suddenly open. Charlie stood up.

"What's going on?"

A young soldier, his expression angry, gestured them toward the exit.

Sidney snagged the doc's arm. "Come on, before they change their minds."

Uncertain, they made their way down the aisle. Uniformed men and women shuffled as far back as possible or ducked behind equipment-loaded desks.

"Hurry it up!" Quinten Fenwick snapped from where he stood in the narrow opening of one tall trailer door. He had a pistol pointed at the guard's chest. "Use the other side."

The doc pushed the left-hand door just wide enough to let them out. The glare of the floodlights beyond made Sid's eyes tear and, with an arm shading her face, she leaped to the ground after Charlie.

" 'Bye," Fenwick told the soldier, and slammed the doors together, wedging the spring steel lever across them. The pounding and shouted threats started immediately.

Charlie, a little haggard, raised a brow at the gun in the scientist's hand. "Hell, Fenwick. The colonel'll have your nuts for this."

"No, he won't. He's dead."

"You killed him?" Sidney's dark circled eyes widened.

"Not me," Fenwick said quickly. "Look. You've got to get out of here. There's a helicopter on the way, and all hell's going to break loose."

The young woman drew a breath. "Where's Caldwell?"

"There's no time—"

"Sid! Listen to the man," Downing growled.

She didn't, only turned and hurried toward the other trailer.

"Dear God! Mrs. Bowers, don't!" Fenwick rushed after her.

The doors were still wide open, the interior clearly visible. The sights and smells caused Sid to freeze on the stepladder. Charles arrived with the scientist.

"What is this?" The old man pushed past Sid. "What's happened?"

"Caldwell happened."

"Is he all right?" Sidney felt a sudden fear.

"Christ! He's the only one who is."

She climbed into the trailer, eyes averted from the death. "John!"

He answered from the distant shadows. "Here . . ."

"Damn!" Fenwick snarled and followed the doc and Sid inside.

Charlie cursed bitterly the whole way, the sleeve of his jacket pressed to his nose. He soon stopped checking for life in the bodies.

"Oh, God," Sidney murmured. "Oh, dear God . . ." So many had died so horribly.

She found Caldwell finally, bound naked to a table in the midst of the carnage. "John . . ." Sid bent close and watched his black eyes open. They seemed fathomless. Some part of her knew there should be fear, but she'd seen him change, witnessed his pain, and now could find only a strange beauty in those eyes and in the clean, sharp angles of this inhuman body.

"Sidney," he murmured, consonants made exotic by that pointed tongue. There was a weakness in his voice.

"Damn them," the young woman cried and fumbled at the straps on his ankles first.

Fenwick gripped her wrist. "He killed those people!"

Sidney jerked away and started on the straps at Caldwell's thighs. "Can you blame him?"

"Sid, think a minute," Charlie said, words muffled in his sleeve. "What are we going to do? This isn't a Spielberg movie. You can't throw a sheet over him and take him trick-or-treating. Or say he's a cousin from out of town . . . *way* out of town."

Caldwell made a sudden noise, a high fluting whistle that rose and fell.

"What in God's name is that?" the doc demanded, alarmed.

"He's laughing," Sid answered, not certain just how she knew.

"Well, at least he's still got a human funny bone. So what are we doing, lady?"

"We're going to get him out of here before the helicopter arrives, then worry about the details."

Gently, she withdrew the long plastic intravenous needle from Caldwell's arm, and freed his wrists. He reached up to caress her cheek with those slender, claw-tipped fingers. His touch brought a rush of confusion.

"My God, be careful!" Fenwick said sharply. "The man he raked last night died within minutes from anaphylactic shock."

Charlie looked troubled. "Get back, Sid. The guy may already have been prone to allergic reactions, but we're not going to take any chances."

Johncaldwell broke the straps from his own throat and forehead, then swung long thin legs from the table and sat upright, heavy head bowed. "The Gatekeeper . . ." he said.

"The damn boxes are in my place," Fenwick told him. "And we're just about out of time." He dared to step closer to John. "What will happen if you open the gate? Are we . . . is humankind . . . in danger?"

"You know the danger that already exists." Caldwell stood, that impossible humanoid body unfolding into the high ceiling, ropy muscle and bone under taut yellow skin. His eyes fixed on the scientist. "I don't know what will happen, Dr. Fenwick."

"I'll tell you what I want to happen," Fenwick said. "Somehow, you've got to fix that gate, then take it with you, out of this world. It must never fall into human hands again."

Caldwell tilted his head side to side. "I agree. That would be best."

VI

"There's something wrong here," Nate growled in a low voice. They'd hidden the Jeep in the same small wash, but this time had come up on the lighted enclosure from below. They crouched now beside the fence, hidden in the deep shadows near the front of the semitrailer that Sidney and the doctor had disappeared into the night before.

Mike single-mindedly cut another link in the cyclone fencing. Each snap with the bolt cutters caused the whole fence to clink and shudder in the stillness. The distant rumble of the generator seemed to be the only sign of life.

"Damn it, it's too quiet. Where is everybody?"

"Having dinner," Mike grunted and widened the hole some more. "Let's just take advantage of the situation." He threw the cutters down, then squeezed head and shoulders through the break. At least, the kid had left the cowboy hat behind.

Nate stared at the hole in the fence. "I won't fit through that, you skinny little jerk."

"Shit! So cut it to size." The deputy stood up in the narrow space next to the cab and put an ear to the trailer's front wall. "We got plenty of people inside by the sounds of it. That should make you happy."

It didn't. None of this did. They were going to get themselves caught smack in the middle of some super top secret mess and end up in Leavenworth. Or shot. Nate shoved his way through his slightly larger cut in the fence. Jesus, this was nuts. The adrenaline was pumping, the fifty-two-year-old heart was thumping, and Detective Sergeant Curtis hadn't felt this alive in a very long time.

Somewhere along the line, he'd lost that adventurous part of him, grown conservative and careful. For Janice's sake, Nate had gone into homicide over fifteen years ago, but he'd always loved working the streets—loved the danger. Only this time, he was riding the ragged edge of disaster with a scatterbrained partner. That partner had dropped to his hands and knees and disappeared under the truck frame.

"Nichols! Get back here."

A long moment passed, then Mike returned from another direction—the rear of the trailer.

"It sounds like they're trying to break the doors open from inside."

Nate frowned. "Sid and Charlie, maybe?"

"Too noisy for just two people."

"Then there is definitely something very wrong here."

"Why don't we just ask them?"

"That's real bright," Nate said. "Why don't we look around first? Just in case."

The deputy nodded, contrite. "Okay, Sarge. Which way?"

Good question. Nate led them along the fence to the rear, then put a cautioning hand out to Mike. A careful peek around the corner showed open ground. He could hear the folks trapped in the trailer arguing. Someone pried uselessly at the doors, but they'd been barred. The kid was right. They might get some interesting answers and maybe even some gratitude just by opening the trailer. And a whole lot of trouble.

"Look at that," Mike muttered and nodded toward the second truck.

One of that trailer's doors was hanging wide open.

"Oh-oh." Uneasy, Nate stepped out into the bright lights.

The deputy beat him across the yard, but had the courtesy to wait. Both doors were wide. "I don't like the looks of this."

"Yeah," Nate agreed, his eyes on the shadows just inside. A still form leaned against one wall. He started toward the ladder.

"You don't want to do that," a voice called. "You really don't."

Charles Downing stood on the concrete slab near the mobile home.

"Charlie!" Mike cried, then the joy faded abruptly. "Where's Sid?"

"She's fine. She's here in Fenwick's place." When Mike strode quickly onto the slab, Charlie blocked his path. "Wait . . ."

Now Nate couldn't resist. "Want to tell us what the hell is going on?"

"There . . . was an accident," the doctor said almost reluctantly. "They're all dead in there. Fenwick says there's a helicopter coming. Any minute. So he and Sid and . . . They went into the mobile home to get the boxes."

"Hanover's?" Nate demanded.

Charlie nodded.

The sergeant felt a nasty chill. "Who's Fenwick?"

"He's a SETI scientist. This was his compound until the military commandeered it." Mike tried to push past, and Charlie caught his arm. "I said wait. There's something else you should know." He paused, head cocked.

Over the steady hum of the generator, they heard the rhythmic thump of a chopper now. No, several choppers. High in the southern night sky, tiny lights could be seen, growing quickly larger. Everything seemed to fall apart all at once. Sidney Bowers appeared with a little man in a white lab coat, both staggering under the weight of the small black boxes in their hands. Mike started toward the young woman and stopped dead. A nightmarish stick figure followed in their wake. Some . . . thing beyond belief.

Nate's mind refused to work for one long moment, then emergency reflexes kicked in.

"We've got the Jeep just down the road!" he shouted to the others. "Forget the gate, it's locked tight. There's a hole in the fence. This way!"

But the creature loped to the gate in question and easily tore it from the track.

"Charles!" That was the little guy, Fenwick, hollering. Downing turned back and had the second box thrust into his arms. "I can't go with you!" Fenwick pushed him toward the road. "Hurry!" Then he turned and ran back toward the mobile home.

VII

They couldn't possibly make it, not with the federal government aware of John Caldwell's existence and the existence of the boxes. Quinten realized that. There'd be no place to hide. A futile and brief moment of freedom was all they could hope for. He stopped near the center of the slab and glanced back. They'd disappeared into the night—John and Charles and Sidney and their two friends, who'd come to rescue them against impossible odds.

The first helicopter arrived, bringing its own icy wind to buffet the scientist. Quinten backed to the mobile home, and, eyes squinted, waved a beckoning arm over his head. The massive aircraft circled low, made a couple of passes over the deserted compound, then returned to settle slowly on the concrete. A helmeted soldier with a rifle in hand stepped down.

"What's going on, sir?" he shouted over the thump of the still turning double blades. "We haven't had radio contact in over an hour!"

Fenwick shouted back, "Equipment malfunction! There's been a little accident, but everything's all right now!"

"Where's Colonel Candliss?"

"With our ... special guest!" He was getting hoarse from all the yelling.

Someone else climbed down from the chopper, a large man, straight-backed, and the floodlights brightened a familiar shock of white hair. The pilot killed the engine and the blades began to slow. In the night beyond the compound, the two other helicopters headed away to the south, back toward George Air Force Base.

"General McKinley ..." Quinten dared to approach, his hand held out.

The general accepted the hand. "Dr. Fenwick, it's been a while."

"Yes, sir."

"There's been an accident?"

"Well, yes, sir. I'll let the colonel explain. He regrets that he couldn't meet you personally, but ..." Quinten smiled.

"Is that blood on your coat?"

"My own, general. I failed to look where I was going earlier."

Fenwick could hardly believe how easily he came up with such logical, sincere answers. His little fantasy world wouldn't stand up long in the face of things, but then it shouldn't have to.

The soldier came to stand beside them. "Excuse me, Dr. Fenwick. Can you explain why the gate is off the track?"

"I didn't realize it was. They were packing everything earlier, perhaps one of the trucks hit it. We've been pretty rushed around here."

"Check it out, Captain," McKinley ordered, then turned back to Quinten. "I'd like to see Colonel Candliss."

"Of course. But the boxes are just inside the house. If you'd like a quick look. They're quite incredible."

Over the general's shoulder, Fenwick watched the soldier cross toward the broken gate, but something stopped him. He gazed at the back of Truck Two. The jig was nearly up, just a few moments more. There were a dozen or more men and women in the trailer—innocent people who had only followed orders.

But Quinten couldn't allow himself to think about that, or anything else. Thinking might remind him what a coward he truly was. John Caldwell and the others needed time, and in order to have that, the government must believe Project Black Box a complete loss.

Fenwick slipped a hand in his pocket and armed the radio detonator as he led the general in through the front door of the mobile home. The room was dark. The MSA and all the supercomputers, along with Quinten's years of hard work, had been destroyed by the damn black boxes. There were also two young Air Force men lying dead in the shadows.

"Where the hell are the lights, Fenwick?"

"Don't worry. In a moment, you'll have all the light you need. I just wanted you to know, McKinley, that I never could stand your ultramilitary paranoia. Over the years, you've diverted more federal funds into the Pentagon for the nuclear arms buildup than anyone. And all you're chasing now is a chance for even bigger weapons. What a shortsighted jackass you are."

The general's face contorted, but Quinten only smiled and pressed the detonator button.

Chapter Nine

MIKE NICHOLS COULD hardly keep the Cherokee on the road. It was too early for the moon, and they didn't dare use the headlights. Curtis had even pulled the fuse on the brake lights. Now the homicide detective, a massive dark form, rode up front in the passenger seat. Charlie, Sid, and . . . John Caldwell were jammed in back.

"If those are Hanover's boxes back there," Nate grunted beside him, "I just want to know how long we've got before they do their thing again."

"One's broken," the doc told him. "Caldwell says he shut the other one down again when he retrieved them from Fenwick's trailer. Don't worry."

Mike was paying more attention to the conversation than he should. The Jeep hit a bad pothole and flew into the air—which was weird considering how slowly they were going. Bright light and heavy thunder followed, and the whole mountain seemed to shudder. Mike hit the brakes, but even at a dead stop the vehicle continued to rock violently. Through the rear window, they watched a glowing mushroom cloud spill into the heavens. It roiled and burned and began to fade within moments.

"They blew the place," Charlies said, disbelieving. "They blew the whole goddamn installation—just to get us."

"Oh, God, poor Fenwick . . ." That was Sid.

Mike felt a small ache just hearing her voice, knowing her near. At least she was safe. He put the Cherokee back in low and sent it slowly down the road once more. The shocked quiet didn't last long.

"Just where the hell can we go?" Nate asked someone, anyone.

"Forget about Sidney's," Charlie muttered. "Best to go to my RV. It'll be crowded, but it's out of town. . . ."

Nate Curtis smacked the door with a fist. "They know where you live, Downing. These guys are gonna scoop us up the minute we step foot in Mojave Wells. We've got to run, but damned if I know where. Not with . . . your jolly yellow giant."

"Maybe we should split up," Sidney said. "I could take John north in the Trans Am, follow the desert basin up into Oregon."

Mike clutched the steering wheel. "No!"

"It was Quinten Fenwick who destroyed the compound." Caldwell's voice in the darkness sounded almost musical, the words distorted, but clear enough.

"How do you know that?" Charlie demanded.

"Candliss wired explosives, and Quinten had the detonator," John answered.

Sid moved on the seat behind Mike. "That's why he wouldn't come with us. He was trying to buy us some time."

"Crazy bastard," Doc said with just a hint of sorrow. "But he's right. They won't know we're not in the ashes with the others."

Curtis tried to turn and thumped a knee or an elbow on the dash. "Shit! You figure that'll get us off the hook? Forensic experts will figure the whole thing out, and fast."

"Wait a minute, Sergeant," Charlie laughed. "This is the federal government *and* the military. They're going to be filing forms and pointing fingers for a helluva long time. And probably trying to hide everything from each other while they're at it." Mike felt a tap on his shoulder. "Home, my dear deputy. I want a shower and a long nap in my own damn bed."

II

Sid leaned her head against the cold glass of the window as they pulled down the road. The Mojave Wells

Trailer Park lay dark and deserted. Mike parked the Cherokee behind Charlie's dusty Mercedes, but left the headlights on, while everyone piled out, milling in a kind of stupefied confusion—everyone, except John. Sidney opened the tailgate and reached in to take his hand. Twice as long as hers, it was still no wider, and somehow the gentle, cool grip of his fingers brought comfort.

"Ta'mirik," he whispered, head near hers. "I thought I had lost you."

Mike rounded the back of the car, then halted just steps away as John unfolded his narrow body and straightened. "You okay, Sid?"

"No," she snapped, irritated at so idiotic a question. "I'm filthy, tired, and hungry." The light was too poor to see his expression, but body language told her enough. Sid shook her head. "Forget it, Nichols. I can't be civil yet. Do you have an old pair of jeans you could loan me? Maybe a shirt and some socks?"

"Sure. You can use my shower, if you want."

After all the madness that had happened, how could that faint hope still be in his voice? Caldwell stirred beside her, his fingers tightening. "No thanks," she said a bit sharply and turned her back on the deputy.

By the Jeep lights, she watched Charles Downing climb the steps to his Winnebago and kiss the door reverently before pulling it open. That made her smile, tired as she was.

"You left in kind of a hurry last night, Downing," called Nate Curtis from behind them. "I turned the TV off and put your wallet under the recliner, but you really oughtta be more careful."

"I intend to. No more house calls. Ever." Charlie yanked the screen door open.

"Doc, wait a sec." Sidney towed John Caldwell by the hand to the steps. "You sure you got enough room for Caldwell and me in there?"

"It's an RV, Sid. It'll sleep six easily." Charlie gazed up into Caldwell's strange face. "Or four humans and an eight foot alien . . ."

"Hey, Doc, what about these boxes?" Mike asked.

"For Christ's sake, leave 'em in the Jeep. Just cover them with a blanket or something." Charlie found the light switch for the front room. "You guys, I want a shower and some sleep. Then I'll worry about all the damn details. Please!"

"And I have the shower after you," Sid insisted.

John Caldwell had to stoop to get in through the door and remained stooped once inside. His dark gaze took in their surroundings, and his nostrils fluttered.

Sidney eyed him. "You need clothing, too. But I don't think there're any big and tall stores around close."

"Do you find this body offensive?" His head tilted to look at her.

"No, of course not. I just thought ... you must be cold."

"I function quite well in a much wider temperature range."

"Lucky you," the young woman said lightly. With a muttered "Age before beauty," Charlie had already disappeared into the dinky bathroom. "Are you hungry?"

"Yes."

"Let's look in the fridge. ..." She frowned. "Can you still eat ... what we eat?"

Caldwell smiled. She understood that odd twist of his mouth as amusement now. "The Ral have colonized much of a galaxy. Indigestion has never been a problem."

"Yeah?" Sid stared at refrigerator shelves stocked mostly with beer. "Well, Doc's cooking will be the true test of a Ral digestive tract, I think."

She served them warmed-over spaghetti, the noodles all mixed in and soggy. Charlie's idea of Italian seasoning seemed to be heavy on the chili powder and light on everything else. And although an M.D., he hadn't bothered to skim the artery-clogging grease off the hamburger in the sauce. Still and all, Sid decided, the taste was divine. John Caldwell didn't complain, though he was forced to sit cross-legged on the tiles in the little kitchen area, and the fork gave him trouble at first.

Sid, after some consideration, finally asked, "What does *ta ... merk* mean?"

"Ta'mirik." Caldwell hooked a last noodle from his bowl with a claw and poked it neatly into his mouth. "It means many things, none of which I can explain. Perhaps when we've dreamed again."

Sidney felt a small tremor. "Forget the dreams. Once was bad enough." She scooped up the dishes and carried them to the sink just as a knock sounded at the door.

It was Mike, standing on the top step, a small stack of clothes in his hands. She wondered briefly how he'd happened to be on the mountain with that big cop from Anaheim, and thought maybe some sign of genuine gratitude would be appropriate, but no . . . that'd have to wait until tomorrow.

"Thanks," was all she could find to say and took the clothes.

"Sid . . ." The deputy kept his voice low. "Let Caldwell stay here, but you come spend the night in the Airstream. . . ."

"Jesus! You just never give up. Nichols, I'm not interested."

That made him angry, his light gray eyes narrowing. "All I'm interested in is making sure you're safe."

"She's safe, Deputy," John said from the kitchen.

" 'Night, Mike," Sid told him firmly and hustled him backwards down the steps far enough so the door could be closed.

"What was that?" Charlie demanded from the back of the RV, wrapped in a huge terry cloth robe.

"Laundry delivery." The young woman stepped around John and headed for the bathroom. "My turn to shower."

Doc raised a feathery graying brow. "If I can help in any way, my dear . . ."

"Get lost, Charlie."

III

Nate Curtis brought a pot of brewed coffee from the camper to Mike's. His brother-in-law, Milt, had managed to install a Mr. Coffee in the tight little living area, and Nate had had enough of instant Folgers. His watch said

1:36 A.M., but he wasn't quite ready to climb onto the camper's lumpy mattress and sleep. Far from it.

The deputy was thumping around inside his trailer, grumbling. He had his cowboy hat on again. Personally, Nate had always hated wearing hats, but Janice had explained that they were an acceptable form of security blanket for some adult males. Mike had discarded his utility belt already, and a gun ought to make him feel a lot more secure than a damn hat.

"Slow down," Curtis snapped, muscling the young man aside so he could get to the dirty coffee cups in the sink. "We just pulled off the snatch of the century, right under the government's nose. *And* got away with it—so far. So what's the problem now?"

"Nothing," the deputy snapped back.

Nate filled his cup, used the last of the milk, and took his coffee to the table. "You ever thought much about UFOs and aliens from space?"

"When I was a kid, maybe." Mike settled his lean hips against the counter. "Can't live up here with all these stars and not wonder just a little what's out there."

"Me ... I had city streetlights for my stars as a kid, and I never cared much for the science fiction movies. 'Course, they weren't so high-tech, back then. But I was into Sherlock Holmes and Sam Spade and Philip Marlowe."

"Never could've guessed," the deputy said dryly.

"Yeah, well, when Arnold Hanover and his family died, I thought I had one great little mystery to unravel. Shit, I almost wish it had been that easy." Nate frowned. "Now, we've got the boxes and we've got John Caldwell, and I still don't know what the hell's going on."

"John Caldwell's dangerous." Mike's voice was tight.

"No shit ... What's the body count now?"

"Then what are we doing? Let's dump the boxes, grab Sid and Charlie, and get out of here."

Nate shook his head. "You never cease to amaze me, son. Ready to zoom off in any old direction at a moment's notice. I think you know your lady friend isn't about to leave Caldwell behind. And I think that's your biggest problem. You're just plain jealous."

"Bullshit . . ." Mike filled a cup with coffee and brought it to the table, then, distracted, spooned far too much sugar into it.

"If the situation wasn't so bizarre," Nate told him, "it'd be worth a good laugh. Caldwell's a threat in a lot of ways, but not to your love life. He isn't human anymore."

"He's still male. . . ."

"How can you tell?"

"How can you miss it? He's got those ugly hands all over her every chance he gets."

"I think you're seeing things." Nate took a sip of cooling coffee. "And as far as I can tell, Charlie Downing's the same damn way around Sid."

The deputy snorted. "Charlie's the same way around anything female. He's harmless."

"Well, gut instinct tells me Caldwell's harmless, too— around Sid." Mike opened his mouth, but Nate went on. "You've got to look at the dynamics of what happened. Those three have been through some hell together. That tends to make folks feel kind of tight. And Sid Bowers may be a mighty fine auto mechanic, but she's still a woman. Most women get maternal when faced with something or someone that's hurt and helpless. Caldwell, as huge and dangerous as he is, is also very childlike."

"So we're supposed to just hang out . . . until the boxes kill us. Or until the military figures out what happened."

"No. We're supposed to get some rest, then decide what to do—all five of us, together."

"Shit," Mike growled. "I can try to rest. But, I'm moving the Jeep to the other side of the park first. I don't want to wake up dead in the morning, or looking like Caldwell."

IV

The Ral had no gods—had never had them. The universe simply existed, and the People went out among the stars because they must. Ral conquered because they could, and the concepts of destiny and divinity were *il'ral'im*—not of the People—and therefore shunned. The Ral absorbed technologies, not cultures.

Johncaldwell, though, had been created of other flesh. Along with the form and attitudes of the Ral, he had retained his human memories and a vague understanding of them. It left him unique among two species, and very much alone. It left him to make decisions no Ral would ever consider.

Unlike humans, the People had no need of sleep. The tired body was rested when necessary, while the mind explored and dreamed. Johncaldwell rested on the fold-out couch bed at the front of Charlie's RV. This involved lying curled to stay within the confines of the mattress. Sidney Bowers slept nearby on a converted kitchen dinette. At the back of the motor home, Charlie moved restlessly on his own bed.

Johncaldwell thought of Mike Nichols and wondered. Obviously, the man had chosen Sid, and she denied him, as was proper, but a faint connection had already been made. Mike Nichols must also be *mirik'im*, the second male. They were all three inexplicably bound by circumstances and need. His human memories would name it fate, his Ral mind refused that.

This was madness—*il'ral* were no more than animals, and the People did not mate with animals. But the urge to bond, to share dreaming, burned in him. The Gatekeeper had made Johncaldwell to repair and open the gate. Beyond that, all choices must be his.

He slipped off the bed and went into the kitchen, hunched against the ceiling. A blue sleeping bag covered the young woman lying faceup on the narrow cushions, one bare arm draped over the edge. Johncaldwell crouched there, watching with new eyes. She didn't stir when he trailed the pad of a fingertip over the exposed skin. Such a strange vulnerable body, so soft, so fragile, and yet he sensed a great strength within.

Dark blond hair spilled over her face, and he brushed it carefully aside, then pressed his forehead to hers. Exhaustion held her deep in sleep, too deep to fight him. In time, he felt certain, she could learn to control the dreams, but now they were his. There was so much more to show her. The Gatekeeper had given him myriad images in its last brief moment of waking.

No dream chamber now, but a high escarpment on an ancient red world with a fading red sun—a destitute planet on the far rim of the galaxy. Here only the elders dreamed. Still half-asleep, Sidney Bowers stared out over the great empty sea basin, then glanced down at the tall, thin, and black-armored body Johncaldwell had given her and cried out.

"Ta'mirik," he said gently. "Don't be afraid. Dream with me."

She held up long, jointed fingers. "John, I'm not ready for this. Stop it, please."

"All right. Better?"

The human female stood with him now. Sidney nodded wordlessly, her attention trapped once more by the landscape.

"What is this place?"

"Tu'ral, our birth world. Abandoned long ago."

"It's so empty. Is there nothing left?"

"We take our past with us . . . here." Johncaldwell touched his head. "In this cliff was once a great city. Come. I'll show you."

He led her along the porous rocky shelf to a stairwell. Stone steps spiraled down into the escarpment, and they paused at the bottom for Sidney to gaze through high window apertures across hazy red distances. The passages led deep into the rock, dusty and bare, as were the scores of wide chambers they visited.

"How can there be light so far back from the cliff face?" Sid asked, intrigued. "It doesn't seem to come from anywhere."

"The People are *ta'ing*—light wielders. It is an art form as well as a simple technology."

"Oh, that makes it all perfectly clear." The young woman smiled. "Archaeologists would be pretty miserable in this city of yours. There isn't a potsherd or a bone or a scrap of anything anywhere."

"We have little and waste nothing."

"What? No shopping malls, no Disneylands? Sounds economical, but very boring. What's the purpose of life if you don't have any fun?"

"But you know the answer, *ta'mirik*. The purpose of life is death."

"Whoa . . . not in my book. But I'm not going to get into any philosophical arguments with you."

"We have no philosophies, only truths."

Sidney grimaced. "Well, we've had groups on Earth all along who think the same way, except truth seems to change with the perspective. What about children? Aren't they the real purpose of life for any species? To perpetuate itself?"

"Offspring are important, but not a reason for life. Existence simply is, until it is no more."

"How terribly Zen of you. I think I'd like to get back to my own dreams, now."

"No, Sidney. A little while longer, please. There's so much you must know. . . ."

Already the walls rippled around them, fading to a dull gold. A fire burned in the center of another stone-walled room, not within the city but in some far distant place on the other side of Tu'ral. An elder sat hunched before the flames, robed in dusty white cloth.

"Old One," Johncaldwell sang in the tongue of the People, "would you share first dreams?"

With infinite slowness, the elder rose. Time had enfeebled him, robbed him of what little flesh a Ral might have. Bone and sinew were twisted with age, shortened, but the huge black eyes, undimmed, regarded his visitors.

"Il'ral," he said and turned his back on them.

"Why did he do that?" Sidney demanded.

"He's insulted by your presence."

"Well, make him behave. I thought this was your dream."

"My dream, yes. But the Gatekeeper's images. In dreaming, there can only be truth."

The young woman flexed her fingers in his face.

"Truth? That wasn't truth—what you did to me when this dream started."

"It was my truth, *ta'mirik*. What I see beyond the human body."

"You think I have the soul of a Ral?"

"The People have no souls."

"Bullshit," Sid snapped, then froze. "You . . . wouldn't . . . John, I don't want to be changed. You can't do that to me!"

Sadly, Johncaldwell agreed. "I can't change you, and the Gatekeeper won't. It has what it needs." He curled a hand around her upper arm. "There's one last thing I want to show you."

The silent Old One, his back to them still, faded away, but not the yellow-red flames of the fire. Instead, the fire spread and separated. They stood in a gutted structure, in a gutted night city overlooking a rubble-strewn street.

"Look," he said and pointed into the smoky shadows.

The first male led them, his eyes searching the way, weapon ready. Close behind, the taller female came, the second male cradled in her arms. They slipped silently into the building.

Sidney backed way. "They'll see us. . . ."

"No. Just watch."

"They're hurt, John. I don't want to watch."

"You asked me the meaning of *ta'mirik*. She is *ta'mirik*—warrior, wife, dreamer. These are her mates."

The female settled to the floor with the unconscious second male. They were close enough to see the dark purple blood that welled sluggishly from a deep rent in the side of the Ral's neck. The first male crouched beside them, fluting a quiet question. His mate hushed him, then sent him to the entrance to guard. Gently, she pulled a long silver blade from a sheath in the forearm of the chitinous black armor, and with the razor edge, opened the injured one's throat.

"No," Sidney gasped.

"They've been cut off from their legion, and she does what she must."

As the life drained from her second mate, the *ta'mirik*

briefly touched his forehead with hers, then laid him aside and stood. The *nom'ng*, a light-pistol, was drawn from her belt. A wide beam of swirling red spread over the body at her feet, and in moments the *mirik'im*'s bones were ash, his armor a black slag.

"I don't understand any of this." Sidney spoke in a low, troubled voice. "Why are they here? What's happened to this place?"

"The Ral happened, *ta'mirik*. If a world submits, it survives. But if there is resistance, we destroy completely. We do not negotiate with *il'ral*."

A muffled keening began. The female mourned in the flickering light of the fires. Sidney, face contorted, strode away.

"*Ta'mirik*, wait."

"Don't call me that! I'm human!" She turned on him, angry, then winked out of existence.

Johncaldwell stared in amazement. Sidney Bowers had taken herself from the dream.

V

She jerked back from Caldwell and came up against the dinette wallboard with a thump. In the darkness, only his eyes were visible, reflecting a faint sheen of starlight from the RV window.

"Get away," Sid whispered, furious, then felt a dreadful ache of sorrow and loss. "No! Stay." She groped for one of his hands and held it tight, unaware of the tears that had begun to flow. "What are you doing to me?"

"We're doing it to each other, I think," John murmured. "We're bonding, *ta'mirik*, as impossible as that is. The adult Ral male is helpless without a female to guide and care for him."

Sidney smiled through her tears. "A lot of human males are the same way."

"But it's not the same, and I'm here alone. When . . . I first shared dreams with you, I accidently forged this connection between us. However wrong, however disastrous that proves to be, it's done."

"It's been so confusing," she admitted at last—to herself as much as to him. "I knew I should be afraid of you, and yet, I've felt this strong need to protect you, keep you safe."

"So it is, *ta'mirik*. You can never be Ral, but you'll never again be *il'ral* either."

Sid gave in to a strangled sob. In John's dreams, she'd watched a *ta'mirik* tenderly open the throat of her mate—one of her mates. She'd seen evidence of Ral destruction, and while her perceptions of them were still muddled, the thought of their arriving in force on Earth terrified her. Caldwell moved onto the narrow bed and wrapped long arms around her. That eased the pain, if only temporarily.

"What will we do now?" Sid asked.

"That's for you to decide, *ta'mirik*. Where you lead, I'll follow."

"Anywhere?"

"Yes."

"And if I tell you not to open the gate . . .?"

"Then it won't be opened."

His answer came readily, without hesitation. It was a power Sidney didn't want. To keep John Caldwell stranded here would be no better than cutting his throat.

Chapter Ten

CHARLES, YAWNING AND scratching the silver hairs on his chest, found Sid still asleep on the kitchen area cot. John Caldwell was nowhere to be found. A long look out the RV's windshield revealed slightly hazy desert daylight and nothing much else. Well, at least the world out there appeared normal, nonthreatening. Then most of the last forty-eight hours came crashing back in one nasty wave. The doc sat heavily in the captain's chair and leaned against the steering wheel, breathless from it all.

Outside, someone mounted the steps, then the door swung open, and Nate Curtis crowded his bulk through the entrance. "Howdy."

"Be nice if you knocked first," Charles grunted.

"So lock your door."

"I did."

The sergeant glanced around. "Got any coffee? Any extraterrestrials?"

"Had one, but I don't know where he's got to. As for the coffee, it's bad for you. Have a beer."

"Not before breakfast," Sidney Bowers said. Fair hair disheveled, she folded her blankets on the kitchen threshold.

"It's two in the afternoon," Charles complained. His head ached dully and his mouth was dry, but sight of Sid eased the misery. Mike's Levi's fit her much better than they did the deputy.

Curtis pushed the passenger-side chair around and sat in it, heavily, his expression troubled. "You know we're sitting ducks here. We've got to get out of Mojave Wells. So where the hell is Caldwell, Sidney?"

"Around somewhere, I suppose." She stared at the blankets in her arms.

"Jesus. The last thing we need is for him to go strolling around the desert in broad daylight. We're trying to keep a low profile."

Charles shrugged. "So maybe he's headed out on his own. Wouldn't bother me much at this point." It bothered Sid, though, and he tried to make sense of the stricken look his comment brought.

The sound of a racing motor sent them to a side window in a rush. They were all jumpy as hell still, but it was only the deputy's blue and white Jeep bumping along the chuckholed road from the far end of the trailer park, coming too fast. The vehicle brakes locked at the last possible moment, and it slid to a halt beside the doctor's convertible. Mike Nichols climbed out, slamming the door behind him angrily.

Curtis opened the RV for him, but he paused at the foot of the steps.

"The boxes are gone. . . . Look what the bastard did to the back of the Cherokee—trashed the window, ripped the damn tailgate right off. How'm I gonna explain this to the sheriff's office?" The young man caught sight of Sidney's pale face at the window, and his expression softened momentarily, then he glared up at Curtis. "I want to talk to Caldwell."

"He isn't here," the sergeant told him.

"Hell!"

But Charles, standing beside Sid, saw movement near Nate Curtis's camper on the far side of the Airstream. Caldwell appeared from behind the aluminum trailer. In the light of day, he was truly hideous, a walking skeletal man with a huge malformed head, hairless and earless. Sidney stirred, headed toward the doorway, and, reluctantly, the doctor followed.

"Caldwell!" Mike found the nerve to latch onto a bone thin arm. "You son of a bitch, why'd you fuck up my car?"

Nate Curtis's questions were a little more pertinent.

"What'd you do with the boxes, John? Did you fix them already?"

"No . . ." The creature shrugged Nichols off, then bent to pull the black boxes from the shadows under the RV. Sidney had pushed her way past Curtis down the steps, and Caldwell put a long hand gently on her shoulder. *"Ta'mirik?* Tell me what you want done with these."

That little display only set Mike off again, and the doc grinned to himself.

"Why don't you just keep your fucking hands off her?"

John tilted his head, lipless mouth twisting. "Do you challenge? Would you be *mirik'ee,* her second?"

"I just want you to leave her alone, asshole. You've caused us all enough misery."

"Mike," Sid warned, "stay out of it."

Caldwell gave a sudden flick of a finger at the deputy, so quick Charles wasn't sure what he'd seen. An alien equivalent of the bird? Only now a flap of skin lay open along the young man's cheek from ear to nose. The exposed flesh and bone remained white a moment, then tiny broken capillaries sent blood rushing into the slash. Mike's shock turned to outrage, and he launched himself at Caldwell, something the doctor would never have expected from the normally quiet, almost timid, deputy sheriff.

Shouting, Sidney tried to wedge herself between them, but Mike had an arm around the creature's neck, pounding at his face with the other fist. Curtis started after them, his hand on the butt of the snub-nosed pistol at his belt, and Charles caught his wrist.

"Don't!" God, things were bad enough. Any moment, John could rip his assailant wide open, just as he had the man at Fenwick's compound.

Instead, Caldwell slung Mike away, and the deputy hit the ground hard. He struggled upright and came on again, only there was something drastically wrong. All the color had drained from his face, and now Charles could hear the air wheezing in his lungs. Fenwick's warning came back in a rush then—an allergic reaction to the claws. It might already be too late for help. Mike managed to get a hand

on Caldwell's wrist, then his legs gave way, and he went
down to one knee, panting.

Downing didn't wait to see more. He turned and fled
into the kitchen. There was epinephrine for bee sting aller-
gies in the fridge along with a few other perishable med-
ications. The disposable syringes were buried in a drawer
under the counter. Panic goading him, Charles raced back
outside. The deputy had collapsed on the sand, unmoving;
the others crouched around him. Sidney moved to give
Charles room, but John Caldwell knocked his shaking
hands aside.

"No! Don't touch him. . . ."

"He'll die!"

"He'll dream. It is our way." The creature scooped
Mike's limp body into his arms and straightened. "Don't
interfere. Come, *ta'mirik.*"

Helpless, they watched Sidney and Caldwell disappear
into the RV with the deputy.

"Christ, this just keeps getting worse and worse," Curtis growled. "If the kid dies, I'm going to shoot that extraterrestrial son of a bitch."

II

They went to the back of the Winnebago where John
laid Mike on the unmade bed. The deputy's lips were blue
and his breath came in short, labored gasps. Blood continued to flow from the slash, but the cheek had begun to
swell. There couldn't be much time left.

"Why did you do this to him?" Sidney demanded,
heartsick.

"You know why. We must be three."

"Well, you're crazy. If you were looking for another
warrior for your little *ménage à trois,* Mike Nichols was
the last person you should've picked."

"This was not my choice. It was yours . . . and his."

"No, John. We're not Ral. Whatever else has happened,
we're still human. Now, you've got to help him, or let
Charlie."

"Ta'mirik, he's yours to keep—to save. You must dream with him."

The thought made fear twist in her stomach. "I can't dream. Not like that."

"You can." Caldwell settled back on his haunches, face peaceful, waiting.

What he asked was impossible. Sidney leaned close to Mike and smelled blood. It had soaked into Charlie's ivory satin sheets. She didn't want to touch the deputy, and had been avoiding exactly that over the past year. And he would die, just as Dale had. Caldwell had killed him—all for some insane desire to create *mirik.* The young woman touched her forehead to Nichols's, eyes closed. His flesh burned with fever, pouring into her.

Nothing happened at first, only a feeling of weary hopelessness, then behind her eyes the heat began to take form and color and substance. The sensations and sounds around her faded. She stood on the grimy concrete floor of the shop. Wind gusted in through the open doors, a hot dry summer wind. A fat red sun hovered near the horizon, and Sid smiled. Since when did the sun set in the north?

"Hell, it's my dream. I can set it anywhere I want." Her own voice startled her. "Mike?" Instantly, he was lying at her feet with bloody face and raspy breath. She squatted beside him and covered his cheek, a gut reflex. First things first. The wound and the blood vanished—willed away. This was a dream, after all. "Mike! Listen to me. The pain is gone. You can breathe again." He didn't respond. "Damn it, Nichols. . . . You listen to me and believe. You're all right, now. Take a deep breath."

The deputy inhaled noisily, his gray eyes finally opening. "Jesus," he whispered.

"No, just me . . . But I am feeling kinda godlike at the moment. Get off the floor. You're getting all dirty."

Mike climbed slowly to his feet, his gaze on the landscape beyond the doors. "The air's hot. . . . And what's the sun doing . . .?" He felt his face, then his chest. "I'm dead."

"I don't think so."

"But we were at the trailer park. . . . Caldwell . . . This isn't right. It's all wrong."

"It's a dream." That only confused him all the more. "I'll show you. Something really astounding this time, I think."

The walls, the world, faded at her command, and a delicious feeling of power swelled. The Ral escarpment resolved around and under them. Mike gaped at the hazy depths of the basin, at the sky.

"It's not perfect," Sidney apologized, noticing that she'd gotten the sun wrong again. "I've only been here once, and my Ral memories are a child's still." Caldwell had said the same thing the first time they'd dreamed.

The deputy stamped a foot experimentally. "Feels real. Christ, Sid, how're you doing this?"

"I'm *ta'mirik*. It's my job to take care of you, and that's what I'm doing."

"Caldwell keeps calling you that. What's it mean?"

"A lot of things, which I'll explain as best I can, but we need a better setting. . . . Something familiar, maybe even peaceful."

She called up a dark Mojave night and a campfire made of greasewood and pungent juniper that popped and snapped, sending sparks into a star-filled sky. The horses stood on the edge of the firelight, hipshot and dozing. Across the flames, Dale stared at her, a faint smile on his lips, but it was Mike, not Dale, and he wore a troubled frown.

"This is too bizarre for me. . . ."

"It's only a dream—just very real-seeming," Sid told him, as much to remind herself. "The Ral use dreams to connect with one another. Our dreams have always been so personal that it's hard to imagine sharing them physically with anyone else."

"That's because we've never been able to."

"That's not exactly true. Some people—identical twins for instance—have been known to share dreams." She shifted, uncomfortable with her thoughts. "I watched John Caldwell change into something alien. God, his suffering was almost more than I could stand, but by the end of it, I'd changed, too. *We* made a connection."

Mike glared at the campfire. "I don't want to hear this."

"He's alone, Nichols. The Ral depend on one another in a way you and I can't really understand. An adult male bonds with a female and another male. She's a *ta'mirik,* and they're her *mirik'im* . . . husbands, I guess. John's chosen us to be *mirik,* his dream mates."

"Not a chance! Don't include me in your weird little fantasy."

"Why not?" Sid demanded. "It's what you wanted all along."

"What?"

"To be with me, right? John's made that possible."

"Caldwell's screwed everything up. I didn't want to be with you . . . like this." The deputy swept a hand out over the fire.

"Mike, I would never have been with you at all." That hurt him. "Not because of you, because of me. I'd never have let you or anyone else close to me."

"Since we could've never lived up to Dale."

Sid smiled. "Well, I think Dale would've had trouble living up to the man I created from my memories. But that's gone now. I still love him, but I know who I am . . . and who you are. Or rather, who you can be. If I let you."

"I still don't think I can do this."

"I don't think you have any choice. We're *mirik,* bonded, and the only divorce is death." Where did this knowledge come from? John had given her some of it in dreaming, but her understanding went much deeper now. She also realized there was something more to do here. "And you must obey me always. I'm your *ta'mirik.*"

She stood and circled the flames, then sat down beside the deputy, hip and thigh tight against his. He stared at her a long moment, then his hand came up to brush the hair from her eyes, and he kissed her so sweetly on the cheek. That was not enough. Sid caught his chin and guided his mouth to hers. Finally he understood. It was as she'd always suspected—Mike Nichols, quiet and retiring, was a truly passionate man.

III

Nate sat with Charlie in the Airstream and fretted. Instinct told the sergeant they should run—just get the hell as far from Mojave Wells as possible. But another deeper instinct made him sit and wait. Whatever was happening between Sid and John and Mike, he didn't dare interfere. Caldwell frightened him, touched him in that place of his deepest, darkest nightmares.

With the sunlight fading to dusk, Nate finally heaved himself up from the kitchenette and headed across the ground to the RV. There were lights in the back and quiet voices. Nate followed them, unaware that Charlie tripped on his heels.

Mike Nichols wasn't dead—by any means. He sat on the edge of Charlie's bed between Caldwell and Sidney. Real cozy. The blood had been cleaned from his face, and though there was still a good deal of swelling, the cut on his cheek had closed into a neat raw line.

"How do you feel?" Curtis demanded.

"Wasted," Mike answered readily enough, but there was a strange little smile on his lips.

"You guys want to tell me just what the hell that was all about? If the three of you are going to do alien love dances, at least let the rest of us know what's going on."

Sidney Bowers cocked her head. "Why, Sergeant Curtis, you're pretty intuitive."

"I'm a cop. I've seen plenty of domestic squabbles in my time. I've also seen folks die over them. Is this one settled, or do we have more of the same to look forward to?"

"It's settled," Sid told him. "But things have changed."

Nate eyed them. Somehow, he didn't doubt that one bit, or that there'd be more revelations to come in this whole crazy deal. If any of them managed to survive. And he thought he understood his own part in everything now—more a witness than a participant. His careful observations might serve history, but more likely would serve to disgrace and ruin him. As madly as some pursued the unknown, this world could hardly deal with what it had, let alone with something from the galaxy beyond.

"There's a car coming!" Charlie shouted from the threshold. "Shit! It's CHP."

John Caldwell continued to stare off into unknown distances, unperturbed, but Mike showed his usual tendency toward panic.

"It's all right," Sid said and patted his hand. "Curtis, go help the doc, or he may crack under the pressure."

That sounded suspiciously like a direct order, and Nate wasn't sure he liked it, but he obeyed. The living area lights hadn't been turned on, and the sergeant stood with Charlie at the door as the CHP cruiser arrived. The driver parked it behind the Dodge Power Wagon and climbed out.

"Mike! Hey, Nichols!" He stuck his head in the Airstream first.

"It's Coffin. . . ." Charlie said quietly.

"Who?"

"Jake Coffin. What'll we do?"

"Stay calm and find out what he wants."

"Oh, Jesus . . ."

The officer headed across the small space to doc's RV, and Downing opened the door.

"Hiya, Charlie."

"Jake. What brings you around?"

"I'm looking for Nichols. The sheriff's department hasn't heard from him in a while, so I said I'd check it out. You see him?"

"He's in here . . . resting," the doc answered carefully. "He . . . had a little accident."

"No shit?"

"He wasn't looking where he was going and ran into the side of the Winnebago. Hit his head kind of hard."

Jake Coffin choked back a laugh. "Christ, what a klutz. I never could figure how a guy with two left feet ended up a cop." The man climbed the two steps. "Can I see him?"

"He's kind of woozy," Doc said, quickly.

"I won't stay long." Jake pushed his way inside.

Both Nate and Charlie looked toward the bedroom, sharing a common alarm, but John Caldwell had vanished. Somewhere.

Coffin paused in front of Curtis, eyes narrowed slightly. "You didn't say you had a visitor, Doc."

"This is, uh, Detective Sergeant Nate Curtis from the Anaheim PD. Nate, this is Jake Coffin."

"Barstow, CHP," Jake finished for him. "Glad to meetcha." He was a small stocky fellow with a bushy blond mustache, and now he gazed up into Nate's face as he shook his hand. "God, you ever play pro football?"

"Nope."

"Sure coulda . . ." Coffin hitched his utility belt and holstered gun around his hips. "In back, Charlie?"

"Yeah, go on ahead." The doc waited for him to get into the kitchen, then whispered. "Where's John?"

"Shut up," Nate hissed and headed toward the rear himself. The patrolman seemed just a little too friendly, a little too pushy.

Sidney had her back to the closed bathroom door. Coffin grinned at her.

"You got the whole damn town back here, Doc? Where you been, Sid? The shop's been closed for the past couple of days."

"Just taking some time off."

"Well, you lost out on a couple of great breakdowns yesterday. He asleep? Hey, Mike."

Nichols lay under a down comforter. He turned to look at Jake, revealing the raw swollen side of his face.

"Oh, man, you really did yourself in. Maybe you oughta see a doctor."

"*I'm* a doctor," Charlie growled from the kitchen, offended.

"Yeah, Charlie, but what if it's a concussion or something?"

"It's not."

Jake waved a fist under Mike's nose. "How many fingers I got up?"

"None, asshole."

"He's fine," the patrolman said with another grin, then

shook his head. "Whatta klutz, man. God, that must hurt. You want me to call in, tell 'em you need some sick leave?"

Sid shifted in the tight area. "Would you do that, Jake?"

"Sure. No problem. Look, I gotta get back on the highway—lot of Las Vegas losers in a rush to get home." The quick grin returned. "That's gonna cost 'em even more. Stay cool, pal." Coffin slapped the deputy's shoulder. "And watch where you're going next time. Jeez." He stopped beside Sidney. "Don't think I've ever seen you in anything but coveralls, Bowers. Or without a dirty face. Not bad."

"Thanks," Sid replied testily. "Next tune-up, I'll wear an evening gown."

"You do, and I'll have to bring my car in to be serviced." Chuckling, Jake Coffin started for the door. Unamused, Nate followed. The patrolman clattered down the steps into the cold night air and promptly stumbled.

"Shit, Doc! This place is booby-trapped. What the hell are these batteries doing down here in the dark? I get acid holes in my pants, and you get the bill."

"Sorry," Charlie called, voice quavering slightly. "I meant to move those."

They watched the officer climb into his vehicle, maneuver it around, then send it over the rutted track to the county road. The taillights bobbed onto the pavement, but Nate's apprehensions didn't disappear with the car. It took some careful thought to untangle Caldwell from the tiny bathroom, and the sergeant grumbled the whole time.

"We've got to get out of here now. That guy was up to something."

Sidney turned to him, brow furrowed. "Jake Coffin? He's okay. That's the way he always acts."

"He's a cop," Nate said. "And there was definitely something else on his mind."

"What makes you think that?" Mike asked from his seat on the bed.

"For one thing, why didn't he mention the explosion on Avawatz Mountain? That's got to be the big news in this area. It must have been seen for a hundred miles around."

When Sid opened her mouth, Nate cut her off. "No. Coffin was sent in here to check us out. They may not have told him why, but they sent him."

Charlie squeezed into the hall. "Everything was destroyed in that explosion. *They* don't even know we're alive. Otherwise they would have been here already."

"Wake up, Doc. Candliss had to have told somebody something. They were packing up to leave the test site. They were going somewhere ... and somewhere there's bound to be a list with your name and address on it." Charlie paled, and Nate went on. "The only reason they haven't come in after us is they want to know just what they're up against. And Jake Coffin will tell them."

Caldwell had taken a seat on the edge of the bed again, next to Mike whose face was even paler than Charlie's. Now the deputy put his head in his hands and muttered, "What'll we do?"

"There's nothing we can do at the moment," Sidney told him. "You need to sleep and get your strength back. In the morning, we'll think of something."

Nate gritted his teeth. "By morning, it could be too—"

"In the morning," Sid repeated, tone firm. She pushed the deputy back gently. "You rest, and I'll bring you something to eat in a bit. Everyone out." She turned off the light, hustling the others down the narrow passage, then pulled the accordion door across the sleeping nook. "Go watch some TV, but keep the sound down."

Pushy damn broad, Nate thought, and felt a twinge of guilt. Janice was just as strong willed and competent. Even with the inaction grating on him, the sergeant retired to the front of the RV with Charlie. Even John Caldwell joined them. He sat on the carpeting, knees and elbows akimbo, staring at the glowing wide screen. Doc commandeered beers from the fridge and passed them around.

From the bizarre to the sublime. There was a Raiders-Broncos game on, beamed by satellite from Denver. Just Monday night football with the guys. Nate glanced nervously at Caldwell and saw two perfect color images in reverse playing across those huge black eyes, saw him lift the beer bottle to his lipless mouth, long clawed fingers curled around it.

Does he see what I see? Does he think like I think? A brief shiver rippled up the sergeant's spine, then someone in a black and silver uniform caught a wild forty-five-yard pass and Charlie let out a subdued whoop. After that, nothing but the game seemed to matter anymore.

IV

Sidney had rarely enjoyed cooking, and tonight was no exception, but for energy and clear thought, the body required fuel. The fridge offered up mostly cold cuts and snack foods. The bread was less than fresh, and she toasted it before making ham and cheese sandwiches. Their eyes glued to the set, the men only grunted when the food was delivered. John, on the other hand, reached up to touch her face and whisper something in the Ral tongue.

"Beloved," he translated, then entranced, his gaze returned to the football game.

Perhaps even the Ral could appreciate the small, contained—if mostly bloodless—war being fought on that green field. Shaking her head, Sid took a sandwich to the rear for Mike.

"Dinner," she said quietly and pushed the door back so kitchen light filtered into the little room.

Starry night shone beyond the wide windows. On the bed, Mike didn't stir. She set the plate on a cabinet and bent closer. The swelling had gone down some more. Maybe ice would help.

"Mike?"

He wrapped his arms around her suddenly, dragged her down, and their heads collided painfully. Red light flared behind her eyes, then came a burst of white into which colors rushed. A mountain glade appeared all around, sweet green grass rolling away toward stands of tall evergreens. Miraculous scents and sounds came on a warm wind, rich with flowers and bubbling water. Birds warbled from high branches.

Mike sat beside her, grinning, proud. The puckering scar on his cheek was gone.

"My God. You dreamed this up?"

"All by myself. Like it?"

"Where are we?"

"Damned if I know. I think it was on a calendar I got in a Barstow hardware store—June '89. I just wanted something different . . . something private and beautiful." He pointed skyward. "Look at the clouds. I could really get to like this kind of thing."

"It's definitely beautiful, but I think dreaming's something we should use for good purpose, not to escape reality."

"Yeah, I suppose," he muttered, halfheartedly. "Just let me practice a little while longer."

"A little while," Sid agreed.

They fell silent, and Mike wrapped an arm around her shoulders, drawing her gently against him. She stiffened, afraid he might ask something more of her—something she was unwilling to give at the moment—but apparently he wanted only the comfort of having her close. Sid relaxed and closed her eyes, drowsy. In the warm sunlight, their troubles seemed far away. Neither of them were aware when Mike's world faded into darkness.

V

Mirik brought comfort, however human his mates. Johncaldwell watched them sleep, snug on the doctor's bed, and occasionally with fingertips, touched one brow, then the other. Their dreams were disjointed, filled with vague fears. The urge to draw them into a dream of his own making was strong, but they needed this mindless rest. Instead, he turned his eyes on the night beyond the windows.

She had not forbidden him the boxes, only told him to keep them and wait. Waiting didn't bother him. There was a time of action and a time of inaction, both being equal, both bringing contentment. The People were not driven by duty or honor. Beauty in war, peace in death. They had no possessions of value and no attachments except to those in their *mirik*—which might be called love, but was something much more and much less than that.

Sidney had embraced the Ral concepts of love without loving and care without caring, but she'd already achieved a detachment from these human emotions before the bonding. Mike would take longer to adjust, but in him, Johncaldwell sensed the darkest urges of the warrior. These made him invaluable to them. Murmuring, the deputy pulled his *ta'mirik* closer, face nestled in her neck. Yes. Each small moment of her life must be perfect, since of them all, she was least likely to survive.

Chapter Eleven

NATE CURTIS DID not sleep well. Restless and uneasy, he spent most of the night trying to decide what next to do, and the answer he finally arrived at terrified him. Just before first light, he gave up sleep altogether and helped himself to a shower in the deputy's trailer, then donned his last set of clean clothes. Outside, he stood a moment gazing into the east. The rising sun had fired the sandy hills to shades of gold and salmon and peach, and even the tiniest pebble on the ground threw long dark shadows.

"Nate?" Charlie stood in the RV doorway, dressed in his oversized robe. "What are you doing?"

"Just daydreaming, Doc."

"Well come inside, then. I've already made coffee."

Gratefully, Nate climbed the steps, aware of a chill from his wet hair. Everyone was up and seated in the warm living room. John and Mike were watching the TV with the sound turned off—a big yellow bird dancing around a number of small children. They seemed entranced. With a nodded greeting to Nate, Sidney held a cup out for Charlie to fill with coffee.

"So what are we doing?" the sergeant asked, accepting a mug for himself.

Sid Bowers smiled, and her cool blue eyes fixed on Curtis, peaceful, and distant—and almost alien. "Could I speak with you alone, Nate?"

"Sure." The thought made his heart pound. "Where?"

"In the back." The young woman stood, lithe and graceful as a dancer, even in Mike's blue jeans and work shirt.

The sergeant followed her through the tiny kitchen area

into Charlie's bedroom. Sidney pulled the accordion wall mostly closed, then took a seat on the bed. Nate sat at the other end, as far from her as the space allowed. She scared him—for some goddamn reason, she scared the shit out of him now.

"I think it's time for you to leave us, Nate," Sid said, voice gentle.

"Yeah," the sergeant admitted unhappily. "I was thinking the same thing. I'm not much help, anyway."

The woman shook her head. "You're an unusual man, Nate Curtis, a good man, and you've been a great help. But if you stay, you'll die, and there's no sense in that." She caught his gaze again. "I want you to live. I want you to tell the world what really happened here. The human race has to know what a frightening place the universe really is—that they're not alone."

"Nothing I can tell them will ever prepare them for the Ral, Sidney." Nate's stomach did a slow twist. "But I'll go, and I'll shout it from the rooftops, if you want. Only you've got to let me do something else first."

The young woman frowned. "What?"

"Give me the boxes, please." When her frown deepened, Nate rushed on. "I have a brother up in Solvang. He's a pilot, and he's got a small twin engine plane. We'll fly out over the ocean, find the deepest trough we can, and drop the boxes in where no one will ever find them . . ."

Again, Sidney shook her head. "The gate is Johncaldwell's only means of escape. He can't survive here, not as he is."

"But that may be the only choice, Sid. His life, or the planet's. You can't take that risk."

"I have to," the woman said. "John's my responsibility. He's my . . . husband."

Nate felt a thrill of fear. "Listen to what you're saying, Sidney. Caldwell's not human anymore. Whatever hold he's got over you, you've got to fight it. You and Mike, both."

"It's too late. But I don't intend to let the Ral through the gate, only to let John through to them."

"Sounds a little too easy. What about you? Will you go with him?"

"No." The young woman managed a smile. "The gate only lets the Ral pass through. Even if it didn't, Mike and I couldn't survive among the Ral any more than John can survive among humans."

The sorrow in her voice was faint, but Nate heard it. The instinct to mother was a strong one, he knew, but the attachment between Sid and John had gone well beyond that.

"What about Charlie?" Nate asked, anxious not to follow that line of thinking any farther. "Maybe I should take him with me."

"He'll leave, but I doubt he'd go with you. Charlie is very attached to his things. Unfortunately, I need the RV, but we'll pack the doc's belongings into the Airstream and hitch it to Mike's Dodge. He'll find another trailer park somewhere safe. Far from here."

Then pull out his satellite dish, his big screen TV, grab a beer, and settle back. Nate entertained the fantasy for only a moment. None of them was ever going to return to what they once were.

"Here," he said and laid his snub-nose .38 on the blankets between them. Sid only stared at it. "I think you guys are going to need this more than me."

"But what if—"

"If I run into any government heavies along the way, they're going to handle me with kid gloves. I'm a cop. Worry about your own ass, lady." Nate stood. "I guess I'll get out of here."

"I'd like to ask one last favor before you go," Sidney said quickly and got to her feet, as well.

"What?"

"Would you drive into Mojave Wells and buy us some supplies. You're a stranger so no one will think twice, and once we start out, I think it's best if we don't stop for anything but gas."

Nate wanted to ask her where they would go and knew it was best he didn't know. "All right. I'm not much of a shopper though."

"This'll be easy. We need lightweight dry goods—crackers, flour, salt, beans, baking soda, Rice-A-Roni, powdered milk. Anything of that sort you think we can use. And can carry with us, if we have to leave the Winnebago."

Smart girl. "What time does that little grocery store open?" Nate asked.

"Eight-thirty. It's open by now. I'll get you some money, their prices are steep."

"No need," the sergeant said gruffly. "I got plenty."

Sidney reached out to lay a hand on his wrist. "Would you check on my horses, too? Hannah promised to feed them, but . . . they might need some hay. A good armload apiece."

"Sure." He turned abruptly and headed back toward the front of the RV, troubled by the touch of her cold fingers.

"We'll be set and ready to go when you get back," the young woman called after him.

Charlie sat at the dinette with his coffee, morose. John and Mike hadn't moved from the rug in front of the television and the big yellow bird still danced before them silently. It brought to mind a bizarre image of a galactic kindergarten class.

"Caldwell." Nate paused near them.

The creature dragged his gaze from the screen. "What is it, Nate?"

"We're parting company soon. Maybe you could clear up a little mystery for me—about the Hanover deaths." John only continued to stare at him with those huge black eyes, and the sergeant went on finally. "Did you kill them?"

"Yes."

"But was it an accident or did you murder them?"

"I was angry at the time. Very angry."

"And you used the box, somehow—even from that distance. How? How does it work?"

"Curiosity?" Caldwell gave a very human shrug of his skeletal shoulders, and his lipless mouth twisted. "What can I tell you that you can possibly conceive? It's stolen technology, taken from a race that thought to conquer the

Ral. They had found a way to trap the forces displaced by ultimate mass—the gravity wave that distorts space is only a side effect, like a puff of air when a door is suddenly opened. Imagine, if you can, the mass of a sun trapped within each small box, sometimes drawing energy, sometimes emitting it."

Nate couldn't imagine that, the thought was mind-boggling.

Caldwell went on. "That conversion of energy produces a wave in the local gravity field. Such power can open the universe . . . or destroy a world. Or simply ripple through the dining room of a professor's home."

"Then you can direct that power," the sergeant muttered, "and kill whenever you please."

"I'm . . . changed, Nate. A made creature. I resonate to and focus the energy the one box emits each time it tries to perform its function and fails. But once the second box is repaired, the two become a gate—with forces too great to be used safely in any other way." Caldwell tilted his head. "Do you understand?"

"Enough," the sergeant said and looked away. "I'm taking off now, but I'll be back in awhile."

Charlie jumped up, almost in panic. "Where are you going?"

"Relax, Doc. It's just a little shopping trip."

II

A shopping trip. Hell. The pickup and camper rocked gently side to side as Nate sent it through the park to the road. The wind had returned, not so strong as before, but strong enough to send burger wrappers and newspaper skittering across the pavement. Twice, he almost slammed on the brakes, convinced that something alive had darted into his path. It amazed him how humanity's trash could be so widespread. He'd heard somewhere that man was the only animal who fouled his own nest. Hell.

The truck hit a pothole and jumped on its springs. Nate looked at his speedometer. Sixty. In too damn big a hurry. After a day and a half of inaction, there was this sudden urge to rush everything. He took his foot off the gas pedal instead, and the pickup slowed just in time for the last curve into Mojave Wells.

The little store and the post office were on the near end of the street, side by side, sharing a common building. Mojave Wells Liquor and Food, the sign overhead said succinctly. Nate pulled up in front and killed the engine, then stepped down onto the oil-soaked dirt. The wind gusted past, ruffling his hair, but other than that nothing stirred in the town.

"What the hell . . ." He glanced down the short main street. There were no other cars in sight, no people, no stray dogs. No sounds either. In the quiet, only the wind sighed. Such emptiness bothered him, but then Mojave Wells had never been bustling to begin with. Perhaps it was Sunday and everyone had gone to church. Try as he might, Nate couldn't remember exactly what day this was, though it must be Sunday, or maybe Monday.

A hand-stenciled piece of cardboard in the store window claimed the establishment was open, but the door was locked. He pressed his forehead to the glass and peered inside. It appeared Sidney Bowers would be doing her own shopping after all, somewhere else. Still, Nate knocked on the door, then rattled it gently. It had an old locking mechanism, worn and loose. One good hard thump against the hand-bar, and the metal pegs popped out of their notches in the top and bottom of the aluminum jamb.

"I could get arrested for this," he muttered and took another quick look down the street before stepping inside.

The small storage room cum office in back was checked first. No surprises there, except that an open carton of Hormel chili had fallen from a stack and the cans lay scattered about the floor. Nate stepped over them to gather several empty cardboard boxes and take them out into the front area. The cash register was wide open and had only a handful of pennies in the drawer. He tucked a hundred-dollar bill neatly into one of the slots. Now, the old urgency came back to push him as he worked his way methodically down the aisles.

Flour, salt, beans . . . Anything sensible and edible that

caught his eye ended up in a box. Dried soup, packets of Stroganoff, cookies. He saved the sixth and final box for Charlie, loading it with lunch meats, pretzels, peanut butter, bread, and a case of beer. Just a little something for poor Doc—for the road.

One by one, Nate lugged the overloaded cartons out to the camper, one eye on the empty road and the other on the shadows of the buildings. His last act within the store was to add a fifty to the hundred in the cash register. Even that probably wouldn't cover the cost, but the prices were too damn high anyway, nearly double what you'd find in the city.

Outside again, he listened to the wind. Something was missing. Everything was missing. Vaguely, he could recall his arrival here, eons ago. There'd been constant white noise then, even at the trailer park, subliminal sounds of distant jets and the almost soothing rumble of big trucks on the highway—a shouting child, a barking dog carried on the wind from town. When had that stopped? Yesterday? Today? The answer eluded him.

The town was empty. He was certain of that now. Every man, woman, and child spirited away to safety. That thought brought a thrill of fear, and then a moment of anger. He'd warned Sid that this would happen. He'd told them to leave right at the beginning. *They* were out there, behind the scattered run-down houses, behind the reddish sandstone hills. His back began to twitch, as if the cross hairs of a gunsight were trained on him.

Then Nate's rational mind kicked in. These guys weren't interested in a lowly homicide sergeant, otherwise they would have scooped him up by now. Best to hustle back to Mike and the others and give them the bad news. But when he finally backed the camper out into the road, he turned it toward the other end of town instead. Hannah's Cafe was dark, the wide parking lot empty. Nate pulled down behind Sid's shop and parked tight against the corrugated tin wall.

The corrals were also empty. Even the donkey's body had been removed. Thorough, these guys. The sergeant felt behind the cab seat and found his brother-in-law's field glasses, World War II vintage and battered, then carried them with him to the rear of the camper. The narrow metal ladder to the luggage rack held his weight well enough, though it creaked and groaned. From the top rung, he stepped carefully across to the garage roof. If there were spies all around, by damn, he was going to spy right back.

The sun-heated tin panels burned through his slacks and through the elbows of his jacket as he stretched out over them, and the binoculars gave him trouble, refusing to focus at first. Cursing under his breath, he did a sweep of the highway first, east to west. It stretched into the distance in either direction, wide and barren. No trucks, no buses, no nothing. Civilization seemed to have disappeared from the face of the earth.

Now, he checked the desert to the west, a sharp magnified view of spiky yucca, clump-grass, and brush. Still nothing. Then something moved, but it was only a coyote. Fascinated, Nate followed the gray-brown animal a short way. It dogtrotted nimbly through the sand, then stopped to nose a bramble, and finally lifted its leg to pee. Business as usual. That made the sergeant chuckle, and told him a thing or two. There was nothing around to bother a coyote, at least not in that section of the desert. He lowered the glasses and rubbed at his eyes. Time to get back, time to figure out some way of getting out of here.

But when he stepped back to the ladder, a tiny glint of light flashed off to the west, well beyond where the coyote roamed. The flash came again, mid-morning sun reflected off glass, another pair of binoculars most likely. Nate didn't bother to use his own, the distance was too great for only a thirty-five field power. Now he knew where some of their trouble lay ... waiting. For what? He couldn't bother with that, either. Not yet.

The ladder complained again under his heavy footsteps, and the ground wind greeted him with puffs of cold, sweet air. The taste of it in his lungs, the hint of wildness behind that gentle touch, brought a strange joy. In the midst of all the insanity, the world and everything in it had somehow become more precious.

Click-click. That familiar sound made him turn—the

hammer of a pistol being cocked. A lone soldier in a splotched tan jumpsuit stood beside the farthest corral, a small caliber Ruger automatic pointed at Nate. Greasepaint of a similar color smeared his young expressionless face.

Nate remembered his .38 back at the trailer park with some regret.

"Take it easy, kid," the sergeant said, hands held away from his body. "I'm not armed."

At this range, sight and sound came almost simultaneously. Light flared at the gun muzzle, the air cracked, and confused, Nate felt himself stagger back a step. A new bright crimson blotch widened near the center of his chest. He looked up, too outraged to make sense of it.

"You shot me, you son of a bitch!"

Silent, his eyes cold, the young man pulled the trigger twice more. Each impact drove Nate against the shop wall. Now there were three spreading stains on his jacket. The dark holes made a small, perfect triangle. Neat pattern, he thought numbly and clamped his hands to his bloody chest. Sharp irresistible pain came hard after the initial shock. Breathing grew suddenly impossible, and a cloud of swirling fireflies obscured his vision.

"Bastard," Nate whispered, then his knees gave way.

III

Charlie made it very clear he didn't care for the arrangements. Mike tried to ignore his grousing while dismantling the doc's satellite dish with Sidney. Each piece freed was quickly carted to the Airstream by John Caldwell and wedged inside. They'd already moved the TV, stereo system, and microwave, though the deputy doubted any of it would work with the trailer's ancient electrical wiring.

"Do you realize how much I paid for the Winnebago?" Charlie demanded.

Sidney stopped to wipe sweat from her forehead. "Doc, I'm sorry. It can't be helped. Now, be useful and get us some beers."

Glum, Charlie moved around toward the entrance side

of the RV and passed Caldwell on his way back from the Airstream. They carefully avoided each other. Mike, a wrench in his hand, paused to watch John's approach—his giant, almost boneless, stride, his flesh all the more yellow in the winter sunlight. Everything had changed between the three of them, John and Sidney and Mike, yet the sight of Caldwell still gave the deputy chills.

He cinched the crescent wrench down over the bolt that held the frame of the dish to its concrete pad and began to loosen it. Sidney worked beside him, warm and real, which was the only thing that made the rest of this crazy business tolerable. John hunkered down beside them, black eyes on Sid.

"Nate Curtis has not returned," he said, nostrils fluttering. "I don't think he will."

She nodded. "I was afraid of this."

"Afraid of what?" Mike wanted to know. "So he decided to just go on home. Can't blame him much."

"No," Sidney murmured. "Nate wouldn't do that, and you know it. I thought there might be trouble, and now I'm certain."

"We've waited too long, *ta'mirik.*" Caldwell's strange lipless mouth mangled the English words.

"It was already too late, the night you changed," Sid told him, her voice dull. "There was never anywhere for us to run. Not on this world."

Mike felt confusion and anger. "Then are we just giving up?"

"We can't," the young woman answered. "That's not the way of the *mirik'im.*" She pulled the bolt she'd been working on from the concrete and stood. "Put the frame in the trailer, John ... then bring the one unbroken box to me."

Silent, Caldwell took the metal piece in a long-fingered hand and lumbered away.

"What are we going to do?" Mike asked.

"We need weapons—more than two pistols and Doc's deer rifle."

"If we're facing the whole damn army, we'll need

rocket launchers. Lots." He leaned closer to her. "This is suicide. You know that."

"No," Sid said firmly. "This is what the Ral were born to—war." She turned and walked away from him, across the barren trailer park toward open desert.

IV

The land seemed suddenly vast around her, and a strong sense of foreboding filled Sidney. With it came a moment of confusion and self-doubt. She looked down at her grime-stained hands. How would she protect her *mirik'im* with this frail body? *Ta'mirik* meant wife and warrior, but she was a mechanic by trade and had had little contact with weapons. Mike was trained in self-defense, but their enemies were many and too well equipped.

She felt the deputy behind her, heard his muffled bootsteps in the sand. A tiny dust devil whirled to life only a dozen steps away, dancing through the withered grasses. It struck the rusted wire field fence that encircled the park and dissipated. God, the beauty of this place left her breathless.

"Hey, you guys, wait for me!" Charlie shouted from the RV. "I've got the beers!"

"No!" Sid called back. "Stay there, Doc. We're going to activate the box."

"What?" Mike said in alarm.

Charlie Downing, M.D., had wasted no time in disappearing back into the Winnebago with his beers.

Sidney pushed the low fence down with a boot and stepped over it, then squatted in the sand to wait. Johncaldwell was already on his way, the black box held in the crook of an elbow. Mike settled beside her, his expression distraught.

"You can't let him start up the box, Sid. It's too dangerous."

"Don't question my decisions," she answered coldly.

The deputy's face clouded and his lips pursed, but he looked away. Johncaldwell arrived.

Sid nodded to him. "I want you to wake the Gatekeeper. Out there . . ." She pointed into the desert. "Where it can't hurt us."

Dutifully, Johncaldwell strode away into the brush, then halted about thirty yards out. He laid the box in the sand and bent over it, his hands caressing the dead black material. Sidney knew the moment it woke, and next to her, Mike took a sharp breath. The earth shifted ever so gently under her, and around her, the air rippled—a tiny shock wave that flashed toward and through them and away before it could be truly comprehended. Still, the menace of that invisible power struck Sid.

She stood up. "Come on, Mike."

He followed, however unwilling, to where Johncaldwell waited. They dropped to their knees in the soft sand before him.

"I want to talk to the Gatekeeper," Sidney said.

Johncaldwell's luminous peaceful eyes grew troubled. "It's *g'ral*—Ral created—and has our mind-set. I doubt it will speak to *il'ral.*"

"I'm *ta'mirik,*" she snapped in sudden irritation, "and it'll speak to me." Then she managed a smile for Johncaldwell. "But we'll dream this meeting. The three of us together."

They crowded in tightly, knees pressed to knees, the box between them. Mike and Sidney touched foreheads, and Johncaldwell leaned into theirs. Beside her, the deputy flinched at Johncaldwell's touch.

"Give me control," the young woman commanded and made the world disappear.

There would be no fragrant evergreens or singing birds, though. She created hard reality within this dream. The landscape returned unchanged, and Mike stared at the black box in front of him.

"Didn't work this time," he said, voice edged with relief. "Too bad—"

The box began to melt, a black liquid that flowed upward, away from the pull of gravity, and the deputy scrambled back, with a shout. The image blurred, then refocused. Now, a tall Ral in night black robes stood in the sand.

"Ta'ame ir ger?" it growled, eyes fixed on its own long fingers, then on the shimmering robe.

Johncaldwell answered in his fluting voice and fell silent. The other looked around, displeasure plain on its alien face.

"I need you to ask something of the Gatekeeper . . ." Sidney began.

"You can ask yourself, *ta'mirik*. It absorbed English from . . . who I once was."

The Gatekeeper, impatient, waved a hand. "You wish to use this tongue, so be it. But you offend me, Johncaldwell. *Il'ral* are not dreamers, and yet, you bring them into dreaming. And do this to me." It indicated its body. "Release me or I'll destroy these animals, these pets of yours."

"You can't," Sidney said from her seat on the ground. "Not for another four hours. Johncaldwell didn't give you Ral form. *I* did."

"I hear nothing. I see nothing." The Gatekeeper turned its back.

She'd witnessed this behavior when she had met the Old One on the Ral world, and it angered her, now, as it did then.

"Don't mess with him," Mike whispered behind her. "Leave him be."

Sidney climbed to her feet. "I'm *ta'mirik*, and I need your help, Old One." She moved around into the Gatekeeper's line of vision. "I want weapons and armor. You can provide those." It stared through her. "I am *ta'mirik* and as such, demand your respect. I demand the right to protect and defend my *mirik'im.*"

Johncaldwell said something rapidly in Ral, and the Gatekeeper snorted with derision.

"Listen to me, Old One," Sidney ordered. "You took *il'ral* flesh and re-formed it so that the gate could be repaired, and you could perform your function. But Johncaldwell as a Ral can't function without his *mirik'im*. You made him, and so I was made—neither Ral nor *il'ral*. I exist and you will see me!"

The Gatekeeper's head turned and its eyes fixed on Johncaldwell. "How can this be? She is an offense to all that we are, and yet this animal reasons . . ." Its voice trailed off.

"Old One," Johncaldwell said softly. "You've been my teacher, and taught me well, but in doing so, you've also learned. The Ral take worlds and technologies, then discard the sentient species. To keep their own race dominant, they've denied the intelligence of others and named them animals.

"But in the time you've been alone, you've been forced to change. You're no longer the single program machine your masters left behind. You've also learned to think and reason. You've even learned another language—something a Ral would never do." Johncaldwell tilted his head. "Don't you understand? You are *g'ral* and *il'ral,* too. Please listen to my *ta'mirik.*"

The Gatekeeper straightened his shoulders, his attention on Sidney. "Speak, then . . . *ta'mirik.*" The taste of the word seemed foul to it.

Sidney's thoughts had scattered, and it took a moment to collect them. "In . . . In order for Johncaldwell to repair the gate, he must survive, and his survival is my responsibility. But our enemies are many and well armed. If you can make a Ral, then it must be within your power to make us weapons and armor."

"I have that knowledge and ability, yes."

Sid felt a sudden hope. "Then you'll help us?"

"I will."

"Tell us what materials you'll need," Johncaldwell said eagerly.

"What I need is beneath your feet. Silica. My energy levels are low, but it is a simple task." The Gatekeeper considered Mike, who stood a respectful distance away, then dipped its chin at Sidney. "Such a *mirik'im* should never have been, but on me lies the responsibility. Leave the dream, all of you, and take yourselves a dozen paces from this place. Go."

They woke with their heads still pressed together. The deputy was the first to disengage, and Sidney could hear his panicked breathing.

"Come on," he growled urgently and grabbed Sid's arm, towing her to her feet.

Johncaldwell took them away from the box, and they stood with him among the windblown bunchgrass, watching, expectant and afraid. For the first time, Sid detected a faint hum on the air, more felt than heard. The hair on her head bristled suddenly, and a darkness formed around the box. The shroud wavered and grew, then quickly began to shrink into itself. Light flared, a cool white light that dazzled the eye, and Sidney blinked.

Now the box lay at the center of a shallow glass crater, within which were scattered a number of items, all of the same material as the box. Oddly, Mike was the first to arrive at the depression. He touched the slick surface lightly and hissed.

"Cold!" A long black rod, wide at one end and narrowing almost to a point on the other, lay near his fingers, and gingerly he pulled it to him, then took it up. "Doesn't weigh much, but the balance is nice. This is the business end, right?" He held the thing up to Johncaldwell.

Johncaldwell tilted his head side to side. "Yes. That's the *pa'ng,* the light-rifle."

"What does it do?" Mike asked.

"It kills."

"I gathered that, but how? Bullets? Laser? Ray gun?" Johncaldwell shrugged. "Light."

"Laser, then."

"No." The Ral pointed a finger. "Those are the *nom'ng*—pistols."

"And these?" Sidney had gathered up three tiny black rectangles, no bigger than dominoes.

"Armor."

"Christ," Mike said, and there was a childlike delight in his voice. "This is incredible, Sid. Like the *Arabian Nights.* The box is your lamp. You just give it a rub, out pops the genie and grants your wishes."

Sid snorted. "As I remember, the genie was usually one nasty customer, just waiting for a chance to do you in." She picked up a rifle, a *pa'ng,* and eyed it skeptically. "These weren't made to be activated with human fingers.

This has claw holes instead of a trigger. How do we get around that?"

"Charlie," Mike stated. "The doc'll have some gizmo or other we can use."

The sun had nearly reached the midheavens, and Sid glanced up into the light. "Well, whatever he does, I hope it's fast, because there can't be much time left."

Chapter Twelve

A DEEP THROBBING sensation pulled Nate Curtis up out of the darkness. Under him, the ground shuddered, and all around, the air thundered, while a burning pressure built steadily in his chest. Indigestion. Janice's turkey stuffing had come back to haunt him with a vengeance. Then memory and awareness flooded back at the same moment, and he opened his eyes, afraid.

There were two dark helmeted heads bent over him and hands that moved quickly to adjust a band around Nate's upper arm. The ground made a sudden slip-sliding motion, then dropped out from under him briefly. Helicopter . . . He was in a helicopter. The uniformed soldiers grabbed bulkheads for support before resuming their ministrations. Giddy with pain and shock, Nate observed them until consciousness faded again.

The clean scent of pure oxygen greeted his return. Slender fingers held a plastic mask over his nose and mouth, and beyond the fingers, he saw the monotonous beige walls and ceiling of a corridor. They had him on some god-awful gurney with old shopping cart wheels that thumped and bumped over the floor. Nate clawed the mask away from his face.

"Where am I?" Those three spoken words left him gasping.

"Easy, Sarge," someone young and feminine said. "This is the military hospital at George Air Force Base." The oxygen was firmly replaced.

"What have we got, Corporal?" demanded another older male voice behind Nate. The gurney stopped. Two men in white coats stood at the foot, one with an IV bag in his hands.

The female answered, "Multiple gunshot wounds to the chest, sir. We've got him stabilized."

"Where's Colonel Wayne?"

"On his way, sir. ETA fifteen minutes."

Nate struggled to tilt his head enough to get an upside-down view of the young woman who spoke. She glanced down and gave him a faint smile. Her brown hair was tied back, and she wore fatigues with corporal's stripes—army, not air force. Hers was one of the helmeted faces from the helicopter.

"All right. Get the patient to pre-op, stat. We'll be ready for him in OR. Move it."

The gurney began its thumping journey down the hall again, and the pain threatened to pull him under. The corporal leaned close to his right ear.

"Wayne is our chest man. He's the best. You'll be fine."

But Nate could hardly make sense of the words. "SOB shot me," he mumbled into the mask. Janice was going to be pissed.

II

The weight of the *pa'ng* brought a feeling of strength and peace. He was no longer helpless in this world. Johncaldwell's fingers entwined the thick smooth stock of the weapon. It had been designed for hands like his. Mike held his less gracefully, but with no less awe, as if he sensed the power it held.

The two of them stood just outside the RV, and though no words passed between them, Johncaldwell recognized subtle changes in the deputy. By sharing a dream, the *mirik'im* had been bound all the more tightly together. John drew his nails along the rifle's black surface, let them snag briefly on the trigger holes. Soon, in the midst of smoke and death, his *ta'mirik* would ask him to open the gate. Then all that should be, would be.

He gazed at the Winnebago door, content to wait. Sidney had gone inside with Charles Downing to search for something that would make it possible for human hands to use the Ral equipment. His otic nerves picked up their sounds—of drawers opened and closed, of frustrated arguments. Finally, Charles stuck his head out the door.

"Bring the damn things inside," he ordered.

Mike went first with both pistol and rifle, and Johncaldwell came after. Sidney met them with a strained smile. Being human still, she worried about time.

"John," Charles said. "Tell me how the weapons work."

Johncaldwell stared at the man, uncertain how to answer, but Sid put the question in a more reasonable form.

"He means, what makes the weapons fire."

John waved three clawed fingers.

"Only claws?" the young woman asked.

"Pressure of the claws. The stronger the pressure, the greater the discharge. Shall I show you?"

"No!" Charles said quickly. "Not in here, for God's sake. But we're talking pressure created by the pull of the claws in the holes—same as the pull on the trigger of a . . . human gun?"

"Yes."

"OK. I think I got it, now." The doctor motioned to the kitchen area. "Set the ones you want done on the table. Sidney . . . drawer next to the fridge. Get me some six-penny finishing nails." He began to rummage in the little space under the sink, then pulled out a small dusty paperboard box. "Plaster of paris—sets up fast. This may not work, but it's the best I can come up with in a hurry. Get out of the way, all of you."

John, his own weapons still in hand, collapsed bonelessly to the living room carpet, grateful to be able to straighten his head. Human residences were tight and confining, and mankind must carefully regulate the atmospheres and temperatures within. Not a very hardy species. He had begun lately to view other humans with a critical Ral eye, though it was a blind eye he turned toward his mates. Still, the memories of his own once-human life were fading, more and more.

The room had been stripped bare, and Mike took the driver's swivel chair for his seat. Sidney stood at a window, watching the desert beyond. Even motionless, she was obviously agitated.

"Ta'mirik," Johncaldwell said gently. "Be at peace. The moment will come no sooner for your worry."

"I'd sooner it didn't come at all." Her tone was harsh, and she scrubbed at her face with open hands. "My God, what am I doing?"

Mike went to wrap arms around her. "Surviving, Sid. You're surviving as best you can."

"I knew there'd be trouble waiting for Nate in Mojave Wells, but I didn't trust my judgment. So I sent him on a bullshit errand just to prove a theory." Sidney shrugged Mike's arms away, and his sympathy. "He may be dead."

"Why should you feel distress over *il'ral?*" asked Johncaldwell, perplexed. "He's not of your *mirik'im*. His value is limited and for you to use as you would."

"I'm *not* feeling distress," Sidney answered tersely. "I'm not feeling anything—no remorse, no sorrow—and that's what scares the hell out of me."

Mike turned troubled eyes on John.

"Hey, is this what you want?" Charles demanded and thrust a *pa'ng* into Sidney's hands.

She checked the rifle carefully. A white substance had been poured or pressed into the holes, and now the pointed tips of three small nails protruded from them in a triangular pattern. Experimentally and very carefully, the young woman curled her fingers over them. The nails appeared snug in their seats.

"Thank God the thing's light, or I'd never be able to aim it and fire." Sid looked at the doctor. "Did you do the others?"

"Let's make certain this one works, before I mess with the rest."

"Outside?" Sidney asked John.

Amused, Johncaldwell tipped his head in affirmation, then led them all back out into the morning sunlight. He brought an empty oil drum and placed it a distance from the RV.

"A narrow beam is achieved with a single . . . trigger.

For the widest beam use all three with an even, steady pressure."

"What kind of range does it have?" Mike wanted to know.

Range . . . distance. Johncaldwell tried to find a comparison for that in human terms. "A mile, I think. Perhaps more."

The deputy raised a brow. "Not too shabby. So shoot the thing, Sid. See if you can hit that itty-bitty barrel over there."

Sidney used the narrow beam first. A faint shimmering light lashed silently out from the rifle barrel, and now there was a large perfect hole in the center of the drum.

"Ouch," Mike muttered. "Let me try that." He commandeered the *pa'ng*.

"Easy," Sid cautioned. "It doesn't take much pull."

Mike used all three triggers, and within moments, had made a pile of slag of the drum. "Jesus H. Do these have safeties?" The tang of hot metal was strong, but very little smoke drifted away on the wind.

"With clawholes there's little danger of accidental discharge." John shrugged. "You'll have to be very careful."

"What about ammunition?" Sidney asked. "Will we need to reload them?"

"Not in your lifetime."

"Great, just like in the old cowboy movies. OK, Charlie, fix the others." She pulled three small rectangles from her pocket, the *in'al*. "Now we're going to try the armor."

The doctor retreated once more into his Winnebago, and Sid held out a rectangle to John. "How do these work?"

A simple matter, the *in'al*. Johncaldwell laid the little block on the back of his wrist and activated it by pressing a clawtip in the single hole. Response was immediate. The *in'al* liquefied and raced up and around John's arm. Quickly, it had covered his entire body, neck to toes to wrists, in a black shield only a single molecule thick, though there were heavier layers at the wrists and on the soles of the feet. And a beltlike thickness at the waist.

"The *in'al* must touch the body. You'll need to discard your clothing."

"The hell I will," Mike grunted.

But Sidney had already begun to shed hers, shivering in the winter air. She held out her wrist to John, who placed a rectangle on it. There was fear and determination on her angular face, and when Johncaldwell released the armor, she gasped.

"You're going to freeze in that," the deputy said. "You'll have to wear your clothes over it."

"No . . ." Sidney ran her hands over arms and shoulders. "I feel fine, warm . . . just right. This is great. Put yours on, Mike."

His face reddened. "I don't really need armor. Honest."

"Come on," Sidney encouraged, smiling. "I've seen you naked before."

"Only in your dreams." Unhappy, Mike shrugged his clothing off, and submitted to the process, eyes squeezed shut the entire time.

"What does it feel like?" Sid demanded a moment later.

The deputy stood with arms out. "It feels like I'm still buck naked, only I'm not cold anymore."

"Admit it. The armor's more comfortable than clothes. It's . . . it's like wearing water." The young woman rubbed an arm, again. "You can feel every touch through the *in'al*."

"Sensitivity is still lessened, but what matters," John said, "is that your frail human bodies are now better protected."

Mike stubbornly pulled on his jeans and shirt. The armor was completely hidden underneath. He was struggling with his boots when Charles returned, carrying the remainder of their weapons.

"What next?" the doctor asked, his gaze shifting from one to the other before it settled on Sidney. "My dear, is that a slinky new leotard? I approve—completely."

"Right," Sid muttered and climbed into her own borrowed jeans and shirt.

Charles handed her a rifle and pistol and gave Mike the second *nom'ng*, then nodded toward what used to be the oil drum. "Could you guys wait until I'm down the road a piece before you start something with Uncle Sam?"

"Then you better get going, Doc," Sidney said gruffly.

They had already hitched the Power Wagon to the little Airstream, but Charles Downing hesitated by the cab. "Am I ever going to see you again?"

Sid looked away. "Not if you're lucky, Charlie."

"I still can't believe any of this," he complained. "I was happy here. I had the rest of my life all planned."

"Shit happens," said Mike with just a hint of amusement. "Drive out the back way, Doc. If the road's barricaded, just stop and do whatever they say. Play along, tell 'em everything you know. After all, we kidnapped you, forced you to help us."

"I can't tell them that."

"You can," Sidney insisted. "You have to. Now go on." She gave Charles a quick hug and opened the driver's side door for him. "Go!"

"This doesn't feel right, Sid," the doc said, face clouded with doubt. "I've been with you in this from the beginning. It's wrong to leave you just when things are gonna get rough."

Sid held back her frustration. "Charlie, I couldn't have made it this far without your help . . . none of us could . . . But the game has changed. I won't be able to protect you."

"I can take care of myself," the man blustered.

"No, Charlie, not anymore. If you stay, you'll die."

That honesty alarmed him. "Well, I'm still coming back for the Mercedes as soon as I can," he said.

Dr. Downing climbed into the cab and started the engine, then sent the pickup forward, dragging the Airstream behind. He waved halfheartedly.

"Be careful," Mike called after him. "The tires are low on the trailer."

Sid watched him go. "Since Charlie's headed south, we head north."

"It's the only other way out of here," the deputy said, suddenly glum. "And they'll be waiting for us in town—same as Nate—sure as shit."

"If they are, they'll be sorry." Sidney gripped the *pa'ng* tight.

This was how it should be—the *mirik'im* together, alone. Johncaldwell considered the black boxes beside the RV steps. He'd thought his greatest desire was to open the gate, but now the desire to face *il'ral* in battle, to bring promised death and destruction to the enemy, was even stronger. Next to him, Sidney's warding impulses were almost as potent, almost as tangible, and whether she knew it or not, she felt the pull of her first mate's urges. Sid shared his longing, and so did Mike in a lesser way. The gate could be dealt with later. Johncaldwell kept silent, content to follow his mates into the Winnebago.

III

"Tell me, Sergeant Curtis, have you always been lucky?"

Nate hardly felt lucky—he felt only pain. The room he'd awakened in was the same dirty beige with a single tiny window. His wrists were strapped down, and an IV line trailed up from the back of his hand. To add further insult, there were crib bars on either side of his bed.

"Lucky . . ." the man in a white coat and thick wire-rimmed glasses repeated. He held an aluminum clipboard as he leaned over the sergeant. "Are you the kind that always has the winning ticket at the church raffle? Or gets two prizes in his Cracker Jack's box?"

"No," Nate muttered, too tired for anger, even though he disliked the fellow's smug tone.

"That's hard to believe. I dug two .25 caliber bullets out of your chest—"

"Three," the sarge corrected him.

"No, two. One found its own way out. Glanced off a rib and exited under your left arm. Not only are you lucky, but you've got tough bones, Sarge. One slug nailed you dead center, but there was enough distance between you and the soldier that it only flattened like a pancake on your sternum. That's still pretty incredible. But I saved the last bullet for

you as a memento." The man had grown animated, gesturing
with his clipboard, expression intent.

"You must have turned, because it entered at an
angle—missed the heart by a centimeter, then somehow
managed to dodge your lungs and every major artery, and
ended up snug against the inside of your right shoulder
blade. Now that's luck of a biblical kind."

Unimpressed, Nate gazed up at him. "How long have I
been here?"

"What?" The man blinked, then mentally changed
gears. "Close to three hours. Not long really, considering.
We had to work fast, so we couldn't use strong anaesthe-
sia. They're eager to question you. You didn't need much
time in recovery."

"Are you Dr. Wayne?"

"Naw. Wayne's too busy to hang around here. I'm Major Byer, M.D. I assisted the colonel in surgery." He
paused. "Are you in much pain?"

"Enough," the patient grunted. The throb in his chest
had spread to every part of his body at some unremem-
bered point.

"I'll call a nurse. We can give you a little something to
take the edge off." Byer checked his wristwatch. "I'd better hurry though. You've got visitors coming soon."

Nate watched him vanish through the heavy, much-
scuffed door. For a hospital, the place struck the sergeant
as more than shabby, less than clean, but then George Air
Force Base had been closed down a while ago. The straps
on his wrists chafed, and his nose began to itch. Hell!

IV

Charles cursed the road, the truck, and the trailer. And
the world in general. He'd never given the idea of cruel
fate much thought . . . until now. The low tires on the Airstream and the added weight of his numerous heavy belongings put a lot of strain on the hitch. This caused the
Dodge to come up slightly in the front end and oversteer
on the worn asphalt.

That wasn't what made him drive so slowly though.

Something unknown and therefore scary lay at the end of
this road. Worse yet, his friends—his closest friends, if
truth be told—were headed in another direction, toward
another fate. Charles considered the future. There would
be a very uncomfortable time spent explaining himself to
the government, and after that . . . After that, there would
be beer and football and soccer. Endless meaningless com-
petitions. And the knowledge that he'd given up the only
game worth playing for the only prize worth winning.
Life.

Now he cursed himself for a coward, but kept on driving. The road wound through dunes and around sandstone
boulders with pockmarked faces. The wind sent threads of
sand writhing over the pavement. At twenty miles an hour,
it would take just short of forever to make it to Kelso, the
nearest town. Assuming the military would let him get that
far. The thought of a roadblock around the next curve
slowed him to 10 m.p.h.

When the ground lurched suddenly, Charles barely noticed, but the thunderclap that followed made him put on
the brakes and swivel his head. A small dark cloud of
smoke rose above the hills to the north where Mojave
Wells lay. In moments, the cloud was torn apart by the
wind, only to be replaced by more smoke.

"Hold on, guys," Charles muttered and climbed out to
unhitch the trailer.

V

Mike drove the Winnebago—that great lumbering beast
of a machine—while Sidney took the copilot's chair, a
pa'ng across her knees. In another life, she might have appreciated such luxury—to travel like a turtle, your house
on your back, and with the elevated perspective that big
rig drivers enjoyed. Now the high, wide windshield only
provided a means to locate trouble.

Johncaldwell had shown them how to attach the light-
pistols to the built-in utility belts at their waists—a clumsy
task under shirts, and Sidney realized they'd be forced to
discard the clothing again soon enough. He had also

shown them where the *tin'k*, the long slender knife, was stored in an almost invisible sheath on the left forearm. Since the Gatekeeper had not provided *tin'k'im*, they rummaged through Charlie's kitchen knives and found three that would fit their purpose. Lastly John explained the single clawholes in each cuff. The right one would remove the armor, while the left one would cause the material to cover face and hands for added protection. These were activated by the perfect sharp point of a clawtip though, so only Johncaldwell could make them work.

At the last curve before Mojave Wells, Sidney asked the deputy to halt the RV.

"Why?" Mike demanded, his foot already on the brake.

"I want to give our friends, it they're out there, something else to think about. Wait here, both of you." That last command made John uneasy. He uncurled from the carpet, tense. "I'll be right next to the RV," Sid promised him.

She stepped outside, eyes on the landscape. Only a mile to the south, the trailer park was still visible in the clear desert air. A gleam of white told her exactly where Mike's Jeep sat, just beyond the Chinese mulberry tree. The *pa'ng* had no sights, and though the rifle was light, it was far too long and felt awkward in her hands. Sidney brought the stock to her shoulder, struggling to find a comfortable position, then took as careful aim as possible. Some inner voice told her a narrow beam would be best for this, so she pulled back gently on a single nail.

Soundlessly the weapon fired. A tight cord of nearly invisible light snapped out, and instantly the target exploded. In the midst of fire storm and thunder, large pieces of twisted metal rose high above the mulberry's top limbs. This was a far bigger blast than she'd expected. Doc's Mercedes, parked close to the Jeep, had gone up as well.

Mike stared out his side window, devastation on his lean face. Sidney turned and ran for the steps.

"Let's go!" she cried.

The Winnebago lurched forward, the deputy growling, "Christ! My Cherokee."

Mojave Wells came into view. Sid scanned the empty streets and hoped for the best. Just let them get past and onto the highway. Let Nate be wrong, let the government be yet unaware of Johncaldwell's survival.

"Where is everyone?" Mike asked, and the old sense of dread filled Sid again.

"Keep going. Don't slow down."

They made it as far as Hannah's Cafe, then Sidney saw the back of Nate's camper behind the garage.

"Stop!" she shouted, and Mike nearly put them into the windshield. "It's Nate. Take us down by the shop."

Johncaldwell curled a hand around her ankle. *"Ta'mirik,* there's risk here. Don't be concerned with *il'ral."*

He was right, and Sid felt tugged by human and inhuman influences.

"Bullshit," the deputy snapped and headed the Winnebago into Hannah's parking lot.

They refused to be left behind this time, and clambered down the steps after Sidney, weapons ready. She stopped them.

"Understand one thing . . ." she said carefully, her eyes on Johncaldwell. "We don't shoot at anything that doesn't shoot at us first."

"Ta'mirik," Johncaldwell said in alarm. *"Il'ral* are animals, dangerous animals. We must kill swiftly."

"Don't question my judgment," Sidney told him, her tone cold and angry. "Obey me."

John bowed his head. "Forgive, *ta'mirik."*

She ignored him, attention fixed on the camper. "Nate?" The camper door was unlocked, but the sergeant wasn't inside, nor was he in the cab of the pickup.

"Sid . . ." Mike said gently. He stood near the back wall of the shop, eyes on the dirt. "It's blood."

Lots of it—in wide puddles that had seeped into the ground. Most of the pools had dried to a rusty brown, but the centers were still damp, still thick and crimson. Sidney's sense of dread heightened, and with it came a sudden wrath. Nate Curtis was not of her *mirik'im,* he was *il'ral,* yet this loss brought anger. John had shared his Ral mind-set with her, somehow imprinted them over her human sensibilities, and the conflicting feelings only confused and hurt her.

Against her will, tears flooded her eyes and spilled over—not for Nate but for herself, for what she had become. Mike shifted uncomfortably, and Johncaldwell stared at her, perplexed, no longer capable of understanding human emotions. *Cold cruel alien,* Sidney thought bitterly, but then his long spidery arms entwined her, drawing her tight against his cool armored body. The back of a claw trailed down her wet cheek.

"Be strong, *ta'mirik* . . . beloved," he murmured. "We are in your hands."

A gentle reminder. She gathered her composure, embarrassed by the lapse—and by her own misapprehensions. Johncaldwell's love was real, and emotions couldn't be exclusively human traits. Around her, his arms tightened, and he hissed.

"They come. The enemy approaches."

VI

This would be the Inquisition, Nate decided unhappily. As promised, the wait was a short one, but instead of grim, uniformed men on the threshold, a single brown-haired head poked around the edge of the door. He recognized her instantly.

"Come in," Nate said, perhaps too eagerly.

"I can't stay," the young woman answered. "Just wanted to make sure you were okay."

"I will be . . . if you scratch the left side of my nose. Please . . . "

She laughed and came toward him, still in olive drab fatigues—not a beautiful woman, but handsome, with heavy eyebrows, strong square chin, and freckles. Her movements were self-assured and yet feminine, and Nate liked her. The corporal scratched his nose, then gave it a tweak.

"I told you Dr. Wayne would fix you right up."

"You did. So what's your name, soldier?"

"Lehman, sir. Corporal Alice Lehman."

"A medic, huh?"

Alice nodded, her plain brown eyes on the door. "In Evac. And you're Detective Sergeant Nathan William Curtis, age fifty-two, Anaheim PD."

"You know a lot," Nate said thoughtfully, "Do you know why I'm here?"

"Could be because you got shot." The answer was flip.

"Then do you know why *you're* here? At a closed-down air force base."

She pursed her lips. "That's classified, sir."

"Alice, some friends of mine are in Mojave Wells. They're good people. I don't know how much your bosses have told you, but there's an honest-to-God extraterrestrial with those friends of mine. *That's* why we're both here. I need you to tell me what you can about this whole operation."

"Sorry." The corporal looked at her lace-up army boots.

"I promise I won't say anything. Come on," Nate pleaded. "They're going to be here any minute to give me the third degree. I deserve a little info, too. Is this strictly army business now?"

The young woman gave a bare nod of her head.

"Have they caught my friends?"

"No."

"What the hell's the army waiting for? We sat at the trailer park for almost two days. Easy pickings. Why didn't they go after us?"

"After the destruction of the Avawatz test site, I think they decided to be careful."

"Just in case John Caldwell has some kind of weapon. . . ."

"Who?"

"The alien. That's his name. So what else? How many men have you got involved?"

"Lots . . . thousands . . . with all the newest high-tech equipment. It looks like Desert Storm out there. The whole area's surrounded, and the roads are blocked. Your friends can't possibly get out."

Nate felt a chill. "Containment . . . The bastards are gonna kill them. Better safe than sorry. Jesus Christ."

They heard the sound of voices out in the corridor.

"I got to go," Alice said quietly. "I don't know anything about extraterrestrials. They told us ... They said there were terrorists with a nuclear device holed up in Mojave Wells." She turned and fled from the room.

Chapter Thirteen

THE FIRST MAN to enter the hospital room had a round fleshy face; a young captain, fair-haired and ruddy-cheeked with an affable smile. His hazel blue eyes said something altogether different, though. The second man, a sergeant, carried a court reporter's stenograph in his arms. They found two metal folding chairs against a wall and brought them to the bed.

"Good afternoon, Sergeant Curtis," the blond one said in a friendly tone. "I'm Captain Andrew Kern, and this is Master Sergeant Jones. We're here to interrogate you."

Ugly word, one Nate had used many times on the job. He eyed them thoughtfully through a haze of pain. "Do I need a lawyer?"

"I am a lawyer, sir."

"But not mine."

"Under the circumstances, we can hardly allow any more civilian personnel to be involved. This is a military emergency, and under the congressional act of—"

"Never mind," Nate grunted. "I've got nothing to say to you."

"May I remind you, sir," Captain Kern said sternly, "that treason still carries the death penalty."

"I want to see someone in authority."

"I hold all the authority here."

Sergeant Curtis snorted as best he could through the oxygen tubes in his nose. "You're a shitty-assed little captain, and I wouldn't give you the time of day, if I knew it. Go find me the head honcho—the guy who's running the whole show. He's the only one I'll talk to." He glanced at the other man whose fingers danced over the keys of the machine in his lap. "You getting all this down, fella? Want me to spell shitty for you?"

Kern had no time to respond. The door opened, and a plump middle-aged nurse breezed in, a small syringe in one hand.

"You'll have to leave, ma'am." The captain's tone had a touch of fury behind it.

"I was just going to tell you the same thing. I have to give the patient a shot," she answered curtly.

"Of what?" Kern demanded.

"A pain medication."

The captain straightened in his chair. "Absolutely not. I need the man clearheaded."

"Are you a doctor, sir?" the woman inquired.

"No, but I'm in charge here, and I order you to leave the room immediately."

"Well, the major has given me other orders. And I'll follow those before I follow yours . . . Captain."

The nurse moved around the two seated men to Nate's side, and he cringed at the sight of the needle, but she only inserted it into a section of his IV tube.

"There," she said and smiled down at him. "Give it a couple minutes to get into your system, then you'll feel much better. I'll be back. . . ." She glanced at the others. "As soon as *they* leave."

"Thanks," Nate told her. Perhaps it was only the promise of relief, but already the pain seemed to be easing off. He watched her exit the room.

"Curtis!" That was Kern, demanding his attention again.

"Send me the guy in charge, and I'll maybe tell him everything I know. I want to talk, but not to you, Kern. You can't do anything for me."

It occurred to him vaguely that he was in no position to make such demands. A gentle lightheadedness had begun. The pain had not gone, only drifted into some distant place. Nate sighed and closed his eyes, grateful for the respite. He could hear Kern, hear his angry tirade, but refused to respond, and eventually there was silence.

II

Mike felt the old panic threatening to overwhelm him. Except for the whistle of the wind, he heard nothing, yet Caldwell stood, huge head cocked, intent.

"Where?" Sidney demanded and pulled free of his embrace. "How many?"

John pointed to the east. "Airships. Large ones, a long way off."

"Get in the RV." Mike caught Sidney's arm. "We'll go back the way we came."

"No!" she said. "We've got better cover here."

The deputy's panic heightened. "A tin shed won't stop bullets." Easterly gusts brought him the faint sound of engines now, the thump of rotors.

"There's nowhere to run, Mike."

He knew that already. "The old schoolhouse has the thickest walls. Let's try for there."

Sidney nodded, then dodged past the RV, headed between Hannah's Cafe and the outbuildings behind it. John Caldwell loped after her, but the deputy hesitated. He'd noticed something strange about John's armor as the alien moved quickly—in shadow it made him nearly indiscernible, and in direct sun, the *in'al* seemed to deflect the light or somehow refused to absorb it. Caldwell was visible, yet his image confused the eye just enough to make it difficult to track.

Sid disappeared beyond the cafe, then John. Mike still took the time to shed his clothes before racing after them. The two had paused against the back wall of Obie's Desert Rock Shop, a flimsy weather-beaten shack.

"What the hell are you doing?" Sidney demanded.

"Lose the clothes," Mike answered breathlessly. "You'll be less of a target. It's got some kind—"

John Caldwell put out a gaunt hand to silence him. "A vehicle . . . very close." His lipless mouth curled into a grimace—or a smile. "It's the Dodge."

"Charlie, damn you!" Sid snarled. She smacked Mike's arm. "Well, go stop the idiot."

"Why me?" the deputy muttered under his breath, but darted obediently through the narrow space between rock shop and post office and, with a quick glance around, out into the street. The big red Power Wagon careened toward him, transmission in low gear, engine wound at nerve-racking high revs. Doc drove like a drunk, weaving all over the road, and Mike went to stand in harm's way with the rifle held over his head. At the very last moment, Charlie slammed on the brakes, and the truck screeched to a stop practically on the deputy's toes.

"Jesus! Your brakes are crap!" Doc leaped from the cab, his .30-.30 in hand. "I thought they got you." Red-faced, the little man growled, "They killed my goddamn car, the bastards. Yours, too."

Mike didn't bother to tell him just *who* had killed his Mercedes. "You shouldn't have come back, Charlie."

"Tell me something I don't already know. Only I couldn't leave you guys on your own. You need all the warm bodies you can find. Where's Sid and John? Let's get the hell out of the open." Charlie gazed into the sky to the east, beyond the hills. "Can't you hear the helicopters?"

Mike heard them. "Doc, turn the Dodge around and get out of here. You can't do anything against armored gunships with that damned deer rifle."

"Wanna bet?" Three dark green choppers had risen above the western rim of the sandstone hills, bristling with weapons. Charlie set his elbows on the hood of the truck and took careful aim with his deer rifle.

"Doc, wait. Sidney decides—"

Charlie ignored him. "This is for the Mercedes, you assholes," he muttered and squeezed the trigger.

The high-powered .30-.30 shell exploded, its sharp report loud even against the rumble of the gunships, and Doc fired off a half dozen more shots, the empty brass cartridges popping from the ejection port in a small, steady stream. The ship on the left made a drunken sideways swerve, managed to right itself, and swung away, headed back over the hills.

"See!" Charlie whooped. "You gotta know where to hit

'em. Aim for the tail rotor. It's just about the only vulnerable place. Saw it on 'Wings,' that Discovery Channel show."

But those well-placed shots had only pissed the other two helicopter pilots off. One came at them, head-on, its tail rotor kept carefully out of view.

Sidney appeared at the edge of the rock shop, waving the two men back to shelter, but the copter swept above them. Charlie ducked down beside the truck just as the chatter of answering gunfire started. No tranquilizer darts this time, the deputy noted. These were armor piercing bullets that punctured a neat row of large holes in the hood of the Dodge, then went on to plow a deep furrow in the asphalt.

In powerless slow motion, Mike watched the line of fire head toward Sidney. She tried to dodge, but it followed her, then her mouth opened soundlessly, and she took a sudden involuntary step back that turned into an awkward jerking pirouette. Around she spun and collapsed in John Caldwell's arms.

Someone began an inhuman shrieking, and vaguely Mike recognized his own enraged voice. The chopper had swung directly overhead, the gunner in the open door searching out the next target. Mike propped the stock of the *pa'ng* against his thigh, the barrel pointed upward, and dragged down on all three nails.

"*Mirik'ee!*" Caldwell screamed. "No!"

The helicopter seemed to be blown straight upward first, but even as it climbed, its shape began to change. The blades drooped, melted, superheated metal flung away by the centrifugal forces, then the machine began to fall, smoke billowing. The third chopper hung over the eastern horizon, but Mike paid it no mind—not with death dropping out of the sky so close.

"Charlie!" he cried. The doc had cowered down near the truck cab, head covered by his arms. "Run!"

They both ran, scattering just before the thunder of impact. Dodge and copter met and exploded, and the concussion slammed into Mike's back like a sledgehammer. He cleared the wreckage at a helpless tumble, hands and face skinned bloody. For a moment, he lay fighting for breath, then remembered Sidney and dragged himself to his feet. Gas-fed fires blazed all along the road, while the pickup and helicopter had become an unidentifiable melted heap on the edge of an empty lot next to the schoolhouse. Though many of their glass windows had blown out, miraculously the tacky wooden buildings of the main street had survived the explosion.

Sidney was on her feet, clutching one shoulder. She stood with John Caldwell near some wreckage in front of the post office. The Ral dragged up a massive piece of smoking metal and tossed it aside.

"Are you all right," Mike demanded of the young woman as he limped toward them.

Face white with pain and sorrow, she turned to him. "I'm fine, but Charlie . . ."

The deputy looked down where John crouched. Charlie Downing's eyes were closed, his mouth slack. His right leg was mostly gone, only shreds of flesh held what was left of the limb to his thigh, while shards of white bone showed clearly through torn muscles and ligaments. Blood spread in an ever-widening puddle under his body. The right arm had been shattered as well, bent into several impossible angles. This is my fault, Mike thought, and his stomach clenched.

"Do something," he wailed. "He's bleeding to death."

Sidney pulled her light-pistol and on its finest setting, cauterized the wounds as best she could. The right leg came free as the flesh burned, and Mike turned away to vomit. Then John Caldwell scooped the unconscious man up into his long arms, heading through the burning debris to the schoolhouse.

III

"You wanted to talk to me?"

The voice came through a sleepy, hazy daydream, and Nate forced his eyes to focus on the man standing alone just inside the door.

"Who're you?" he asked, his tongue thick and uncooperative.

"Avery Sands."

Avery ... Sands. Didn't ring any bells. He wasn't military, but dressed in gray slacks and a fine light blue dress shirt—no tie. The clothes were quietly expensive. The man in them was slender and young, with baby-fine blond hair. No more than twenty-five, Nate decided, then changed his mind and added another ten years for the slightly stooped shoulders and faint creases at the corners of Sands's brown eyes.

"You a bigwig?"

"Big enough," Avery Sands answered with a hint of amusement. "Biggest around here anyway."

"But not army?"

"No, but I'm running things."

"Yeah? So who's your boss?"

"The president ..."

Nate blinked. "No shit?"

"No shit."

"Well, haul up a chair, man. You and I have got some serious discussing to do."

"Gladly." The chair skidded across the tiles, and Sands paused to lean over Nate. "Do you need anything? Thirsty?"

His mouth was bone-dry. "Water, please."

Sands reached behind Nate's head and brought a plastic cup with a straw to his lips, then afterward unstrapped the sergeant's wrists and elevated the head of his bed.

"Damned torture devices. Better?"

"God, yes." Nate scratched his nose for good measure, but found that only his right arm worked. To move the left one brought searing pain. "Are you the only guy around here, Sands, who isn't a class-A asshole?"

"Oh, I'm an asshole." The man laughed pleasantly. "Ask just about anybody. So best not cross me." Those brown eyes remained kind, though, thoughtful and intelligent.

A thought occurred. "How come I'm not in quarantine

with the rest of you turkeys walking around in space-suits?"

"Caldwell's condition was determined to be caused by genetic manipulation. We ran a few tests while you were in surgery even though we didn't expect to find anything. You looked pretty bad when we brought you in, but you didn't look diseased. Besides, most bacteria and viruses are animal specific anyway—despite H. G. Wells's climax in *War of the Worlds*. What little humans and extraterrestrials will have in common, probably won't include too many illnesses."

Nate couldn't make sense of most of that. *War of the Worlds?* "In other words, since I didn't die from being around Caldwell, you decided to take a risk."

"That's about it." Sands grinned. "So tell me all of it. Everything you can."

"I will, but I'll want some things in return."

"Like what?"

"Like a chance to help my friends, if possible."

"Believe it or not, Sergeant Curtis, that's exactly what I want to do. I can't prove it to you, and I can't make any promises, but I'm in a position to be very big help when the time comes. If you'll take a chance and trust me."

Nate stared into those ingenuous brown eyes. "Have I got any real choice? Don't you want a tape recorder or something?"

"Got one." Sands tapped his blond head. "Eidetic memory. I can't forget anything. Go ahead."

Nate closed his eyes and tried to assemble his thoughts, then began the whole crazy tale, starting with the Hanover case and ending with his being shot in Mojave Wells. Avery Sands listened, mostly silent, but interrupting now and again to ask pointed questions about even the smallest of details, which convinced Nate that the man wasn't just intelligent, but more likely brilliant. The recitation didn't take all that long. Nate, veteran of countless police reports, told mostly the facts and kept his personal observations to himself, unless asked. Some information was carefully held back. He liked Avery Sands, but wasn't about to hand him everything.

When Nate finally fell silent, Sands stood up again, agitated.

"So . . . So your alien didn't blow the Avawatz test site. It was Fenwick, my kindly scientific colleague playing the damned martyr."

"He didn't want Caldwell's black boxes to fall into human hands," Nate said. "And, by God, he was right. I'm telling you."

Sands's eyes hardened. "Well, by killing General McKinley, he only made things all the worse. McKinley was a good man, and might have saved us a lot of misery. Things are in a hell of a mess now." The grief left his voice abruptly. "You say Caldwell can use the boxes as a weapon. That's how the Hanover people were killed . . . and Colonel Candliss and the others—before the explosion. But the range is limited to the proximity of the alien or the boxes. Right?"

"To the best of my knowledge."

"Do you realize," Sands muttered, "what it could mean to mankind if we could get a hold of Caldwell alive . . . and the boxes?" He turned away, fretting. "But the machinery is already in motion. The safety of our country comes first."

Nate took a short aching breath. "What do you mean, machinery?"

"I'm not a madman like Candliss, willing to risk everything for the sake of knowledge and power. We're prepared to sterilize the area if we have to. Contain and sterilize." When the sergeant frowned, Sands went on. "A bomb, Curtis. If we can't neutralize your alien, there's going to be a small nuclear accident, as soon as the wind changes. So close to L.A., we've got to head the fallout east. And if you ever repeat any of this, I'll deny every word."

"Damn you!" Nate sputtered. "What about my people? What about Sid and Mike and Charlie?"

"We're doing everything we can to get them out first."

"Like you got me out?" The sarge touched his chest lightly.

"That was an unfortunate accident. The soldier's been

remanded for court-martial, but the poor boy was scared to death. This whole business has everyone jumpy. You caught him off guard, and the corporal just lost it."

Nate mulled that over for a moment. "You're sure there's no one else running this show?"

"What? No. Damned sure. Everyone reports to me, and I report directly to the president."

"Well, you better start checking around. That kid wasn't scared, and I didn't surprise him. It was the other way around. He knew I was unarmed, but he shot anyway. He meant to kill me."

"But he didn't kill you."

"That's not the point, Sands. I'm a cop. I've seen plenty of men doing just what they were told." Nate held his frustration in check. "He shot to kill, because someone ordered him to. Someone besides you." A chill rippled through him, and he pulled the oxygen tubes from his nostrils, thinking he might have the strength to get up. "And that means those bastards intend to kill my friends, too."

"Easy, Sergeant, easy." Sands leaned over him again to hook the tubing back around his ears. "I'll put my men on this immediately. If we've got another renegade officer, I'll find him. I promise you. Somehow we'll get your people out of there alive."

But the chill only grew worse. Nate closed his eyes, afraid.

IV

The third helicopter, still hovering over the sandstone hills, made a move forward, and Mike, teeth gritted, swung his light rifle to bear. One short burst of energy was all it took to convince the invaders to turn tail and run. Sidney and John, with his gory unconscious burden, slipped through the entrance of the schoolhouse—but not before Caldwell had given the locked door a solid kick that sent it crashing inward.

Mike followed, heartsick, filled with rage at himself and the hostile world around him. The single classroom inside was cold with ancient abused desks scattered about.

There were open books on several of them. A green chalkboard with a half-finished lesson plan on it covered the front wall. Class had been dismissed in a hurry.

Caldwell deposited Charlie Downing in a heap on the floor, almost callously, then unhooked his *nom'ng* from his utility belt. Sidney only stared, numb. For a moment, the deputy stood frozen too, unable to believe what he saw, but when John pointed the pistol at the injured man, that awful rage took over.

Mike flung himself the short distance, tackling the alien low, and they stumbled over the unknowing doctor, then floundered into a pair of desks. The wrist with the gun was caught hard in Mike's hands, but Caldwell's superior strength wrenched it free.

Somewhere behind them, Sidney began to wail. "Stop it! Stop it!"

John slung the deputy away, and, airborne, he tumbled over the teacher's desk and into the chalkboard. It seemed to take forever to get his feet back under him. Caldwell had returned to stand purposefully over Charlie.

"He's gonna kill Doc!" Mike cried. "Sid, don't let him do it!"

At the touch of her fingers on his arm, the alien turned huge glimmering black eyes on Sidney. His nostrils fluttered and whistled.

"To the human mind, the Ral seem cruel," he said gently. "But even we do not leave *il'ral* in such pain. Animals are not left to suffer slow deaths."

Mike rushed to Sidney's side. "You can heal him, Sid. Just like you healed me."

"She didn't heal you, *mirik'ee,*" John answered. "She ordered you to heal yourself, and because you believed in your mate, you obeyed." He gestured at Charlie. "This is not a cut cheek. Do you truly believe he can repair such damage? He's not *mirik'im.*"

"It doesn't matter." Desperation made the deputy's voice quaver. "I'll take him. I'll find help. He doesn't need two arms and legs to watch football and drink beer." He looked at Sidney. "Let me try . . . please."

The young woman's face was impassive. "No, Mike,

your place is with us. Johncaldwell's right. We can't allow *il'ral* to suffer."

"This is Charlie!" Mike shrieked at her. "Not some animal!" He grabbed her by the shoulders and shook her hard. "Forget *il'ral*, forget *ta'mirik*. You're Sidney Bowers, and this is the doc we're talking about—the guy who risked everything to come back and help us."

"Mirik'i," Sid muttered at John, and the alien caught Mike's wrists and dragged him back. She stared down at the mangled body. "Charlie isn't *mirik'im*, but he's still my responsibility. Go away, both of you. Guard until I call you."

"No," Mike moaned, disbelieving, as Caldwell forced him toward the schoolroom's back door.

V

With care, Sid removed the outer trappings of her humanity, her jeans and shirt and boots, until nothing remained but the *in'al*. Cold air found its way through the sleek black garment, but her body stayed warm. Charlie lay pale and unknowing on the hard floor. His life's blood leaked slowly from the massive wounds, and his breath came labored, harsh. Even unconscious, the agony made his eyelids twitch.

Someone other than Sidney Bowers sat down beside him and gathered his upper torso tenderly in her arms. *Ta'mirik.* In some strange way, Charlie Downing was one of her children, too—her mate, her brother—and so his death would not be *il'ral'im*. She slid the knife from its forearm sheath and caught Charlie's chin firmly with her left hand, tilting his head back.

The sharp edge cut through the skin, deep and deeper, until the jugular vein opened wide and hot blood gushed. Sid dropped the blade and bent to press her forehead to his. White light flared.

"The pain is gone, Charlie. Forever lost," she told him. "Come with me. Dream."

The dreams were fleeting, but time slowed in this place. Her hand in his, she brought him to the Ral world, then even farther, into realms of beauty and color that she had no idea existed in her mind. They watched galaxies form, saw the gaseous birth of stars. He stared at it all in silent awe, eyes filled with joyful tears. Finally, she brought him back to his own world, to a familiar reclining chair before a familiar big screen television. Warm desert sunlight beamed through the RV's windows.

"The game's about to start," Sid whispered and placed a cold bottle of beer in his right hand.

Charlie watched the players run onto the field, then smiled up at her, iron gray hair mussed, eyes peaceful. "Australian football's my favorite."

"I know."

His image faded from the chair, and she found herself alone in dream. Chest tight, Sid woke with Charlie dead in her arms. Blood covered the floor. How could so much blood be in so small a body, she wondered. The *ta'mirik* stood. A remembered song came to her, though the words were twisted by her blunt human tongue. Keening, she pulled the *nom'ng* and set its wide beam on the body, then watched Charlie's features darken and char and turn to dust.

VI

Empty desert stretched around them, quiet and wind-blown. Only an occasional puff of dark smoke seen between the buildings reminded Mike of the helicopter attack. Now the skies were clear, the afternoon drifting toward evening. John Caldwell sat close to him on the playground's rusting merry-go-round within a large fenced sandbox behind the school. Every little while the tall alien gave a push with one foot so that the old machine creaked and turned, reminding Mike of his childhood here.

But those memories were brief. "She can't do it," he told himself dully. "Not Sid."

"She does as she must," John answered, his eyes on the horizon. "Why do you fight what is, *mirik'ee?* Accept."

"Accept nothing, asshole,". Mike snarled. "We're human, Sid and me. *Il'ral.* Animals."

"No. We three are bonded, *mirik'im* always."

"She won't kill the doc."

Caldwell tilted his head, listening. "Charles Downing is already dead. She sings his death song even now. She honors him as she would honor one of us." His black eyes considered Mike. "You're confused and troubled, second husband. If there is time, we'll dream again, and you'll remember what you are."

Furious, Mike pushed himself upright and started away, but John snagged his arm and hauled him back. "She'll call for us when she's ready."

"Let her call. I don't plan to be here." He tried to shrug John's clawed fingers off. "If the bitch can kill Charlie, then I don't want any part of her."

In a lightning move, Caldwell's hand caught the deputy by the throat, his claws sinking into the flesh. "You will not speak or think of her in such a manner. You are *mirik'ee* now, and you belong to her, even as I do." His fingers loosened. "The female of our species is short-lived. She is forbidden to form a *mirik'im* until she has produced a litter of young, otherwise our race would have died out long ago. Her instincts drive her to protect us at all costs. Do you understand?"

"No," Mike growled.

"Some *mirik'im* survive battle, but never the *ta'mirik.* Those males who outlive their wife return to the *hol'al,* where the children are raised. In time, they become elder dreamers and guide the Ral. Their lives are long and so is their sorrow. No one ever forgets the love and devotion of his *ta'mirik*—however fleeting."

John Caldwell bowed his great head. "By making Sidney my *ta'mirik,* I have destroyed her chances of bearing a litter. She will die without passing on her courage and strength.

"There will be nothing of her in the *hol'al.* Should we live, there'll be nothing but our memories of her. Her line will be lost forever."

That familiar sense of dread had returned to Mike. "Sidney is human, damn you."

"Is she?" Caldwell drew a fluting breath of air. "Love

her, Mike Nichols. Obey and please her in all things. I see her changing moment by moment. She leaves what she once was behind and becomes the fierce warrior wife. She is our *ta'mirik,* and her life will not be a long one."

There Sidney was now, a black shadow on the back steps of the school building, beckoning them. The late sun had taken on a reddish hue that colored the white walls behind her and turned her dark blond hair a soft auburn. Despite her alien detachment, despite the dark-circled eyes and drawn features, despite all she'd done, Mike still couldn't imagine anyone more beautiful than this woman. Charlie was dead, and that made his chest ache, but Sid was alive, and that managed to cancel much of the pain. It didn't matter what John Caldwell said. Somehow, someway, Mike would keep Sidney safe from harm.

Chapter Fourteen

AVERY SANDS WENT away for a short while, though it felt like ages to Nate before the door opened again.

"So tell me more," Sands said conversationally, and seated himself once more by the bed.

Nate groaned. "I told you everything."

"Not everything, I think."

"What about my people?"

"I've done what I can for the moment, Sergeant. Now we wait."

"Wait, hell. I want out of here," Nate snapped. "I want my clothes and a ride back to Mojave Wells. If I can just get close enough to talk with Sidney . . . to make her understand."

"Why Sidney?"

"Because she's running the whole show. Both John Caldwell and Mike Nichols will do anything she says. It's the way the Ral run things—with females in charge. Threesomes—two male, one female."

"A triumvirate," Sands said thoughtfully. "How did the deputy and the woman end up connected with Caldwell like that?"

"I'm not sure. The whole business is so bizarre. Caldwell isn't human anymore. Ugliest damn thing you ever laid your eyes on and dangerous as hell—yet, there's something . . . compelling about him." Nate drew himself up short. "Look, Sands, you've been kind, but I don't know you, and I'm not really sure I can trust you."

Avery Sands's lips twisted into a wry smile. "I generally instill more faith in people. Look, the major says no way you can leave here." He held up a hand when Nate drew an angry painful breath. "But you're going, only you're gonna be one sorry son of a bitch if you leave that bed."

"It can't hurt any more than it already does."

"Wanna bet?" Now Avery grinned, and that made him look about seventeen. "We can't leave just yet. There's a visitor on the way, one I think you'll be happy to see. So tell me more while we wait. Tell me all you know about Caldwell's boxes."

Nate shook his head. "I don't know that much, and a little bit of knowledge is a dangerous thing."

"No knowledge could be deadly. Come on, Curtis. What little you've said has already scared the shit out of me."

For a long moment, Nate Curtis studied the man's open youthful face, his guileless brown eyes. It seemed impossible for Avery Sands to be working for the government. Trust was something Nate had little of, and honest men were hard to find, but Sands was his only hope in this whole tangled mess. Reluctantly, the sergeant repeated what Caldwell had said about the gate and how it was powered, and now Sands seemed to age as he listened.

"I'm a scientist," he said finally, heavily, "a physicist, but you're moving in realms that I can't even begin to follow. The mass of a sun in a tiny box? How can that possibly be? Could he have meant the energy of a sun? But even that's beyond belief."

"The fact that he exists is beyond belief. He said it would be difficult to explain everything in terms that I could understand. But it has a lot to do with gravity."

Sands frowned. "Gravity. Mass ... Science believed that gravity was the result of the distortion of space by mass—that it sent out energy waves, like ripples on a large galactic pond." Brows furrowed, he pondered. "Imagine the fabric of space-time stretched across the universe—each mass creating dips and depressions in that fabric that eventually smoothed out with distance. The heavier the mass, the deeper the hole. And the ultimate mass would create a rip in the fabric of space-time—a black hole.

"But there's something else involved with these boxes, if the Ral have found a way to trap that kind of mass. There's a balance to everything in nature—or so we believe. Black holes pull everything within their gravitational reach into them, including light. Theory has it that that light and mass go *somewhere*, that at the far side of a black hole is a white hole.

"If the boxes both draw energy and emit it, then the Ral may be using both black and white holes to control the distortion of space-time. Lord, it sounds like science fiction, but that's the only possible explanation I can come up with.

"We really have no physical evidence that black holes even exist—as anything other than visible anomalies." The man's eyes widened suddenly. "My God, if the Ral have the technology to tame black and white holes—That's got to be it! The ultimate displacement of space, a gateway to anywhere—maybe even *anywhen*."

Nate, who had followed very little of that speech, said innocently, "So, what happens if you drop just a little atom bomb on those boxes?"

"Mary, Mother of God," Avery Sands muttered and crossed himself. The thought amused Nate—religion, politics, and science, all rolled up into one contradictory young man.

"If we had the boxes, we'd have the universe," Avery said just as fervently, a moment later.

"Or destroy the world," the sergeant reminded him. "Face it, Sands. This is a no-win situation. Blow the boxes and we blow ourselves. Open the gate and all John Caldwell's friends will move in on us. The Ral don't believe in sharing. To them, we're animals. There's only one thing we can do . . ."

Avery looked up. "What?"

"Take those damn boxes and drop them in the deepest ocean around."

"But we'd lose so much. This is technology so alien

that we may never discover it on our own—not in a million years."

"So let's be happy with what we've got! Let's take care of what we've got, and stop inviting folks from the other side of the galaxy over for dinner. Blind trust is a dangerous thing, too."

Someone knocked on the door, and Sands jumped in his chair. "Shit. It's our visitor. Come on in, fellas."

Pudgy-faced Captain Kern entered first, escorted on either side by an MP.

"I don't want to see that bastard," Nate growled.

"What the hell's going on, Sands?" Kern demanded, round face flushed with anger.

Avery stood up, shoulders slumped, hands jammed in his pockets. "We seem to have a problem, Captain. My orders have gotten a little . . . distorted somewhere along the line of command. I had a talk with Corporal Estavas. He says he was told to shoot on sight, and to shoot to kill."

"Well, he's mistaken," Kern snapped, a little too quickly. "He misunderstood. Or maybe his sergeant did. I passed on the orders that came through Major Conners word for word. Capture at all cost, and shoot for protection only. It was Curtis's fault. He went after the corporal, and Estavas had to defend himself."

"Bullshit!" Nate grunted.

"Easy," Sands told him and turned his attention back on the captain. "You've been kissing all the right asses, all along, Kern. Including mine—just to keep yourself smack in the middle of all this. In fact, you've got ass-kissing down to an art, and, Mister, I've had mine kissed by some of the best." Avery's smile was grim, but Kern only grew angrier. "I don't know exactly what you're after, but it's probably a fast ride up through the ranks, maybe even a presidential appointment. I've a good mind to break you, Mister—"

Another knock at the door pulled Sands up short. "Come," he said irritably.

A young soldier ducked inside with a many-folded

piece of paper which he thrust into Avery's hand. "Sir! From Colonel Harris, sir."

Sands opened the page and scanned the numerous paragraphs of type. In the time it would have taken Nate to read the first line, Avery'd finished, the message crumpled tight in his fingers.

"Gentlemen, please take Captain Kern to the stockade. I'm sure the corporal will enjoy his company."

Kern reared up, snarling, even as the MPs directed him to the door. "This is an outrage. You have no right to hold me! You can't prove any wrongdoing." Then the door closed on them.

"Any reply, General Sands?" the messenger asked.

"Tell the major we'll be there directly."

"Yes, sir." The boy snapped a salute, did a neat reverse on one boot toe, and left the room.

Nate was still swallowing his own shock. "You lied, you bastard. You said you weren't military."

"It was a half-truth. I'm army reserve."

"You're a fucking general . . ."

"So I just found out," Avery said and waved the paper under Nate's nose. "It hardly matters now. We've got fatalities."

"Who?" Fear made the sergeant's heart pound.

"A helicopter went down. All six aboard were lost. That's Kern's doing, the SOB. I thought you said Caldwell didn't have any weapons?"

"He doesn't. . . . Just the boxes."

"That chopper was shot down—or rather melted down. One of your people took it out with a black rifle of some sort, a goddamn alien ray gun." Avery had been pacing, and now he stopped dead. "Wait here."

"Where are you going?"

"To get us some clothing. I've got to make a quick call to Washington, then you and I are going to try to save what we can of the situation."

II

Sidney sat in the shattered glass from the school windows, her back to the wall, Mike beside her. John had left them alone on her orders, gone to retrieve the black boxes from the Winnebago. An internal numbness had descended on her, and her *mirik'ee,* in desperate need of comfort, remained neglected. She felt his shoulder tight against hers and found no comfort for herself, either.

Charlie was no more, and his face, his voice, had vanished from her memories, just as Nate Curtis's had. Occasionally Mike would send quick glances at the blackened flooring with its heap of fine gray dust, then she'd feel him shiver. A second husband was always the least self-assured, yet somehow the most stable—his sensitivity brought balance and accord to the *mirik'im.*

John returned silently, unnoticed in the fading afternoon light until he hunkered down before them. The boxes were set on the floor at Sidney's feet.

"Shall I wake the Gatekeeper, *ta'mirik?*"

"Yeah, sure. Call the genie," Mike muttered dully.

"No." Sidney shifted her *pa'ng* to her left hand, its black barrel pointed toward the ceiling. "I want you to repair the second box, John."

Johncaldwell hissed. "It is already done."

"When?" Sid asked, shocked.

"The night after we returned from Avawatz . . . while you slept. A simple thing, easily done."

"When you trashed my Jeep," Mike accused.

Sid put her free hand on John's arm. "Why didn't you tell me?"

"Because it was done without your permission, *ta'mirik.* It was wrong. I thought only of myself, of escape."

"I should have let you go then." Sidney closed her eyes. "In trying so hard to make the best choices, I've managed to make all the worst ones. It's time for you to leave, Johncaldwell. It's time to open the gate."

"No!" Mike cried. "Sid, you're forgetting why you didn't have him open it in the first place. The Ral. He'll lead the Ral back here." He glared at John. "Go on, tell her. Tell her what you'll do."

Johncaldwell shrugged. "I am Ral, *mirik'ee*. How can I be other than what I am?"

"See?" the deputy growled in exasperation. "Open the gate and it's the end of mankind."

"Is that so terrible?" Sid murmured softly, amazed at the sense that made. "All things end. Even the Ral will perish in time. It makes little difference."

John's great dark eyes seemed to swallow her, and a pain started deep inside. He would return to his people, and she would find herself alone. Even more alone than she'd been before, hopelessly caught between their worlds. Mike would survive. Still so firmly human, he'd forget his *mirik'im*, but not Sidney.

She dropped the rifle and flung her arms around Johncaldwell's neck, pressing her cheek to his cool alien face. "I'd go with you, *mirik'i*. First husband."

"Only Ral may pass through the gate." Fingerpads touched her brow. "And they would never accept *il'ral*. No, wife. Let me stay here and fight. I would rather die with you."

"Let him stay," Mike said, clutching his own *pa'ng*. "We can't possibly win, but we can sure do some damage before we're done."

"And leave the boxes in human hands," Sid reminded him. She pulled back from John. "No, *mirik'i*. You have to leave, but try to remember what you once were, then close this particular gate behind you—for good. Can you do that?"

Johncaldwell's head tilted. "No, *ta'mirik*. Even if I disable the gate, the Ral will repair it. You must close the gate from this side."

"And leave the boxes for mankind to experiment with," Sidney muttered.

"I'll show you a way to remove the lenses and make the gate inoperable, but the power will still be there—the danger."

"Then somehow we'll hide them. Perhaps Nate's idea is the best, after all." Sid took a deep breath. "Go, Johncaldwell. Open the gate. Join the Ral and never return."

The air around them grew suddenly charged. A great gust of wind shook the walls, then came a crack of thunder and the roar of jet turbines.

"Jesus!" Mike yelled, leaping to his feet.

They could see the glow of afterburners as a jet veered up and over the hills to the east. Another followed close behind.

"Hurry!" Sid called to John, but already both aircraft had turned in the distance, headed back, higher now. The first launched its missiles, one from under each wing, and their screaming descent nearly deafened her. They struck at nearly the same instant. Mojave Wells's tiny housing tract at the north end of town turned to light and fire, while the schoolhouse floor reared under their feet.

Johncaldwell grabbed Sidney's left wrist and stabbed a claw into the hole in the cuff. She felt the material liquify again, rushing up over her face to cover nose and mouth, eyes and ears. At first there came a suffocating sensation, then she remembered the touch of air through the body of the armor and drew a deep breath. Her senses still worked, hearing—even sight, though not as her eyes might see. Beside her, Mike had become a midnight figure, limned in a strange faint glow, and there beyond the windows, where the conflagration raged, she could discern in one swift glance the range of temperatures—Kurlian hues that danced and flared with varying intensity.

Then the second jet boomed past, a light trail streaming behind it. It swung back toward them and loosed its missiles as well.

"Down!" Johncaldwell shouted, and they dropped to the floor as the world disintegrated around them.

The *in'al* deflected the heat and much of the flying debris, but to lie at the center of such a firestorm terrorized Sidney. Only Johncaldwell's fingers tight around her arm kept her from tumbling away under the force of the blast.

He had somehow found a grip on an exposed floor joist. But Mike . . . Where was Mike?

The fury died back, leaving them still immersed in flame, and Sidney dragged herself upright. Every bone felt bruised, every joint throbbed from concussion. The school building had been leveled, and the street beyond was now a deep ragged crater filled with fire.

"Mike!" she cried over the crackling blaze. "Mike!"

No answer came. Johncaldwell dug through the remains of the building's front wall and recovered the boxes and all three of the *pa'ng'im*. Sidney, with careful steps, searched the rubble for Mike, refusing to think him dead.

"Here!" John called from behind her.

The explosion had thrown the deputy beyond the back wall, buried him under shattered wood and plasterboard. Worse yet, a heavy roof beam had pinned him from shoulder to hip.

"The *in'al* doesn't make us invulnerable, after all," Sid said as John uncovered the unconscious man.

"No, *ta'mirik*—only much more difficult to kill."

"Is he alive?"

Johncaldwell looked up, lipless mouth quirked in a smile. "Yes. Our husband is strong."

Thick smoke obscured the evening sky, but the sound of the jets drew Sidney's attention westward. They were high, caught in the light of the setting sun, speeding away. A sudden rage filled her. Mojave Wells lay in ruins. These creatures had attacked without provocation, they had destroyed Charlie, and possibly taken her *mirik'ee* from her as well. Now, certain of their victory, the aircraft sped home.

She snapped the rifle to her shoulder—so much easier to sight using the *in'al* vision—and tugged all three triggers. The trailing jet rolled to the left, one spin, two, then came apart in midair, oddly without its fuel igniting. Something shot outward from the wreckage and dropped earthward. A parachute opened to break the fall of the pilot.

The first jet's course grew erratic, but even at so great a distance, even in the midst of evasive maneuvers, Sidney

followed easily, the *in'al* and the *pa'ng* helping her track
her target. This time there was no escape for the pilot. The
craft exploded in a brilliant flash of white light, and coldly,
Sid turned the rifle on the man beneath the gently dropping parachute. He struggled briefly, then was still. By the
time the chute found the earth, nothing remained of the pilot but charred bones.

"Bastards . . ." The deaths of the enemy brought an
ecstasy she'd never known, a rush to Sidney's head that almost made her weak.

"Kicked ass, huh?" the deputy said weakly, his eyes on
her, filled with pain and concern.

John had carried Mike away from the building, out into
the cool sand where Sidney stood. He'd removed both
their face and hand armor, and Sid held out her wrist so he
could disengage hers as well.

"Are you all right?" she asked, and dropped to her
knees beside Mike, noticing his white drawn face.

"I think my back's broken."

"Oh, God. Nichols, you're such a klutz. What can we
do?" Sid looked at John, but he made that strange sideways nod.

"Dream, *ta'mirik.* I'll guard."

"But a broken back," she said in panic.

Johncaldwell laid a hand on her shoulder. "You should
know a thing, my wife. Your dream powers are stronger
than the Rals'. Even the Gatekeeper knows this." He
stared at her. "There are limits, but you can do no more
than try."

Mike waited in pain. She leaned down to kiss his lips
briefly, then touched her forehead to his. Warm sunlight
and birdsong greeted them immediately with the soft
scents of pine and green grass, the sounds of rushing water. Mike's meadow spread away to distant mountain
peaks.

"You remembered," the deputy muttered.

Sidney ignored the comment, her mind on other matters. "I want you to let go of the pain, Mike. Right now.
Give it up." She closed her eyes, a vision of him deep in
her mind. "This isn't just your back. There're ribs broken

on the right side, and some internal bleeding. Start there first and repair the damage."

"Sid." There was doubt in his voice. "I don't think I can . . . this time. Charlie couldn't be helped. This is almost as bad."

"What?" she demanded, angry. "I haven't told you to think, only to obey. The doc was far worse. Now do this for me, *mirik'ee!* Remember the wound on your face. Remember how it felt as it closed and healed.'"

Mike brought a hand to his injured side, and even in dream, the movement brought agony, a strangled sound from his throat.

Sidney gazed down on him grimly. "Try, husband. If you can't function—if you can't end your pain—I'll be forced to end it for you as I did for Charlie."

His pale gray eyes widened with understanding, then came fear and anger. Good. Sid stood up, arms crossed, and strode away from him, across the sweet grasses of the dream meadow. Tiny creatures, field mice perhaps, tunneled away through the thick sedges, scattering ripe, heavy seed heads as they went. Above, great white clouds puffed and scudded before the wind. Yes, her dream powers were strong. Peace and beauty lay on every hand, but it hardly touched her.

She hadn't lied to Mike. They couldn't leave him to suffer or fall into enemy hands. Among the trees, a small bubbling rill halted her, and she settled on the stony narrow bank, mind emptied, to watch minnows flash silver in the sun. In time, she heard his quiet footsteps on pine needles, then his arms closed around her from behind.

"Satisfied?" he murmured in her ear.

She let his strong hug fill her with pleasure. "Yes." His lips nibbled on her lobe next, and his hands found her breasts, stroking them through the *in'al.*

Abruptly Sidney let the dream go. Acrid smoke replaced fresh mountain air, and fire shadows danced around them.

"Damn," the deputy grunted from where he still lay on the sand.

Johncaldwell squatted nearby, his rifle across his lap. "He's better, I think."

"Just fucking dandy," Mike muttered, dragging himself upright. "Now what?"

Sidney noted the slight drunken sway, but the man was definitely better.

"Now," she said, "we open the gate."

"Perhaps not yet." John pointed a long clawed finger to the west where the barest opalescent glow of sunset survived on the rim of the Shadow Mountains. Well to the left, flame still flickered in the wreckage of a jet, and smoke boiled away in the wind.

"What?" Sid demanded.

"Machines. They began while you dreamed. Big machines, moving toward us across the desert."

"We'll hurry then."

The Ral motioned with a hand. "They've stopped."

A high-pitched whistle began, growing louder as some unseen thing or things approached in the air above them.

"Damn!" Mike shouted over the shrill clamor. "Mortar fire!" And the first barrage struck.

III

"What took you so long?" Nate snarled.

Avery Sands threw a bundle of khaki clothes on the bed. "Finding something to fit a man your size." He, himself, was already in fatigues with inauspicious gold stars on either shoulder. "I matched the boots to your shoe soles. Let's get you out of here before Major Byre catches wind of what we're up to." He pulled the IV gently from Nate's hand and jammed a less than sterile thumb against the puncture.

Nate stared at the clothing across his legs. "There're lieutenant's bars on the shirt."

"No civilians on this run, Mister."

"I think they frown on impersonating officers."

"I just drafted and commissioned you. All right? Jesus, Curtis, you're a pain in the ass. We'll tell 'em you're my XT expert."

"Hey!"

Major Byre had already found them out. With the middle-aged nurse for reinforcements, he stormed into the hospital room, white coat aflutter.

"Sands, you're going to kill this man."

"Back off, Byre," Avery said. "Either help me get him dressed or get the hell out." He caught the nurse's eye. "You got any little pills around here that'll keep the sarge ... the lieutenant ... on his feet for the next few hours?"

She looked at the doctor, who gritted his teeth and nodded, sending her from the room. Nate gritted his own teeth as the two men helped him upright on the bed. The pants were bad enough, but donning the shirt brought tears to his eyes.

"Hey," he said breathlessly to Byre. "The helicopter that went down ... Do you know who was in it?"

The major's face went blank. "Why?"

"Just tell me. Was Corporal Lehman on board?"

"God, no. That was a combat craft. She's on the medical evacuation team."

Nate sighed heavily and noticed Sands giving him an odd appraising stare. All that mattered, though, was that little brown-haired gal was OK. The nurse returned while Sands laced up the boots. She backed in, towing a wheelchair with packets stacked on the seat.

At Nate's frown, she snapped, "You'll damn well ride while you can." A small brown pill bottle was pressed into his hand. "One every three hours. No more than that, you hear? And *no* alcohol."

Avery Sands laughed at that. The nurse had brought a sling for Nate's left arm, one that strapped front and back like half a straitjacket. There were bandages, too.

"In case the bleeding starts again." She was angry, concerned. "Men are such fools."

"And women are so wise," Avery answered with sincerity, then, quickly, kissed the lady on the lips. That ran her out of the room for good, mumbling and red-faced. They helped Nate into the chair, a half-assed lieutenant in a rumpled uniform.

"Be careful, for God's sake," Major Byre said as he let them out the door.

"What's the speed limit in these halls?" Sands called back, already in motion.

The general hardly slowed for the corners, and the draft felt cold against Nate's cheeks. They turned down a last corridor and banged out through double doors into icy desert evening.

"General, sir!"

The daylight faded quickly, and in the heavy dusk, Nate made out the tall man standing near them on the cracked pavement. On a grassy concourse across a narrow parking lot, there sat a monster helicopter. Their exit from the building had been a signal, and now the twin turbine engines began to whine, the double blades above began a slow turn, gaining speed.

"Shit," Avery hissed. "I forgot jackets. We'll freeze our butts off up there. Sergeant, find us some flight jackets, quick."

"Yes, sir." The man dashed away toward another building.

General Sands wheeled Nate over the rough ground, as recklessly as before, only now there was considerable pain involved. The bay door on the chopper waited, open and wide and dark.

"Easy!" Avery growled when arms reached down to help Nate up inside.

He was guided to a seat in the darkness and a heavy helmet plunked unceremoniously on his head. The jackets were handed up and Nate struggled his one good arm into a sleeve, grateful for the thick material.

"Harness him in, damn it! He can't do it himself!" Sands shouted.

The thunder of the engines through the open door was muted by the helmet, and there were voices in Nate's right ear—the pilot speaking with someone in the bay. The door was slammed shut, leaving them with only a dim reddish light to see by. Everyone settled into their places, and Nate made a quick head count. Five, including himself and Sands. He also noticed the minigun bolted to the flooring near the starboard door. No time to worry about it though. The ship launched skyward. His stomach bottomed out, and the blood rushed from his head to his feet.

"You OK?" Avery asked, a tiny voice inside Nate's empty head.

He found himself slumped forward against the harness ... drooling, for shit's sake. Embarrassed, the new lieutenant wiped his mouth with a sideways glance at Sands, there in the next seat.

"How long will this trip take?" he managed.

"Mojave Wells ETA, ten minutes. I've instructed the pilot to hang at two thousand feet about a mile out."

"Why so far?"

"Because I want a good look at the situation first." Avery was silent a moment. "I haven't been able to get in touch with Harris."

"The colonel? Why not?"

Another long silence. "He's unavailable, for some reason. But I have my suspicions. To him, I'm still Avery Sands, presidential adviser and all around busybody. He's an old war dog, and he takes dead soldiers very personally."

"The downed chopper? Harris knows, doesn't he ... what's really ... "

Sands hissed into his mike. "This isn't a secure channel, Lieutenant. He knows. But everyone's got a secret agenda, Curtis. *Everyone.*"

"Even you?"

Avery's answer turned to static, and when it cleared, the general demanded, "Come again, Lieutenant Holmes?"

"You better get up to the cabin, sir. Right away."

"Don't say any more." Sands hit the breakaway buckles on his harness, but when Nate fumbled for his, the man pushed him back. "Stay here, damn it." He moved gracelessly across the shuddering floor to the forward ladder and climbed out of sight.

Sometime soon after, Nate's helmet speaker crackled and went dead—communications neatly cut off. Everyone has a secret agenda, Sands had said. The pain and the equipment-cluttered walls closed in on Nate suddenly. He felt caught up in a whirlwind, swept far beyond any sense of reality. Strangers. They'd been strangers to him only days ago, pieces of an interesting puzzle, and yet now he knew he couldn't give them up without a fight. Not even John Caldwell, tall gaunt alien creature.

The vibration of the engines seemed to grind through him. He missed the damned hospital bed, of all things. At least it sat still. What the hell was Sands doing up there? But the headphone crackled back to life in Nate's helmet, then a pair of boots appeared on the top rung of the ladder, and Avery descended into the bay.

"Open the door," his voice called. "This one," and pointed to the one closest to Nate's seat.

Someone jumped to obey, and ice cold wind rushed in. Sergeant Curtis felt nothing, noticed nothing beyond the red and yellow glow of fires on the desert far below. Sands, fighting the wind, found his seat.

"Mojave Wells," he said, the bleakness in his voice apparent even through the helmet's tiny speaker. "Harris called in a pair of air force jets, and they laid a few Side-winder missiles into the town. Your friends took out the jets as they were leaving—from over a mile away."

"They're still alive, then."

"Were, anyway. Harris's company's been lobbing mortars at them ever since, along with some tank fire."

Even now, Nate could see puffs of brighter light flowering among the fiery wreckage of the town. "Stop him!"

"I'm sorry, Nate, but I have to agree with Harris. This has gone too far. There are too many casualties. Damage control is going to be a nightmare as it is. We can't use nuclear weapons to sterilize the area, but it has to be sterilized."

Nate grabbed Sands's wrist with his good right hand. "You mean kill them?"

"Curtis, your friends have changed. They're shooting down helicopters and jets—"

"Who shot at them first! I can stop them if you'll just take me in there."

"And get us shot down, too?"

"Then set this chopper down here and let me out. I'll walk in."

Avery's laugh was anything but humorous. "You can hardly stand, let alone walk."

"I could make it in a Jeep."

The helmet crackled with empty static for a while, then, "Lieutenant Holmes, head for the colonel's field HQ, top speed."

"Thanks," Nate muttered, exhausted.

Chapter Fifteen

THE MORTAR FIRE drove them away from town, out into the desert to the west and directly toward the enemy. But then, the enemy lay in any direction they might go. Mike watched the night with the *in'al* vision, something close to infrared, yet not. Mostly he saw three-dimensional outlines of things—brush, rocks, yucca plants, and Joshua, and he stumbled some at first until his mind began to make connections with what the vision showed him.

Sidney insisted on leading them, slender glowing lines just ahead. There'd be the better part of a half-moon later, but not this early, which was actually to their advantage. He knew the enemy had night vision, too, sophisticated Starlight scopes with which to track them, and wondered if the *in'al* might be hiding them. The mortar fire had so far remained concentrated on Mojave Wells.

Beside him, John Caldwell moved with his strange sinuous stride over rough terrain that shuddered continually under the impact of the shells. The black boxes were held snug in one arm, his rifle held in the opposite hand. Mike set one foot in front of the other mostly out of reflex. Exhaustion dogged his steps, and sharp twinges of pain continued to radiate from his spine just below the neck. The ribs ached too, but to a much lesser degree.

When Caldwell left them, he wondered, would the marvelous ability to dream disappear with him? Or was it as Sidney had suggested? That mankind had always had the ability without realizing it. Either way, the deputy felt certain that John Caldwell's transformation had transformed them all, and that these were somehow irrevocable changes. The thought depressed him utterly. His stomach

225

growled, empty for far too long, but the adrenaline kept his teeth on edge, producing a sense of energy.

"Here," Sidney said in the darkness, her voice barely heard over the whistle-scream of flying mortars high above them. She had paused in a sandy depression that hid them from any eyes to the west. "Rest, *mirik'im.*"

John set the boxes down, then settled next to them. Sid made herself comfortable as well, and Mike, groaning, sat beside her.

"Can we take this stuff off our faces now?" he asked irritably and held a wrist out to Caldwell.

The Ral complied at Sid's nod. For a moment after, Mike felt blind, his eyes adjusting slowly to the starlight—and the firelight well behind them. They must be about halfway between the town and the opposing forces. This seemed to be no-man's-land, and somewhere ahead, soldiers launched the mortars. Their constant *thump-whoosh-shriek* made the deputy's eardrums ache.

"How long?" Sidney asked above the racket. "How long to open the gate?"

Caldwell considered that, his face turned toward her, his enormous eyes reflecting the yellows, reds, and golds of Mojave Wells. "It should take no more than a few minutes."

"I want you to take all the weapons and armor with you. They don't belong here any more than you do."

Mike felt a touch of panic. Never mind, they'd be forced to walk naked out of the high desert on a winter night. To give up the weapons, though—their only power and protection—was insane. He clutched the *pa'ng* possessively, afraid to speak his mind. Sidney looked around her.

"Is there room enough here?"

"Yes," John answered.

"Mike and I better leave, then."

"There's no danger, *ta'mirik,* when both poles of the gate are activated. Stay. It is a marvelous thing to witness."

Sidney nodded, her hands folded on her knees. Mike had no such faith in alien things, but he remained. For a long moment, Caldwell considered the boxes, then rose to carry the first along the lower edge of the depression. He searched the ground carefully until something that suited him was found, and knelt to scoop away the sand.

The deputy saw dark porous rock underneath, and to this John secured the first box. The second was carried only three paces from the first—three of the Ral's long-legged paces. But the distance had widened another pace by the time he found the needed anchoring rock. At last, he returned to the first and inserted a claw underneath.

A small tingling sensation rippled through Mike. With the awakening of the second box, the tingling became a dull vibration felt even over the ground-shuddering impacts of the mortars. The deputy licked his lips, resisting the urge to run. Raw power washed over and through him. John Caldwell strode back to his *mirik'im.*

"It's ready."

"Then we'll say good-bye," Sidney said, and Mike heard pain in her voice.

When she tried to rise, John's fingers curled around her arm. *"Ta'mirik,* please. One last dream before we part."

"Too dangerous—"

"I'll stand guard," Mike offered, though the thought of them alone in dream together brought its own particular brand of misery. But jealousy seemed so petty.

John Caldwell glanced his way. "No . . . This must be a final dream for our *mirik'im*—for all of us." He turned back to Sidney. "We'll be gone only moments, I promise."

Not happily, she gave her permission, and they gathered close, cross-legged, knees touching, then leaned foreheads together. John's dream, this one. They stood on another cliff overlooking a great black ocean, whose waves and swells remained perfectly still. Stars, hard tiny pinpoints of light, reflected from the water's surface. The ground was scattered with heavy frost crystals that crunched underfoot.

Mike gazed around him. Tall slender growths that might be trees rose on either side of them. He reached to touch the nearest, and it shattered under the pressure of his fingers, falling soundlessly into a heap.

"What is this place?" he demanded and heard the words in his head, not his ears.

John answered, "A world the Ral found long ago. It was much like your Earth. The *il'ral* here were a gentle species that prized what they called 'justice.' They defied us and we took their sun. The Ral have no word or concept for justice."

Took their sun. Mike shivered, staring up at the endless night sky. The crystals underfoot must be this planet's frozen atmosphere.

"Why are you showing us this?" Sidney asked quietly.

The voice that answered was human. "Because this John Caldwell is nearly lost to me." The young man who had driven a wounded old Jeep into Bowers' Garage stood next to them, but the image was distorted somehow—not quite right. "Once the gate separates us, that small bit of humanity left to me will die, and this is what I'll become." He gestured at the world around him. "A destroyer of civilizations. I've made you my *mirik'im* and asked you to love me, but it would be far wiser to fear me."

"I'm your *ta'mirik,*" Sidney reminded him. "You said you'd obey me."

"And I will so far as I can. But the Ral must obey their elders, too, and they will ask about your world. In dream, only truth is spoken. You can shut the gate down and disable it, but even so, we'll find Earth again one day. In time."

Sid looked into the young man's pale face. "Humans aren't like the gentle *il'ral* of this dead world, John. In a lot of ways we're as savage as the Ral, only we've had no way to get off our planet and were forced to be content to kill each other. But we're too clever, too inventive, and we're getting close to leaving Earth. We may even meet you head-on, out there somewhere." She pointed at the stars. "Whatever happens, happens. You told me once that the only purpose of life is death. If that's so, then go to your people, find a new *ta'mirik,* and follow her into battle."

John Caldwell's human eyes were shedding starlit tears, and Mike saw tears in Sidney's eyes as well. Their combined grief dragged at him.

"Sidney!" The shout echoed over the glass-surfaced sea, directionless and urgent. "Mike!"

He turned and turned again, confused by the shadowy alien landscape. The voice wasn't familiar, and neither John nor Sid seemed aware of it.

The deputy stepped between them, between their mutual sorrow. "Get us out of here, quick!" There's someone coming."

II

The helicopter made a dizzying turn in midair, heading away from Mojave Wells. Nate clutched for armrests that weren't there. No one had bothered to close the door, and the rim of the world outside seemed to make impossible shifts of position before the craft finally righted itself. The engines began a deeper throb and acceleration pressed Nate back in his harness.

"Hang in there, Lieutenant," Avery Sands said. "It isn't far."

It wasn't, not for a jet helicopter. Soon, they slammed to a halt in midair, then dropped earthward like a stone. Nate swallowed his heart and watched as bright floodlights came into view. The pilot, despite his crazy acrobatics, set the chopper down gently. Someone came to unstrap Nate, then assisted him to a ground that insisted on swaying for a while yet. Avery had disappeared immediately into the busy crowd that hurried through the field headquarters. There were tents and trucks and equipment in all directions.

"This way, sir," a young private shouted with deference over the chopper's engines and thumping blades. "General Sands said to bring you directly to the command center."

Nate was having trouble staying upright under the downwash of the rotors—a walk of any length just might be beyond him. But the kid led him to a Jeep and helped him in. The short ride hurt, bouncing over the sandy desert floor of the encampment to a tent that looked no different than all the others.

"Get the lieutenant some coffee," Sands ordered as

Nate entered. "And one of those cinnamon rolls. Sit down, Curtis, before you fall down." He turned to the man beside him. "Colonel Harris, this is Lieutenant Nate Curtis. He's the XT expert on my team."

The colonel's nostrils flared slightly. "How the hell do you get to be an expert on XTs? He looks half-dead to me." Nate discounted, the man went back to poring over some maps laid out before him.

Colonel Harris was sixtyish, whip thin with only a faint gray stubble to cover his head, and he didn't look like he had much of a sense of humor. Nate sank into the nearest chair and found that it offered up a view of the radio equipment stacked on other folding tables. Two soldiers in sand-colored cammies worked with microphone and headset. Black coffee and roll arrived.

"Milk and sugar, sir?" asked the helpful private.

"Milk, thanks." Powdered creamer was what he got.

Avery Sands came to lean near, speaking in an undertone. "Take one of those pills with the food. It's going to be a long night."

Nate balked. Rolaids and aspirin were the extent of his drug use, and he didn't like taking even those, but the tough guy attitude wore thin in the face of so much pain. He fished the little plastic bottle from his pocket and dutifully swallowed a pill.

"If you want to take a little drive into the desert tonight, General, I won't stop you," Harris looked up from his maps. The accent on general had been caustic. "There's nothing left alive out there. Guaranteed."

"Then why the hell is the mortar and tank fire still going on?"

The colonel grunted. "Might as well get a little practice in while we're here."

"I want it stopped. Now," Avery said, and when Harris only crossed his arms over his chest, "I'm a scientist and desk jockey, Colonel, but I'm also your superior officer—for the time being. So follow orders, or I'll have the president give them to you direct."

"Call a cease-fire, Sergeant," Harris snarled to one of the radiomen.

It was only in the silence afterwards that Nate realized he'd been listening to faraway thunder all along.

"I want a Jeep, gassed-up and ready to go, outside this tent in five minutes." Sands took a sip of his own coffee and made a face.

Harris shifted uneasily. "My advice, sir, is to wait till morning. In daylight we can spot anything that might still be out there."

Sound advice. The shelling had stopped, but Nate felt a sudden wave of anxiety at the thought of waiting. He didn't want these people finding the *mirik'im* first.

Avery noticed his unease. "Thanks anyway, Harris. I don't think we've got that much time to waste."

"Then I'm sending an escort with you," the colonel said.

Nate's answer to that was sharp. "No." He glanced at Avery. "I don't want us to look like the enemy."

"Curtis," Sands told him, "there isn't much chance of our looking like anything else."

"All I need is a bullhorn. If they hear my voice . . ." He faltered, aware of Harris's full attention on him. "No escort, no weapons. I can do this, Sands. Give me the chance."

"You heard the man, Colonel. Bullhorn, no escort." When Harris started to protest, Avery shook his head. "What are you so worried about? There's nothing alive out there. Guaranteed."

Colonel Harris straightened his shoulders. "If there's a chance I'm in error, and you're killed . . . sir . . . then—"

"The Prez would be pissed," Avery agreed. "But if you disobey my orders, I'll be pissed. Extremely pissed." Even pleasantly spoken, those words carried weight.

"Yes, sir." Harris's face had reddened all the way up into his scalp. He barked orders at the hapless private and sent him running, then stalked from the tent.

Avery Sands grinned at Nate's perplexed expression. "I told you. I've got a nasty reputation."

"And it helps to have friends in high places," Nate added wryly.

"Bullshit; I am in high places. Get much higher than me and you'll get a nosebleed."

Despite the pain, Nate chuckled, then sobered. "Can we trust him not to send anybody after us?"

"We'll discuss that later." Avery sent a quick glance at the radiomen and muttered, "Remember what I said about secret agendas."

The vehicle arrived, and Nate followed Sands out of the tent. The blond scientist climbed behind the wheel while Harris stood tight-lipped near the driver's side door.

"We've got a thirty-square-mile containment area, General. There's a lot of desert out there. Do you have any idea where to search?"

"Do we?" Sands asked Nate who had climbed in beside him with a little help from the private.

"No."

Avery sighed. "It's definitely going to be a long night."

"The bullhorn's in back," Harris said. "And there's a two-way radio under the seat. Call if you get in trouble. We'll be there quick."

"Not too quick," Sands advised, "or I might think you've disobeyed orders." He jammed the idling Jeep in gear.

They lurched forward through the encampment, headed off into the desert toward the distant faint glow that had once been Mojave Wells. The seat belt held Nate secure, but the rugged jolting terrain brought swirling red specks before his eyes.

"Slow down," he managed, loud enough for Sands to hear.

The man geared down. "Sorry." He took the next rise at a more careful pace. "Curtis, you've got to have some idea of where they might be. It won't do us any good to wander in circles the rest of the night."

"Just take me to Mojave Wells ... to the trailer park south of town. That's where ... I last saw them. We ... might be able to pick up a trail from ... there." The words grew labored, too painful to voice. God, the ache in his chest ...

"Well, use the bullhorn while we're at it. Might get lucky."

Nate cursed bitterly, soundlessly. "I don't think ... I can."

Avery Sands brought the vehicle to a halt and reached behind him for the bullhorn. "I'm not sure I can drive and work this thing at the same time. But I'll try."

Would they respond to an unfamiliar voice? That thought worried Nate. They might—with weapons fire—if they were still alive. The Jeep started out again.

"Mike!" Avery bellowed through the horn, fighting the steering wheel with one hand. "Sidney!" He'd slowed even more, perhaps in hopes of a reply. Twice more, he called, then sent the vehicle forward at a faster pace, bearing slightly south of the gutted town.

III

Outside the dream, Mike heard nothing—not even the thunder and blast of the mortars. The night desert, ordinarily filled with myriad nocturnal sounds, lay silent and still.

"I swear I heard someone shouting my name," he mumbled to the others.

"A dream within a dream," suggested Sidney. "At least the shelling's stopped."

John Caldwell, head tipped, stood motionless beside them. "I hear a single small vehicle. There." He pointed south and west of them. Then his great black eyes grew larger. "Someone does call your names, but it's a voice I haven't heard before."

"Come out, come out, wherever you are," Sidney sang, with amusement. "Fat chance. Is it headed our way?"

"No."

She climbed to her feet. "Wish your eyes could see as far as your ears can hear, my love."

"*Ta'mirik,* we can intercept it easily, if you wish. It's moving slowly."

"No sense ..."

Now Mike could identify the grind of a four-wheel

drive. The wind brought the sound, then blew it away again. An odd sense of urgency struck him, overpowering the sense of danger.

"Let's go after it," he said and gripped the *pa'ng* tightly, amazed at his own eagerness, his bloodlust. The longer they put off opening the gate, the longer he would have the alien weapons. "I doubt they'll see us since we're wearing the *in'al*. If it's a trap, we can blow the bastards away."

"The gate . . ." Sidney frowned, unhappy again.

Caldwell uncurled, long spidery limbs and bulbous head framed by a star-filled sky. "The gate will stand whether we return or not, and the universe will be little affected, either way." He bowed his head. "What is your wish, *ta'mirik?*"

"I want you safely off the planet," the young woman growled in irritation.

"Let me know when you've made a decision." Mike used the butt of the rifle to pull himself up, took a quick bearing on the sound of the vehicle, then headed out at a fast dogtrot.

He knew they'd follow. They were meant to be three, a greater strength lay in that number. *Mirik'im.* Three. Three, soon to be two. And those two would find themselves individuals and alone again. The magic circle would be broken, and Sidney would forget her *mirik'ee.* Mike pushed himself harder until the icy air rasped in his lungs. The armor cooled the body, massaged calves and thigh muscles with every forward stride, while the sounds of the vehicle grew nearer.

IV

There was something dark moving beside the Jeep. Maybe. Nate stared with tired, pain-blurred eyes, yet couldn't focus on it.

"Sands," he said finally. "I think there's—"

"Jesus!" Avery shouted and slammed on the brakes at the same time.

At five miles an hour, it wasn't a very painful stop, but

Nate grabbed the edge of the metal dash, gaze trapped by the figure standing in the headlights. A shadow creature, it had no face, no features, and for some reason, that terrified the detective.

"Nate?"

The feminine voice came from beside him, and he found another shadow, its grotesque eyeless head so close to his window that he reared back in horror.

"Nate Curtis!" the one before the vehicle cried joyfully.

"Nichols? What in God's name's happened to you?" Nate pulled even further back from the window, away from the Sidney-creature.

"It's armor. Ral armor. Watch." Mike reached out an arm beyond the headlamp beams, and something black and disgusting slithered away from his face and hands. "Great, huh?"

Nate felt only revulsion. Beside him, Avery Sands hadn't moved, not a muscle, though his mouth hung slightly open. John Caldwell had moved into the light finally, dressed in the same sleek black armor, face and hands uncovered. Those alien eyes, huge and dark, were fixed on the driver of the Jeep, and Nate couldn't tell if it was curiosity or hostility in them.

"Who's he?" Mike demanded, brandishing a long stick-like weapon. "Good guy or bad?"

"So far, good," Nate answered.

"Well, he's toast, otherwise." The deputy offered them a feral grin.

Sands seemed to hear none of their exchange. His attention only on John, he slowly brought a hand up and crossed himself.

"Holy Father, thank you," he muttered and came to life suddenly. "John Caldwell!"

The scientist bounced from the vehicle, circling into the headlights to halt before the alien. Both Mike and Sidney had darted to Caldwell's side, weapons raised, and Nate thought he understood a little, now, the power and strength of the threesome.

"May I see your hand?" Avery asked John, reverence in his voice.

After the slightest hesitation, Caldwell offered him the right one—the left held a black object very much like a pistol. Sands touched the clawed fingers, felt the many joints, almost caressed the tight sallow flesh.

"If only . . ." the man said wistfully. "If only I had a decade to spend with you—what I might learn. There are so many questions you could answer."

"You might not like those answers," Caldwell told him in his strange fluting voice. "But there's no time. My *ta'mirik* has made other decisions."

"Sidney, your *ta'mirik.*" Avery seemed to notice her for the first time. "A matriarchal triumvirate. Mother and wife, all in one. The British, in another age, would've said you've 'gone native,' Sidney. Why is it we human beings are never satisfied with what we are? Always eager to become something else. We mimic, we mirror. Has it helped us or harmed us, do you think? This chameleon-like aptitude?"

The young woman glanced at Nate. "What's wrong with this guy?"

"I think he's in shock," the sergeant answered. "It's impossible to believe until you actually see—"

"Sex!" Avery exclaimed, his hands tented before him, as if in prayer. "How do the Ral procreate? Are two males required for fertilization? Are human and Ral sexually compatible? Have the three of you tried it—"

Mike reared back in offense. "You're one sick son of a bitch."

"No, he's a scientist," Nate said, the words breathless.

Sidney, scornful of Avery's questions, walked away. "What happened to you, Curtis?" She returned to Nate's side of the Jeep. "You don't look well."

"I had a little accident on my grocery run. I got shot."

She peered close. "You're in pain. I might be able to ease it."

As she'd helped Mike with his allergic reaction to Caldwell's claws. Something in her cold blue eyes told Nate to decline. "Thanks anyway. Where's Doc? Did he leave?"

That brought an odd silence, then Sidney smiled. "Yes, he left." The smile faded. "Why are you here, Nate?"

"This guy—Avery Sands—stopped the mortars. He can offer you safe passage out."

"Safe passage to where?"

Sands answered, "Not very far, I'm afraid. I know how Candliss treated you, and there's no excuse for his behavior. He was a renegade and had no real authority, but now he's dead. I'm a presidential adviser—a scientist—but I'm primarily interested in John Caldwell's mind, not tissue samples and brain scans. Though if he'd submit to those tests, it'd be a great help." He glanced at Sidney. "All I have to offer him is life, comfort, and a very small amount of freedom. It's unfortunate, but under the circumstances—"

"Stop," Sidney snapped. "A Ral would prefer death to what you offer. John saved your lives. I saw a military vehicle and wanted to destroy it, but John insisted we look closer. Go away, both of you. You aren't safe with me."

That speech was too gently spoken and all the more frightening because of it. Nate saw the distress in Avery's face.

"Please, I'll do everything within my power to see that you're justly treated. Consider this, what other options do you have?"

Sidney gazed at the man. "I've already told you that death is preferable. But we have an alternative. I'll even let you observe the destruction of the gate, scientist, so you can tell all the others that it is absolutely ended." She walked into the desert.

John Caldwell followed, but Mike lingered behind a moment to speak with Nate.

"John's opening the gate, Sarge. Maybe you should have your friend just take you back. You look like you should be in a hospital, not hanging out in the desert."

Avery still stood in the glare of the headlights, his eyes on the retreating shadowy forms. Nate shook his head.

"I've been in this from the very beginning. Think I'll stick around for the end."

"You should know, Charlie's dead," the deputy said tonelessly. "We sent him off, but he came back. It was the chopper crash. He was . . . in a bad way, we couldn't save him."

Nate felt the raw emotion just under the surface of that empty voice and understood it. "I'm really sorry, Mike. Poor Doc. I'll miss him."

"Me, too."

Mike turned abruptly and trotted into the dark after his team.

"Come on, General," Nate growled to Avery. "Sidney gave you an invitation. Let's go."

Sands climbed behind the wheel once more. "This is all so unbelievable. We've dreamed so long of first contact, and now . . ."

"Me, I'm hoping this is our first and last contact." Nate gripped the edge of his seat with his good hand as Avery swung the vehicle in a tight turn. "We're not ready for visitors. We may never be."

"You're a cynic, Curtis. Growth of any kind is dangerous and painful, but necessary. In the thousands of years since the Ral first visited Earth, we've changed a lot. They must have, too. It's foolish to assume they'll still be hostile."

"And it's crazy to assume they won't be," Nate snapped.

Chapter Sixteen

JOHNCALDWELL SHORTENED HIS stride to match Sidney's. So small and fragile this *ta'mirik,* and yet, a resolute strength emanated from her, a cold determination that not even her internal confusion could counter. His own more simple emotions were held tightly in check. This was her decision, and he would obey. In one way or another, he was bound to lose her.

The night around him smelled of sulphur and nitrates, of woodsmoke and hot plastics and metal, but only faintly. The fires of Mojave Wells were dying back to a ruddy glow in the east. He had been born to this world originally, and yet it appeared alien to him, now. Their *mirik'ee* followed, the deputy's footsteps softened by the sand, while the engine rumble of the military vehicle and the whine of its worn gears made it difficult to discern the lesser noises.

Somewhere ahead, the Gatekeeper waited patiently, that gentle vibration more felt than heard. Sidney felt it, too, for she went unerringly toward that one spot in the desolate desert landscape. A half-moon hung just above the eastern horizon, bringing, finally, a cold blue light. A short time later, they found the gentle depression in the ground and the black boxes still secured to their rocks.

Mike arrived soon after, with Nate and Avery Sands close behind. The scientist parked his Jeep a respectful distance away, but with the headlights pointed directly at the *mirik'im.* John had studied Avery Sands carefully with all his senses, not just eyes and otic nerves. This man was nothing like Quinten Fenwick, neither timid nor terrified by those things he desired most. Sands was in many ways as alien to the human race as Johncaldwell, but used that strangeness, that superior mental strength, to his advantage.

The man climbed from his vehicle now, and with Mike's help, brought Nate Curtis to the edge of the sand bowl and seated him there to witness.

"It's time, Johncaldwell," Sidney said with infinite calm.

She reached out her right wrist for the *in'al* to be removed, but John, with a glance at the others, shook his head.

"Keep the armor, *ta'mirik*. And the weapons. They're your only defense against your human enemies, or against the Ral if they should come through the gate."

Frowning, Sidney accepted John's reasons, but the deputy looked overjoyed, his *pa'ng* hugged close to his chest. Johncaldwell pulled the knife from his arm sheath, and before Sid or Mike could react, chopped the blade hard across the claw on the smallest finger of his left hand. Lightning reflexes let him catch the small object before it could be lost in the sand. He held the sharp, curved nail out to her.

"This is so you can close the gate behind me, and remove the *in'al* when you need to. Or raise the face shield. There's a pocket on your belt to carry it in."

Sidney hesitated, then reached out to take the claw. John showed her where to peel back the black material of the belt and open the little pouch. There were few moments left to them, and Johncaldwell searched for a reason—any reason—to draw those moments out. The glare of the headlights hurt his eyes, and he strode across the ground to the vehicle to search out the switch to turn them off.

In soft blue moonlight, he returned to the others, pausing beside Nate. The man's pain radiated from him, though he kept himself seated straight, his face carefully devoid of internal suffering.

"To the Ral, all *il'ral* are animals," John told the sergeant. "We're taught they have little worth and less intelligence. Yet I've been forced to see the flaw in this logic." He crouched to lay a long-fingered hand on Nate's arm.

"In you, and in Charles Downing—and among my human *mirik'im,* I found great strength and courage. Creatures who think and care and love are not animals. I want to remember you when I leave this world."

Nate managed a wry smile. "I won't forget *you,* John Caldwell."

"Come," John said to Sidney. "I'll show you how to shut down the gate."

"May I watch?" Sands asked.

Sidney lifted her chin. "So you can start them up again? Not a chance. Just stay back. *Mirik'ee.*"

Dutifully, Mike came to block Avery's view as John and Sidney leaned over the first box. Only Nate, seated nearby, had a clear view of their actions. Johncaldwell scooped the sand from beneath the first pole. Its gentle hum tingled through him.

"I insert a claw in the first hole of each end, then in each of the two center holes," he murmured to her. "Like this." He brought her fingers beneath to feel the row of indentations, then pressed a claw tip into each in the proper sequence.

The muted hum became a sudden buzzing, and the box liquified, flowing skyward, until a slender black rod trembled above them—taller than John. Sidney gaped at it, eyes huge.

"Here," Johncaldwell told her. "There is a single claw hole at the base of either side. Use the one nearest you and the gate will close here. The box will re-form. This particular rod is the Gatekeeper's pole, the guidance system. Its box can be programmed to open the gate on other locations. There are special codes involved that even the Keeper doesn't know, but must respond to. I have no knowledge of them either."

He pressed the hole at the base and the rod poured back into its original shape, returning to the quiet hum. "The second hole on either end of the underside will loosen the boxes from their anchors. When the third and seventh holes—again from either end—are pressed, the lid will open." This procedure John demonstrated, and the twisting myriad hairs of colored lights appeared.

Now Sidney gasped. "So beautiful."

"There are tiny lenses that create the curcuits, here between the fins. The clawtip will remove them. This purple lens." John pointed carefully. "If you take this lens from both boxes and throw them away, the boxes are useless—the gate closed, possibly forever. Mankind has no technology or materials capable of reproducing the lenses. Yet." He tilted his head, gazing into her eyes. "Best to hide the boxes, *ta'mirik*. Hide them well."

"Yes," she nodded.

The lid was reclosed, the gate pole re-formed, and John led her to the second box. Regretfully, he initiated the sequence. The rod raced upward to match its mate, only instead of black, this one glowed a radiant white. The buzz became a rumble of raw power. Between the poles, a shimmering silver curtain appeared, mirrorlike, yet transparent, too.

Sidney stepped before it in awe. Her distorted reflection danced in the gate, but beyond that, she saw tall, lithe figures in white gowns gathering to stare back at her. She felt a presence behind her, and expected Johncaldwell, only to see Avery Sands dart toward the curtain.

"No!" she screamed at him at the same time as Mike and Nate.

At the last moment, the man stopped and, seemingly mesmerized, pushed only a hand through the gate. His shriek of agony came instantaneously, and he fell back in the sand, the right hand wrapped tight around the left wrist. The left hand had been translated by the Gatekeeper, and being *il'ral*, had been rejected. Horribly rejected. Sand's shriek turned to strangled sobs. Sidney stood frozen. Even with eyes averted, she could still see in her mind the ugly bloody mass of bone and tissue. Avery's fingers had reversed, pointed back toward his arm, and the skin had been turned inside out, muscles and tendons and blood vessels all visible.

Nate, ill as he was, crawled the short distance to the injured man and wrapped his own jacket over the ruined flesh.

Johncaldwell stood over them. "You should have asked. The gates let nothing but Ral pass through them."

"I had to try," Avery groaned through his tears, "to see if there was any chance to treat with them, communicate with them."

The gathering beyond the curtain had grown, and Sidney felt a touch of panic. These were Ral, numerous huge black eyes watching what transpired beyond the gate. The rippling lines distorted much of her view, but the Ral seemed to be dressed in the white robes of elders, not the *in'al* of the warriors. Still, how long before the warriors would be summoned?

"John!" she called. "Go through. Quickly."

Without question, he obeyed, but she saw in the broad planes of his face misery, loss, even the urge to rebel. Two long-legged strides, and he slipped through the shimmering silver curtain. Beyond it, Sidney watched other black armored Ral appear in the crowd, headed toward Johncaldwell and the gate.

"Sid!" Mike cried, and she dived to the Gatekeeper's rod, fumbling for the claw in her pocket. Her fingers grew clumsy, and the shiny, curved nail nearly fell to the sand, but she got it turned right and found the hole by touch.

The dark pole melted into a simple black box again, and the gate—and Johncaldwell—were gone. She knelt there on the ground, face buried in hands, and gave way to heartbroken tears. Not even Mike's arms around her helped.

"Beloved," he whispered finally, "can you help Sands? He's in really bad shape."

"How?" Sid muttered. "I offered to help Nate, and he refused. John's right. They aren't *mirik'im*. They won't believe."

"You could make them believe, *ta'mirik.*"

"Don't call me that. Not anymore. Not ever again. It's over."

"Is it?" The deputy pulled her around to face him, then pushed his forehead to hers though she tried to dodge.

It was to her desert night that he took them, with the

horses beside the crackling campfire. To the first and only place where they'd made love.

"I don't want to be what I was before," Mike said vehemently. "I want to be your *mirik'ee*—forever. And you'll never be just Sidney Bowers again, no matter how you try. Johncaldwell isn't dead. He's where he belongs, where you sent him. You should be happy, not sad."

Sidney's jaw tightened. "He's where he belongs. But where do we belong?" Angry, she took herself out of his dream and back to reality.

Avery Sands's muffled agony continued, and Sid, dusting nonexistent sand from her *in'al*, went to squat beside him.

"Let me see the hand," she demanded harshly, but unwrapped the jacket with gentle moves. The sight made her ill. "I can heal this, if you'll let me."

The man, face contorted, stared up at her. "I don't . . . understand."

"You don't need to understand, only obey me."

The strength in her voice had trapped him already. She sat close and pulled his head to her, pressing their foreheads together. Dreaming had become second nature to her, and Sid swept him into it with her easily. But to overwhelm such a strong man would take something beyond his imagination. The final world that Johncaldwell had shown her might be just what was needed.

Avery Sands lay gasping on the crystal-strewn ground, but the awe of his surroundings had taken his mind from the pain.

"What have you done?" he managed to ask.

"Brought you to another part of the galaxy. Look at your hand. It's healed."

She had made it so in dreaming, but it would be up to him to make it so in reality. Sands flexed the fingers of his left hand, in no less awe.

"Stand up," Sid told him. "I want you to see what was once a thriving world like our own, full of life until the Ral took its sun away."

The man got slowly to his feet, eyes on the frozen sea

below them. "The Ral took their sun? Dear God, what powers they must have."

"Oh, yes. Powers beyond understanding. These are the sentient creatures you've searched the heavens for. The very ones you wish to begin a dialogue with." Sidney touched a long slender "tree" and watched it shatter and fall soundlessly.

"How are we here?" Avery asked.

"The Ral are dreamers. They create at will in their minds. Their elders use dreams to instruct and guide the People, because in dreams for them there is only truth."

"And you? How can you create all this? You're human."

"Not entirely. Not anymore." Sidney couldn't hide her bitterness. "In many ways, I'm Ral now. I understand the simplicity of their existence and envy it. They follow no gods, have no religions. They live to die—not for honor or reward—but simply to continue their species. They conquer because they can. They take the technology of conquered races, but nothing else. To them all others are *il'ral*—not of the Ral and, therefore, of little worth. This . . . this principle has served them for millennia."

"Then they simply take what's useful to them and destroy the rest? No one ever survives them?"

"Some do. If a race submits, the Ral coexist with them, appropriating what they want and need. Humans would never submit though. They're too independent and aggressive, so they would be destroyed."

Sands shook his head wearily, the empty silent planet seemed to weigh heavily on him. "You still admire them," he accused.

"I do, yes. But as much as I am Ral, I'm also *il'ral,* unacceptable in their eyes."

"But you could use this gift of theirs." Avery held out his hand. "Dream healing is a miraculous feat. If you could teach it to others—"

Sidney gave him a nasty laugh. "And be told these are divine powers granted by God? I'd be revered and hated, a freak. But it doesn't work that way. I'm *ta'mirik*—or was. I heal in dreams, but my *mirik'im* heal themselves in the real world, because they have faith in me, believe in me."

"Then . . .?" Sands made a fist. "I may wake up and . . ."

"Yes. But listen to me, Avery Sands. Mike's back was broken during the missile attack, and he healed himself. You have that power, too. Every human does. I know that now."

Avery smiled. "I don't know why, but I believe you."

"Good. Then let's return."

"No, wait. There's something else you know, Sidney. Even with your partial Ral mind-set, you still know the worth of every sentient and nonsentient being." The man stared at her in the starlight, eyes nearly as black as Johncaldwell's. "You and Mike are part of Caldwell's triumvirate. Nate explained the *mirik'im* to me—as much of it as he understood. There's nothing any of the rest of us could do to convince the Ral to accept us as anything but animals, but you three might have a chance."

Sidney frowned. "What are you saying?"

"Open the gate one more time and go through to John Caldwell."

"Only Ral can pass through the gate. You learned that the hard way."

"But you're very nearly Ral—you think as Ral, you wear their armor, you use their weapons. When we first saw you, that armor covered all of you, face, hands, everything. If it's impervious enough to save you from missile fire, then it should protect you from the gate. The gate might not even know there's a human body underneath."

"And if that works, what then?"

"You might be able to save humanity . . . and a lot of other sentient races. You might prove to the Ral that we aren't useless animals." Sands's lips pursed. "Or you might die. But even I could see how strongly connected the three of you are. Do you really want to live out your life without John Caldwell?"

"No," Sidney said and ended the dream.

Mike hovered near in the moonlight, and Nate sat beside them, his breathing ragged.

"Look." Avery held out his left hand, normal, functioning. "You should let her help you, Curtis. She's incredible."

Nate only trembled and looked away.

"We saw," the deputy muttered, tone subdued. "We saw your hand change while you dreamed. Scared the shit out of me."

"Mike," Sidney said sharply. "We need to talk."

"If it's about taking the rest of the gate apart and getting out of here let's just do it."

"No. I want the gate opened again. I'm going through."

"What?" the young man demanded. "Are you crazy?"

"With the *in'al* completely covering me, I should make it all right." She gazed at him, sadly. "Mike, I can't live without Johncaldwell. I don't want to live without you, either, but I can't ask you to come with me."

"You don't have to ask," the deputy growled. "I might be able to live without Caldwell, but not without you. So how do we work this? The gate still needs to be closed from this end."

Sidney looked at Nate, who was far too ill, then at Sands. "You'll have to do it for us. Can we trust you?"

"Guess you'll have to," Avery said.

"He'll do it," Nate told them. "I trust him, but I'll make certain."

Mike shifted his *pa'ng* impatiently. "Let's do it, then. Before I have too much time to think."

Impatient herself, Sidney still took infinite care in showing Avery Sands how to use the claw to work the gate, to shut it down and remove the lenses. The man took it all in easily, and Sid finally turned to Nate.

"What you said before ... about finding the deepest part of the ocean and dumping the boxes ... Promise me you'll do that as soon as possible."

"Wait!" Sands argued. "If I disable them, then at least let us keep them for study purposes. If you'd just let us analyze and try to duplicate the material they're made of, it could advance—"

"Warfare," Sidney sneered.

"All right. That may be true, but it could also help us

defend ourselves against the Ral, if they should find their way back here again someday."

"No," Sid snapped. "There's a greater chance you'll destroy this world. Your understanding of the powers involved is too limited. Nate! Promise me."

The sergeant's murmured, "Yes," turned into a painful bout of coughing that bent him over.

"And you, too," Sidney said, her eyes on Sands.

He was angry, his teeth gritted, but he nodded. "OK. I promise."

"What?"

"I promise to let Nate do whatever he needs to with the damn boxes."

"All right. Open the gate."

Mike Nichols came to stand beside her, rifle ready. She engaged the *in'al*'s face and hand armor for them both, then handed the sharp clawtip to Sands.

"I love you," the deputy said gently to Sid as Avery Sands inserted the claw underneath the Gatekeeper's box. She had no time to answer. The black liquid shot skyward, thinning into a tall, slender wand of power. The curtain appeared, silver-blue with the *in'al* vision and wavering, but the scene beyond it had changed. Armored Ral far outnumbered the white-gowned elders. Johncaldwell stood in their midst, his face too distorted by the shimmer to decipher. As one, all heads turned toward the reopened gate.

A tiny voice in Sidney's head screamed a warning against such insanity, but she'd already taken a step forward, and felt Mike close behind her. Should the Gatekeeper reject them, their deaths would be horrible. Should it let them pass, death might still await them among the Ral.

The rippling silver curtain seemed to snag them, enfold them in a thick sticky substance, then Sid broke free into a world that wasn't dream. The elders glowed with *in'al* sight—their robes, their serene faces. Cold stone walls encircled the small crowd that towered over Sidney and Mike. The air here, filtered through the armor, was thin, and brought a bitter taste to the tongue, and the gravity felt slightly greater.

"Ta'mirik!" Johncaldwell cried in distress. His arms were trapped by warrior hands, and his weapons were gone.

A slender armored female stepped toward Sidney, and instinctively, the young woman swung the rifle barrel, but long-fingered hands reached from behind her and wrenched the weapon away. Someone snatched the *nom'ng* from her belt. Mike Nichols, caught in other hands, managed to fire his *pa'ng* into the air. The stone ceiling exploded above them, showering the group with heavy chunks of rock and plaster. An elder in a white robe was felled, surrounded immediately by horrified Ral.

Fluting cries of outrage filled the room, and Sidney, the slick black material of her wrist grasped tightly, still slipped loose and jerked the knife from her arm sheath. She slashed her captor across his unprotected face and dark purple blood flowed freely. Her thin grasp on reality had failed. Here, in the midst of a milling throng of armored warriors, she and Mike had no chance whatsoever, but the need to attack, to fight, drove her on.

Somewhere in the craziness, she heard Mike's shouts, but two male Ral, their faces now shielded with armor, had thrown the deputy to the floor, his nose and lip bloodied. His *ta'mirik* slammed through the crowd, finding an inhuman strength deep inside. She caught one Ral around the throat with her elbow and flung him aside, then latched onto the second. The effort was futile—a fist caught her hard on the side of the head, then half a dozen bodies crashed into hers all at once, bearing her to the stone flagging beside Mike. Her arms, like the deputy's, were forced behind her back and the wrists fastened.

Dazed, they were dragged upright to stand before an elder—the only one in white robes edged with silver. With a feeble, shaky hand, he reached out behind them to put a clawtip in the holes that uncovered their faces and hands. Sidney laughed at the shocked intakes of air that their human ugliness brought from the entire group.

"Il'ral," someone snarled, and Sidney felt death very close.

"Wait," the elder cried in Ral, and she recognized the word. *"Il'ral ga nir in'al?"*

This ancient one questioned the possession of armor by animals—that much she also understood.

"I am *ta'mirik,*" she said angrily, fighting for the breath to carry her words. Her head throbbed. *"T'wa ta'mirik!* That is my *mirik'i.*" Sid nodded at Johncaldwell, who had not resisted, so had not been bound.

Her mixture of Ral and English confused them just enough for Johncaldwell to pull free and push his way through the warriors. Then they were three again—Mike and Sid and John—power in the *mirik'im*—the mates. Sidney sensed their energy bind with hers. Even in the midst of their own troubles, she was still aware of the gate behind them, alive, open, its omnipresent hum of power heavy in the atmosphere. Mentally, she cursed Avery Sands. Of course, he would wait until the very last minute, intent on seeing how humans would fare among the Ral.

Anger and rage filled the room. Only the eldest's presence kept the alien *mirik'im* alive.

"Hy't," he said to John imperiously. (Speak.)

An unforeseen chance—Johncaldwell spoke in halting Ral sentences, as if uncertain what to say or how to say it. Sidney could make out some small part of his speech about the broken gate and how he was *g'ral,* made from human genetic material to repair the damaged pole. But when he began to relate the choosing of his *mirik'im,* there were ominous rumblings of disgust among the Ral.

The eldest barked a single word, and all but two of the warriors backed from the chamber through doors on either side, taking the injured with them. Now, only a handful of white-robed elders stood with the aliens, who were held tightly in check by their Ral guards. The ancient one, fleshless and decrepit, found an austere stone chair at the back of the room and seated himself. The other white-robes sat at his feet, since there were no other chairs.

"Yaz," he said to the *mirik'im.* (Come.)

Sidney glanced back at the silver curtain of the gate and saw Sands watching. And Nate. "Close it," she mouthed to them, then was forcibly led with her husbands to the eldest. A high-fluting joyfulness sounded from somewhere beyond the room, unmistakably laughter. A dozen huge-eyed Ral raced in through a doorway—children, only slightly smaller than Sidney, in short brown robes. At sight of her and Mike, they halted in confusion, the laughter fading away.

"SSShoo," an elder said gently—at least one word held in common with English.

The children stared without fear or even anger, only curiosity. Somehow that gave Sid hope as they scattered out the doors once more. One brave child halted and even dared to touch her lightly on her naked face before he darted past her to stand behind the eldest's chair. Sidney found the Old One's shrewd eyes on her.

He turned his attention to Johncaldwell again and spoke rapidly. This time, Sidney could not find sense in the words, but the sense behind them was clear enough. They were accusations, harsh and cold. Caldwell looked at Sid, devastation in his broad, angular face.

"The Old One says that because I am *g'ral* I am blameless in my behavior. But that I must forget my *il'ral mirik'im* and enter the *h'rik* where another female may choose me as a mate." John's sorrow washed over Sidney. "He says you and Mike are destructive and dangerous and, therefore, must die. He tells me to close the gate now, until they decide how to deal with Earth."

"Like hell!" Sid snarled, but blocked the deputy when he started forward. *"Te'h,* old man! Hear me? No! These are my *mirik'im,* and no one takes them from me. Or my world."

The eldest tilted his head as if to better understand her, while those at his feet only stared emotionlessly. No one feared *il'ral,* because no Ral feared death. Sid turned back to the gate. Avery Sands stood as close to the curtain as he dared, and once again she told him silently to shut down the gate, her face conveying her desperation. God, you fool! she cried mentally. If they close the gate from this side, the Earth and everything on it is lost.

Unwillingly Sands finally moved to kneel beside the Gatekeeper's pole. The eldest sang a sudden command at

Johncaldwell, and Sidney remembered that Ral must obey their elders, too. His reflexes were far quicker than Avery's, but he still arrived too late. The gate vanished, leaving a blank stone wall in its place. Gone. Her world gone forever. Sidney had no time to mourn.

She expected anger, even a quick death from these creatures. Instead, the eldest only gazed solemnly at her, then again spoke to Johncaldwell, slowly so that she might catch as much of the meaning as possible.

"I am old and I have seen many things, but can this be? Could an animal be so ingenious as to defend its planet and be so determined to defend its mates?"

"She is my *ta'mirik*," John insisted. "Not *il'ral*. She dreams."

That stunned the rest into horrified silence. The eldest considered this a long moment.

"Animals do not dream."

"Then my *mirik'im* are not animals," John answered him simply. "Our second husband dreams as well, but my warrior-wife's dream powers are greater even than mine." He offered the eldest a twisted, lipless Ral smile. "They may even be greater than yours, Old One."

The eldest's nostrils fluttered in agitation.

"A challenge," one of the elders muttered, and was echoed by the others. "*Il'ral* cannot challenge."

Sidney glared at them. "But we do, we challenge your stupidity and ignorance—your refusal to accept intelligence in creatures other than yourselves."

John translated her words, and they didn't please the Ral elders. All but the Old One, who remained serene throughout. The child behind him stood with a small clawed hand upon the eldest's shoulder, black eyes intent, absorbing everything, revealing nothing.

"We have never denied the limited intelligence of others," the Old One said gently, and waited for Johncaldwell to make his meaning clear, "only ignored it as being of little consequence to us. Animals can be clever and imitative and even useful at times, but the People are far superior. This we've proven over millennia. How does intelligence serve creatures with bodies so frail that they die easily and young? What good are you as mates to Johncaldwell when your lives would end long before his?"

"All *ta'mirik'im*'s lives are short."

"Ahhhh," murmured the elders seated on the floor, and beside her, Sidney felt Mike's distress.

"Perhaps yours will be shorter than you realize," the Old One said. "You would have us believe you are Ral . . ."

"No," Sid answered. "I'm human, but I want you to believe that I'm not *il'ral.*"

"Then I will give you the chance to prove this . . . in dreaming."

Again the elders murmured, heads tilting side to side in agreement. John translated, and an uneasiness spread over Sidney.

"The *mirik'im* test themselves continually in contests against one another. Such dream exercises strengthen the powers of body and mind. You'll use the *K'ral.*"

"No!" cried Johncaldwell. "We've been together only a short time. My *mirik'im* have no experience with Ral combat."

"But," the eldest said with scorn, "your *ta'mirik*'s dream powers are greater than mine."

"What?" Sidney demanded. "What did he say?"

"He . . . he plans a contest for us with another *mirik'im.*"

"What kind of contest?" Mike glanced over the inscrutable alien faces that watched them.

"Dream combat with ancient Ral weapons—curved double-edged knives and swords."

The deputy drew a breath. "We should be all right. It's just dreaming, isn't it?"

"You've only seen the healing aspect of dreams, Mike Nichols." Johncaldwell stared at Sidney. "The power of the dreamer can harm as well as heal. These combats are usually exercises—rough play—but deaths occur occasionally. But this exercise will be anything but usual. They can't let you survive, either of you, and perhaps not even me. We defy everything the Ral have stood for over the ages."

"Can we refuse?" Sidney asked.

"Yes. And die as *il'ral. Ta'mirik,* that they have deigned to speak with you at all is proof enough that you have shaken them deeply. We must fight, beloved, but I told you once that your dream powers are beyond the Rals'. I believe in you. We can win this contest."

Mike didn't look so certain, but, hands still bound, he leaned to kiss her lips, and left them liberally smeared with his blood. "Let's just kick their Ral asses."

Chapter Seventeen

NATE HAD NO real idea of how much time had passed, but the eastern sky seemed to be lightening even as Mojave Wells died back to coals. Despite the devastation, there seemed to be a few of the buildings still partially standing. Or perhaps it was just a trick of the shadows, a trick of his exhausted mind. He fumbled the little brown bottle from his jacket pocket and swallowed another pill dry. God, the taste was horrid, and the damn thing stuck in his throat.

But Avery Sands crouched beside the first box, statue-still, undecided, and Nate knew he might have to some-how, someway, forcibly help the man keep his promise. The second gate rod, slender and straight, still hummed to itself.

Voice rough with fatigue, Nate called to Sands. "Do it, Avery. Shut the other pole down."

"Lord, what have I done?" Sands groaned, his hands on the slick black material of the box. "I talked them into going through, because I wanted to and couldn't. I've killed them."

"Don't do it!" Nate warned. "Don't open the gate again."

"They might make it back, Curtis. I should give them that chance."

"No, damn you! Sid and Mike don't belong here any more than John Caldwell. They deserved the chance to reason with the Ral."

"You saw how the Ral reasoned. Mike and Sidney are prisoners."

"But their lives aren't worth risking our world. Sid would be the first to tell you that. You're not God; you can't control any of this. You made a promise. Now keep it." The length and force of that speech left Nate almost too weak to sit upright. He fought to master his body and mind. "It's nearly light, Avery. Harris and his people will be here soon. I'm sure they already know exactly where we are. Shut down the other gate pole and hide the boxes in the Jeep." Nate paused. "I'd help, but . . ."

Avery Sands finally looked at him, face shadowy in the moonlight. "Just rest, my friend. I'll keep my promise." But his movements were slow, dragging. He inserted the clawtip in the hole of the second rod, and it became a silent box once more.

The boxes were then freed from the rock anchors and carted one by one to the vehicle, where Avery pushed them under coils of rope and folded tarps.

"The lenses," Nate muttered. "You forgot to remove the lenses."

"I didn't forget. I'll do it later when there's time."

"Do it now, Sands."

"No," the general snapped and pointed his chin to the west.

Nate heard it, then, the rumble of motors. A line of military trucks bumped over the rough ground, moving rapidly toward them.

"You're real sick, Curtis," Avery said. "You don't remember a damn thing that happened. Just let me do all the talking. You lie back and play unconscious."

Nate Curtis let himself slide with relief into the cold sand. As it was, he didn't have to feign unconsciousness. The darkness came all too easily, obliterating the pain at last.

II

After a moment's quiet conference with the eldest, the male child was sent from the chamber, but his luminous black eyes remained on Sidney all the way to the exit. She had learned to read Johncaldwell's facial expressions well and didn't see abhorrence in the child's eyes. No, if anything, there was a subtle attraction to this exotic female creature in their midst. And Sidney, *ta'mirik* and mate to a Ral, saw only beauty in the boy's features and movements.

"What's happening now?" Mike whispered.

Johncaldwell cocked his great head. "The young one has been sent to the *u'het* to find a *ta'mirik* named Helgess. She and her *mirik'im* will prepare the dream chamber for us and gather the *tin'kim*—the *K'ral.*"

"Great," the deputy growled. "Knives. I don't like sharp things, and I hate being stabbed or slashed. Why can't we use the *nom'ng,* or our rifles, in this so-called combat?"

"The eldest decides," John said simply.

"And anything he decides will not be in our favor," Sidney added with a touch of fatalism. "Whatever it takes, they'll make certain we lose this contest."

Mike's jaw hardened. "The bastards are cheats."

"No," the young woman sighed. "They're Ral."

As one, the group of elders rose from the floor, straightening their robes. The ancient one motioned to Johncaldwell and spoke.

"What'd he say?" Mike demanded.

"He says your light weapons will be returned to you should we survive combat—since then you'll no longer be animals."

The eldest nodded and led them all from the room. There were winding stone corridors, invisibly lit after the fashion of the deserted cliff dwellings Sidney had once visited. None of the chambers along these halls had doors, only openings. Some were dwellings with austere furnishings, some held groups of children seated on the floors, listening to white-robed elders that wandered among them.

"Is this the *hol'al?*" Mike asked John. "Where the children are raised?"

"*Mi'n,*" Johncaldwell answered with a hint of sadness. "Yes. And where the surviving *mirik'im* live and work—unless they are chosen by another *ta'mirik.* But it is rare for *mirik'im* to accept another wife."

Sid listened with only half a mind. Every sight and sound was marvelous and new—so very alien. The bands that secured her wrists were tight, but the Ral guard's hand on her elbow kept her from stumbling off-balance. They passed another room, far larger than the rest, that held bustling young male adults who worked over great round bowls with steaming contents. Food, Sidney decided, aware of strange, but alluring, scents. Her stomach reminded her urgently that it had been empty for far too long. Mike sniffed the air appreciatively.

At last, they followed long spiral staircases upward into the outside world. The land stretched around them, covered with a short red grass, occasionally relieved by strange twisting trees whose foliage was a dull rust color. Distant jagged mountains formed the horizon in even direction, and overhead, in a pale blue sky, were two remote blue stars that served as this world's suns, providing a dim, dusky light.

"The oxygen's thin," Mike commented, "but not too bad. Tastes strange, though. And I feel kinda heavy."

"The question is, can we fight in this world?" Sidney said.

Johncaldwell murmured, "We fight in dream, in the mind. You can imagine all the air you like there."

They followed the elders a long distance across the broad red field to arrive at another stairwell. Something took flight at their approach, a bird of sorts, with narrow wings that moved so quickly it reminded Sid of a hummingbird, though it was far larger.

"Does anyone know where we're going?" Mike asked as they started clumsily down another spiral stair.

"These lead to the *u'het*, the warriors' quarters." John followed them at the very rear of the group. "This world is called *Ha'ral*. The Ral have held it since the gate to Earth was first set and lost. There are underground cities all across the planet and many more military bases. Armies are sent by gate and by ship when new star systems with viable worlds are discovered. Through dreaming, the People have instant communication with every occupied planet within the galaxy. This is why we are so formidable an enemy. Time has no power over us."

"How long do they . . . can you live?" Sidney asked.

"Again time has little meaning. Some of the eldest here are thousands of your years old."

They had found the corridors of the *u'het*, much wider than those in the quarters they had left, and far more busy. Beautiful lithe creatures in black armor moved about in all directions.

"Do not stare," Johncaldwell advised them. "It's impolite, even insulting, among the warrior *mirik'im.*"

None of those they passed even took notice of the *il'ral* strangers in their midst, though they acknowledged the elders with gracious dips of their heads. The rooms along these halls were larger, too—huge barracks with sleeping mats set in threes all across the floors.

"Kind of crowded," Mike commented. "How do they . . . I mean what if they want some privacy . . . to . . . say, make love?"

Johncaldwell's mouth twisted. "They dream."

"OK, but what if they want the real thing? You know . . . sex in the flesh?"

"Dream sex is for pleasure, *mirik'ee.* Real sex is for procreation only, and I told you, that happens before the *mirik'im* is formed."

The deputy opened his mouth again, other—no doubt more graphic—questions on his mind, but Sidney narrowed her eyes at him, and he dropped the subject.

The end of one long corridor opened on the largest chamber yet with a high, vaulted ceiling and strange, swirling designs carved shallowly into the stone floor. It was empty of life. In the distance a square, boxlike building stood alone, free of the outer walls of the chamber. From where they stood, Sidney could see no windows or doors in this separate room.

"The *pyn'ar,*" John said in a low tone. "The *u'het* dream chamber."

There was movement at the one entrance to the large hall. The male child entered first with a long cloth-wrapped object in his arms, heavy, by the way he moved. Behind him came three warriors—obviously a *mirik'im* by the unconscious symmetry of their movements. Their *ta'mirik* led them, nearly twice Sidney's height, slender and graceful. Now, Sid couldn't help but stare. As they neared, she noticed a long thin scar on each of the male's faces in the exact same place as Mike's.

"They don't look so tough to me," the deputy said, but without much conviction.

Their Ral guards pushed them roughly toward the *pyn'ar* in the wake of the elders. There was no chair here, and the white-robes helped the eldest to sit upon the floor near one wall of the dream chamber. The male child brought the cloth-wrapped object and unrolled it at his feet. Within glittered a single sword and knife. The sword somewhat resembled the scimitar of Earth, only wider and razor sharp on both inner and outer edges of the curved blade. Instead of a pointed tip, the end was rounded and held three curved spikes, shaped exactly like large versions of Ral claws. The knife was a *tin'k,* the extremely long, needle thin blade that fit in the arm sheath of the *in'al.*

"Observe," the Old One said. "These are the only weapons you may dream. You may not use the *in'al* to cover the face or hands. And combat is confined to the *pyn'ar.*"

Sidney listened to John's translation, though she understood most of what had been said. The thought of six combatants in the one tiny room brought a touch of fear that she carefully hid—especially from Mike and John.

"Yaz," said the eldest to the other *mirik'im.* They came forward with a dip of their heads in deference. "This is Helgess, *ta'mirik,* and her first husband, Nurn, and second husband, Kimn." The Old One nodded to Sidney. "This is Zidney, who claims to be a human *ta'mirik*—her *mirik'i,* Johncaldwell, and human *mirik'ee,* Mike. Zidney wishes to prove they are *il'ral* of worth. She claims to dream." The eldest's mouth twisted wryly. "If this proves untrue, then the animals will die animal deaths."

Helgess listened solemnly, her huge dark eyes on Sidney, curious and yet contemptuous. Her husband, Nurn, came only to her shoulder in height, and Kimn was even shorter, but power and supreme confidence emanated from them. Sidney felt John and Mike behind her, close, offering her their strength and comfort.

"If you're through with the introductions," she said with contempt of her own, "then let's get on with it."

The eldest glanced at John, who explained.

"Ral are never . . ." The Old One searched for a word, and John supplied it.

"Fi'na . . . hurried . . . impatient."

"Mi'n," the eldest agreed.

"Well, humans are. Loose our hands," Sid demanded.

"Dream them loose." The Old One signaled the guards and Sidney and Mike were forcibly seated against one blank wall of the dream chamber. John settled beside them, while the other *mirik'im* disappeared around a corner—perhaps to seat themselves at another wall.

"Begin," the eldest said with some relish, and the elders murmured their assent.

John leaned his head against Sidney's, and Mike did the same on the other side. Control of this dream would be hers—unless Helgess proved the stronger. White light flared in her brain, and she found the chamber John had shown her in their very first momentary dream, long ago.

Their hands were free, but first things first. Sid willed the claustrophobic walls to spread away—doubling, then tripling the space within the doorless, windowless place. The weapons were formed next. Having only seen them the once, and never holding them, Sid imagined them as closely as possible, but with one change. She made them of the black armor material, incredibly light, yet incredibly strong.

Mike hefted his appreciatively, one in each hand. "If they're allowed to cheat, but we're not, this may just piss them off."

"Our *ta'mirik* defines truth in ways other than the Ral," Johncaldwell told him, "but it's truth all the same."

"Where are the others?" Sidney asked, worried.

John smiled. "I told you your dream powers are superior, but remember, time passes far more quickly here. They have yet to dream themselves into the chamber."

He had barely finished those words, when the others arrived. They materialized at the center of the room, back-to-back, swords in one hand, knives in the other.

"T'mey," Sidney said sarcastically, which meant both hello and welcome, and observed their momentary confusion at the size of the chamber, their opponents' black weapons.

Helgess pointed her chin at Johncaldwell. "So you dream well for your hu-man mates, *g'ral* brother."

"She thinks I've done all this," John muttered to Sid.

"Let her," the young woman answered. "We need all the surprises we can muster."

"So what now?" Mike demanded. "Do we pair off, one at a time, or go for a free-for-all?"

He got his answer immediately. Helgess, silver blade a blur in her hand, came at Sidney without warning. The deputy, closest, blocked the stroke with his own black scimitar, but the strength of the blow knocked the blade from his grip and sent him stumbling backward.

John drove forward at the enemy *ta'mirik,* his own strength nearly matching hers, and managed to kick Mike's sword across the floor to him. The man scooped it up in time to defend himself against Kimn, the second husband. Sidney dodged a blow aimed at her head by Helgess's *mirik'i* and danced away in hopes of gaining time to figure her defense.

Nurn only followed all the quicker, and this time his scimitar's outer edge caught her a blow to the side of her head. Sidney went with the force of it and saved herself from an impact that would have opened her skull. Instead, the scalp above her right ear was laid wide. Hot blood poured down over neck and shoulder.

Her rational mind sent the pain signals to flood her other senses, dulling them. She knew this was dream, and she could heal herself, but Nurn gave her no chance. Blade swinging, clashing against hers, he forced her back and back toward one of the walls. With disaster and death only inches away, Sidney dodged low, beneath the slashing sword and stabbed upward with the long *tin'k,* under the Ral's narrow chin. It was pure luck, that stroke. His own overconfidence had given her the opening, and her own desperation had forced her to take it. The sharp tip of the knife popped through the tight leathery skin and buried itself to the hilt through tongue and palate, then into the creature's huge brain.

He dropped to the ground, legs and arms jerking spasmodically, the knife still deep in his flesh. A shriek of dismay filled the chamber. Helgess beat Johncaldwell aside and rushed to Nurn. The threat of her blade made Sidney dart away along the wall. It was then·she noticed the faces blended in the stone. The elders also dreamed, watching the trial through the walls.

The combat had paused. Each contestant stood with poised weapons as the *ta'mirik* drew the *tin'k* from below Nurn's jaw. Helgess would heal him, Sidney assumed, and so the battle would continue. But the *mirik'i* did not hear her commands, could not obey them. So death was possible in dream. Then again, the eldest would not have set up this contest, if that weren't true. But what she had done still chilled Sidney. Helgess began to keen, and her pain was Sidney's pain. For the *ta'mirik,* her own death was far preferable to the loss of a husband.

Her keening died abruptly, and Helgess rose to stand over her dead mate. Now Sidney felt her anger, her rage, all hidden behind that careful Ral exterior. But it wasn't Sidney that the female came after. Instead, she leaped with feline grace toward Mike. A husband for a husband, then. Kimn saw his *ta'mirik*'s intention and went for the deputy, as well, only to meet Johncaldwell.

Mike didn't seem to understand what was happening. He stood his ground a moment, then confused, dived away from Helgess's first charge. The length of leg, the innate superior reflexes of the Ral, gave the humans little advantage. Helpless, Sidney raced after the *ta'mirik,* but the female spun gracefully on the ball of one foot and followed Mike.

He tried to turn and face her, to bring his weapons up in self-defense—too late. Helgess's sword caught him in the back, parting the black *in'al* as if it were merely cloth. The three-clawed tip broke through the front, bits of flesh carried with it. Sidney arrived just as the *ta'mirik* tore the blade free. Mike made no sound, his face white with shock, while red blood gushed from the wound. Brow furrowed, he dropped to his knees, then slid bonelessly to the stone floor.

Helgess howled in triumph, standing over her victim. Now it was Sidney's turn for rage. The female would keep her from Mike until he was finally beyond dream help, would let Sid feel her husband's suffering the entire time. Sidney's rage turned inward—at the frail human body that could do nothing against the strength and power of this Ral. And now she knew that not even the *in'al* provided protection. She buried her face in her hands.

Truth. Truth in dreaming. Johncaldwell, still caught in deadly battle with the second husband, had shown her his truth, his vision of her, in one of their dreams. She realized now, it was her truth, too. Dream! Pain came, a deep agony that wasn't Mike's, but her own. Muscles and tendons stretched, bones lengthened. The sharp tips of clawed fingers pressed into the taut skin of her face.

Whatever the human form that dreamed beyond these walls, Sidney was Ral now. She saw the world from a greater height, and the dusky light seemed brighter to these large black eyes, the weapons smaller in such long-fingered hands. Her otic nerves heard the disconcerted mumbles of the elders from the walls, the deputy's stertorous breathing. Even the slash on the side of her head flowed with a thick purple fluid.

While Helgess stood stunned by her enemy's transformation, Sid drove suddenly at her, leading with sword and knife. The *ta'mirik* moved to meet her.

"Mike!" Sid shouted, even as metal clanged against the strange black material of her weapons. "I'm here to help you, to take the pain away! Now, heal yourself. Do it!"

Helgess feinted with the *tin'k* from the left, then swung her sword at Sidney's already bloody head. The young woman's Ral reflexes helped her parry the blow. A quick glance aside showed her Mike curled in a fetal position, blood still pooling under him.

"Damn you, Mike! Bastard! I need you—I love you! Close the wound! We can't let them win."

Finally he began to respond, and his relief from the agony swept through her, bringing a heady dizziness that nearly cost her her life. Helgess came at her hard, driving her back, step-by-step, each blow deflected only just in time. This body might be new to Sidney, but it answered every demand with lightning quickness. Then, as suddenly, the female Ral eased off, something else on her mind.

Now, she began to back away, and Sidney became the aggressor. From the corner of her eye, she could see Johncaldwell at the far side of the chamber engaged with Kimn. The enemy Ral struck a blow to Johncaldwell's shoulder, but the armor deflected the blade. Why? Why not for Mike before? Dream, the answer came. Helgess, too, was a powerful dreamer, capable of changing the structure of the *in'al.* Sidney continued her careful strikes, defending her own body from the female's sudden thrusts.

Mike still lay in a heap on the stones, and now, Sid knew what Helgess intended in her slow progress back across the room. She would finish him there, while the deputy was too weak to protect himself. Sidney tried to force her to the side, away from Mike, but Helgess would not be turned.

"Mike!" Sid cried. "Pick up your sword."

He tried, human fingers stretched toward the dark blade, then the female Ral was there, standing over him. Sidney doubled her effort, though her Ral form grew tired. The great lungs labored for air. Helgess blocked Sid's blade with the *tin'k* and raised her sword over Mike.

"Not this time, bitch," the deputy growled and wrapped his legs tight around her ankles. He twisted to the side, though the move brought a muffled cry of pain from him. The female's legs were dragged out from under her, and down she went, flailing.

Helgess struck the ground hard, her sword skittering away out of reach. Sidney dropped her own scimitar, and flung herself onto the fallen *ta'mirik,* then caught the hand with the knife that plunged toward her throat. The female's other hand raked at her face, claws digging deep, yet Sid hung on, desperate, head held high to keep the claws from her eyes. Slowly, she forced the blade tip around until it pressed against the *ta'mirik*'s neck. A tiny drop of purple blood welled.

"Min'ta," Sidney said through her teeth. (Sister.) "I have killed my *min'ta's mirik'i.* My shame and sorrow is without end. John!"

Breathlessly, Johncaldwell translated. Kimn had lowered his weapons, his eyes on his *ta'mirik.* Helgess's struggles ceased.

"I dream, *min'ta,* even as you. I love my husbands, even as you. The elders have sent us against one another to prove me *il'ral."* Sidney kept her blade tip at the *ta'mirik's* throat. "Am I *il'ral, min'ta?"*

Her great dark eyes were filled with suffering and sorrow over the loss of a husband, but Helgess fluttered her nostrils. "I cannot say what you are, but you are not an animal."

"What can I do, *min'ta,* to gain your forgiveness for what I've done?"

Helgess looked away. "Forgiveness is not a consideration. Nothing will bring Nurn back to me, but that is the price of combat." John's translation carried the same sadness as in her voice.

"Then there is only revenge?" Sid asked.

"Not for me. Here and now, there is only death."

"So all we can do is fight and die to please the elders? I don't want to kill you, Helgess. I've hurt you enough already."

Johncaldwell spoke up. "The Ral have no word for mercy, *ta'mirik."*

"Then perhaps they should invent one," Sid said angrily. "I'm not an animal. I'm hardly human, anymore, but I'm not a Ral, either." She flung the *tin'k* away. "I'll fight if I must, *min'ta,* but let this end now. I've proven my worth."

Sidney climbed wearily to her feet and closed her eyes, let the bones shorten, the muscles shrink, felt her face, bloody and scratched, change back to its familiar human shape. Suddenly the gravity weighed more heavily on her, and her lungs ached with lack of oxygen.

Helgess had moved only enough to bring herself to a sitting position. She didn't reach for sword or knife. The elders' faces, set in stone, came forward, their bodies slipping through the wall—even the eldest, supported by the male child. The Old One's anger was obvious.

He sneered at Helgess, his voice full of scorn, and she, spent, still managed to climb to her feet to tower over his shrunken form. She spoke rapidly, also angry.

Johncaldwell came to stand beside Sidney. "She says she has lost a husband, but gained a sister—one she will defend if need be." He touched her lightly. "You felt her pain and loss, *ta'mirik*. You begged her forgiveness for the death of her beloved. These are things only a Ral female truly understands. She is still confused by you, but accepts that part of you that *is* Ral. The eldest is bitter only because he knows he has lost."

"Has he?" Sid demanded. Johncaldwell was as bloody as the rest of them. He'd lost two fingers from his right hand. Mike, sitting in his own blood, still looked white and weak. "We're a mess. Let's heal ourselves and get the hell out of this chamber."

The need for one another was strong. John and Sid sat next to Mike, tight together, bodies in contact. This was new to Sidney, healing injuries that existed in dream, not in reality. In a way it proved easier. They woke against the *pyn'ar* wall, heads touching. But though the wounds had healed, the bodies still felt the aches and exhaustion of such physical exertion. John took the thin black bands from their wrists.

The white-robed elders still sat in motionless rows on the outer floor, the milky nictitating membrane covered their eyes as they continued to dream. Sidney gathered herself up with the wall for support, then used it to take her around the first corner. The Ral *mirik'im* lay against the stone, their heads together, dreaming. All but Nurn, who would never wake again.

Once she had been a wife, then a widow, and a half-assed mechanic in a little desert town called Mojave Wells. That was light-years away and ago. Now, Sidney Bowers had killed—friend and foe alike. She had taken lives with these two hands. Her eyes traced the lines of her palms, the creases of her fingers. Irrevocable changes had taken place for good or ill.

"Sidney," Mike said softly.

She turned and found one of the elders stirring on the floor. He got up, stiff and awkward, and came to them, then gave Sidney a careful nod.

"Ne'pyn huuu'man ta'mirik," he said and touched her hand, his mouth twisted into a tentative smile.

John smiled, also. "Well dreamed, human *ta'mirik.*"

"Thank you," Sid replied. *"Gil'ma."*

"Yeah, *gil'ma,*" Mike echoed, pleased.

The others still argued among themselves in the dream chamber. The truth of what happened could not be denied, though. This was a start, she thought. But only a start. Over and over again, she and her *mirik'im* might have to prove themselves more than animals. The news would spread across the Ral-held galaxy—of the humans who lived among the People on *Ha'ral.* There would be challenges, but there would also be those who would defend them, who would listen and learn.

And there would be time to dream with her husbands, to share the pleasures of their lives together, alone and untroubled by reality.

"Gil'ma," she said again and felt Johncaldwell's strong slender arms wrap around her shoulders from behind. In turn, she wrapped her own arms around Mike Nichols.

Mirik'im.

Chapter Eighteen

NATE CURTIS WAS rushed back into surgery in that early morning light, then lay unknowing in his hospital bed for three days, unaware of Avery Sands's constant visits or the man's worry and guilt as he sat beside the patient. On the fourth day, Nate woke at mid-afternoon, muzzy and dry-mouthed, but reasonably pain-free. He stared a moment at the dirty beige ceiling before it dawned on him where he was—again. And that he was alive.

"Thirsty?" a familiar voice asked.

"God, yes," Nate croaked and watched Avery Sands, once more in casual, if expensive, civilian clothes, bring a cup and straw to his lips.

"The nurse says just to take sips at first," the man advised. "Your stomach's forgotten what it's like to have anything in it."

So Nate sipped, letting the wonderful liquid drench every part of his parched mouth.

"The doc was right, you know," Avery said tonelessly. "I nearly did kill you, dragging you out in the desert that night."

The desert. The gate. John Caldwell. Mike and Sidney. The memories flooded back in a confused jumble. A touch of panic followed.

"Easy, pal," Sands muttered. "It's all over."

"The boxes ..."

Avery looked him in the eyes. "Gone. They took them with them. Remember?"

"But—"

"Remember?" Avery repeated and shifted his eyes to

269

the side as if there were someone else in the room to over-hear.

"Yeah. I remember."

"I've been to Washington, D.C., twice in the last four days. Both times, I was raked over the coals. First by the president, then by the Joint Chiefs of Staff."

"Fun, huh?"

"Extremely. I gave them the whole story, and it didn't make them happy. And where there was once a sleepy little desert town named Mojave Wells, there's a great smoking hole in the ground. Oh, it's all explained away, of course. War games. Take a tacky falling-down town, evacuate the people, and then use it for target practice. Public domain and all that. No big deal."

"Except to the townspeople."

"Yeah, well . . ."

"What about me?" Nate asked, the panic returned.

"Like I told everyone. You don't know nothing. And the way you looked when they brought you in, no one's going to doubt it." Avery glanced away. "Of course, what went on before, that's another matter. You'll have to make a statement, but I'll be present to make sure no one tries to get heavy with you. Your brains have been so scrambled, though, if your story doesn't make a whole lot of sense, no one's going to complain."

"That's me—just a big dumb, scramble-brained cop." Nate allowed himself another swallow of water. "How long will they keep me here?"

"Another three days, the doc says. They're going to start you on some exercises, a little walking. The major reluctantly agreed that you'd be able to drive yourself home."

"In what?"

"Believe it or not, the only thing left standing in Mojave Wells was that camper-truck of yours. We had to put new tires on it, but the engine runs fine."

"Oh . . ." Nate's scrambled brains had drifted onto another track. "Are they OK, do you think?"

"Our friends? I doubt we'll ever know. Best to just forget any of this happened and get on with your life."

My boring, predictable life, Nate thought sadly. Janice would be home soon from Hawaii. That thought soothed him. Once away from this place, he would never speak to anyone of what had happened here—except Janice. She would help him sort things out, make sense of it all. A warm feeling of love swept over him. Boring and predictable his life might be, but Janice made it worth living.

"I'm up to my ears in paperwork," Avery said suddenly. "I really need to go."

"Wait . . .What about Colonel Harris, and that little prick of a captain?"

"Harris has packed up his tents and gone home—disappointed as hell. Poor guy. As for Captain Andrew Kern . . . all charges were dropped and he's got himself a post in Washington. God help us. But that's the military for you." Sands stood up. "What might have been the biggest scientific discovery of the ages turned out to be a big fat nothing. You and I saw something, but there's not a single piece of physical proof to corroborate it. We're back to square one."

"And still sending out invitations with your radio telescopes. . . ."

Sands shrugged. "It's important to humankind to know they're not the only ones in the universe."

"We can tell them that," Nate said with a shiver.

"Without proof, who'll listen?" Avery leaned close and murmured. "We've got the proof, and I've been tempted, Nate. My God, you don't know how I've been tempted to just play with the boxes—but I made a promise to Sidney Bowers, and I'm doing my best to keep it." He backed away from the bed. "My advice to you, Sergeant, is to take your medicine, eat your spinach, and get the hell out of here. I'll be back later."

II

Avery Sands never returned. Nate asked after him several times and got vague answers from nurses and doctors. Mr. Sands was in Washington, Mr. Sands was in Colorado, Mr. Sands was out of the country. Books arrived, courtesy of Mr. Sands—Joseph Wambaugh novels, which was a little like a busman's holiday—but no Avery Sands. He even failed to show for Nate's interview with a snippy young lieutenant who came to tape the sergeant's statement. Incredulous and amused, the fellow made it very clear that Nate's story belonged in the *National Enquirer,* and Nate had to agree. After that, other than doctors and nurses, the sergeant had no other visitors.

Since the hospital seemed to have been built before the invention of television, Nate dutifully stared at paperback pages that usually put him to sleep. By the promised third day, he was deathly sick of bed rest and had decided there was a certain point in the course of hospitalization when one ceased to get better and began to get worse again.

The nurse came to bathe, shave, and dress him that morning, one final humiliation. The bandages had been reduced to 4x4 gauze pads taped over the wounds, and the shirt he donned was not his own, but fit well enough. The wheelchair arrived, pushed through the door by a smiling Corporal Alice Lehman. Overjoyed to see her friendly face, Nate had to resist the urge to grab her in a bear hug. Not only would that be painful, it likely wouldn't be appreciated.

"What are you doing here?" he asked instead, aware of his own silly grin.

"I wanted to say good-bye, sir." Her freckled face colored slightly in embarrassment.

"I thought everyone had pulled out already."

"Most have. My team leaves this afternoon." She wheeled the chair to the bed. "Lucky you. You get to go home, now."

"Yeah, lucky me . . . Hey, I can do that."

The nurse was trying to push a sock over his toes. She stood back to observe his slow progress. Bending still brought considerable pain, but determined, he got both socks and shoes on.

"Very good, Sergeant Curtis," the nurse said patronizingly, then laid a business envelope in his lap. "You're to see your family doctor immediately on your return. These are your medical records. And this"—she laid two small bottles with the envelope—"is your medication. Follow the directions carefully. The major says you're to limit your movements for the next few days and rest often."

"Yes, ma'am." Nate slipped envelope and bottles into his jacket pocket.

"Have a seat," Alice said, seemingly as eager to be out of this place as Nate.

He was weaker than he'd expected, but bed to chair was only one step. Once he was settled, Corporal Lehman swung the wheelchair around and headed out the door. The halls were deserted, the floor gritty with sand. Nate wanted to carry on a conversation with the corporal, but for some reason, his head seemed empty.

"Your vehicle's right outside, sir."

"Thanks, Alice . . ." He fought an inner confusion. "And thanks for taking such good care of me, when . . ."

"Just doing my job, sir," the young woman said gruffly.

"Nate. Call me Nate."

"Nate, sir," she agreed with a hint of impishness.

They found a door somewhere in the labyrinth that let them outside. His brother-in-law's pickup and camper was parked on the narrow asphalt walkway.

"Christ!" the sergeant growled.

It had new tires all right, but he also had a close, clear view of the driver's side of the vehicle. Gary was going to kill him. The perfect blue-gray paint job had been bubbled and scorched away. The thin metal walls of the camper had warped from the tremendous heat. Nate took his first tottering steps to the truck door and peered inside. Someone had spread a woolen army blanket over the seats— what was left of them. The sergeant didn't have the heart to look underneath.

It hardly mattered if the insurance covered Sidewinder missile damage, his brother-in-law's pride and joy would never be the same. Alice came to pull the door open for him. That, too, was warped, and he didn't have the strength to jerk it loose.

"The motor pool replaced all the hoses and fan belts and electrical wiring," Lehman told him. "Most of it works, except the right turn signal. The tires all exploded from the heat. There was this RV parked next to your camper that got blown completely away. They figure it somehow protected yours." She offered him a sympathetic look. "At least it runs."

Nate nodded, speechless.

"The camper's a mess inside. Mr. Sands said to just leave it all alone ... that you'd know what to do with it when you got home." The corporal smiled at him. "Want some help into the cab? Can't stay much longer; I'm on duty, soon."

"No," Nate answered, distracted. "Just point me the way out of here."

Her directions were concise, careful, and would take him off the base and out to the highway. Home. Suddenly, he wanted to be home. *Needed* to be home. Alice waved to him as he pulled away, though he couldn't remember climbing into the vehicle or starting the motor. He'd never see her again—never see any of them again. The two men at the guard station waved him through without a second glance, and he found the freeway exactly where Corporal Lehman had said it would be.

The drive down off the desert reacquainted him with his body. Other than his pants fitting a lot more loosely and an occasional sharp pain in his chest, everything seemed to work. Still a little weak, though, but that would pass with time. He wondered if the army would send him the medical bill. Probably not. And there was really no reason to mention any of this at the police station. The Hanover case was very definitely closed.

The Orange Freeway had some leftover morning traffic on it, still. Monday. This was Monday. Twelve days ago, Professor Hanover and his family had died over their Thanksgiving dinner. Or was that twelve years ago? It felt like a lifetime. The city all around him had taken on an alien atmosphere. Smog dimmed the horizons, diesel smoke from big rigs hurt his lungs, and drivers avoided him as if the camper had something catching.

His own street looked strange, and for a moment, Nate felt hopelessly lost and afraid, but Janice's roses were still in bloom—red, yellow, and pink—lining the narrow walkway to the front door. The camper wouldn't fit in the garage—too high, even if there'd been room. Wearily, the sergeant parked it at the curb and climbed out of the cab. Jesus, little more than two hours out of bed, and he was ready to get back into one.

It took some courage to survey the overall damage to Gary's rig. The camper would have to be replaced, but the truck itself, with some sanding and bodywork and a good paint job, might survive. He doubted Gary would ever forgive him though. Someone had padlocked the camper door. Nate considered that a moment—an expensive laminated steel padlock. He checked the car keys, and sure enough, a shiny new key had been added to it.

The lock came off easily, but the door was warped and jammed tight. It took some straining and a broken fingernail to finally free the door from the jamb. His brother-in-law's neatly packed things had been knocked down from cupboards and shelves and tossed to the narrow floor. The mattresses were overturned and Nate's dirty clothes piled on top of it all. A strong stench of scorched fabric permeated everything.

He was too damned tired to deal with any of this just yet—except maybe his clothes which could be thrown in the washer. Pants, shorts, shirts . . . black box. Nate froze, eyes trapped by the slick, smooth material, a cold sickness in his gut. The second box lay under another pair of pants. A much-folded piece of paper was wedged underneath, and he pulled it free.

It was from Avery Sands. "Curtis, There's only one man on this planet I'd trust with these, and it isn't me. I just couldn't remove the lenses. I couldn't destroy such marvelous technology. No one knows these exist, except thee and me. Do with them what you feel you must—drop them in the ocean, or keep them for a day when we might actually be ready to meet the Ral. I have the key, still—John Caldwell's claw, pierced and worn on a chain around my neck. Just in case . . .

"I'm sorry I couldn't be there to say good-bye, but I'm a sentimental kind of guy and would've embarrassed us both. If our paths fail to cross again, I wish us both good long lives. Yours, Avery Sands."

Exhausted, Nate still took the time to lug the boxes, one by one, into the garage and set them in a dark, little-used corner beyond the Datsun and the Oldsmobile, then finally let himself into the house. God, he wished Janice was home, but she wouldn't arrive until day after tomorrow, lightly tanned and smelling of white ginger. Then there would be three people who knew of the existence of the boxes—"thee and me" and Janice.

As for deciding what to do with the boxes . . . that, too, could wait another couple of days. Panic and worry would be of little help. Nate wandered the empty house for a while. The bed looked inviting. Instead, he ended up in the dining room, seated at Janice's computer desk. By following her last lesson, he managed to turn the computer on and call up the word processing program. The blue screen stared back at him, a blank page.

With two fingers, he began to type slowly.

"A young lady named Sidney Bowers made me promise to get the facts straight about what happened. So I will, as best I can. Sidney's gone now—I don't know where exactly, but she's not on this world anymore. And that's what I have to tell you.

"We are not alone in the universe. I understand that now, and I'm afraid. Perhaps we should all be afraid. Perhaps we should think twice before we invite what is out there, here. But I'm getting ahead of myself. I should start this at the beginning. Sidney would want it that way.

"You see, not very long ago, there used to be a little desert town called Mojave Wells . . ."

AVONOVA PRESENTS
AWARD-WINNING NOVELS
FROM MASTERS OF SCIENCE FICTION

WULFSYARN
by Phillip Mann   71717-4/ $4.99 US

MIRROR TO THE SKY
by Mark S. Geston   71703-4/ $4.99 US/ $5.99 Can

THE DESTINY MAKERS
by George Turner   71887-1/ $4.99 US/ $5.99 Can

A DEEPER SEA
by Alexander Jablokov   71709-3/ $4.99 US/ $5.99 Can

BEGGARS IN SPAIN
by Nancy Kress   71877-4/ $4.99 US/ $5.99 Can

FLYING TO VALHALLA
by Charles Pellegrino   71881-2/ $4.99 US/ $5.99 Can

THE MAGICAL *XANTH* SERIES!

PIERS ANTHONY

QUESTION QUEST

75948-9/$4.99 US/$5.99 Can

ISLE OF VIEW

75947-0/$4.99 US/$5.99 Can

VALE OF THE VOLE

75287-5/$4.95 US/$5.95 Can

HEAVEN CENT

75288-3/$4.99 US/$5.99 Can

MAN FROM MUNDANIA

75289-1/$4.95 US/$5.95 Can

THE COLOR OF HER PANTIES

75949-7/$4.99 US/$5.99 Can